Bollywood Nights

Bollywood Nights

Shobhaa Dé

NEW AMERICAN LIBRARY

New American Library
Published by New American Library, a division of
Penguin Group (USA) Inc., 375 Hudson Street,
New York, New York 10014, USA
Penguin Group (Canada), 90 Eglinton Avenue East, Suite 700, Toronto,
Ontario M4P 2Y3, Canada (a division of Pearson Penguin Canada Inc.)
Penguin Books Ltd., 80 Strand, London WC2R 0RL, England
Penguin Ireland, 25 St. Stephen's Green, Dublin 2,
Ireland (a division of Penguin Books Ltd.)
Penguin Group (Australia), 250 Camberwell Road, Camberwell, Victoria 3124,
Australia (a division of Pearson Australia Group Pty. Ltd.)
Penguin Books India Pvt. Ltd., 11 Community Centre, Panchsheel Park,
New Delhi - 110 017, India
Penguin Group (NZ), 67 Apollo Drive, Rosedale, North Shore,
Auckland 1311, New Zealand (a division of Pearson New Zealand Ltd.)
Penguin Books (South Africa) (Pty.) Ltd., 24 Sturdee Avenue,
Rosebank, Johannesburg 2196, South Africa

Penguin Books Ltd., Registered Offices:
80 Strand, London WC2R 0RL, England

Published by New American Library, a division of Penguin Group (USA) Inc.
Previously published in a Penguin Books India edition as *Starry Nights*.

First New American Library Printing, June 2007
10 9 8 7 6 5 4 3 2 1

FOR MY HUSBAND, DILIP

CONTENTS

PART ONE

PART TWO

Waqt ne kiya kya haseen situm,
tum rahe na tum, hum rahe na hum.

(Ah the exquisite cruelty of Time,
you are no longer yourself, and I'm no
longer I.)

KAIFI AZMI IN *KAAGAZ KE PHOOL*

PART ONE

Kishenbhai

LIGHTS OFF! KISHENBHAI REGISTERED THE HARSH COMMAND OF the studio lackey with disdain. How many times in the past two decades had he heard those words? A thousand? Ten thousand? As darkness descended in the shabby, suburban preview theater, he eased his feet out of his white Rexine *chappals,* reached for his Pan Parag *dabba,* belched discreetly and touched the *panch-mukhi rudraksha* around his neck. A reflex action.

Or it was most times, anyway. Tonight's film was special. He had more than just his money at stake. Kishenbhai wanted *Tera Mera Pyaar Aisa* to be a box office hit. Not so much for himself. But for Aasha Rani. His Aasha. She was no longer his, of course, he corrected himself swiftly. But she had been. And her rise to fame had begun in this very theater. It was an event he would never forget. His first film. And hers. His premier hit. And hers. His first love. And hers?

The man in the bucket seat next to him had already begun to fidget. Kishenbhai cursed under his breath. This two-bit *bhangi* in a synthetic electric blue *kurta-pyjama* was Gopalji this evening. Gopalji my foot, he'd silently snorted. He was no Gopalji. He was a scavenger from the gutters of Bombay. And today this same son of a bitch was a producer. A big-time, big-bucks producer.

3

Bastard! Seven years ago he'd been a servile unit hand in Kishenbhai's production company. Oh yes, he'd had his own production company then. A banner of his own. K. B. Productions.

At that time Gopal had been nothing but a fucking *bhadwa* who fetched *paan* for the director and whores for the hero. Kishenbhai remembered him well. *"Abey saale!"* he'd call out to the shifty-eyed sidey, "Get me my *beedi* packet." Fetch, he'd say and off Gopal would scamper to bring him his Dunhills from the car. He was useful and resourceful. He could iron the heroine's taffeta petticoat without burning holes into it. He knew where to get camels at a day's notice for a song picturization. Why, the bloody bugger even pancaked faces when the makeup man fell ill. Gopal had made himself indispensable. And detestable.

Kishenbhai recalled the day he'd sacked him. That was nasty. But inevitable. Gopal had overstepped. He had made a pass at Aasha Rani. Kishenbhai didn't want to think about it. He forced himself back to the present. Deafening music while the credits rolled. Why did all Hindi films (even the arty ones) insist on raucous ear-splitting noise during the all-important opening sequences? Was it to shock the audiences to attention or to numb and deaden good sense? *Jaaney do* . . . he was beyond caring. This was what the bastards wanted. And this was what they got.

Aasha Rani hadn't bothered to show up for the preview. She wasn't expected to. In any case, she now had a small theater attached to her swanky Bandra bungalow. Plus a dubbing studio. Good business sense, Kishenbhai mused. Who was her guru? Whoever it was had gotten her to part with her precious money. Kishenbhai laughed silently at the image his mind suddenly conjured up: "Aasha Rani, darling, part your legs, you can part with the money later." She deserved whoever it was. She deserved what he was doing to her. Scheming bitch! *Chalo chhodo,* all women were the same. All *filmi* women, at least. No exceptions. Not one.

When Kishenbhai discovered Aasha Rani she had been nothing. A "dhool ka phool," the film rags gleefully dismissed her. An awkward, ungainly, overweight girl from Madras. And so dark. Chhee! Kishenbhai didn't like dark girls. He'd always gone for *doodh-ke-jaisi-gori* women himself. His own swarthy complexion was worked over with Afghan Snow and Pond's Dreamflower talc, a part of his daily postbath ritual. Aasha Rani had laughed and laughed when she'd found him at his careful toilette. But that was later. After she had officially become his. No, he hadn't married the bitch or anything. But it was known in their circle that Kishenbhai had gotten hold of a new *chidiya.* It was a signal to all others to keep their paws off. But Gopal had deliberately chosen to ignore the commandment. Gopal had always felt one-up on Kishenbhai. Because Gopal was from Himachal Pradesh. Very fair, and with light eyes.

Anyway, here she was now. Beautiful sequence. Well shot. Aasha Rani was very finicky about the opening shot. Yes, Aasha Rani had certainly learned all the tricks. She knew her face better than anybody else. She knew she had a difficult nose. And a heavy chin. But she also knew that once her eyes were the focus and her lips properly pouted, nobody bothered about anything else. Kishenbhai searched the image on the screen and found the mole above her lips. She used to hate it in those days. "*Nikaldo na,*" she'd plead with her makeup man. It was Kishenbhai who had convinced her that the mole looked very sexy. That it drew attention to her mouth. These days she darkened it. He tried to stop thinking about old times and to concentrate on the song she was moving her lips to. Still the same Aasha Rani—terrified to open her mouth too wide lest her crooked dogteeth showed up on the screen.

Soft-focus lens, a backlit shot, three-quarter profile—everything just the way she wanted. He let the words of the song engulf him. Nothing special—though the sound track had a minute or so of suggestive panting. The visual had her in a Jacuzzi, one slim leg sticking out. It was supposed to be a fantasy sequence in which the heroine dreamed of her wedding night. Aasha Rani had really let herself go for this one. He watched as she caressed herself with a cake of soap. The camera panned her body lovingly, lingering near her breasts. Those breasts. Gopal farted in the next seat. Kishenbhai shifted uncomfortably. Despite himself, he was beginning to feel aroused. Shit! he thought. The bitch still gives me a hard-on.

Gopal nudged him. *"Kyon ji—kya cheez hai."* Kishenbhai pretended he hadn't heard. The scene shifted to a honeymoon suite in a five-star hotel. Aasha Rani in full bridal finery. Why were brides in Hindi films unfailingly North Indian? The same red-and-gold sari, the same jewelry, the same *mehendi,* the same *bindis.*

In the beginning she never wore red. *"Chhee!"* she'd say, "I'll look so dark in it." It was her dress designer who had convinced her to wear bright colors. "No *rey baba,"* Aasha Rani had resisted, "Mummy says don't wear gaudy clothes." *Mummy says.* In those days every sentence of Aasha Rani's began and ended with "Mummy says." Did she still talk like that?

How he hated that mummy of hers! A belligerent cow with ghoulish *kaajal*-blackened saucer eyes. "Geetha Devi" she called herself. Geetha Devi and he hated each other from the very start. But then, Geetha Devi hated everybody. "Mummy is not like that," Aasha Rani tried to explain when he'd cursed her one day. "Mummy does that to save me," she'd continued. "From what?" Kishenbhai had thundered. "Men," Aasha Rani had answered simply. And his anger had disappeared. He'd reminded himself that she was just a child. A fifteen-year-old. With a forty-inch bust.

Kishenbhai turned his attention back to the screen. Shit! She still wore those bloody falsies! She didn't need them; he'd told her a hundred times. But mummy had insisted. So had all the producers. *"Achcha lagta hai, yaar,"* they'd said, looking at the rough cuts. *"Kya achcha, saala pahad dikhta hai,"* he'd answered.

Aasha Rani had great tits. Kishenbhai could vouch for that. After all, who had bought her all those bras from St. Michael's? She used to beg him each time he went to London, "Don't get me anything else . . . just soft toys and bray-si-yares" (as she pronounced it). Kishenbhai used to take great pride in asking the salesgirls to help him look for black-lace, three-quarter-cup, underwired 38-Cs. He'd imagine them admiring him, envying him.

And her menagerie of stuffed toys! *Toba:* pink kittens, blue rabbits, silky black leopards with yellow eyes, polka-dotted pandas, even a four-foot giraffe. "My zoo," Aasha Rani would giggle coquettishly, clutching a teddy bear as she posed for the centerfold of a *filmi* rag.

He could never understand her fetish for toys. "You don't know about my childhood," she'd tell him, hugging a doll. "I never had anything to play with—no toys, nothing." He'd heard the story before. The father who had deserted them. The mother who had been left with three girls to raise. The poverty. The deprivation. The struggle. He didn't mind getting her these things. Though he did feel faintly foolish walking through customs with the huge fluffy monkey she'd asked for. What kind of animals, Kishenbhai wondered bitterly, did she like now?

The opening sequence ended with a tight close-up of Aasha Rani's face. Why did she still use those silly false eyelashes and the colored contacts? Why? She had beautiful eyes. Blacker than the moonless night sky. Innocent as a virgin's. It was amazing. Here she was, so many men and so many films later, still looking vulnerable, innocent, pure.

Kishenbhai had gone through a quarter of his Pan Parag. He got up to go for a quick pee. He knew he wouldn't be missing a thing. Perhaps one more tuneless song, a rape or a dacoity.

The loo was filthy, with cigarette stubs thrown in the stained urinals. There was no water in the solitary basin. Kishenbhai reached for his handkerchief and wiped his fingers. He knew some men who didn't bother to do that. He was finicky about such things. After all, he had touched himself; a few drops of urine were bound to be there. And the same hand for eating later? *Chhee, chhee.* Once again he thought of Aasha Rani. He'd asked her once whether she washed herself after peeing and she'd been shocked by the question. In those days everything used to embarrass her. She'd blushed and nodded her head. "Good!" He'd patted her on the back. "These Punjabi bitches never bother. Dirty creatures. All *chamak-dhamak* outside and filthy inside. Moldy bras, stained *chaddis,* smelly underarms. *Chhee! Bekar* fucks." She'd frozen at the sound of that forbidden word. And today? Today, the prudish Aasha Rani was all fucked up and fucked out.

Kishenbhai went back into the theater and tried to concentrate on the film. The hero looked too young for her. Kishenbhai couldn't remember his name—what was it—Amar something. How old was he? Did he even have pubic hair? *Chikna-chikna* face. Eyes the color of melting caramel. A rosebud mouth. In Kishenbhai's time, he wouldn't have stood a chance. Forget about fucking, could this fellow frig? What would he look like without those fancy clothes? Had Aasha Rani seen him naked? He'd heard makeup room stories, but those were floated about every star all the time. And in Aasha Rani's case, more so. This young fellow wasn't her type anyway. And then he asked himself—was he? Would anybody today believe that he, yes, he, Kishenbhai, had been the first man in her life? That it was he who had had her first—not by force, or brutality, but with tenderness and love? Yes, love, whatever that crap was.

SHE HAD LAIN THERE on an impersonal hotel bed watching him with those innocent eyes as he undressed carefully. "Do you know you are the first naked man I'm seeing, besides my cousin, but he was only a boy?" she'd commented. "Aren't you afraid?" he'd asked, climbing out of his trousers and folding them neatly. "Of you? No. Not at all. Why? Should I be?" Those eyes had regarded him coolly, and he'd wondered briefly if she was as innocent as she looked.

"Do you know what we are going to do? Has anybody told you about . . . about sex?" he'd stammered, sounding a little foolish to himself. "Nobody has told me, but I've read about it in books. *Amma* never talks about such things. And my sisters are so silly, they only giggle and giggle when people kiss in English films." "This involves more than kissing," he'd said, removing his socks. He was down to his underpants now and feeling ridiculous. "Oh my God!" Aasha Rani had suddenly screeched. He'd jumped. "What happened?" "That mark!" she'd said, her hands over her mouth. His hands had flown to his thigh. "Oh, that? Didn't I tell you? I got it when I was twenty. Some crazy fight

9

after shooting. Too much booze, too little money. All-around frustration . . . We had real *goondas* in the industry then. Thugs. I owed someone money. He came to ask for it. I started to fight and *phatak*—out came a knife. Twenty-nine stitches. I don't heal very well. Or very quickly." And with that, he'd climbed out of his briefs and into bed.

For the first ten minutes, Aasha Rani had traced her long nails along the jagged edges of his wound, kissing the tiny bumps where the stitches had joined his torn flesh and crooning into his groin. He'd felt himself growing against her soft cheek and had pulled her up. "You know *baby-jaan,* at this rate I will fall in love with you. Become your *gulam*. That will destroy me, and it might destroy you." She had closed her eyes and snuggled up to him trustingly. "Let's not think about all that; just love me."

He hadn't been able to take his eyes off her breasts. "When did you get this big?" he'd asked, caressing one and then the other. "When I was thirteen. I got my periods early. Ten and a half. *Amma* was very angry. As if it was my fault. I felt terrible. I started growing and growing after that. By the time I was twelve, I was already wearing size thirty-six. I hated my breasts. Nobody else had such large ones. I couldn't skip or run or jump around like other girls my age. I couldn't wear *pavadai*. Even my dance guru made me feel conscious. He told *Amma,* 'This girl should wear saris. Cover her up.' I think it's God's curse."

Kishenbhai had propped her up on a pillow and said, "You're beautiful. Just look at your breasts. Beautiful. Works of art. Perfect." "All the men I meet these days want to touch them," Aasha Rani had said tonelessly. With a jealous leap he had covered her body with his and entered her. "Never let them, do you understand? You are mine. Only mine. These are mine. All mine."

Her eyes had remained open throughout. Not a sound had escaped her lips.

HERE SHE WAS AGAIN. It was a disco scene in which she was wearing an outfit that exposed most of her midriff. Aasha Rani looked good in gold, especially if her makeup and accessories were coordinated. This was the dress that had created a trend in film cabaret costumes. Instead of the usual glittering sequins or dyed feathers, her dress designer had come up with coins. Not real ones, of course. These were made out of tinfoil and linked together with delicate chains. She wore a flesh-colored bra and nearly invisible beige bikini panties underneath. Her tights were spangled Lycra, clinging to her legs. The uplift of her specially constructed bra was such that it gave her a deeper cleavage than her natural one. The Tina Turner wig was an inspired touch, like the gold-painted ropes around her neck. She looked straight out of a Hollywood sci-fi film. Kishenbhai noticed her navel had a rhinestone stuck in it. It reminded him of something.

Of course. Their first meeting. Kishenbhai had just gotten back from a matinee show of *Cleopatra* and was enthusing about its finer points (i.e., Liz Taylor's beguiling belly button) to his friend Venky, outside the gates of the studio. Suddenly a dark, fierce dragon lady had elbowed herself viciously through the crowds thronging the gate and positioned herself in front of them. Then she had addressed Venky, who didn't seem to recognize her. "Geetha Devi," she had said, and the name registered dimly. He'd gathered that Venky was once employed as a lab assistant in a studio she had some connection with in Madras.

Kishenbhai had mistakenly thought that it was Geetha Devi

who wanted the break and had still been laughing silently to himself when she'd pushed her daughter forward. "Meet Viji." It was like seeing Elizabeth Taylor in the flesh. Kishenbhai had sprung into action. Brushing out the creases in his safari suit and smoothing the few strands of hair he had left over his bald patch, he'd presented himself with a flourish: "Myself Kishenbhai, producer, actually speaking, assistant producer. Madamji, I'm on the lookout for new talent. I'm knowing everyone in the industry. What is your good name? Is your *beti* knowing dancing? Actually I'm knowing everybody—dance directors, music directors, cameramen . . . all big big producers, *hero-log,* heroines, everybody. These days demand is good. South Indian girls are good. No *khitpit,* no *faltu nakhras.* In Bombay all are liking South Indian girls too much, maybe I can get baby a role . . ."

Amma hadn't really needed convincing. She was desperate. She had consulted perfunctorily in Tamil, with Venky who had been discouraging. But *Amma's* mind was made up.

Bas. Cleopatra had been forgotten and the three of them had walked down to a poky South Indian joint. It was there, over lukewarm *kaapi,* that he had given them his visiting card, noted their address in Matunga, warned them not to approach anyone else, and fallen irrevocably in love with a big-bosomed, innocent-faced girl-woman.

WATCHING AASHA RANI'S FACE genuinely light up for the first time in the film as, clad in leather, she viciously booted the villain of the piece, Kishenbhai wondered about Aasha Rani's thinly disguised hatred for men. Perhaps it had something to do with *Appa* and the way he'd mistreated her mother. Or maybe she felt soiled, used, exploited by them. She often told him bitterly: "All of you are just the same, but wait, I will show you. I will do to men what they try to do to me. I will screw you all—beat you at your own game!" Kishenbhai used to laugh indulgently and say, "*Chhodo, chhodo,* women are like delicate flowers. It is our privilege and duty to take care of you." "Then why don't you take care of your wife instead of warming my bed? Or isn't she a woman?" Recalling their old conversations now, Kishenbhai agreed with Aasha Rani. Most men were *haraamis.*

Kishenbhai remembered his attempts to discourage her from getting involved with Akshay Arora. *Saala* hero! He knew his type—only too well. But Aasha Rani was blind to reason. "Don't try to stop me, Kishenbhai. I'm in love. I will kill myself if anything happens to this relationship. Akshay is my *jaan!*" Her words had nauseated him. *Jaan!* She'd even picked up the meaningless terms of endearment that *filmi* types bandied about. What *jaan?* And whose *jaan?* These heroes were nobody's *jaans.* They lived entirely for themselves, and for the next fuck.

But who was he to moralize? He was not her father nor her brother. He was just an ex-lover. In the film industry nothing was as worthless as a discarded paramour. Especially one who was a professional has-been. What would he have told her? "Don't sleep with that *maderchodh*"? She would have replied, "Didn't you too sleep with me? Where were your scruples then? You also had a wife. And children. You used me. You exploited me. So how are you any different from Akshay?" And she would have been right. Except that there was one important difference. Somewhere down the line Kishenbhai had made a *bewakoof* of himself. He had fallen in love with Aasha Rani.

Kishenbhai was getting terribly restless. What *bakwas* films people made these days. The money scene was so dicey. Idealistic distributors like him lived from one film to the next. It was different when he'd started his career. He'd made his mark as an independent producer. People respected him in those days. But success in this business was a short-lived affair. Two or three big flops and *khatam*. He hadn't expected that to happen to him. But it had. From owning a Pali Hill bungalow (just a stone's throw from Deepak Kumar's) and two Ambassador cars (air-conditioned, with tinted windows) here he was: a nobody. Promoting Aasha Rani had been a stroke of genius. Had he had the means, he would have launched three or four more films for her with himself as producer-director. Now, all he could be was the middleman.

Kishenbhai's first film with Aasha Rani had gotten off to a bad start. On the *mahurat* day itself, there had been an accident on the set which had destroyed one section completely. "A bad omen," someone had said. That had scared Aasha Rani. As it was she'd been reluctant to work in the film. "I'll never be able to do the role," she'd said when he'd narrated the story to her. "How can I play such a woman?" It took a lot of convincing to make her change her mind. Aasha Rani lacked confidence. *Amma* had spent hours working on her, reassuring her that she could do it; that Kishenbhai would be standing behind her at every step. "That is the problem, *Amma*," she'd groaned. "That is why I'm nervous."

Kishenbhai too had felt inhibited at first. But he'd bought the story only for her. If she didn't want to do it, he wouldn't either. It was a bold theme, of course, but he knew how he was going to handle it. Aasha Rani was worried about some of the scenes, particularly the rape one. And that other sequence that had her in a wet sari. She was also terrified of snakes, and this film was full of them. In fact, the *mahurat* shot had her caressing one. "Why couldn't you think of something else?" She'd shuddered. "Why snakes?" "Trust me," he'd said. "Snakes hold a special attraction. Once you get over your initial fear, it will be OK. Besides, these snakes aren't poisonous."

The snakes and the hero, Aasha Rani had hated both. "What kind of a story is this?" She'd reacted petulantly. "My hero is also a snake." "That's why I have signed Shrikant. It wasn't easy to get him. He wanted another heroine, not you. After a lot of buttering and *chamchagiri* and a fat signing amount, he finally agreed. Besides, no distributor was willing to back the film without a big hero," said Kishenbhai. "Hero-*shiro* . . . what about me? Such a silly role. All I do is get raped and dance with snakes. What sort of a movie is this?" "A hit, *baby-jaan,* a hit! Have faith in me."

Kishenbhai had been unprepared for Aasha Rani's reaction. He'd been sure Aasha Rani would be grateful and submissive. She was so young. And this was her first Bombay film.

Amma hadn't been too convinced either, but Kishenbhai had softened her with a generous advance. "If this film clicks," he'd told her, "just mark my words: Aasha Rani will become a star. I'm going to picturize three songs on her which will make India dance! *Arre kya baat hai*—just listen to them if you don't believe me."

Amma and Aasha Rani had agreed reluctantly. Later, in bed, Aasha Rani was thoughtful. "I need good costumes, *hai na?*" And he knew that she'd given in. Just as he'd thought she would. She'd learn, he told himself. All the girls did once they settled down.

Nagin ki Kasam had been a modest hit. After a shaky start it had gone on to gross more than three times the initial investment. With the film behind him, Kishenbhai hoped he would now be regarded as a "hit filmmaker."

KISHENBHAI HAD MADE SURE Aasha Rani's debut didn't go unnoticed. He had celebrated her triumph—with a vengeance. What a *shandar* party he had thrown for her. Everybody had come to it. Amirchand, yes, even Sheth Amirchand. And Ramniklal. South Indian producers, financiers, *woh saala* Hiru. Bastard. Right there and then he'd come to ask, "How much?" as if Kishenbhai were some third-rate, *chaalu* pimp. *Amma* had spent the evening concentrating on that Bengali Babu, Sudhendu Bose, solely because he had two or three hit films to his name.

Kishenbhai's heart swelled with pride at the memory of how Aasha Rani had looked that night. How stunning in her white-and-gold Benarasi sari. *Amma* had wanted her to wear a clinging *salwar-kameez*, but Aasha Rani had refused. Kishenbhai had suggested a sari, and the two of them had gone to Kala Niketan to buy it. Fifteen hundred rupees it had cost him. Without the blouse. But how wonderful his Aasha Rani had looked in it. He'd told her to put lots of *gajras* in her hair and lots of bangles on her wrists. She had teased him: "Glass or gold?" He'd taken the hint. He had gone home and, without asking his wife, quietly picked up the bank locker keys and had gone and removed ten gold bangles from his bank. Each bangle was solid; must have weighed over two *tolas*. He'd put them on Aasha Rani's arms while she smiled into his eyes.

His wife had discovered the theft soon enough. *Toba! Toba!* What hell she'd created! "Get them back right now," she'd screamed, "or I'll saw them off her wrists. I'll kill her! Have you lost your senses completely? Next you will sell our house—and give the money to her. May she rot, may she die. Evil home-wrecker. God takes care of her type. She will never know happiness! You take it from me!"

Amma had been equally furious. "You are asking Baby to return the bangles? What kind of a man are you? Baby's heart will break. Do you know she hasn't taken them off since you gave them? *Gave.* She did not come and steal them from your house. She will cry so much. You can buy your wife new bangles, but don't make Baby feel bad. How do you expect her to concentrate on her career if you keep upsetting her like this?"

Not daring to go home without the bangles, Kishenbhai had gone to a moneylender in Kalbadevi. He'd pawned his watch, gold chain, ring, cigarette case and lighter. Yet he couldn't raise enough to buy ten new bangles. The price of gold had doubled since he'd bought those for his wife. In desperation he had gone to a friend's office and borrowed the balance and rushed in a taxi to Zaveri Bazaar. It was hot and sticky. As usual, the small lane was already overcrowded with thousands of hawkers selling vegetables, plastic mugs, stainless-steel utensils, ready-made clothes, even stolen watches, on the narrow footpaths. He hadn't gone into any of the glittering showrooms of established jewelers. He'd have had to pay double for the same item. But these smaller fellows had such a limited choice. Quickly he had selected a pattern closest to the ones he'd taken from his wife. Paying for the bangles he had sped home in the waiting taxi to his wife, but she was not placated.

She had chucked the bangles at him, saying, "Throw these into the gutter. What have you brought? These are not half as heavy as mine. Don't think you can fool me like this. Go take the new ones to the *rundi* and bring me back my original bangles.

I wouldn't pass these on to my sweeper-woman—even hers must be heavier. And don't come home without my bangles."

Amma had taken one look at the new bangles and turned her face. "How can I show these to Baby? She will fling them in my face. These! Where did you get these? Are you sure they are made of gold? Let me see, so light, how many *tolas*? Four? Tch! Tch! Those must be twelve at least. No, *baba*, we cannot accept these." Kishenbhai had pleaded with her. It was no use.

Finally, he had struck a deal. "As soon as I raise money for the next project, the first thing I will do is buy ten *tolas* of gold for Aasha Rani. This much I promise you. But till then, accept these and give those back. My life is at stake." Reluctantly *Amma* had gone and fetched the originals. "You don't buy anything from anyone," she had said. "You give the money to me. I will go to Matunga to our own South Indian jewelers there. They keep genuine articles. Their gold is real. I don't trust all these Marwaris and Gujaratis. Look at the color, just look at it; call this gold?" Aasha Rani had sulked for a while, but the excitement of meeting new people at the party that evening had improved her mood. She had made some useful contacts—Sheth Amirchand, for instance. In the week after the party, the Sheth's man had phoned twice, and the Sheth had even sent his car for Aasha Rani. Unfortunately, she'd been away at the studio. But *Amma* had been home and had done her best to find out more about the Shethji. Her best industry contact, a fixer called Rizvi, had said: "If the Shethji has shown interest in Aasha Rani, take it that her career is made."

KISHENBHAI HADN'T BEEN AS ENTHUSIASTIC about the Shethji's interest. He remembered storming into Aasha Rani's newly hired

Andheri flat on what turned out to be their last day together. "Have you slept with him?" he had stormed. He remembered she had been lying on a Rexine sofa—her head propped on one armrest, and her feet on the other—reading back issues of *Showbiz* magazine. In one corner of the room was a TV covered with a tablecloth and topped with a vase full of gaudy plastic flowers. The other corner housed a small cabinet with a glass front. In it were displayed a stainless-steel dinner set, a photograph of Aasha Rani, three brass *natarajas*, two brass *Oms* on wooden pedestals, one Tanjore doll and a chipped Air-India maharajah. Every detail was still so clear in his mind.

Aasha Rani had regarded him briefly and gone back to her magazine. Kishenbhai had been beside himself. After all that he had done for her, pawned his wife's jewels, staked his all on the film that had made her, even given her a name. *Chalo chhodo*, those were material things, but he'd also given his *dil*. "You filthy prostitute!" he had screamed at her. "Whoring your way to stardom! What has Shethji given you, what have all those others given you that I haven't? What is my *gunah*, my great sin, that I am being betrayed like this?"

Aasha Rani had looked at him steadily. "You financed and produced my first film, Kishenbhai, but you extracted payment from my body. You call me a prostitute, but you forget that you were my first pimp. So don't throw *ahsan* on me. I owe you nothing!" And she had said it again: "I owe you nothing."

It was a scene that haunted him constantly. All these years later he still wondered how it might have been had he handled Aasha Rani differently. If he hadn't lunged at her like a jealous husband. Like a man possessed. But he had not been thinking rationally. He had grabbed her by the hair and shouted, "You're

mine, you're mine, mine!" Aasha Rani had struggled to free herself, and her face—if it had been terror he saw there he would
have stopped—but it had been loathing. He'd become like a *jaan-
war* then. *Chhee,* even he felt ashamed. Luckily *Amma* had come in
just then. He had let go of Aasha Rani, who had picked up her
magazine and had walked out of the room, stopping at the door
only long enough to say, "I don't want to see this man again.
Ever."

But was it so wrong, what he had done? He was a man of
honor when it came to such things. She was his woman. His. It
was impossible to accept that she could have allowed another
man to touch her body. His property. But she had. And she
hadn't even pretended to be sorry. Maybe, just maybe, if she'd
asked for forgiveness, if he'd felt that she was genuinely repen-
tant, if she had sworn never to do it again . . . What the hell,
what was the point in thinking of that now?

For some odd reason he'd decided to beseech *Amma,* who was
still standing by looking thunderstruck. She'd be on his side,
he'd thought. Instead *Amma* had turned on him like a viper. "How
dare you accuse Baby of all these things? From where do you get
the guts? You filthy rapist. Are you a saint yourself? Haven't you
also enjoyed my daughter, exploited her? And now you want explanations? Confessions? What have you done for us besides making that two-bit film? After that? Was it your face on the screen
or hers? Did you do her dancing for her? Did you slog in the studios, shift after shift? Did you stay for hours in the sun? Or walk
barefoot on ice like my Baby? She is free to go with whoever she
wants. Besides, Shethji has promised her two more films. He is
the one who will make her a star, not you."

Kishenbhai had not met Aasha Rani since that day. But that

didn't mean he had forgotten her. But what to do? These days she refused to answer his calls, refused to meet him. What crime had he committed? He asked himself that often enough. He had genuinely loved the girl—in his own way. But he was a *shaadi-shuda* man—a married fellow. He had made it clear, both to *Amma* and to her, that he would never leave his family. What did they expect? It wasn't as if Aasha Rani was desperate for a husband. Not at that point, anyway. She was just starting her career. OK, so he had slept with her, *chalo,* he could be accused of having used her body. But his point was simple: If it hadn't been him, it would have been someone else. The industry was full of *bhooka,* sex-starved men who had *chidiyas* like Aasha Rani for breakfast. She was lucky she'd found him. And he'd helped her. Had she forgotten that? Most of the others just fucked and forgot. No roles, no nothing. It was he who had given her such a first-class screen name—Aasha Rani. It had turned out to be lucky, just as he had predicted. He recalled the day he had re-baptized her.

They had been on their way to Niteshji's office. Aasha Rani was so distracted staring at the smart office girls at bus stops that she didn't hear Kishenbhai saying, "Asharani. *Haan yehi naam theek hai.* Aasha Rani. *Dekho,* when Niteshji asks you your name, don't say 'Viji.' It doesn't sound right. It's old-fashioned and crude. Say 'Aasha Rani'; that sounds fashionable and grand, like Devika Rani—oh ho—what a star she was. *Kya cheez thi.* Now, say it to yourself a few times: *'Aasha Rani, Aasha Rani, Aasha Rani.'* I like it! Remember from today, you are Aasha Rani— Sweetheart of Millions." The extra "a" in her name was his idea as well. "It's different. Something new. Novelty," he had explained to her. But what really convinced *Amma* was its numerological significance. The extra "a" made all the difference between success and failure.

ON-SCREEN AASHA RANI was gyrating seductively to vaguely familiar music. As the camera closed in on her face, she caught her lower lip between her teeth and moaned suggestively. Haplessly, Kishenbhai followed suit.

Aasha Rani 🐦🐦

AASHA RANI PRESSED HER FINGER TO THE BELL AND HELD IT
there. The new maid appeared, flustered and awed by her starry
impatience. Without quite looking at her, Aasha Rani asked for a
cup of coffee.

The girl came back with Nescafé. Aasha Rani flung the cup at
her. "Don't you even know how to prepare good coffee? Where is
the damn filter?" The maid looked stricken and said, "Madam, in
Bombay people drink this type of coffee." Aasha Rani saw red.
"Don't tell me about what people drink in Bombay. I know it too
well. They drink piss and think it's coffee! I want mine done the
way we do it in Madras. Don't ever bring me this rubbish again!"
The maid hung around with a surly expression. "What do you
want now?" "Madam, *saab* coming for dinner or shall I tell the
cook to just make *dahi bhath*?"

"Goddammit. Tell him to make whatever he wants!"

"But, madam, Akshay *saab* doesn't like *dahi bhath*. What about
murgi?"

"Just make what you bloody well want." Aasha Rani's voice
was shrill.

* * *

AKSHAY HAD OBVIOUSLY FORGOTTEN her birthday. Just as well, she thought bitterly. How did it matter? What was he to her anyway? Yet, she couldn't move from the telephone. Akshay was not that selfish, that thoughtless. A call? Just one lousy telephone call? Even his secretary could have made it for him. My God! What if he was sick? In the hospital? If that ever happened, she'd be the last to know. Maybe there was an income tax raid on at his house even at this moment. Maybe Malini had had an accident; perhaps *she* was dead.

She wanted to call but didn't dare. That again was one of the rules. She could never make calls; she could only receive them. She thought of contacting Linda and asking her to phone him; kind of pretend she wanted an interview and then pass on her message. No. Akshay would be furious if he knew Aasha Rani discussed their relationship with journalists. Bloody newshounds. The gutter-press who wrote filth about the stars, about him. No way.

Aasha Rani sat by the phone and waited. She didn't even go to the bathroom. She had a cordless machine but didn't trust it. What if it conked out just when he called? At the crucial moment? He'd think she was out shooting and hang up. Bloody instruments, she cursed, transferring her anger to the phone. Never work when you need them. She picked up the receiver to check whether there was a dial tone. There was. Perhaps her line had been dead earlier. That happened often enough. Shit! These *bakwas* phones—how she hated them. Maybe Akshay had tried and gotten no response! Still, he could have sent the driver over. What was the distance, anyway? Hardly anything. Maybe the driver was on Malini's duty. Then how could he carry a message for her? Akshay could've driven over in his BMW. He did that often enough. But maybe the BMW was in the shop for repairs. Last week he'd said it was giving him trouble. Poor chap! He had so many things to worry about. That lousy car was always acting up. Like his lousy wife. Two days of running smoothly—and back to the workshop. She'd told him so many times, "Get an Indian car, get an Indian car," but no. He was so stubborn. *Bas*—he was crazy about foreign cars. Toyota, Honda, Mercedes, BMW—that van!

Maybe he was sitting at home waiting for Malini to return. He couldn't take a cab after all. And that elder brother of his—*chhee*! Another one! Always lecturing him. All that fellow thought about was money. And more money. No self-respect. No compunctions about freeloading off his younger brother.

Ajay had heard the rumors about her and Akshay. She didn't give a damn. Naturally his brother was going to side with the wife. So what? All these relatives were just the same. Like *Amma*. What did they care about the people who slaved in the studios to make money for them? Nothing. But they wanted to control their lives, all right. They wanted to tell them who to marry, who to sleep with, who to act with, who to be nice to, who to ignore, who to snub.

AASHA RANI WENT UP TO her bedroom—all gauzy pink drapes, quilted bedcovers and pink heart-shaped cushions trimmed with lace. There was a king-size double bed pushed against the wall, and a dressing table littered with uncapped jars of makeup. Her stuffed toys were arranged on a low shelf that stretched the length of the room. And the floor was covered with clothes. She went and stood by the window. This was so unfair. On Akshay's birthday she had canceled all her shooting, thinking this was one day he would really want her to be around.

They had celebrated his birthday two weeks earlier with a quick tryst in the penthouse suite he maintained at the Holiday Inn. She had found a couple of telltale hairpins on the carpet, which he'd waved off nonchalantly. "Tch! Forget it, darling. Malini had brought me some *masala* milk from the house during a story session and napped here, while I was busy with that *chootiya* in the next room." Aasha Rani had let it pass. It was Akshay's birthday and she wanted to make him happy. Very happy.

She had unbuttoned his shirt and kissed his glistening chest softly. Akshay was practically hairless, and she liked that. She recalled all the hirsute, sweaty men she'd been forced to lick—all over—whose body hairs would get into her mouth and make her feel nauseated. "Don't stop, Rani," Akshay had pleaded. Aasha Rani hadn't needed prompting. Her mouth had worked its way down while her fingers unzipped his jeans. He was wearing her favorite briefs, those lethal black ones. How smooth he was— almost like a woman, she thought, as she flicked her tongue over him. He had propped his head on his arm and watched. "Don't stare," she had protested. "I feel shy . . ." "You . . . and shy? I like watching your head move while you suck me. Do you want to deny me the pleasure?"

Aasha Rani had wordlessly reached for her bag, which was right next to the bed. "What are you doing?" Akshay had asked. "Lie back. I have a present for you," she had said. "But you've already given me one." "That was only the beginning. This is something special; you'll enjoy it." And she'd pulled out a small bottle. It had filled the entire room with its heady, spicy fragrance. "Oil?" he'd asked. "Special oil we use for ceremonial baths. Your body will smell of it for a week—now relax; let me give you a massage." And with that Aasha Rani had mounted him and, pouring a palmful of the divine-smelling oil over his erection, had slowly begun massaging him between his thighs. She moved like a lithe dancer, her hair falling all over his chest, her breasts moving above his face, her nipples occasionally brushing his lips. "You sexy woman, where did you learn all this?" Akshay had groaned, surrendering himself to her ministrations.

Two hours later, as they slept coiled up in bed, there was a loud thumping on the door. Akshay had jumped up and thrown a towel in her direction. His face was pale, his eyes panic-stricken. "It's her!" he'd hissed. "You have to get out of here fast. Malini must be on her way up; that's the secretary warning me. *Chalo, chalo,* move it, get dressed!"

Her eyes had been heavy with sleep. He had shoved her off the bed, thrown her clothes at her, and said harshly, "Are you deaf, woman? Didn't you hear me? Out! My wife's here!" Aasha Rani had sat on the edge of the bed, clutching the clothes flung at her, and had refused to budge. "If you are shitting in your pants, you leave. Why should I? She isn't my wife. I'm staying right here. I don't care whether it's Malini or Goddess Sita herself!" she had finally said. Akshay had lunged toward her, eyes blazing with anger. At that precise moment there was another knock. The secretary's voice was apologetic. "Sorry, boss. It's OK. Madam doesn't know you are upstairs. She has gone straight to the health club."

Akshay's arm had fallen to his side as he'd collapsed in Aasha Rani's lap, saying, "God help me! I nearly died then." She had made no move to touch him.

* * *

THE PHONE RANG and she snatched it up. Wrong number. Shit. This was proving to be another ghastly birthday. The calendar seemed to leer at her. As it had on that day she'd turned fifteen. She remembered how she had woken up early and lain in bed hoping that *Amma* would let her have her best friend Savitha over for the day. A special treat. After all, it was her birthday. Maybe she'd get a new *pavadai*. But *Amma* had chosen that very day to steer her family from rags to riches, cashing in on the only solid assets she had in the world: the forty-inch bust of her fifteen-year-old daughter.

Looking back, Aasha Rani realized how methodically *Amma* had geared up for her first big move. From the time she'd painted herself garishly and left with dubious uncles in the evenings to the time she'd forced Aasha Rani to "perform" in blue films when she was not quite twelve, there was only one thing on her mind: to save enough money to get Viji to Bombay.

"DON'T CALL ME *AMMA* in front of people," her mother had hissed into her ear at Victoria Terminus. "Call me Mummy; remember that, Mummy. In Bombay everybody calls their mother Mummy not *Amma*."

She had nodded docilely. She was tired and sleepy. It had been a long train journey from Madras. And her first one. *Amma* had gotten her new clothes for Bombay. She had hoped for a new *pavadai* for her birthday. Instead she had gotten a blouse and skirt. And so tight-fitting! She remembered being barely able to breathe in the blouse. And the bra! *Chhee,* so thick and uncomfortable! She'd looked at herself in the small mirror in their home before leaving for the railway station, and her eyes had filled with tears.

"*Ai yaii yo,* what has *Amma* done!" Her sister, Sudha, had laughed and teased her. "Look at you, look at your bust! You look just like a she-buffalo!" "Please don't make me wear this; it looks so horrible," she had pleaded to *Amma. Amma* had glared at Sudha. "You shut your mouth or I'll smack you hard. Viji is going to Bombay to become a big film star. What do you know about such things? She will be famous and rich, while you will still be wallowing in mud." The girl had sniggered. "Film star, film star, ha, ha, who will look at such a fat, dark and ugly girl?" *Amma* had run toward her, palm raised, but she had scampered ahead and continued her taunts. "And look at her name. Viji! Can you imagine a film star called Viji? Viji, Niji, Piji." Aasha Rani had tears streaming down her face, streaking the pink powder her mother had generously dusted her face with. *Amma* had merely picked up the Rexine bags with the price tags still on them. "We will see which one of us is right. You can make fun of Viji now, but one day she will be a big star. Dance, sing, act, while the rest of you stay here in this hell-hole and rot! Viji can do anything, everything. She is a good girl. She listens to her *amma.* I will make her a star."

THE COFFEE ARRIVED. It was awful, but at least it wasn't Nescafé. She'd been in Bombay for so many years now, but she still hadn't gotten used to drinking instant coffee. Aasha Rani got up to change out of her kimono. Just in case. She waded past the mess in her bedroom: clothes, shoes, handbags, Akshay's *kurtas,* jeans, Jockeys littered all over the carpet. She started flinging *kurtas* impatiently out of her cupboard. Her hand stopped on a shiny, pink, flowered one. She picked it up and touched it lightly. She remembered it well. She'd worn it that morning when Kishenbhai was escorting her to her first big interview. The day that she'd stopped being Viji. And become Aasha Rani. It was a name Kishenbhai had given her. It happened in a taxi. That was right.

That day they were on their way to see Nitesh Mehra. He wasn't the renowned producer-director he was today, but he'd made a few reasonably successful films with newcomers. The Godfather of Unknowns. He took chances; he gave breaks. He could sniff out talent. Or rather, he knew instinctively what the audience came looking for. He'd announced a new film: a light-hearted musical comedy with a double role for the heroine, the trade rags informed knowingly. A fresh face. Already hundreds of hopefuls were jamming the studios. Kishenbhai had told *Amma* that her daughter stood a good chance provided she stayed out of the picture. *Amma* had bristled. "Viji is my child. I know what is best for her. Who are you to tell me anything?" Kishenbhai had reasoned that many a budding film career died prematurely because of interfering mothers. "Nobody likes *lafdas*. Let him meet her first and then we'll see." Reluctantly *Amma* had allowed Aasha Rani out of her sight. But only after cautioning her: "Don't sign anything. Don't say anything. Do as you are told. If the man says 'dance,' you dance. Do disco if he wants disco. Do Bharatanatyam if he wants Bharatanatyam. But do not go alone into a room with him. Do not take off your clothes. Stay with Kishenbhai and let him do the talking. Don't slouch. Stand tall and straight. If he asks any questions, you just say, 'Speak to Mummy'—not *Amma*. Will you remember?" Aasha Rani had nodded and climbed into the waiting cab.

Niteshbhai operated from a cramped office in the legendary "film building" at Tardeo. In this sprawling complex were housed over a hundred film production companies. Nitesh's office was like all the others—false ceiling, plastic flower bouquets, garish carpets and innumerable phones. Aasha Rani gaped at the publicity stills plastered on the walls. It was Nitesh's frequent boast that he made films for money—first and last. He was not an aesthete, he sneered. He made movies for moolah—mega moolah. "*Arrey, chhodo yeh sab* art-fart *ki baatey,*" he'd say to journalists who accused him of crassness. "My movies sell. They're seen by millions. I give audiences three hours of *masala*. That is all. See it. Flush it. Forget it. But see it. At least I'm better than all those pseudo art-film wallahs whose films win awards in Timbuktu. Nobody watches them—even when they are shown free on Doordarshan! *Bilkul faltu; ghatiya cheez.*"

Nitesh had given Aasha Rani a thoughtful once-over. "Big tits," he had observed matter-of-factly to Kishenbhai. Then he had turned to Aasha Rani and asked, "Can you dance? Bharatanatyam? Kathak?" Aasha Rani had nodded and looked to Kishenbhai for verification. "Of course she can dance. Give her a screen test, *yaar*. High class. Top class. *Kamaal ki cheez.*" Nitesh hadn't been convinced. "Hindi *aata hai*?" he'd asked her. "These southie females can't speak a word of Hindi, *yaar,*" he'd explained to Kishenbhai. "The producers spend a packet on Hindi tuitions and end up with Hindi-speaking actresses who *still* sound as if they're talking *Madraasi*. Southies and Bengalis. Same problem. Nice eyes, nice tits, lousy accents."

Nitesh had ordered coffee all around and a *tambaku paan* for himself. He had turned to Kishenbhai and asked, "Have you got a cassette? Screen test, *hai*? Wait, let me call Dada." He had reached for a bell under his monstrous table and had asked a peon to summon Dada, the makeup man. Kishenbhai had turned to Aasha Rani and explained, "Dada is the best. He will make you look like an *apsara*." Dada had come in and stared impassively at Aasha Rani. "Forehead *ka* problem *hai, saab*," he had said flatly, "stringing *karna padega*." Nitesh had instructed him to go ahead and do whatever was necessary. It had been Aasha Rani's first makeover. And the most crucial one.

Dada had worked on her face for close to four hours: reshaping her eyebrows, altering her hairline and redefining her plump cheeks with quick strokes of plum-colored blush. Aasha Rani's hair had a kink to it. It was frizzy around her face. Dada's assistants had taken care of that with hot tongs that stretched out the curls and straightened the tresses till they fell in a dark curtain.

Nitesh had remained unconvinced. "What are her thighs like?" he had asked Kishenbhai with a gleam in his eyes. "Why?" Kishenbhai had asked, keeping his face expressionless. "*Arrey baba*, these days you need heroines with thunder thighs! All these Southie girls have them. Don't you see those hot films from there? *Sab undoo-gundoo bhasha mein*." "Those are from Kerala, *yaar*," Kishenbhai had clarified, "and the girls are Malayali." "Same thing, *yaar*, what's the difference?" Kishenbhai had pulled out some stills of Aasha Rani—"Here, take a look for yourself," he'd said, and thrust them into Nitesh's hands. "Figure *badi achchi hai*," Nitesh had said after a minute. "But she'll have to put on weight on her thighs. I told you—men like *tagda* thighs." "When can we fix up the screen test?" "Let me see; I'll have to fix up a good cameraman. Next week? Phone *karna, yaar*."

THE MEMORY OF HER SCREEN TEST was indelibly etched in Aasha Rani's mind. For more reasons than one. After all, it wasn't just her career that was launched. It was also the launch of the most-talked-about romance ever to hit the film industry. The scandalous saga of Akshay Arora and Aasha Rani.

She'd left it all to *Amma* and Kishenbhai. Funnily enough, she hadn't felt nervous at all. Ever since she could remember—let's see, how old was she when *Amma* had pushed her in front of a camera and said, "Dance, Baby, dance"? Five? Six?—Aasha Rani took instructions well. It had never occurred to her that she had a choice in the matter. And so it was when they had all waited for Niteshji and the cameraman to turn up. Her test was to be squeezed in between takes. The film being shot on the studio floors was a mega-epic blockbuster-in-the-making called *Jeet*. Aasha Rani, *Amma* and Kishenbhai were shunted into an inconspicuous corner while the sets were rearranged for the next scene. She had watched, fascinated, as nimble-footed lighting boys clambered around on makeshift bamboo props like agile monkeys playing with coconuts. There had been all-around chaos, with lots of people shouting orders simultaneously.

The set had represented a deluxe luxury bedroom, the Indian filmmaker's idea of how the rich lived and lolled. Aasha Rani had thought it was the most gorgeous room she'd ever seen. Velvet bedspreads, brocade curtains, Rexine love seats, pink telephones, gilt-edged mirrors and a fountain! She had turned to *Amma,* her eyes large and wondrous. "Can we also have a room like this?" she had asked. *Amma* had laughed and nudged Kishenbhai proudly. "Did you hear what Baby just said?"

Film technicians ran to and fro, jumping neatly over snake-like wires crisscrossing the studio floor. "Light check, sound check!" someone had shouted. The three of them were in the way, and someone had come up and roughly pushed them aside. Aasha Rani had ensconced herself on a large water drum. *Amma* had sat on a packing case. Kishenbhai had stood around trying to chat up the dance director—a broad, fierce, ugly-looking woman called Komal. At one point he had beckoned to Aasha Rani. "Come and meet Komalji, the industry's most *mashoor,* top-class dance director." Aasha Rani had walked over and the woman had pinned her with an unfriendly stare. "*Naach aata hai?*" Aasha Rani had nodded. "She's very good. Best in Madras. You should see her on the screen—too, too good! Dancing since she was four," Kishenbhai had said persuasively. But the choreographer's interest had drifted and she had begun instead to tear apart the heroine of the film being shot. "Bloody whore! Can't dance two steps, and acting so high and mighty. All these heroines are the same. Come from the gutter and behave like queens after one hit. They think we haven't a clue about their past. This bitch is no different. I knew her when she first came to Bombay. Her name was Rosy. *Arrey,* she would sleep with anything that moved, even the spot boy . . . just so she could bum a *beedi.* And look at her today! I tell myself, 'Don't care about these sluts. They are here for one day and gone the next. But your work goes on.' I see hundreds like her. Two-film wonders. Trick some sucker, get him to produce a film, and *bas,* they think they're Queen Elizabeth. I told the director, '*Baba*, this woman is impossible. She has two left feet. She cannot follow even simple one-two, one-two steps. *Jaane do,* I will give her easy things to do. She can jiggle her breasts and flash her thighs—that's all.' *Dekho,* she is supposed to be rehearsing with us just now. But where is madam? In Akshay Arora's makeup room, parting her legs. She thinks he'll recommend her for his next film. High hopes! He is not such a fool, *yaar.* He will sleep even with a eunuch if he has nobody else! This *rundi* should realize that."

Aasha Rani had listened intently, hanging on to every word of Komal's colorful Bombay-Hindi. Then, while Komal had nattered on, Aasha Rani had caught sight of the most devastatingly handsome man she'd ever seen. He was dressed in white pantaloons that ruffled at his ankles, red shoes, red cape. His eyes were dark and brooding. His thick hair slicked back. And he had walked as if he owned the place.

She saw studio hands jump out of his way. Someone rushed up with a chair. Someone else had run to fetch a glass of water. He had passed within three feet of Aasha Rani, and she had felt the hair on her arms stand on end. It was as if she had been hit by a high-voltage jolt of electricity. Totally unnerved, she reached out for support. There was a sudden loud splash. Everyone had frozen. Aasha Rani had lost her balance and had fallen into the drum, soaked to the skin, and spluttering for air. The mystery man had helped Aasha Rani out, a sardonic smile playing on his lips. In her confusion she hadn't noticed that her drenched skirt had climbed up to her crotch. Flushing and blushing furiously, she had pulled herself up, muttering, "So sorry, so sorry." He'd stared at her, looked down at her exposed legs, shrugged and walked away.

"That was Akshay Arora," Kishenbhai had said reverently.

AASHA RANI OFTEN recounted her dramatic encounter with the megastar in her subsequent interviews. He, in turn, would also mention it, saying with an easy laugh, "I'm convinced it wasn't an accident. She planned it all. How else would I have noticed her?" And notice her he had. For a few minutes after the incident, an oily, disgusting man had slithered up to Kishenbhai and asked, "*Yeh kaun hai?* Akshayji wants to know."

Kishenbhai hadn't wasted a minute. "She is the latest discovery. Four, five big banners are interested in her, but we want her to wait and sign the right film. She has worked in the south, but now she is going to be launched in Hindi films. Raj is interested. Nitesh also. Shekhar has been calling every day. After the Dream Girl, Aasha Rani is the one. Aasha Rani—the Sweetheart of Millions!" *Amma* had also rushed up and belted out her part of the routine: "My baby is only going to sign for big banners with topmost heroes. We don't mind waiting, but no small side roles for her. She is going to be a big star!" The man had leered and gone back. They'd seen him whispering into Akshay's ear. But nothing had happened. Not for a year or so, anyway.

Aasha Rani's screen test had finally been shot at eight thirty that night. They'd gotten nothing to eat, nothing to drink and when she'd asked for the loo, someone had pointed to a dingy corner of the studio and said, "Go there. Don't make a fuss." Kishenbhai had gallantly tried to block the narrow passage leading to the smelly corner till Aasha Rani had finished relieving herself. He had noticed that Aasha Rani's stamina was beginning to waver and had managed to get her a packet of soggy biscuits, which she'd gobbled greedily. She had then timidly asked *Amma* for some *kaapi*. *Amma* had hissed, "No *kaapi* here. Keep quiet and wait—there will be plenty of time later for food. Concentrate on your test now." Aasha Rani had nodded miserably and tried to keep her mind off piping-hot *sambhar* over ghee-soaked *bhath*.

The screen test had been an anticlimax. It had turned out to be one of those *gaon-ki-gori*, village-belle-bathing-in-pond scenes, where all that was required of her was to look drenched. She had managed easily. She was getting quite adept at crashing into water.

Two weeks later, Niteshbhai still hadn't called. It was then that Kishenbhai had stepped in, offering to finance the film himself. One way or another.

THE PHONE RANG AGAIN. "Happy birthday, *baby-jaan!*" Aasha Rani hung up immediately. Today Kishenbhai was the last person she wanted to talk to. Her first lover. And her first pimp. Between *Amma* and Kishenbhai there was nothing they hadn't resorted to. Nothing she had been spared. Her first "customer" had come her way at her first *mahurat* party. Dully, Aasha Rani's mind went back.

Kishenbhai had insisted on her going to the party, saying, "You must be seen by the people who matter." He'd wangled an invitation to it through the financier of the film—a Sindhi with enough *surma* in his eyes to give a Kathakali dancer a complex. This man had a strange name: Vishnu M.D. He was known throughout the film industry only by those misleading last initials. The only words he had spoken when he saw Aasha Rani were, "She's dark, but *chalegi.*" Kishenbhai had winked and shoved Aasha Rani forward, whispering, "*Chalo* uncle *ko* smile *do.*" *Amma* had gotten her new clothes for the occasion—a hideous, candy pink sari from a bazaar in Dadar.

Kishenbhai had handled the *choli.* "*Kuch* sexy *banao,*" he'd instructed the tailor. And sexy it was. A backless, stringy affair with padded *katoris* so sharply pointed it was a wonder she hadn't hurt someone. "Very nice, very nice!" Kishenbhai had enthused while *Amma* warned her to keep her arms down, so as not to reveal her hairy armpits.

So there she had been with her long, fluid arms glued to her side, in an ensemble that did nothing for her, looking terrified and feeling miserable. "Another Southie *idli*," she had heard someone remark as they went past the foyer toward the swimming pool. She had glanced at herself in a mirror. Why had *Amma* done this to her? Why couldn't she have worn a skirt and blouse or a *salwar-kameez?* And the makeup—*aiiyo,* it was terrible. The maroon lipstick, the glittering *bindi,* the eyeliner that made her eyes look like Ravana's, the tons of blush like an angry rash and, of course, the layers of light-colored foundation to make her look fair.

Fair, fair, fair. *Amma* was obsessed by her color. Even her beautiful, black, naturally wavy hair had been hennaed and pulled and ironed into an improbable coiffure. The straps of her stilettos had already cut blisters into her feet. She had wished she'd come there as an invisible girl, for she was curious to see everyone and everything but not be seen herself.

How beautiful it had all looked! Just like in all those Hindi films she watched, even though she didn't follow a word. Even the palm trees in Bombay were different from the ones in Marina Beach. Straighter, taller, prettier. They had had fairy lights in them and looked like graceful dancers swaying in the sea breeze. All around the pool were clustered hundreds of expensively dressed people— hundreds! She hadn't known or recognized anyone. But they had all looked so impressive—the women like dazzling store mannequins, the men pomaded and sleek, just like in TV ads. There had been a band playing on one side, while waiters had cut through, expertly carrying trays full of drinks. Hesitantly she had reached out for one. The bearer had ignored her outstretched hand and kept walking.

Kishenbhai's eyes had raked the crowd, combing it for contacts.

Amma had been like a tigress on the prowl, looking for the right prey. Aasha Rani had caught sight of an attractive man in white—Oh my God! Akshayji! He had looked stunning. The girl with him had looked good too. But why had she not been covered up properly? *Chhee* . . . her shoulders had been bare, naked. Didn't she feel shy or cold? Aasha Rani had shivered on her behalf and continued staring. The girl was throwing her head back and laughing all the time. She had had swarms of people crowded around her. Akshay and the woman with him had looked like a god and goddess—dressed all in white, and looking beautiful. Who was she? Aasha Rani had wondered, and decided to ask Kishenbhai. "Oh, her? She's Anushree, a Tamil star—like you will be soon." Aasha Rani had gasped. "That girl a South Indian? Can't be! She is so fair. And look at her clothes! She isn't wearing anything, I mean, she's not wearing a sari." Kishenbhai had laughed. "These days top heroines don't wear saris; they have their own designers who make special clothes. You will get one also." "But I could never wear something like that. *Chhee!*" "You will, of course you will."

The party had continued, with lots of film stars turning up and greeting the producer. At one in the morning people had still been arriving in droves, and there was no sign of dinner. Aasha Rani had been dying to eat and get home to bed. Just then the man with the *surma* in his eyes had come up to Kishenbhai and said, "*Chidiya tayaar hai?*" Kishenbhai had come over swiftly to Aasha Rani's side and said softly, "M.D. has a room here upstairs. Go with him. He will feed you. M.D. is an important man. Treat him nicely. He can help your career. Don't create a scene or anything. All you have to do is . . . is . . . what you do with me . . . *bas*. It will be OK. Tomorrow morning I will come and take you home." Aasha Rani had pleaded with her eyes and looked beseechingly at *Amma*—who'd simply averted hers.

Looking back on that night, Aasha Rani would conclude it wasn't all that bad. Surma Eyes could have been a lot worse. Besides, he'd had quite a bit to drink. She'd always heard that drunks gave women a hard time. *Amma* used to be in tears often enough when *Appa* showed up stinking of liquor, with bloodshot eyes and speech that slurred. But this man had passed out on the bed like an exhausted bull after a halfhearted attempt at disrobing her. She'd sat around uncertainly, wondering what to do. She didn't dare make a noise or pick up the phone in case he suddenly awoke. So she had stood by the window and gazed at the people below.

The party was still going full swing—bright lights shone in the pool. There stood Akshay and Anushree. My! How elegant the two of them had looked. She had stood transfixed, watching the slow choreography of the guests as the crowd undulated and steered. After a long time she had drawn the curtains and, stretching out on the carpet, had gone to sleep.

The next morning Surma Eyes had been in a foul mood. He looked ridiculous in his net *ganji* and long, striped underpants. She had looked at the chains around his neck—two gold ones and a *tulsi*-bead *mala*. He had pulled her roughly onto the bed and said, "*Kapdey uttaro.*" She had looked slightly puzzled, as her Hindi had still been at a rudimentary stage. Seeing her hesitate he snarled, "*Saali rundi, soona nahi?* Behave like fucking virgins, these bitches!" Aasha Rani had undressed slowly. What she had really wanted was a steaming cup of *kaapi.* She had kept her mind fixed on that and had taken her clothes off mechanically. He had watched her doing this with a scowl on his face. He'd then picked up a pencil from the table and had dug it deep into his ear, rooting for wax. He'd sniffed the wad he'd unearthed on the tip of the pencil, then grabbed her roughly and shoved her on the bed. She had closed her eyes and thought of coffee, of Madras, of her friend Savitha, of the broken dolls she so dearly loved.

His hands had been like sandpaper against her naked skin. He hadn't shaved, and his stubble cut her face. He had belched and filled the room with the smell of bum whiskey, greasy kebabs and onion *pakoras*. His spongy, hairy paunch had been squashed against her abdomen even as he had squeezed her nipples, pinching them till they hurt. He had kneed her legs apart. *"Ooper kar,"* he had commanded. *"Kya?"* she had asked. *"Saali poochchti hai, 'kya'? Aur kya? Tangdi!"* He had placed his hands below her knees and shoved. "You are like a concrete slab," he'd said. "Move . . . excite me . . . stimulate . . . don't just lie there like a corpse, a *murda*." Automatically, she had begun shaking her pelvis, rocking back and forth. He'd grabbed her shoulders and had begun thrusting himself brusquely against her. Aasha Rani had thought, This is it. The worst is now over. The beast will spill, get off and leave me alone in peace. Just a few moments more, that's all. Galvanized by the thought she'd gyrated her pelvis violently and a small scream had escaped from her mouth. That had seemed to excite him. He'd dug his fingers deeper into her neck and had hammered away. He came finally, grunting like a wild pig.

AFTER THAT EXPERIENCE it was all the same. Most times, she didn't even bother to look at the man's face or body. She just ceased to react. What difference did it make who he was and what he did? Kishenbhai sent her, Kishenbhai fetched her and in between she didn't know what was happening. But once Aasha Rani overheard a conversation between *Amma* and Kishenbhai. *Amma* was saying, "I don't mind your sending Baby here and there; I know it's all a part of the business. I trust you. But what about her health? These men, are they all right? Do you know if they are diseased? We must take Baby for a proper checkup. We have some money now. You are keeping track of all her earnings, aren't you?"

Kishenbhai had said something in a low voice. Then she'd heard *Amma* again. "It's time Baby got a good film. After all, I didn't bring her to Bombay to become just a prostitute. If that was what I'd wanted for her, we could have started our own *dhanda* in Madras itself. Don't think people don't have money there. We also have millionaires. They would have paid anything for my baby."

"HULLO . . . AASHA RANI?"

"Amar?"

"So you recognized my voice, *yaar.* I'm *sooo* flattered. Look, remember that scene in our movie—where the director cut to a bolt of lightning just when our lips were to meet? I'm, like, suffering from this continuity problem . . . could I . . . that is . . ."

Aasha Rani giggled coquettishly. If Akshay was going to play hard-to-get, then she would show him. Amar was a *chikna,* light-eyed stud, desperately young, and desperately enamored. Her latest costar. She was quite fond of him and had even suggested his name to Niteshbhai, recommending him profusely for his next blockbuster. And she didn't really mind the idea of having Amar over. And in bed.

"I'm alone now."

"Great, *yaar*. I've even gotten you a priceless present—a full-size blowup of me. I know it's your birthday; I mean, who doesn't!"

It was nice to have someone else do the groveling for a change, mused Aasha Rani. Sometimes with Akshay she felt that all the passion, all the need, was only from her side. His attitude was condescending, like he was granting her a favor. Bastard! Putting the phone down, she changed out of the outfit she'd put on specially for Akshay into an oversize T-shirt that hung to her knees. The kind of stuff teenyboppers like Amar would be appreciative of. Wildly.

The full-size blowup had gotten Aasha Rani thinking. She'd dabbled in that sort of stuff too. Poor baby-faced Amar. What a lot he had to learn. She smiled for the first time that day. And thought of Dhiru.

"Baby," *Amma* had said one day, "what we really need are some top-class pictures of you. Some really artistic, good photos."

Amma's idea of "top-class" photographs had turned out to be topless; namely bare-all shots of Aasha Rani taken by a horny photographer called Dhiru.

Every starlet hitting Bombay made an obligatory trip to Dhiru's studio. He specialized in cheesecake shots. His modus operandi was simple: He'd lure them into his makeshift studio with vague "modeling" offers. Once he had them captive, he'd start working on their vanity. "*Sachchi, kya pyaari* figure *hai*. You should feel very proud of your body. I have photographed *hazaar* film stars, but I have yet to see such a figure. *Chalo,* let's shoot some *Adivasi* shots. *Arrey,* all producers just love them! After all, most of our films are about villagers. You will have to wear such

43

costumes when you become a star. I have arranged for one today; take a look!"

The "tribal" costume in question was rarely anything more than a scrap of a knotted *choli*—more like a bra—and a knee-length *ghagra* ("This way they can see your lovely legs also"). Once the starlet got into this attire he'd pose her with a *matka* between her legs or get her to sprawl invitingly on the floor against a laminated backdrop of the Alps. Another favorite was the famous "waterfall shot." He'd get the "model" to drape herself in a diaphanous white muslin sari, blouseless, as all Hindi film village belles usually were. The first few shots would be restricted to the standard "*gaon ki chori*" ones. Later, once the "atmosphere" warmed up sufficiently, he'd tell the girl to go into the bathroom and throw some water on herself. If she hesitated he'd take some water from a plastic jug and sprinkle some on her. After the first shiver or two the girl would be fine. He would then pour the entire jug or stand her under the shower—it was that easy.

With Aasha Rani, he had tried another strategy. Taking *Amma* aside, he'd said, "Your daughter is beautiful. Someday she will be a star. She has a good bust. We will concentrate on that. Let us photograph her in a sari with the buttons of her *choli* open. That will look sexy and really classy." *Amma* had readily agreed and got Aasha Rani to dress in a flimsy georgette sari. She'd pushed the blouse off Aasha Rani's shoulder, opening the first three hooks. "Enough?" she'd asked Dhiru. "*Theek hai*—for the first shots," he'd answered.

In an hour's time he had worked his way through ten rolls of film; exposing that much more of Aasha Rani with each successive exposure. She was almost naked by the time the session was finished. "OK!" Dhiru had said. "Sign these release forms and I'll show you the pictures day after tomorrow."

A few months later, Aasha Rani had spotted a life-size calendar for a television company in a crowded shopping center and stopped to stare—there she was in next to nothing, beaming at the world from under the caption, which read "The Whole Picture: Only on VTS Television." She'd blushed at the sight of her nipples. They'd been enlarged and retouched. The poster calendar was glossy, sexy. After the initial shock Aasha Rani had smiled to herself. Dhiru was right. She did have a beautiful body.

Dhiru's photographs had had the desired effect. Particularly after they were published by *Showbiz*. An eager reporter had even traced Aasha Rani to the depressing hovel in which they lived. "We would like to interview you," she'd said. *Amma* had been jubilant. "Let's go to the *Showbiz* office immediately. *Arrey,* this is good news. Once they write something about you, *bas,* then we won't need Kishenbhai, Niteshbhai or any other *bhai.* Baby, looks like our dreams are going to come true." Your dreams, Aasha Rani had wanted to correct her mother, but said nothing.

Aasha Rani had seen *Showbiz.* Everybody read it—cover to cover. Even in Madras. She had known that if she got a writeup in it she'd immediately get the attention she'd been craving. But after that? She had wanted to wait. She'd wanted to sign a film before being picked up by the press. Her instincts had told her that that was the way to do it. That was the route she would have preferred. She had tried reasoning with *Amma.* "Look, they will treat me differently once I have a big banner behind me. Now, I'll be just another starlet, a nobody with big boobs. That's all."

Amma had been outraged. "You *kal ki chokri,* you chit of a girl, how dare you talk like that to your *amma*. No arguments. Now, get dressed, put on that bell-bottom pant and come on. We should go there immediately!"

Aasha Rani had held out. "I'm not being stubborn, *Amma*," she had said, "but I want to do it my way. I want to become a star on my terms. Not in this manner. They have contacted me. I have not gone begging to them. I will see them when I'm ready. Not now." *Amma* had glared at her. "Conceited girl. You will have to be taught a lesson. Wait till I tell Kishenbhai." "Who is Kishenbhai, anyway? Just a pimp. That's all. What can he do to me?" Aasha Rani had challenged. The next thing she knew *Amma* had struck her. One stinging slap right on the face. "Don't you dare speak to your *amma* this way," she had raged. "I have not sacrificed my life, my youth, my everything for this. You will obey me at all times. If I say 'do this,' you will do it. Understand?"

Aasha Rani had rushed out blindly. Her cheek had felt raw, but it was the expression in *Amma*'s eyes that had scared her. *Amma* was beginning to look manic. Crazed with ambition. Was their position that desperate? Money. It had to be money. She had gone to a public phone booth and called Niteshbhai. This was the first time she'd phoned anybody on her own. At first she couldn't get the words out. Finally, she spoke, and her own voice had surprised her. There was no hesitation at all as she had purred to him, "I think about you all the time. Especially at night when I'm in bed . . ."

WHEN SHE HEARD Amar's car pull up the driveway Aasha Rani tugged the neck of her T-shirt off one shoulder and positioned herself at the top of the stairs. Amar took them two at a time, bounding up like a little boy. Flushed. Excited. And somewhat drunk.

"*Chhee,* you're smelling," Aasha Rani said as he swooped to kiss her. "Does your mummy know what her *raja beta* is up to— drinking and doing *ashiqui?*"

"My mother doesn't talk to me since I left home to become a star. She still thinks I'll come around and take the IAS." He laughed. "But my dad's a great fellow; you'll like him, *yaar.* He's always encouraged me; he'd probably be proud of me having made it to Aasha Rani's bed! Hey! What's with all the toys, *yaar?*"

Later in bed, with Amar asleep beside her, Aasha Rani thought bitterly how different her parents were from Amar's. A mother who looked the other way when Kishenbhai led her to her first "client," a father who probably didn't recognize her. She was nothing but an unwanted bastard child. For everyone to exploit.

Akshay Arora

BY THE TIME AKSHAY REMEMBERED AASHA RANI'S BIRTHDAY, IT
was much too late. He was at dinner with the family—a treat for
them—when he noticed the kitchen clock. "Oh shit!" he said,
and Malini looked up sharply. "Forgotten something?" she asked.
He said quickly, "No, nothing important."

It was ten at night. Aasha Rani would never forgive him he
thought. He'd even told his secretary to buy a Kanjeevaram sari
and a pair of gold earrings. What had the bloody fellow done
with those? Oh God! Supposing he'd given the jewelry to Malini?
Was that why she had snapped at the dinner table? Malini couldn't
be fooled. She must have known who the gifts were for. Or at
least gathered that they weren't meant for her. When was the last
time he'd gone and bought her a present? For their first wedding
anniversary. After that she'd gone and ordered whatever she
wanted at the family jeweler's and presented him with the bill.
This suited him fine. Saved him the hassle of scratching his head
for ideas. It made her happy too, so long as he picked up the tab
without questioning her. She, of course, planned his gifts months
in advance and made a production out of the presentation ceremony. Making sure everybody got to hear about what an imaginative, thoughtful wife she was. Invariably her unique gifts got

into the gossip columns and received wide publicity. But Akshay didn't begrudge her her small victories. It must have been pretty hard for her when she gave up her career for him and found herself out of the limelight. So what if she got mileage out of small things, like the *pujas* she organized on his birthday or the exclusive parties she planned? Maybe he could tell her he was going across to Ajay's house to discuss business, or he could say he'd suddenly remembered an urgent meeting with that up-country producer who was chasing him for dates. She would simply ask him to send the secretary instead. This was terrible. Akshay knew he had messed things up for himself: Aasha Rani was fiercely possessive. Plus, he knew Aasha Rani would find out sooner or later that he'd spent most of the day in his trysting suite with that new starlet, Shabnam. And then there would be hell to pay.

It was all such a laugh, really. Here he was haplessly trying to conceal his infidelities from his wife *and* his mistress! For Aasha Rani was as cloyingly devoted as his *patni*. Maybe he should get rid of her—after all, his father's doom had been spelled in much the same way when, blinded by lust, he had sunk all his money into the vacant, cold, reptilian eyes of his greedy *rakhail*. Akshay thought of the life they had been forced to lead when his dad went bankrupt, and shuddered. He had vowed to get himself out of it. And it had taken years. Would Aasha Rani now be the force that sent him reeling back to that squalid chawl?

IN THOSE DAYS Akshay Arora's ultimate measure of having "made it" had been the owning of a spectacular bathroom. It was a childhood fetish. A throwback to the time he'd had to queue up to share a stinking lavatory in a dilapidated chawl. His was not the usual poor-boy-makes-good film story. As a kid he'd seen better days, but briefly. He could not remember very much about those years, though his older brother, Ajay, used to tell him of the time the family lived in a neat bungalow in Chembur. That was when his father was a successful producer. They'd even had a car and servants. Akshay only faintly recalled an old house with a small garden outside. He must have been around three or four at the time.

His most vivid memories were of the Dadar chawl, where the family moved after his father went bankrupt backing an ambitious film, *Mehboob ki Nigahen,* which collapsed at the box office. Along with the failure of the film, Akshay's father's health, too, fell into decline. He lost his fire, his wife and his mistress in one fell swoop.

Akshay grew up a lonely child with just his older brother for company. A brother who tried to be everything to him—mother, father and friend. But it was hard for two young boys and an alcoholic father to keep going. The chawl life helped in that there were always neighbors who cared. They were often strapped for money. Akshay's father had taken to hanging around various film units as an assistant. There was no steady income, and the little that trickled in was often drunk away. But the boys coped. They'd had to. Akshay's aunt took care of the school fees, and their grandfather pitched in with the grocery money as and when the situation became desperate.

Akshay didn't hate his father; he felt sorry for him. It was Ajay who detested him. "Papaji let us down. He destroyed our future. Mummyji ran away because of him," he'd tell Akshay bitterly. Mummyji was, in fact, living not too far from them. She'd made a new life with their father's old friend, a cameraman from the days of power and glory; the same friend who used to hang around sycophantically when Akshay's father was still big-league. Akshay could never understand why his mother had abandoned them and gone off with "Suresh Uncle." Ajay tried to explain: "Mummyji was disgusted," he'd point out. "Papaji made her give up all her jewelry, her savings, everything, for this film of his. And why? Because he wanted to make his girlfriend a star. That same green-eyed bitch who is doing mother roles today. He thought *Mehboob* would click and she'd make it big. Idiot! As if it were easy. The film went grossly overbudget, and nobody could stand her. She couldn't act to save her life. Wooden face, high-pitched voice. But Papaji was totally *fida*. He even brought her home once or twice. Before Mummyji got wise to their *chakkar*." Akshay just couldn't relate to all these old tales. He only knew he had to break away and make money. Big money. Quick money.

His heart wasn't ever in studying, and this upset Ajay enormously: "*Arrey yaar,* I want you to become an engineer, go abroad, get a good job. Why are you wasting your time like this? I mean, *yaar,* I don't have brains. But you have everything—looks, brains, everything." Except money, Akshay would think as he stared at himself in the mirror. It was true; he was striking, with his mother's fine features and his father's height. But the last thing he wanted was to become an engineer. "What do you want to become in that case, *yaar?*" Ajay would ask in exasperation. "I don't know," Akshay would say, and stare some more into the mirror.

He'd made it through school, and nearly made it through college. Meanwhile, Ajay had found a job as a junior salesman, selling toiletries and medicines. In school Akshay had acted in plays and enjoyed the experience. College was different. The plays they picked required "emoting," as the pretentious directors of the play would never tire of telling him. For him acting was a lark. A fun thing. He loved horsing around and improvising. Ajay disapproved of his acting, even for kicks. "Concentrate on studies," he'd reprimand each time Akshay broached the topic. So he'd tried to concentrate, but it was hopeless.

Once, just for the heck of it, he'd decided to audition for a TV play without informing Ajay. He'd bagged the role—and more. He was asked to try out for a newsreader's job—strictly on a freelance basis—but with promises of regular assignments if he clicked. Akshay had done surprisingly well in the audition and was told to present himself the next night for a trial run. It helped that Akshay spoke Marathi without a trace of a Punjabi accent. Ajay was furious. Akshay surprised himself by holding out. "This is something I'd like to do for myself. Besides, we need the money." Ajay agreed on one condition—TV newsreading was to be regarded as nothing more than a hobby.

From TV news, he moved on to a TV serial playing a dashing detective. This was when he made a fair amount of money and, more important, got attention. Strictly small-time. But several people sat up and noticed. The fact that his Punjabiness didn't make itself evident each time he opened his mouth won him a lot of praise—and a cover feature in a Marathi movie mag. Suddenly everyone was talking about Akshay Arora. From then on, Akshay didn't ever have to worry about money. Or bathrooms.

Ajay capitulated shortly after Akshay's first big success— a Marathi film by the name of *Prem Tujhe Majhe,* in which he played a love-struck police officer. "You need someone to organize things for you," Ajay announced, and dumped his junior salesmanship to become Akshay's agent. The film industry was beginning to evince interest. One of the producers was a distant uncle, who had pretended not to know them when Papaji's luck ran out. Ajay was triumphant. "*Ab aagayaa line pey salaa.* Now we can show him. He is offering you a role, *haramzada. Chalo,* we'll also teach him a lesson. Let him come to us. Let him crawl. We'll see his piddly film. Don't speak to him if he phones. I'll handle everything."

Akshay was relieved to have Ajay manage his affairs. He had no head for business himself. And in Ajay he discovered a hard, shrewd side that assessed a deal in seconds and decided what it was worth. "Money speaks to me, *yaar,*" Ajay laughed the first time he negotiated an attractive contract for Akshay.

With Akshay's successful debut into Hindi cinema, Ajay decided it was time to move out and buy a fancy car. "Never mind the cost, *yaar,*" he said. "In this *dhanda,* appearances count. Look swanky and they'll treat you swanky. Look *sadela* and that's the treatment you'll get." Akshay knew they couldn't really afford the bungalow at the Juhu Vile-Parle scheme, nor the sleek Honda Accord that rolled up to their chawl, but he went along with Ajay's plan. He was only too anxious to get out of the dreary two-room tenement once and for all. The neighbors gathered to wish them good-bye. They were all set to climb into their gleaming car and zoom off, when suddenly their old man dug in his heels and refused to budge. Startled by his response, they stared at him. Ajay took his arm and tried to drag him out of the dingy hovel. No way. "This is now my house. This is where I belong. This is where I want to be," babbled the old man. Ajay pushed Akshay toward the car and said, "*Chalo bhai, chalo,* we'll deal with him later. The old buddha's quite senile."

Akshay's new house was close to the Sun 'n' Sand hotel. Yet, it took him more than a year in that posh locale before he could pluck up enough courage to saunter across.

It had been one of the most thrilling moments of his life. Sun 'n' Sand symbolized showbiz. It was glamour and sin, success and sophistication. The place to be seen. The favorite haunt of the rich and ritzy. This was where they partied and frolicked. He'd seen photographs in dozens of film magazines. He'd watched the poolside dances in hundreds of films. He'd known all the stories that surrounded the hotel. The deals that were sealed in the coffee shop, the starlets who were bedded in the suites upstairs, the stormy story sessions that went on behind closed doors—even the fights and knifings that erupted when the action picked up! And there he had been, standing uncertainly at the entrance, feeling gauche and stupid, wondering where to go.

The lobby wasn't all that impressive now that he actually stood in it. Besides, Sun 'n' Sand had competition from a clutch of gleaming new hotels angling for the film crowd, which they tried to woo with state-of-the-art health clubs, ethnic food, coffee shops, trendy bars and pretty front office girls. The swanky Centaur, the upstartish Sea Princess, the impersonal Ramada Inn and the industry's current favorite, the Holiday Inn. Yet, the Sun 'n' Sand had managed to retain a charm of its own. The service was friendly, the bar full and the old glamour a little faded, but still tangible.

Someone had walked up to him, startling him for a minute. "Excuse me, are you Akshayji?" a female voice had asked. Akshay had panicked: Oh God! He'd been recognized. Maybe he wasn't supposed to be there. Maybe they were going to throw him out. He'd nearly run toward the exit. The young girl had persisted. He'd looked down nervously at her—she held an autograph book in her hand. This was some kind of mistake. The girl had been persistent. "Please sign," she had said, and he'd suddenly felt intensely foolish. "No pen," he'd stammered. "I'm not carrying a pen." He'd looked around wildly and just at that point the manager had walked up to him, a Parker in one hand, and flowers in the other.

AJAY DIDN'T REALLY HAVE TO worry about Akshay's career. He had scored thirty hits in ten years! Beating the reigning superstar by a wide margin. There was no doubt about it: Akshay was definitely number one. And it was Ajay's shrewd handling that had gotten him where he was. Had he left the business aspect to Akshay he would have messed it up entirely. Chosen the wrong films, made all the wrong moves. As it was, each time Akshay ditched a producer and ran off to Khandala or Alibag, it was left to Ajay to sort out the mess and *manao* the unit.

Ajay stared at the pile of files on his table. Income tax returns, contracts, schedules, scripts—*baap re baap*. He had no time for his family, no time for himself. From the minute he opened his eyes in the morning, it was Akshay, Akshay, Akshay. Sometimes he wondered what all those delirious fans saw in his brother. Agreed, he was a good-looking fellow. But there were so many who were better-looking than him. *Chalo,* he could act. But only certain roles. Rakesh Kapoor was more versatile, and that new chap—Shaban—a better dancer.

Ajay glanced up at a poster of Akshay's first film—*Kismet Ka Karz.* What had he done in it? Danced, fought and died. Like every other hero in every other Hindi film. Yet the crowds had gone wild.

As he continued to stare at the picture his eyes traveled down to Akshay's crotch. The artist had painted a prominent bulge between his legs. He peered more closely. Oh my God! So that was it! Akshay's crotch! Feverishly, Ajay began leafing through other publicity stills. God, there it was again. Akshay had almost thrust it into the faces of his fans. He looked at Akshay's glossy pinup pictures in various magazines. No, it wasn't a coincidence. Akshay always made sure his trousers were well filled out. Here was another still—this time he'd stuck a gun into his pocket. Crotch shot after crotch shot. Akshay was unfailingly photographed from a low angle!

Ajay sat back. The mystery of Akshay's magic finally unraveled in his mind. Akshay had symbolically fucked his way to the top. Every woman in the audience believed he was doing it to her and her alone. While every man thought he was Akshay— screwing the women of the world.

THE ENTIRE FILM INDUSTRY knew Akshay to be a mean, spiteful bastard. Unfortunately, he was also a successful bastard. And that made all the difference. "I'm the only hero who can command a price," he would boast. It was true. Akshay had screen presence. Charisma. Star quality. This baffled producers, who unanimously hated his guts and couldn't really see anything much in him beyond his mean eyes and flared nostrils. Directors, too, testified that Akshay was no Dilip Kumar. And he was a positive pain in the arse to work with. A collective nightmare for everybody involved in the making of a film.

When Aasha Rani first came on the scene, Akshay was still riding high—but only just. Akshay had suffered his first pricey flop. Aasha Rani had just had her first pricey hit. Watching her gyrate in *Taraazu,* Akshay realized that there was only one sure-fire way for him to hold on to his niche at the top. And it involved Aasha Rani.

Souten ka Badla, their first film together, went on to break box office records, and Akshay was back in the running once again. But only when working opposite Aasha Rani. "Lucky pair," cooed superstitious financiers on seeing their names across a contract. Lucky or not, Aasha Rani had been delighted. Working together ensured that they spent all their time in each other's company. She saw Akshay through a besotted woman's eyes.

On-screen they worked amazingly well as a romantic duo. "Chemistry," gushed the *filmi* rags, while fans swooned over their love scenes. One particular duet was picturized in a train coupé in a manner so suggestive that it was a wonder the scene escaped the censors. It had Akshay making thrusting movements at Aasha Rani, in breathless tempo with the train's insistent "chook-chook-chook" (which, incidentally, doubled for song lyrics). Every so often the camera zoomed in for a tight close-up of Aasha Rani's face, which she would contort to express orgasmic nirvana. All this, coupled with cuts to pistons moving vigorously up and down, had the crowds going wild. Entire *Chitrahaars* were devoted to the song. Every *dhaba,* every street-side barbershop, every red Maruti seemed to vibrate with the energy of their love.

The only person who wasn't ecstatic about the star *jodi*'s success was Mrs. Malini Arora. Having gauged Akshay's reaction at the dining table, Malini knew there was something afoot. And she had a fair idea who with. Definitely not just one of the fucks. Akshay's glib lies had deepened her suspicion. Normally he would not even bother to keep his liaisons secret. After all, he needed sex. And Malini was hardly an enthusiastic partner.

She was aware that Akshay had chosen her to be his wife after much deliberation. It was obvious he wasn't looking for a glamour girl or an intellectual. He was not lying when he told the press on the day he was to wed her, "I want a homemaker. Someone who will be a good mother to my children. I don't want to marry a painted doll, some cheap film girl who will flirt with all my friends. Malini is the right woman for me." Malini, in turn, had explained her decision to quit her career. She was a *ghazal* singer who was just beginning to get noticed, when Akshay proposed to her. "My husband means more to me than a career. I believe a wife's place is in the home, not in a recording studio. Akshay is an old-fashioned man. I will never displease him." A cheeky reporter had asked her, "But what about his affairs? Will you tolerate them?" Malini was tight-lipped. "I trust my husband. He will never do anything to hurt me."

Everyone in the industry knew, however, that on the night before the wedding itself, after the mandatory stag party that generally preceded the big moment, Akshay, sloshed senseless, had driven straight to the house of Silk Simki (the easiest lay in filmdom) and stayed there. Even before their honeymoon was over Akshay had betrayed her trust at least half a dozen times. He was an indiscriminating womanizer. And a champion hypocrite. Malini had promptly been converted into the film industry's *bhabhiji*.

For her part Malini rather liked the image and cultivated it assiduously. Soon, it got to her appearance as well. She began wearing expensive, duly dignified saris and pulling her luxuriant hair back into a no-nonsense bun. Strictly no makeup apart from a smudge of *kaajal*, and no sparkle in the eyes either. Her singing came to a full stop as per the premarriage contract, and the only time she permitted herself the luxury of a song was when she sang her morning *bhajan* while performing her daily *puja* in the elaborate *puja ghar*. In quick succession Malini produced two sons and miscarried a third. Visitors to their sprawling bungalow marveled at her quiet taste and impeccable housekeeping. Akshay and she entertained little. ("No *filmi* parties for us, *baba*," she said in rare interviews.) But the truth of the matter was that both hated to spend money. If ever the children visited Akshay on the sets, he made sure the producer paid for their cold drinks and snacks. The entire industry knew him as a *kanjoos*, but nobody dared say as much. Malini didn't scrimp when it came to jewelry for herself, though. She had worked out an ingenious excuse: "It's for my future daughters-in-law," she'd explain to her guests. "The way prices are shooting up these days, it's better to buy jewelry when it is still affordable." Watching the boys as they toddled around outside, this remark always raised laughs, but Malini maintained a grave expression.

Akshay didn't interfere when she went looking for diamonds. It was an expensive upper for Malini, but it assuaged his guilt. He also pushed her into "social work." Malini was associated with half a dozen causes and bullied lost souls to save themselves, when she wasn't buying invaluable trinkets. The industry wallahs felt sorry for their *bhabhiji* and continued to indulge her quirks. Akshay didn't like her to attend his *mahurats* because he was superstitious and believed his film would flop if she witnessed the premiere shot, so the considerate film wallahs sent her the proceedings on video, to watch at leisure in the luxury of her understated beige-and-salmon-pink bedroom.

It was on one such video that Malini first noticed Akshay and Aasha Rani slyly exchanging glances. She replayed that particular portion half a dozen times to make sure and then kept quiet about it. Yes—she was certain she wasn't imagining things. She had passively watched her husband flirting with his heroines during *mahurats* dozens of times and had never spared it a thought. But this was different. She'd had an inkling that something serious was afoot ever since she had accidentally put a tape into her player thinking it had *bhajans* on it and had heard a husky voice addressing erotic love poems to her husband. Initially she had found it difficult to identify the woman. Was she a new singer? A besotted fan? Some unknown admirer? But the words were far too intimate and knowing. At one point the woman had cracked a joke using one of Akshay's favorite endearments, "*Jaanu.*" That had convinced Malini this was someone Akshay was sleeping with on a regular basis.

When he got home from the studios that night, she'd deliberately played the tape and waited to see his reaction. He'd just come out of their designer bathroom (all granite, chrome and crystal) holding a towel around his middle. The voice had startled him enough to make him let go of the towel. Malini had stared at her husband and thought how foolish he looked standing there, with his cock all shriveled and limp, his eyes like a stricken goat's. But Akshay had recovered quickly enough to say, "Oh, I've been looking for that tape. This female, I forget her name, sent me a demo tape to pass on to the producer. Desperate woman. Wants a break as a songwriter." Malini had stared at him coldly and asked, "How come she calls you '*Jaanu*' throughout?" Akshay laughed uneasily. "Silly bitch. She must have read that interview of mine where I mentioned I call you that in my loving moments."

Malini had looked at him with contempt. What a desperate liar her husband was. But she wasn't the typical *filmi* wife. She would not throw a tantrum or get hysterical. That would achieve nothing. She'd wait and watch. The video more or less confirmed her suspicions that the woman was Aasha Rani, but she needed more proof. She needed to hear her voice. On an impulse, she phoned Aasha Rani one night, but her secretary answered and Malini hung up. She had never been troubled by any of Akshay's liaisons before. In fact, she'd never even questioned him about all those heroines who'd given a blow-by-blow account of their sizzling sorties with Akshay to film journalists who thought it worth their while. This time, however, she felt seriously threatened, because she sensed that this woman was not just "one of the fucks," as she mentally categorized the others, despising them for their "animal behavior."

Malini hated sex. Or perhaps she hated sex with Akshay, who did tend to have a sadistic streak. In fact, she often felt she could happily do without it for the rest of her life, despite the fact that she was just in her early thirties. She told herself that Akshay was "allowed" his flings, since they rarely slept together. He had a ready excuse when he got home tired from the studios, and she feigned a migraine on the rare occasions he still bothered to make an amorous move. Now that she had done the considerate Indian-wife thing and given him two male children, she felt freed of all conjugal responsibility. Sex was one area she hated to discuss, particularly with Akshay. She wondered why it was made the focus of everything in life. Akshay loved watching Swedish blue films—especially those of the more sadomasochistic variety. How could human beings behave this way? she'd wonder, averting her eyes from all the heaving bodies on the screen. She knew Akshay often masturbated in bed, and even that put her off. What was he—some kind of insatiable monster? Could he think of nothing but sex? The bed would shake rhythmically, and she'd lie awake in the dark hating the man next to her, thinking, Why does he do this? He has two children—two fine sons—isn't that enough? It never occurred to Malini that bearing progeny and enjoying sex were two different things. That being a wife and being a whore were not all that different. She needed Aasha Rani to educate her.

THE CONFRONTATION CAME a few months after the night Malini had questioned Akshay about the tape. She had vowed never to bring up the topic again, but it wasn't easy to keep her silence—particularly since every movie-mag hoarding in the city screeched about the same thing: Akshay's *chakkar* with Aasha Rani. Is it serious? Or is this just another publicity stunt?"

Malini was desperate to talk to someone. Someone decent and respectable. Someone who understood wayward husbands. But she could think of no one she could trust. Feeling insecure and depressed, she resorted to her favorite pick-me-up: jewelry shopping.

She decided to go to her favorite jeweler—Tribhovandas Bhimji—and to visit their new, ritzy, Arab-trap showroom in the Oberoi hotel. Just driving all the way to South Bombay, chasing a bauble, was soothing enough. While she was trying on the latest in enameled gold bangles, she heard a familiar voice. "Helloji," cooed Rita, who always spoke like she gargled with *gulab-jamun* syrup each morning. Malini was almost glad to see her.

Rita was the film industry's self-proclaimed avenging angel

and Agony Aunt. A powerful woman, whose husband was the closest thing to God in the business, Rita had, over the years, made it her business to mind everybody else's. She also had the softest and fattest shoulders to cry on. Malini paused midbangle and greeted her warmly. For a minute or two, both of them discussed the crazy price of gold, the absurd markups in these shops and the mad way diamond prices were escalating.

The starstruck shopgirls fawned and gushed over the two of them. Film wives were their best customers. But they were also the hardest to please. So fussy. And they could never quite resist haggling over the price of the jewelry box the ornaments came in. But the money they brought in ensured that their crassness, their inevitable late payments and their patronizing manner had to be put up with. Malini waved her bangle-laden arm under Rita's nose and asked, "What do you think? Pretty, no? But *baap re baap,* just look at the prices!" Rita stared politely and then got to the point. "Malini, what are you planning to do about Aasha Rani?"

Malini knew it was no use either playing dumb or even telling Rita point-blank to lay off. She thought quickly and concluded that it was best to enlist Rita's help and support. "I am stuck," Malini said. "I don't know what to do; please help me." Rita loved the sound of those three words—"Please help me." They were irresistible and oh-so-sweet. "Of course I will, Malini. In fact, I've even thought of a plan. Let me fix up a meeting between you two. My place. That bitch won't be able to refuse if I invite her. *Arrey*, what is she? A girl from the gutters of Madras. No class, nothing. A bastard child with a madam for a mother. We all know about her. She'll get so nervous she'll probably pee in her panties. I've got to go, Maliniji; I have a Red Cross meeting. I'll phone you after I've fixed the date." And with that Rita sauntered out, leaving Malini with reservations about the whole plan.

Akshay would be furious if he found out. They had an unwritten agreement that Malini was to keep out of his professional life. He was sure to tell her this affair was a "professional" one. Hah! But Malini would not swallow that shit any longer. She would go to Rita's and meet Aasha Rani. Akshay's wrath could be dealt with later.

RITA HAD ASKED MALINI to arrive early, saying, "I'll brief you on how to tackle Aasha Rani." Malini had wondered what to wear. Something exclusive and intimidating, of course. But the colors? She settled for beige. Akshay always told her it complemented her complexion. And the jewelry? Should she even bother with it? What would that *bhangan* know about fine jewels? She probably wore gaudy *Madraasi* rubies herself. Unless Akshay had been educating Aasha Rani. Like he'd educated her. She had often wondered how a chawl type like Akshay had such refined taste. Of course, his estranged mother was quite a lady, even though Malini found her blue-rinsed hair a bit too precious. Anyway, he knew what looked good on women; you had to grant him that. Finally, Malini settled for her "basic pearls," as she called them. Simple, elegant and undoubtedly priceless. Let that slut see what class was all about.

Rita was her usual self—synthetic from head to toe. She wore her hair sprayed stiff into a dome, like a crash helmet. The generously applied turquoise eye shadow, the fluorescent pink lipstick painted half an inch over the lip line and the rouged cheeks colored like out-of-season tomatoes were all set off by a sleazy, shimmering Punjabi suit of Dubai crepe de chine and a film of perspiration. She's just trying to help, Malini reminded herself, and kept her face impassive as she climbed the steps of Rita's massive bungalow by the sea. Rita stood at the entrance and flashed her teeth that showed up lipsticked to a luminiscent pink. Six tetchy poodles yipped at her ankles. Poor woman, an empty womb and a wayward husband.

The house looked like the houses of all prosperous Bombay film producers—like an expensive set gone wrong. Of course, these days the younger moguls called in socialite designers to do up their homes. But Rita fancied her own creativity. She believed she had great ideas, which the house faithfully reflected, starting with the awesome front door made of mother-of-pearl ("I had it done specially for me by craftsmen near Jaipur," she told visitors). There was the obligatory winding staircase in the middle of the drawing room, and a gigantic chandelier the size of a small closet. Rita held all her parties here with great pride and pointed out all her latest acquisitions ("See those marble pillars? Last week").

Malini recalled some of the earlier evenings at Rita's as she went through the obligatory ritual of greeting. She had seen Aasha Rani at one of them. She was a *faltu* at that time, a nobody. But Malini had noticed her. Noticed her body and felt ashamed of her own. Aerobics. Rita had suggested aerobics at one of their coffee parties. So Malini had tried going to a health club a few times, but she was not made for leotards. She had looked dumpy and horrible. Rita's voice cut through her reverie. "*Kitni sweet lag rahi ho!*" she was saying. Ugh! She hated the word "sweet." Malini didn't feel "sweet" at all. Sweet, my ass, you Technicolor cartoon. Take a long look at your own *thopda* first. Instead, Malini smiled and kissed Rita's rouged cheeks. Poison. Imagine wearing Poison at that hour. Like a cheap call girl.

They went inside and Rita held her hand. "Don't worry. Akshay will come back to you. Leave all to me. I'm expert, *yaar*. The number of *filmi* marriages I have saved. *Toba!* I've even lost count by now. Your husband must have been seduced by that whore in his weak moments—all men have them. *All!* Or she may have used *jaadu-tona*. Black magic. Who knows? We shouldn't rule anything out. Women are so cunning these days. Always after other people's husbands. Her mother is the schemer. Maybe she trapped poor Akshay. And these South Indians! They just can't leave our men alone. Their own must be impo, *yaar*. They look pretty limp. Have a pastry, *ji*, the samosas are too good. Don't let that bitch boss you. Don't beg and plead with her. These women are like *nagins*. Snakes. They understand only one language: threats. You tell her you will ruin her career. That she will understand. If even then she argues, tell her that you'll get *goondas* to cut off her breasts, slash her face or throw acid all over her. Strong-arm tactics. These females respond only to that. Good words, polite behavior, forget it, waste of time."

Malini pretended to listen but her mind was really on something else. She could hear Aasha Rani's taped voice crooning words of love and desire. Malini had never ever done that with Akshay. Not even when they were courting. She used to sing for him, of course, but those were borrowed words, the words even her audience heard. Malini worried about that. She had stopped making Akshay feel special in any way. In fact, her contempt and impatience were only too apparent. He sensed it too, but when he asked, she'd snap back, "You don't try your *herogiri* with me. I'm not one of your obliging starlets or *chamchis*." So Akshay just left her alone.

It was ironic, she thought to herself, that Bombay's reigning stud couldn't get as much as he wanted of sex at home. In the beginning, she used to pretend that she liked having sex, since it was important to her to keep Akshay "satisfied." After a point, she'd stopped doing even that. She'd "allow" him to make love, as she lay there impassively, with a martyred expression on her face, letting him know that it was *his* desire, *his* uncontrollable urge, and the sooner he got it over and done with, the better for both of them. While he was doing his "business" she would go over the words of a favorite *ghazal* in her mind and plan her next day's schedule. It was amazing the number of mental chores she accomplished while Akshay was grunting away—his face contorted, his body sweating despite the air-conditioning.

She loathed "the act." And everything associated with it. She hated his breath, his favorite cologne, the curly hair in his armpits, the gold chains around his neck, even the moles on his thighs. She dreaded the nights when she could anticipate "the act." She always knew when he was feeling horny and resorted to little tricks in order to avoid his advances. She'd ask him coquettishly if he would like another drink, knowing a little extra alcohol in his bloodstream would make him sleep like a baby. Or she'd prolong her good nights in the children's room. Sometimes, she'd even stage a fight with one of the servants. When all else failed she'd fall back on the worldwide excuse women who lack imagination trot out: "Not tonight, darling, I have a headache."

Suddenly Malini became aware that Rita had been nattering on about *her* sex life: "Of course, sweetie, it hasn't been easy being married to Kailashji. You know, he's a very demanding man in every way—and so much temptation! *Arrey*, every day he has beautiful women falling at his feet, begging him to let them into his bed. But I told him from day one: 'Look here, *ji*. I am your wife. You give me proper respect. I don't want to know about your *lafdas*. If you have any affair, just be sensible and don't let me know or find out. In public, you have to give me the honor I deserve. What you do behind my back does not concern me.' Believe me, sweetie, it has been so many years now—nineteen, this month—and we are happy. As happy as a film couple can be. I have my friends, my work, my shopping, my kitty parties, my foreign holidays; what more does a woman want? That way Kailashji is very considerate.

"He never questions me about my spending. He allows me to buy whatever I want, whenever I want. I know about his girls. I have felt hurt also, in the past. Once especially when that witch, Babli, had him completely under her spell and he had started spending weekends in Pune with her. But I put a stop to that. I said to Kailashji, 'Look here, *ji*. Enough is enough. This woman is using you. Looting you. Better give her up, or I will commit suicide. That will bring disgrace to you. Plus, my soul will haunt you forever.' He saw my point. *Chalo,* so he lost a few *lakhs* and the film he made for her flopped, but at least he came back to me. We women have to be firm. And stand up for our rights. Sometimes men can be foolish. They can get carried away. It is our duty to bring them back on the right path. That is what wives are for."

Malini silently nodded her agreement.

Rita made the introductions smoothly. Malini was surprised to see how warm and friendly she was toward Aasha Rani. And surprised by Aasha Rani's attire as well. She was wearing a simple *salwar-kameez*—white *chikan,* with an ordinary *bandhani dupatta.*

She looked like a college girl. Hardly any makeup. Her hair pulled back in a casual ponytail. She had good skin, Malini noted. Dark but good. And, of course, nobody could help but notice her bust. What breasts! Malini could see the outline of her bra: a lacy, pretty one, very like her own. Had Akshay given it to her? Of course, it was what went into the bras that made all the difference. Aasha Rani's breasts were magnificent, firm and proud. Malini clutched her sari *pallav* more closely around her shoulders. She had to admit Aasha Rani was attractive—in an earthy sort of way. Plus, she was amazingly relaxed. Imagine! The girl has nerves of steel—so cool, so composed—as if she had nothing to do with the mess. An innocent bystander.

Malini pictured her naked and in bed with Akshay, then quickly thrust the image from her mind. She imagined her giving Akshay a blow job with those full, luscious lips. She hated performing fellatio herself, and Akshay had realized this quickly. He'd given up asking these days because he knew the answer—a hasty and dismissive, *"Chhee!"* Maybe that was what attracted him to this woman, Malini figured. Maybe this girl even swallowed it all. Ugh! She nearly threw up just thinking about it.

Aasha Rani touched Rita's feet, settled down comfortably on a settee and waited expectantly. Malini was beginning to feel uncomfortable, but Rita expertly took over the proceedings and got the summit under way. "Tell me, darling," she said sweetly to Aasha Rani, "what is all this nonsense with Akshayji? It's not nice. Very naughty." Aasha Rani regarded her coolly. "Is it? Why?"

"Arrey! What do you mean, 'Why'? *Baba,* he is another woman's husband. You can't destroy someone's marriage like this. It is not done, darling," Rita screeched, quite taken aback. Aasha Rani,

looking far from penitent, stared at Malini and said, "I'm not the one who's breaking up her marriage. She has broken it herself."

"Now look here, Aasha Rani. This is not the correct attitude. We have called you to settle this matter. You must be reasonable."

"Why don't you call Akshay and tell him to stop seeing me? Why are you after my blood?"

"Because we women should sort out matters between ourselves. We should not involve men. Poor Akshayji—*bechare*—what can he do if women like you throw themselves at him? He is only a man."

Malini, who had been silently listening to all this, suddenly spoke up. Her carefully controlled facade broke without warning, and in a voice that was shrill with rage and hysteria she screamed, "Look here, you bloody *kutti,* we all know your type—stealing our men, wrecking our homes. Do you have no conscience? It makes me sick to hear all your stupid love talk on the tapes. Shameless slut!"

Aasha Rani didn't say anything for a while. Just watched as Malini caught her breath, her face contorted and ugly. Then she said softly, "Let me show you your face, Malini. Just look at the hatred in your eyes. Is this how you greet your husband when he comes home every night? And you wonder why he comes to me?"

"Bitch! *Haramzaadi!* Whore! You are teaching me about my husband? How dare you? I didn't expect you to be so shameless. So unrepentant. It's your background, of course. How can a *rundi* have morals? She will sleep with anyone who pays her. Akshay may screw you in the makeup room or the gutter, but it is my bed he comes to at night!"

"So? What does that prove?"

"It proves that he is my man. My husband. He may sleep with dozens of prostitutes like you. But I am the one he respects, whose home he regards as his own."

Aasha Rani smiled. "Well, in that case, why are we all here? You should feel very happy, very satisfied. I didn't want to meet you. And I don't want to change places with you either. If you can't manage your marriage, ask yourself where you went wrong."

Malini screeched, "You can stick your bloody philosophy and lecture-*baazi* up your ass. Just give my husband back to me!"

Aasha Rani picked up her bag. "He is not a toy I have bought in the marketplace that I can 'give him back.' I have not taken him in the first place. It is up to you to hold him or lose him."

Malini screamed, "*Sex!* That is all you have—*Sex!* That is what women like you use. Cheap bitches—part your legs and let any man in. Sex, sex, sex, dirty, filthy sex! Perverts! You must be a pervert. What do you do to him—hah? Suck his cock? Or suffocate him with your breasts? He will get tired of you, like he has of all the others. Eventually a man needs his wife and children. You will see. But my curse is upon you. You will never be happy. You will never marry. You will die as you are, without *sindhoor* in your *maang*. And then you will remember this day and regret it. But it will be too late!"

Aasha Rani got up and walked toward the mother-of-pearl door. Something told her to whirl around just in time, and the copper vase Malini had hurled at her whizzed past. Recovering herself admirably she said, "OK, Ritaji. Give my regards to Kailashji. And dear, dear Maliniji, instead of being the *bhabhiji* of the entire industry, try being the wife of just one man. And yes, do suck his cock sometimes—he loves it."

After Aasha Rani's exit, Rita and Malini sat around for a long time, their composure shaken. "Never make the mistake of allowing the industry to pity you. That is the end. Don't plead with the other woman—attack her instead. Don't reduce yourself to a victim—make her one." Rita's instructions kept coming, but Malini was barely listening. "Men are all the same—animals," she repeated bitterly, "and we women, such fools."

"Look at it this way, sweetie," Rita crooned. "You have his name. You live well. He is good to you—I mean, there is no violence in your marriage. Akshayji doesn't beat you or anything. What more do you expect? Romance finishes the morning after the wedding night. After that, what? Boredom. Men like variety. We women have to put up with that and switch our minds to something else. Why don't you play rummy? It's relaxing. It will take your mind off all this. Of course, at this point you hate Akshayji. That's normal. In any case, most women hate their husbands—it's a fact. They hate marriage. That's also a fact. But what else can they do? What is the choice? The only way to make a marriage work is through sex—and most women hate that too. But the day a man feels that his woman has lost interest in sex, and therefore in him, the relationship is finished and he starts looking elsewhere. Aasha Rani and her kind are always waiting. We have to pretend. All wives have to pretend. Just shut your eyes and part your legs, whether you feel like it or not. Because if you don't some other woman will. A wife is acting all the time—this is the world's best-kept secret. But I am telling you, act, act, act; that is what she has to do. Boost his ego, make him feel like a king even when you really want to spit on him. Everything is decided by the bed. On the bed. If he finds you cold, *bas,* you have lost him. No woman should be foolish enough to be honest with her husband where sex is concerned."

* * *

AKSHAY MUMBLED SOMETHING and left the kitchen table to brood in his study. Malini followed him out with her eyes. Would she never be rid of that bitch? she thought bitterly. If looks could kill Akshay would have needed his stunt double at this point. Sex maniac, her eyes said. Bastard, obsessed with the bloody "act." He was incapable of understanding her sensitive and artistic nature. He mocked her religion, he scoffed at her music and he loathed her. For what? For giving up her career? For docilely agreeing to his every whim and providing him with a home he could be proud of? For sacrificing, yes, sacrificing everything to be *Mrs.* Arora? What did he see in that sleazy slut for whom parting her legs was a reflex action? "O Lord, give me peace," she said, and went to her *puja* room. A lilting *bhajan* would have eased the burden of her frustration. But Malini believed in denial. Repressing her anger, turning aggression inward. So that instead of dissipating, the rot set in within.

Closeted in his study, Akshay poured out a stiff measure of Scotch and knocked it back neat. He felt his mind clear. Perhaps it was more sensible not to have called Aasha Rani. Bloody woman was so possessive. Got to be embarrassing sometimes. And she wasn't content to keep things private. No—she'd have them doing made-for-each-other interviews for every *filmi* rag in the business if she were allowed to. He was getting a bit tired of her insisting on coming to the studios, where he was shooting, with a *dabba* of hot Southie *khaana,* at the stroke of one. Like a bloody devoted *Bhartiya Nari*. He had noticed the unit hands avert their faces and hide their smiles. She always seemed to react to things disproportionately. Especially where he was concerned. Swinging from hysteria one minute—at having found him in the arms of a nubile starlet—to dog-eyed devotion the next. A bit weird. Like he was her obsession. Like she was trying to prove a point. It was like being pushed into a pit of quicksand. The deeper you got in, the worse it got. If only he could talk to Ajay. Aasha Rani was suffocating him. If she was to be believed, she had never been too keen on her career. But he was. Akshay liked the heady sense of power, loved the way the crowds adulated him. And loved the cash. Abruptly, he made up his mind: He had to extricate himself from Aasha Rani's clutches, before her manic, destructive love pitched him over the edge. To oblivion.

Akshay poured himself some more Scotch and drank deeply. Very deliberately he picked up the phone receiver and dialed. The film industry was a ruthless place. A bit like a jungle. And the laws that applied were the same. The survival of the fittest. The victor and the victim. Poor, stupid bitch, he thought as he heard the phone ring at the other end.

Shethji ❦

Discarded Lover Boy Seeks Revenge, said the caption under a flattering, soft-focus photograph of Aasha Rani in *Showbiz* magazine. Amused, Aasha Rani read on:

Akshay (Rambo) Arora has started his 'Screw Aasha Rani' campaign with a vengeance. First stop: Nitesh (Big Banner) Mehra's office, where Rambo staged a *dharna* demanding that Aasha Rani be dropped from his forthcoming film, or else! Industry wallahs know all about the Nitesh–Aasha Rani *lafda,* but that's an old story now. Rambo wants to rake up fresh dirt. This has to do with the Puritan Princess's pukey past—porno. It seems the luscious Aasha Rani can be lascivious too . . . for a price, naturally. In her *kadka,* hard-up days, she was forced to act *nanga-panga* in those sexy *sambar* films shot in sleazy Madras hotels. Akshay claims some of them were Nitesh's babies. He is threatening to circulate them widely unless . . . *bechari* Aasha Rani. How will she explain her sizzling *bachpana* to the new *bachcha* in her life?"

Aasha Rani's amusement had faded by the time she got to the end of the article. Her first reflex was to reach for the phone and call Akshay. Cheap, bloody bastard. Her hand remained on the phone, while her mind raced—no, that wasn't the answer. He was probably waiting for her to make precisely this mistake. God! Oh God! Suddenly, she felt desperately alone, and sick. So. Her big romance with Akshay was off as suddenly as it was on. Why was he doing this to her? His secretary must have told him that she wasn't as viable a commodity as she used to be. God! Was her star rating beginning to slip? *Amma* had warned her. Kishenbhai had warned her. Maybe this was just a part of Malini's smear campaign. Or Linda's. Or Ritaji's. Was there no one she could trust? And that porno session? Dammit! She was just a child at that time. It wasn't her idea. She just did what she was told. She obeyed *Amma*. Besides, nobody had asked her whether or not she wanted to do those sickening films, and nobody had listened when she'd cried herself hoarse and protested. Her mind flew back, back.

Amma had taken her aside to the bathroom and pinched her arm savagely. "Don't be stupid. These films will not be shown in the theaters. Nobody will know you have done them. There is a lot of money involved. I have committed on your behalf. We can't let all these people down." Aasha Rani had whimpered, "*Amma,* please don't; I'm so scared. That horrible man. How can I take off my clothes in front of all these strangers?" *Amma* had released her pincerlike grip on Aasha Rani's arm and said patiently, "Think of it like going to the doctor's. Don't you allow him to examine you? Haven't so many doctors seen your body? Examined it? These people are the same. They see bodies all the time. It doesn't make any difference. Besides, that man won't *really* do anything. I mean, it is all *acting.* You just pretend and follow the director's orders. Close your eyes and think of other things. Think of your poor sister and your *amma* struggling to make you a big star. Do you know Sudha hasn't paid her fees? Her dance teacher was also asking for money. We need a pressure cooker; come on, there's a sweet girl. Wipe your face. Remember, nobody can do anything to you while *Amma* is in the room. Not actually."

Aasha Rani had gone into the tacky room, which had been cleared of furniture. An ugly, synthetic fur rug had been spread on the floor. Four extremely bright, harsh lights were focused on it. The cameraman had positioned himself by the door. The director was sitting on a stool, fanning himself and chewing *paan*. An aluminum tray full of cold drinks sat in one corner. "Ready?" the director had asked, looking at *Amma*, not her. "We have to finish in two hours and then rush the tapes to the lab." She saw the "hero" with a towel around his middle. He had looked like an impoverished coconut seller picked up from Marina Beach. Ugly, ravaged, with filthy teeth, and hair in his nostrils. He scratched himself incessantly and had looked bored. Someone handed him a funny-looking cigarette. *"Innu voru dam addi."* He had dragged on it deeply and said, "OK, I'm ready." *Amma* went and sat on a rickety chair. The director had gestured to Aasha Rani—"Lie down there and remove your clothes." The cameraman had asked, "Do you want shots of her undressing also?" "Why not?" the director had replied. "OK, lights, silence. Camera working," said the scruffy assistant. Aasha Rani had unbuttoned her blouse. *"Seekram,* fast, fast action, please" the director had urged.

She had hesitated when all her buttons were opened. "Brassiere, brassiere," the director had said, "quickly, open quickly!" Aasha Rani had looked at *Amma*. She had gesticulated with her hand, indicating how the bra was to be unhooked. Aasha Rani had shut her eyes and reached for the clasp. "*Wah!*" she had heard the director say. After that, she hadn't really registered anything. She had only responded to the directions. Along with her eyes, she'd also shut her mind.

The *Showbiz* snippet had upset Aasha Rani more than she cared to admit. She left the studios early—unable to concentrate—and now, lying in her massive pink bed, still clad in the garish disco costume she had worn for the shooting, she thought of *Amma*.

If only she had been around. She would have shooed the gaggle of domestics who had gathered on the landing to whisper about Aasha Rani's "state." She would have ordered hot *kaapi* and told her that Akshay was a swine—hadn't she told her so all along? In fact, *Amma*'s exile from Bombay had been decreed by Akshay. Akshay, who, *Amma* had announced, was nothing but a loser. A sniveling, weak womanizer. Who cheated on his wife. And on his mistress.

Bastard, Aasha Rani thought, reaching for the bottle of Black Dog that she kept handy for Akshay. I'll show the guy. She remembered suddenly that Akshay had said something about a *mahurat* party at the Rooftop Club. She hadn't figured on the list of invitees: the producer was a relative of Malini's. But she would go, nevertheless. Bloody *bhabhiji*. She looked at the crass costume she was dressed in. *Chalega*. A bit tarty, but revealing. Served the purpose. *Bhabhiji* would look like a bank clerk in comparison. She rummaged through her bag for the car keys and walked to where her metallic silver Toyota stood. "Driver, *chalo*."

The car cruised up to the foyer of the hotel, and a flunky

leaned down and opened the door. She tried to focus on him, unsuccessfully, and walked unsteadily into the hotel. She made it across the lobby somehow and stumbled into the lift, which zoomed her up to the rooftop restaurant. Blearily, she looked around, cursing herself for touching that bloody bottle. There were over a hundred invitees—not just film industry guests, but society people—industrialists and businessmen. She shouldn't have come. And it was close to eleven o'clock. Another mistake. All the men would be pissed. Akshay couldn't hold two glasses, and he must have had at least six by now. *Chalo,* that made two of them.

Aasha Rani searched the crowd. There he was. He was coming toward her. Carefully. The way men do when they're drunk and insist they're not.

Akshay stared at her and shouted, "Why have you come here?" Aasha Rani stammered, "My shooting got over early. Third shift canceled . . . I thought . . ." At that point she spotted Malini, who was staring stone-facedly at her. Akshay lurched toward her. "Bitch! Don't you know your place? Following me around. I don't like my women spying; you are a spy! Wanted to catch me with someone, didn't you? Get out, get out!" Aasha Rani continued to stand there.

Everybody was watching the two of them. Akshay, his suit jacket askew, came up close to her and caught the ends of the pink chiffon *dupatta* around her neck. "You heard me—*Out!*" he yelled. "I am sorry, I am really sorry," Aasha Rani started to say. Before she could finish her sentence, he struck her hard across her face. She looked up, stunned—he struck her again. By then, Malini had joined him. She screeched, "Beat the bitch! Kick her out! How dare she come here!" One more blow across her mouth and Aasha Rani fell to the floor. Akshay kicked her prostrate form and ground the heel of his shoe into the side of her face. Aasha Rani could taste blood as it flowed from her nostrils. She lay there sobbing.

Not a single person in that plush reception hall came toward her. Akshay stood watching, egged on by Malini and another film wife—"Teach her a lesson! Finish her off! Whore! Stealing husbands, destroying lives!" Aasha Rani struggled to her feet unsteadily and limped out through the hideously carved doorway.

WHEN SHE WOKE UP the next morning, Sheth Amirchand was sitting by her bed. This was the first time he'd come to her home. He looked concerned. "So you've heard," Aasha Rani said.

"Heard? *Arrey*, all of Bombay has heard. The entire industry thinks you're *paagal. Chhee*, throwing yourself at the worthless *hijda*—he's not man enough for you. He can't even take on his wife. Where is *Amma*? Where is Kishenbhai?"

"I don't need anyone. I don't want to see anyone. Thank you for coming."

"Aasha Rani"—the Shethji's tone was clipped—"I don't normally bother myself with deluded *bachchis* like yourself. You fuck one woman, you fuck them all. But I thought you were different. Intelligent, and *bindaas*. When I first met you at Kishenbhai's party I thought, This *chidiya* will go far. And I was right. Now that your career has taken off, it's stupid to throw it away. Akshay is a *matlabi, haraami* bastard, with no mind of his own. To forsake your career on account of him—and to be bashed up in public— is idiotic. Snap out of it! *Apni* lifeline *par lao*." And saying that, he picked up the ends of his *dhoti* and left her room.

Sheth Amirchand was a shadowy figure. A member of Parliament. He said he hated politics, but was forced into it by the love of his people. He was there to serve them, nothing more. It was difficult to get a fix on the Sheth. There were rumors galore about his nefarious activities, but nobody knew for sure. There was talk of his controlling a drug cartel, of his taking cuts on every big land deal that was clinched in Maharashtra, of octroi rackets and licensing scams. They said he was a front man for several underworld dons who financed his elections. But the Sheth managed to disassociate himself from every scandal. It was whispered that the sort of clout he had ensured that nothing too adverse appeared about him in the press. He surrounded himself with heavies who were dubbed the Topiwalla Brigade, since they all wore white caps with his symbol on them—a *sudarshan chakra*. It was said he deployed his goons to settle any differences that might crop up with his adversaries.

The *sudarshan chakra* was more than a mere symbol. It was an ingeniously designed weapon that beheaded enemies who messed around with the Sheth. The list of people who had disappeared under mysterious circumstances was awesome.

The Sheth relished his hold over the city. He encouraged and furthered the "Godfather" image, but insisted he was nothing more than a protector of the weak. His private life was shrouded in secrecy. His wife and children were installed somewhere near Bhuj in Kutch, and their whereabouts were staunchly guarded by his squads of henchmen. He lived in an ugly penthouse in Worli with a Muslim mistress, a nautch girl from Lucknow who'd been "rescued" from a Bombay brothel by the Sheth's trusted lieutenant, also a Muslim, called Abbas Miya. Lubna, the dancing girl, had been with Amirchand for nearly five years but was now fat and undesirable. The word was out that Sheth Amirchand was on the lookout for someone new, someone young, slim and preferably famous. As they said in his circles, "Lubna *begum ab buddhi ho gayi hai*. Too old and stale. The Shethji needs a change." Lubna wasn't quite thirty.

Kishenbhai was small-fry, but Amirchand owed him. When both of them were starting off, Kishenbhai had helped him clinch a few easy deals and get into the film industry, which in those days was a closed place that did not encourage outsiders. Once Amirchand had succeeded in getting a toehold in the inner group, he hadn't required Kishenbhai. But over the years, the two had kept in touch. A premiere here, a *mahurat* there, a charity night somewhere else, and Amirchand would show up as the chief guest just to let his old friend know that he, Amirchand, didn't forget past favors.

Occasionally, Kishenbhai would pass on some starlet or the other, generally with a request to help her out of a crisis—perhaps an abortion, or maybe a request to free her from the clutches of a blackmailer or an extortionist. All it required was for the Shethji to pick up a phone and voice concern to the local *dada* who did that particular beat. The Topiwalla Brigade was notorious for its ruthless methods. And they always branded their victims. Any unclaimed body with a *sudarshan chakra* stamped on its forehead and there were no marks for guessing who'd done it.

But the Shethji disdained gang wars. Those were for amateurs, for his flunky to handle. He concentrated on the big stuff—gold and drugs. He'd given up the prostitution and protection rackets long ago, since the returns weren't as attractive. But he still maintained his links with the film industry. That represented glamour and fame. Also, his Dubai counterparts appreciated gestures like sending a film troupe across for a weekend's entertainment program. Lubna Begum rounded up pretty dancers and "disco queens," some of whom had hit the big time, and were now lording it over lesser women in the harems of Kuwait and Muscat.

ON THE EVENING of the party Kishenbhai had organized for Aasha Rani after *Nagin Ki Kasam*, Amirchand had had eyes only for one woman: the tall, dusky girl in a white-and-gold sari. Inquiries had revealed she was Kishenbhai's new find—an actress poised for a megabreak and a megacareer. Amirchand had sized her up. Definitely big-time *maal*. Why was she wasting her talents on a *chhota-mota* like Kishenbhai? At best he could make her a B-grade heroine. But this girl had A-grade potential. She needed a backer. Someone with muscle. And money. He decided to find out more about her. All he needed was one private meeting.

Aasha Rani was most flattered when the summons from Amirchand's office arrived. Totally lacking finesse, his minion had delivered the message bluntly, crudely and explicitly: "Shethji *ne bulaya hai*, Shethji *bola aaneko. Paisa-vaisa bad mey vasool.*" *Amma* had been even more thrilled. She had run to break the news to Kishenbhai. When he heard what the Shethji wanted, Kishenbhai's face paled. He didn't say anything. He was shocked that the Shethji had made such a request in the first place. How could he? It was against ethics to make a play for someone else's moll. The Shethji was poaching. And he was blatantly taking advantage of his superior position. Kishenbhai was in a fix. He knew that Amirchand was aware of him and Aasha Rani. But how could he refuse to comply? The heavies would be at his doorstep the next morning. They were capable of anything. Kidnapping his child; throwing acid in Aasha

Rani's face. He was also furious with *Amma*. She knew how fond he was of her baby. She was aware of the fact that he didn't promote any and every hopeful he came across. Not with such zeal. Did she really think he'd exult at the news?

Amma had feigned injured innocence. "But surely, Kishenbhai, you didn't think I knew about your feelings for Baby? Does she feel the same way? I don't mean to hurt you, but even supposing I believe you are sincere toward my daughter, does she have a future with you? Can you . . . will you . . . make her your wife? Give her respect? Treat her well? No. The answer is no. You have your own family—your own problems. We have ours. I'm interested in what is best for my daughter . . . for her career . . . her future. I want to see that she has enough money. That she settles down properly. That's all. Let her go to the Shethji and find out what he can do for her. We'll wait and see. *Theek hai?*"

It wasn't *theek hai* at all. But what could Kishenbhai do? Aasha Rani—what was she to him? Not a wife over whom he had a right. There was no question of either his "allowing" her to go or her seeking his "permission." Supposing he were to put his foot down and express his displeasure? What would happen? She would laugh in his face and go right ahead with whatever it was she wanted to do. Ridiculous. Never before had Kishenbhai found himself in such an absurd position. He felt impotent and small. He was also certain that Aasha Rani would capitalize on the opportunity, which, of course, she did.

SHETH AMIRCHAND'S MANSION crawled with bodyguards and armed toughies who lurked around trying to look dangerous. Aasha Rani had smiled at them, but they'd remained sullenly expressionless. She had dressed with care—wearing one of her two imported bra-and-panty sets. The pink, lacy one. She'd considered wearing a black outfit, but *Amma* had dissuaded her, saying, "No, no, no, Baby—you will look very dark. Wear some light color . . . wear yellow . . . golden yellow." This time Aasha Rani had decided against a sari. She wanted to look youthful and different. The *salwar-kameez* she chose was a flattering one, with a snug bodice that showed her curves to advantage. She wore heels. Some men liked them; some didn't. She calculated that the Shethji would be impressed, since he wasn't very tall himself. She brushed her teeth with Neem, rubbed Black Monkey brand tooth powder over her gums, tucked a cardamom pod into the corner of her mouth and looked at herself in the mirror. Nice, she thought, before adding a glittering golden *bindi* to her forehead. On an impulse, she grabbed a stick of disco dust and rubbed some spangles between her breasts. Over her shoulders. Around her navel. And between her thighs. The spangles had shone on her skin like a thousand stars in a moonless sky. Perfect. She could take on the Shethji . . . and half a dozen others.

Aasha Rani was asked to wait in a small, air-conditioned room with padded walls, thick carpeting, two telephones, an intercom and a low, velvet-covered settee. As she sat down, she noticed the mirrored ceiling and a cleverly concealed door which blended with the wall. After fifteen minutes, a woman walked in. At least, she thought it was a woman till a gruff voice informed her, "Shethji *raah dekh rahe hain* . . . he has sent me to prepare you for him." Aasha Rani's puzzled expression led the person on. "*Arrey bhai,* don't stare like this. Haven't you seen a *hijda* before? Don't waste time. Let me get you ready. Remove your clothes quickly. I have to check whether you are free of skin infection. Shethji is very particular about cleanliness. Then I have to rub you down with diluted Dettol, check your vagina and insert a diaphragm. No *jhanjhats* here. All you women are the same—screw a thousand men, get your womb filled by one of them and then come and *phasao* the richest one. No time to waste now."

Aasha Rani felt his coarse hands on her. There was no point resisting. She sat down passively and began removing her clothes. She felt sorriest about the shiny disco dust that would come off with the antiseptic scrub.

The *hijda* disappeared briefly and returned with a jar of petroleum jelly and a new-looking housecoat. Expertly, he inserted the diaphragm after asking her to lie back, holding her knees in her hands. Then he told her to turn over. "Why?" she blurted, her curiosity getting the better of her. "I have to make sure your body is ready to receive Shethji wherever the mood takes him," said the *hijda*, and inserted a fingerful of jelly into her anus. "Put on the housecoat and come with me. Your belongings will be waiting for you in this room later. So will a car, just outside. Don't ask me when. All that depends on Shethji. The longer you take to satisfy him, the better. Oh yes, one more thing—he will offer you whiskey. But don't drink it. He has a solid *nafrat* against girls who drink. That is his way of testing you." Aasha Rani looked at his ugly, lipsticked face and followed him meekly.

The Shethji's room was white all over. Like a hospital room, only plusher and crammed with electronic toys. Aasha Rani held up her hand to shield her eyes from the glare of an enormous chandelier that hung in the center of the room. The Shethji, clad in a spotless white *dhoti-kurta,* was busy issuing instructions over a white cordless phone. Without sparing her a glance he waved her to a chair beside him. Aasha Rani bent down and touched his feet. For a moment he was thrown off balance and stopped mid-sentence to stare at her. She smiled sweetly and ran her long, lacquered nails along the length of his arm. The Shethji ended his phone conversation abruptly and lunged at her, his *dhoti* flying.

He had surprisingly soft hands, like buttered *pao*, Aasha Rani thought. His nails were neat and obviously pampered. He began sniffing her all over like a frisky dog. After a minute, he explained, "Allergies. I can't stand perfume, sandalwood, soap, *attar,* talcum powders. I was checking whether *Mastaan* has done his job." Her housecoat was wide open and she was lying back languorously against velvet bolsters, her mind wandering as it always did when she handed over her body to a man. It didn't matter who he was and what he was doing to her—it all felt the same. But her mind remained her own and she guarded that jealously, hoping she wouldn't have to make conversation. The Shethji, however, clamored for more. Savagely, he jerked her out of her reverie and commanded, "*Gandi baatey karo mere saath.*" One of those ones, Aasha Rani thought tiredly. He wanted her to talk dirty. As if it wasn't enough that she was acting dirty. And she with her language problem. She hadn't mastered the art of erotic talk in Hindi. She began haltingly, and it seemed to excite the Shethji. "*Aur bolo, aur bolo,*" he urged. She thought of her blue film days and smiled ironically at the memory. Kid stuff . . .

It must have been around five in the morning when she woke up wondering where she was, what she was doing and with whom. There was nobody in the room, just an eerie blue night-lamp glowing. Was she in a nursing home? She smelled of Dettol. Her body ached and felt sore. What had happened? Generally she remembered all her sexual encounters vividly. This one was a blank. Her head felt heavy and her mouth felt like it was stuffed with cotton wool. Funny, she couldn't recall a thing. She groped around in the dark and found her dressing gown. How was she supposed to find her way out of this hell? She staggered toward the blue glow and found some switches. Blindly, she punched a few buttons and the chandelier exploded in a burst of blinding light.

Good God! So that was where she was! She remembered a few details—the Shethji sniffing her armpits, the Shethji asking her to repeat a few words whose meaning she did not know, and asking her to perform acts she had not performed before. She remembered him sticking his big toe into her mouth and it hurting, crushed ice on her breasts, but that was before the drinks—a small sherbet for her and a tumbler full of whiskey for him. That was it, the sherbet—God knows what it had been laced with. But it had transported Aasha Rani into a hallucinatory world. She was weightless and floating. Her head was full of colors and sounds. Her senses had been heightened to an extent that she experienced no pain even when the Shethji entered her savagely from behind and whipped her with a small leather thong. She was far away in some distant world, listening to birdcalls and looking at a dozen rainbows . . .

She noticed an envelope lying on the settee. On it, neatly typed, was the amount inside—thirty thousand rupees. For services rendered. Not a bad market price, she thought. She had had to work much harder for just a thousand in the past. And thirty thousand was what she had earned for ten blue films, shot over a month, in filthy hotel rooms. She knew she didn't have to count the money. She knew she wasn't going to take it either. *Amma* would be furious, but Aasha Rani had it all worked out. She wasn't prepared to settle for just thirty thousand with this man and call it quits. She wanted more. Much more. And she'd get it. But first, she'd have to forfeit the notes lying invitingly in front of her. Money she badly needed. But she'd recover it from the Shethji twenty times over. Later. Aasha Rani was confident of that much. Confident that he'd need her again. And again.

Her gamble paid off almost immediately. The Shethji's man arrived at her house the next day to demand an explanation. She didn't want *Amma* to handle this one. She decided to deal with it personally. "Please tell Shethji I consider it my duty to please him. It gives me pleasure to see him happy. There is no price for such joy. I will be there for him whenever he wants me. In fact, I'll be waiting for his *hukum* . . ."

The Shethji sent for her that night. This time, he took a few minutes to actually chat with her. He told her she had played her cards well. "*Shabaash ladki.*" He laughed. "You are a cunning little fox—I like that. The other girls have no brains. They grab whatever I throw in their direction and run. But you, you knew that this was nothing. Not even a *baksheesh.* You realized it was a test. Smart woman. You will go far. Fame will come to you if you have any talent, which I believe you do. I will watch you, watch your every move. I have not decided yet whether to make you my permanent keep. Women create too many complications. It is easier to use them and discard them. Replacements are always more stimulating. I think you know that too. For a woman to hold a man's interest, she has to offer more than just her body. Your mind interests me—you could be of use to me. But first I will see how you perform—not just in bed, but on the screen too. Don't worry; I'm not a possessive man. You are free to sleep with anybody you choose. I know about your *lafda* with Kishenbhai. His wife had come to me to stop you from seeing her husband. I know about all the others—your past, blue films, *arrey sab kuch janta hoon. Chalega.* The industry is such. You have to survive."

Aasha Rani chose not to speak and instead silently began pressing his feet, massaging his arches, cracking his toe joints. "Aah," he moaned, "that feels good." She continued, working her way up to his ankles and calves. Then she stopped abruptly, and pressed herself against him. "I want to dance for you. Show you what I'm capable of, prove to you how good I am. Do you have music here?" The Shethji opened his eyes, reached out and pressed a button. Music filled the room. But it was Hindustani classical. "Not this." Aasha Rani breathed heavily. "I want something sexy, something slow." He pressed a few more buttons and, amazingly, got a Western number, an old Marilyn Monroe song, "I Want to Be Loved by You."

Aasha Rani stood up and started swaying. Her fingers moved to the top button of her housecoat. Gradually, taking her time over every motion, she began a tantalizing striptease. The Shethji sat up. His hands reached into the soft folds of his *dhoti*. His excitement was tangible. "Don't stop," he begged, "don't stop."

Amirchand was so pleased with Aasha Rani's performance that he decided to do something about her nonexistent career. A few strings strategically pulled, a few words of gentle persuasion from the Shethji himself, and Niteshji was falling over himself to get Aasha Rani to play the lead in his latest spectacular extravaganza. The title song of the film—"Love, Love, Kiss, Kiss," turned out to be the biggest hit song of the decade, and with it, Aasha Rani's career swung into the fastest track in filmdom. The popularity of the song, and Aasha Rani, took everybody by surprise. There was nothing much to the story line either. It was standard boy-meets-girl, boy-loses-girl, boy-gets-girl stuff. A normal *masaledar* formula film. But that one song catapulted *Taraazu* into becoming the biggest money grosser of all time, shattering several box office records in the process.

Aasha Rani was as astonished by its runaway success as the rest. As she was by the avalanche of publicity that came in its wake. Fan mail arrived by the sack. And each time she stepped out of her house, she heard the opening bars serenade her from everywhere: "Love, love . . . sigh . . . sigh . . . kiss . . . kiss . . . click . . . click." What was it about the song that drove a nation wild? The lyrics were simplistic at best and far from suggestive. Was it the beat that did it? Or the sharp "click-click" of fingers snapping in between the words? Perhaps it was the throaty sex appeal of the singer's voice—an unknown college girl called Neeta (whose destiny was soon to change with the release of the song). Whatever it was, "Love, Love . . ." had become such a countrywide craze that it was impossible to get away from its beat. Street-corner Romeos teased young girls as they passed by, urchins cleaned windscreens at traffic lights with the song on their lips, lovers crooned it across compounds, street bands played off-key versions at wedding *baraats*. Swinging teenagers discoed to it in fashionable nightclubs. And it was Aasha Rani who walked away with the credit.

Overnight her price skyrocketed to eight lakhs per film, and offers for *Taraazu* clones poured in. Aasha Rani shrewdly refused to duplicate either the film or her hit song. The movies she signed on, in the wake of her stupendous success, were those that showcased her versatility. Three swift hits followed. One of them, *Mein Khoon Karoongi*, was a crime thriller that had Aasha Rani dressed like a cross between a female Lone Ranger and Rambo. Armed with a submachine gun, she shot her way to the top of the charts, while *Khoon* raked it in at the box office. Two other songs written especially for her busted the pop charts.

The producers decided to capitalize on the Aasha Rani craze by organizing "Love, Love, Kiss, Kiss" entertainment nights all over India, starting with Bombay. They decided to invite Sheth Amirchand as the chief guest. Aasha Rani was expected to be present, but not onstage. The number was to be danced by young unknowns. Naturally, there was a cause involved; she forgot what it was—the blind, mentally handicapped, spastic—whatever.

Amirchand was known to patronize several charities. His favorite one was a school for orphans. He often said that orphans were the most deprived, the poorest of the poor on earth, and no amount of money was generous enough to compensate them for the loss of their parents. It was said that Amirchand was an orphan himself. But nobody knew for sure, especially as he spoke very little, preferring to let the other person do all the talking. His largesse was reserved for people who touched some unknown chord in him. It was impossible to find out just who would win the jackpot, when and for what reason.

What appeared like arbitrary, erratic behavior to outsiders, was in fact, a methodical plan known only to Amirchand and his two trusted lieutenants. Even though Aasha Rani was still in favor, and he sent for her frequently, he rarely allowed her to ask him any questions, particularly about his past. This suited her fine, since she didn't encourage questions about her past either. He'd been generous with Aasha Rani after that first meeting. And pretty kind too. Diamond sets to wear to her first big premiere night, a couple of lakhs in a fixed deposit account, and the best gift of all—a deluxe, air-conditioned makeup van to take her to and from the studios! Her gleaming, refurbished, remodeled

Isuzu had become the envy of the other stars. It was as sleek as it was functional. And she loved it. As she sped down the highway, beyond the airport, on the way to Film City, she'd relax on the foam bed at the back, switch on her favorite *ghazals* and dream of a marble palace by the sea. Except that in her dream the sea was not the Arabian Sea that surrounds Bombay, but the Bay of Bengal that laps the shores of Madras.

THE MORNING AFTER she'd been beaten up by Akshay, Aasha Rani decided she was too depressed to get out and about. So she ordered the new maid to get her breakfast in bed. When the maid came up with the tray, there was an unaddressed envelope lying on it. Aasha Rani opened it curiously. A Gulf Air ticket to Dubai. First class. On the back of the ticket there were two sentences, written in black ink: "He's not worth it. *Jao, aish karo.*" Accompanied by a barely perceptible *sudarshan chakra.*

The trip to Dubai was just the diversion Aasha Rani needed. She was going to make the most of it. "Don't worry about money," the Shethji said when she phoned to thank him. "Sheikh Mushtaq and his men will take care of everything. You shop for whatever you want, anything at all. Buy up Dubai—*bas,* forget Akshay and come back quickly."

She was met at the airport by a bunch of strange-looking men, most of whom spoke Malayalam. Aasha Rani felt instantly at home. They were dressed like the stuntmen in Hindi films, with flashy gold watches, rings and chains. One of them caught hold of her arm and said, "Boss wants you." Aasha Rani was hustled into a waiting stretch limo with tinted windows. Inside she saw a short, good-looking man dressed in white, sitting at the far end.

He held out his hand and said, "*Salaam-ali-kum.* Welcome to Dubai." She got in next to him. Her tough escort climbed into the front seat next to the driver, who had a glistening bald pate. She noticed two Sten guns in front, and a snub-nosed revolver between her and the man in white.

As the man beside her seemed to have no desire to engage her in conversation, she looked out of the window. The car was speeding by a creek that had dozens of dhows floating on it. The silence grew. The man in front hadn't spoken a word and seemed very tense. The driver looked back and said, "All clear, boss." The mysterious stranger placed his hand over Aasha Rani's. "He's gone. We've shaken him off. *Bhaag gaya saala. Ab* relax, *meri jaan.*"

Later, she found out that the man in the car was the Gold King of Dubai, known simply as "Badshah"; wanted in half a dozen countries, including India, on charges of armed robbery, murder, narcotics and smuggling.

Badshah wasn't turned on by Aasha Rani. He preferred his girls white and preferably blond—a variety there was no dearth of in Dubai. His palatial beachside villa housed a harem that was admirably international; four Thai masseuses from Bangkok, a Cockney waitress from Liverpool, an Australian au pair and a French barmaid.

Badshah's hospitality was lavish, but he didn't sleep with Aasha Rani. The last thing she wanted to do at this stage was to meet men, and she was only too content to look around and talk to the other women. She got her shopping done, plus she had her body dextrously worked over by the Thai girls, who giggled at the size of Aasha Rani's breasts ("like melons") and took turns rubbing coconut oil over them. Aasha Rani found their ministrations most pleasurable and thought of Akshay and how unpleasant he turned out to be. But that was past. The Thai girls asked her flirtatiously whether she wanted to try a "sandwich massage." Game to try anything once, Aasha Rani agreed readily.

It was an experience so sensuous, so arousing, so complete, that it was weeks before she could forget the feel of two, smooth, soft, oiled, practically breastless bodies on either side of her, touching, licking, stroking every naked inch, making her skin tingle and come alive in a way she couldn't have imagined possible.

When she returned to Bombay a fortnight later she had with her two VCRs, two CDs, enough makeup to fill three trunks, and had experienced some of the greatest orgasms of her life. When the Shethji looked out for you, she thought as she arrived home, you got nothing but the best.

Amma ❦

THE FIRST THING AASHA RANI DID ON HER RETURN WAS TO
race up to her bedroom and turn on the answering machine.
Narinder Gupta, the director of her latest venture, barely con-
cealing his anger at her unexplained vacation in the midst of
shooting, had called to say that the unit was moving to Manali,
where the rest of the film was to be shot, in two weeks' time.
There were no messages from Akshay.

Aasha Rani wasn't too keen to go to Manali. Her costar in the
movie was an aged lech whose extramarital *cheez* had just left
him, while Narinder Gupta, a devoted family man in Bombay,
was wont to let the exhilaration of a new place go straight to his
libido. Dubai had still not prepared her for life without Akshay,
and she was in no mood to spend her time in the hills fending off
the advances of the various men in the unit. She decided she
needed a chaperone and on an impulse called Linda, her reporter
pal from *Showbiz* magazine. Her cheery irreverence would do her
good. But Linda was up to her neck in work. "My editor is a real
bitch, *yaar*. She'll never give me *chutti*. Sorry, darling, got to go,
I'll call you back."

It was at times like this that Aasha Rani longed to have *Amma* back with her. She must have heard of the rooftop incident. *Amma* had warned her about Akshay so many times, especially about his sadistic tendencies. Indeed it was because *Amma* had spoken up once after Akshay had beaten her that she had been banished to Madras. At the time Aasha Rani had hated her. Mostly because she was so blinded by her love for Akshay, but also because (even though she was reluctant to admit this to herself) she resented the way her mother had exploited and used her. Still, for all her faults, she was her mother, and when she was down and out, on days like these, she missed her.

Aasha Rani pulled out her old family album from the back of her cupboard and gently blew the dust off the cover. Sitting down on a large floor cushion, she flipped through old sepia-colored photographs of the family that once, a long, long time ago, she had called her own.

God! *Amma* had looked beautiful. But after a few years with *Appa,* by the time she was twenty, *Amma* started putting on weight. They were not staying together then. For *Appa* already had his own family: the formidable Girija with her three sons—Aasha Rani's half brothers. *Appa* had already been married when he'd whisked away *Amma*—a fledgling, fifteen-year-old aspiring danseuse—to the big, bad city of Madras. *Appa* had bought a bungalow for *Amma* a few years later. After Aasha Rani's birth. By then, all of Madras had known about them. But *Appa* was so powerful, nobody dared to say a word. *Amma* had often talked about that period. *Appa,* as the owner of Madras's biggest and most successful studio, controlled a large chunk of the South Indian film industry. "Your *Appa* was a real movie mogul," *Amma* would tell her. "Everybody came to him—music directors, film

directors, heroes, heroines, sound recordists, extras, dance mas-
ters, stuntmen, everybody! He was generous, but not gullible.
The films he backed were hits—big hits. The songs from those
films were on everyone's lips. Madras swayed to the music from
his films. And the posters! *Appa* was the first one to start the
craze. He had larger-than-life cutouts displayed in all the prominent corners of the city. He was the one who thought of putting
tinsel on the painted clothes of his stars, so that they gleamed in
the night. He created his own stars—they were loyal to him and
nobody else. You should have seen them at our home! They'd
come like humble servants, begging for a role in *Appa*'s next film.
We entertained them all—politicians, businessmen . . . even a
few smugglers!"

Aasha Rani particularly liked looking at her mother's photographs at various film functions, when she dressed up in gorgeous
Kanjeevarams and wore fabulous jewelry. "What did you do with
all this?" she'd ask *Amma,* who would promptly lose her good humor and change the subject.

Piecing *Amma*'s life together, Aasha Rani knew more or less
what had happened. How *Appa* had lost interest in her. How
Girija had humiliated her and called her a common prostitute.
How *Appa* had abruptly cut off all money, leaving *Amma* with no
choice but to sell all her jewelry—and the clothes off her back.
That was when the nightmare had begun. Moving out of their
luxurious bungalow and into some ugly little place in an overcrowded, filthy area.

When *Appa* had left, *Amma* had aged overnight. She had
looked worn-out and middle-aged, though she must have been
in her late twenties. Aasha Rani remembered a succession of

dubious "mamas" turning up at their place and taking *Amma* out on mysterious missions. On those occasions *Amma* would make an attempt to dress up. Put *kaajal* in her eyes, flowers in her hair and rouge on her cheeks. She'd come back late in the night, smelling strange and looking sleepy. But the next morning, she'd be up on time as usual to give the children their milk and send them off to school. On those days they'd come home to *dosas* and *uttapams; Amma* would look relatively less harassed and in a more relaxed mood. Through all this, *Amma* made sure Aasha Rani continued with her dance lessons. The gurus in that locality were not all that good, but Aasha Rani progressed well enough. Thanks to *Amma*.

As SHE FUSSED about her house in Madras, seeing to lunch, organizing Sudha's dance class, keeping track of her errant "husband"—most of *Amma*'s waking thoughts were of Bombay. Of her daughter Viji. That silly girl was going to lose everything in her absurd obsession for that wife-deserting flop hero, Akshay. How many times had she warned Viji against him? How many times had Kishenbhai tried to make her see reason? But it was to no avail. Viji had deserted her own mother for Akshay, packing her off to Madras now that she was a big star. Now that Akshay Arora had replaced everyone and everything of importance in Aasha Rani's life. What did she see in him? What kind of security did he give her that she couldn't? What kind of love?

Did Aasha Rani enjoy being beaten? She hadn't really seemed to mind—that time when Akshay had whipped her mercilessly in her makeup room. When *Amma* had gotten the door broken down to save her daughter. The sin for which she had been banished to Madras.

The *Dil Ke Katil* incident had been one of many. *Amma* had been hanging around the studios as usual when Akshay had walked in from a neighboring set and, without bothering to glance in her direction, had marched straight up to Aasha Rani's makeup room, where she had been changing her costume for the next scene. Locking the door behind him, he had started to abuse her. At first his voice could be heard only by the terrified makeup man and the hairdresser standing outside, but soon the decibel levels went up considerably, and even the people hurrying around the studio floor could catch some of his yelled abuses and the sound of smashing furniture. *Amma* had been alerted, and she came rushing up frantically.

"Open the door, Baby," she had shouted, pounding on the door. Akshay had continued to hurl abuses at Aasha Rani while she had sobbed pathetically. *Amma* was hysterical. She had summoned some studio hands and had asked them to force open the door. The producer and director had come along to see what was going on. One of them had knocked loudly on the door, identified himself, and had requested Akshay to open up. Just then, another loud crash and a sharp cry were heard inside. *Amma* had urged the workers to break down the door. The flimsy plywood door didn't require much muscle.

The astonished people outside had seen a naked Aasha Rani cowering on the couch opposite the dressing table with Akshay poised to strike her with his belt. The room had been totally trashed: The costumes were in tatters, and there were jars of makeup scattered all over the floor. *Amma* had rushed in and thrown a tablecloth over her daughter. Akshay had stridden menacingly toward her, saying, "It's because of you—what sort of a mother are you? This girl is nothing but a pricey prostitute, and you her pimp, her madam. Screwing this man and that. Kishenbhai and Amirchand and maybe even her own driver and sweeper! No morals, nothing. You can't call yourself a mother—you are scum. A wretched exploiter of your own child. You think you have made your daughter a big star—but it is her life you have ruined! How do you sleep at night? Doesn't your conscience kill you?"

Amma had been rendered temporarily speechless. When she had found her tongue it was Tamil. A torrent of invective had followed, and she'd spit a couple of times. She'd been an awesome sight, arms akimbo, eyes blazing. Her hair had come undone, and the flowers she had worn after her morning *puja* hung from her loose tresses at comic angles. *Amma* had lashed out at him: "You are just jealous of my daughter's grand success, not her other lovers. You can't bear it that she has beaten you. Today, she is a bigger star than you—ask these people. Her name sells. She makes more money. But you—shameless fellow—running after women when you have a wife at home! My daughter is not married. She is free to see anyone, any time! She is not your property, understand?" The producer and director had tried to calm her. In the meantime somebody had phoned the police. They had arrived, screeching in a van, and run up to see what was going on. *Amma* had looked at the inspector and said, "Arrest this loafer. He tried to kill my daughter. And he assaulted me. Look . . . just look . . . he has done all this. He has damaged the property, broken everything. He is a *goonda*—arrest him."

The inspector had smiled tolerantly and winked at Akshay. "Well, hero, you thought you were acting in a film, didn't you?" Akshay, calmer now, had slowly buckled his belt and said, "*Chalo,*" to the policeman. *Amma* had watched as the two of them had strolled off the set, Akshay with his arm around the burly cop. The director had turned to Aasha Rani and nodded. "Twenty minutes and on the set—the unit is waiting, madam. Important scene. But first, please have a cold drink."

COMING BACK FROM DUBAI to a Bombay devoid of *Amma* and Akshay depressed Aasha Rani. She had nothing much to do till shooting began, and the thought of spending her time in an impersonal house without anyone to talk to upset her further. She hadn't seen Sudha in years, and she missed *Amma*. Abruptly pulling out an overnight case, she flung a few clothes together and yelled for her driver. "Take me to the airport. I'm catching the next flight to Madras."

It wasn't much of a homecoming. When Aasha Rani arrived at the bungalow, ironically named "Matruchchaya," only her pet dog came out to greet her. Where was everybody? *Amma?* Sudha? She walked into the living room and sighed—it looked horrible. An absolute mess! No matter how much money she sent these people, they would never learn. Those curtains! The sofas! Plastic covers over everything! Gaudy, hideous bric-a-brac. And those plaster of paris statues—where on earth did *Amma* get them? She'd told them to hire a decorator. She'd even told them to get one from Bangalore. But no! *Amma* liked to pinch pennies where she could, and look at the result.

She called out to the servants. An old woman came running out of the kitchen and stared at her. "Who are you?" she asked. "I'll tell you who I am. But first you tell me who you are. Bloody cheek—who are you, who are you!" Aasha Rani yelled. The old woman fled and came back with a servant boy. He took one look at Aasha Rani and said, "*Ai-yai-yo* Love, Love, Kiss, Kiss." She flung her handbag in his direction and screamed, "Where is *Amma?* Where is everybody?"

Suddenly she noticed Sudha standing on the staircase—the one that led to the bedrooms upstairs. God! How she'd changed, Aasha Rani thought. Why, she looked almost pretty. Nice figure. Lovely eyes. Lustrous hair. And fairer than her. Much fairer. Sudha kept staring wordlessly, till Aasha Rani cried out, "What's the matter with you? Do I look like a ghost? Where's *Amma?* What's happening?"

Sudha rushed down the stairs and hugged her tight. "It's *Appa,*" she sobbed. "Dead?" Aasha Rani asked without any emotion. "No . . . stroke . . . *Amma* has gone to the hospital to see him. You must go also."

Aasha Rani was puzzled. "But why should I go to see him? I haven't seen him in years. Since I was a child. He hasn't bothered about any of us either. Now that he's dying, why does he care whether we see him or not?" Sudha said, "It's not *Appa* who has asked to see you—see us—it's *Amma*. It's important to her. Do it only to make her happy." "No. I hate that man. He is cruel, heartless, indifferent. A real bastard who abandoned all of us and never showed his face again. What does he want now? More money? Wasn't it enough that he ruined *Amma*'s life and ours? Is he bankrupt totally? Worried about his hospital bills? Fine, I'll pay those—but I will not see him. Never. Tell *Amma* that." Sudha started to weep. "Forget the past. He is our father, after all. And he may die——he wants our forgiveness. *Amma* is ready to put everything behind her. Why don't you also make up with him? He's very proud of you. So are we all. He wants to see you properly married . . . settled down. Don't break his heart. He is old now. What he did to us was bad, but it was so long ago. So much has happened since then. Please, *akka*——go to him."

Aasha Rani was tired, hungry and at her lowest. She felt hard and embittered. She brushed Sudha aside harshly and said, "Let him die like a dog. Why should I care? Did he care when we were starving? Did he come to our help when *Amma* had to go around begging for work? I have no feelings for him. My father died long ago. I don't know who this man in the hospital is . . ." "*Akka*, what has happened to you? Why have you become so unkind?" Sudha said between sobs. Aasha Rani stared stonily at her. "What would you know about the life we faced, *Amma* and I? You were too young then. One day when you are older, I may tell you. Today, you can call your *akka* names. It's all right. But I know what I'm doing and saying. I never want to see *Appa*'s face again. Not even at his funeral."

Aasha Rani stormed into her room and slammed the door. She was very possessive about it. "My room," she had told *Amma*, "is mine. I don't want any of our ratty relatives to use it in my absence. I don't want you or Sudha to use it either. And nobody is allowed to open my cupboards. Tell the servants too."

She was breathing heavily. All she wanted was to be a carefree seven-year-old again and lie down in *Amma*'s lap while she rubbed hot coconut oil into her dry scalp. She wanted to cry. For what? she asked herself. She felt so weary, physically and emotionally drained. *Amma* used to tell her to pray at such times. She'd stopped doing that too. What had God done for her, anyway?

She stared at her room. The same revolting pink that her room in her Bandra bungalow boasted. Pink wall-papered walls, pink silk bedcovers, pink lace-edged pillows. Pink, pink, pink. It was a pink nightmare, down to the pink basin and pink bidet in her pink-tiled bathroom. Whatever had given everybody the idea that she liked pink?

She opened her wardrobe idly and saw a row of unused clothes. Sudha had probably bought them straight off the peg of some local boutique. Taking one desultory look, Aasha Rani decided she hated each and every one of them. Rifling through the lingerie drawer she came across a tiny plastic box. She picked it up—it had an image of Lord Venkatesh in it. *Appa* had given it to her when she was no more than five. She remembered the occasion vividly.

Amma and he had gone on a pilgrimage to Tirupathi to seek divine blessings for his new film. It was his biggest to date: a huge production. *Appa* had a lot riding on it. If the film flopped he risked losing everything—his studio included. She remembered giggling insanely at the sight of his bald head after he'd made the traditional offering of his hair. He'd looked so funny! "I'm India's Yul Brynner now." He'd laughed with them, setting them off again, even though they hadn't the faintest idea who Yul Brynner was. *Amma* had explained the power of faith and the miracle of Tirupathi: "If Venkateshwara grants *Appa* his wish, we will go back next year and perform a *maha puja* there . . . all of us."

But that had never happened. *Appa's* film was a success, all right. But his relationship with *Amma* had collapsed. Maybe *Appa* had gone back alone. Or maybe he hadn't. And that was why the gods were punishing him today. She held the small talisman in her hand and stared at the image. Tirupathi—she'd go there someday. When she needed the kind of solace only God provided. But today she had other things to do. God could wait. She replaced the talisman in its box and buried it deep in her cupboard.

Linda

AASHA RANI CAME BACK FROM MADRAS WITHOUT MEETING *Appa*. Somehow she hadn't been able to bring herself to. *Amma* had been so angry with Aasha Rani that she had chosen not to talk to her unless absolutely necessary. Aasha Rani, on the other hand, was bewildered by *Amma*'s devotion to a man who had caused her and her children nothing but pain.

The Manali shooting was on schedule, and Aasha Rani was beginning to dread it. It was just too much of an effort being social, and the thought of indulging the director and costar in their occasional ruttishness quite repulsed her.

When she got home from the beauty parlor on the evening before she was to leave for Manali, she found the door of her bedroom ajar. Her first thought was that Akshay had come home. Inside Linda was helping herself to Aasha Rani's makeup. Turning a lavishly painted face and batting her eyes, she beamed. "Guess what, darling, I'm coming—I told the editor you're having an affair with the spot boy!"

Aasha Rani smiled in spite of herself and thought back to the time she had first met Linda.

* * *

Aasha Rani had been shooting for her first multistarrer, a big-budget film in which she had two major dances. A woman had called from *Showbiz* magazine and had asked for an interview. "I'll ask Mummy," Aasha Rani had automatically responded. She'd heard the stranger laugh over the phone. "Why should you ask Mummy?" she'd mocked. "Can't you decide for yourself? No, don't say anything; let me come and meet you now." And so, she had.

Aasha Rani had been terribly impressed by Linda's casual smartness. She oozed confidence; she spoke good English and carried a large handbag, which she patted and said, "My office travels with me." Aasha Rani hadn't understood the remark but didn't dare say so. She'd giggled nervously and asked her to sit down.

Instead of pulling out a tape recorder or a writing pad, Linda had sprawled out on the settee in the makeup room and declared, "I envy you, I really do—you are so young. So beautiful and so successful. Had I been a man I would have wanted to marry you." Not knowing how to react to that, Aasha Rani had coquettishly giggled some more and offered Linda a cold drink. "*Nahi baba,* I don't drink on duty."

Aasha Rani was nervous and looked around for *Amma.* "Don't worry; I'm not a child molester. Or a rapist," Linda had said, and Aasha Rani had been flummoxed by her boldness. How could a woman talk about raping another woman? For that matter, how could a woman even say the word rape? She'd sat on the edge of her seat waiting for the interview to begin. Suddenly Linda had jumped up from the settee and asked, "Hey! Do you have any pads on you? Not writing pads, *yaar,* sanitary pads. I think I've got my period. Damn! I always go wrong when I'm on the pill." Startled by the comment, Aasha Rani had sent for her makeup girl and told her to quickly arrange for a packet. "Thanks, *yaar,* you're really a sweetheart; don't mind if I smoke, do you? Chumming makes me tense."

There was a knock at the door accompanied by a "Madam, *chaliye ji,*" which indicated that the shot was ready. Aasha Rani had jumped up. "Relax, *yaar;* you don't have to rush just because the producer says so. Keep them waiting. That way they give you more *bhav.* Here, let me handle it." And with that she'd opened the door and told the boy, "*Kya hai? Madam ko disturb mat karo. Madam so rahi hai.*" The amazed fellow had stared dumbly. "*Chalo phooto!* She will come down when she's ready." She'd slammed the door in his face and laughed. "See? It's easy. Don't be too cooperative with these bastards. They'll take advantage of you." Aasha Rani had marveled at her panache and had timidly asked, "How many years have you been in this line?"

"Let's see, five? Six? No, it's seven. I started when I finished college in Jaipur. I was a real *bindaas* girl, *yaar.* On my own I decided to come to Bombay and become a film journalist; don't ask me why. The first place I applied to was *Showbiz.* I got in immediately. Now ask me why? Because I was confident. I just pushed my way into the editor's cabin and said, 'Hire me. If you don't like my writing then fire me.' She must have been impressed. I got the job. She's a real bitch, my editor. You must have heard of her— Kamini Singh. *Bas,* now I'm a queen. A gossip queen. Everybody is scared of my pen. You'd better be nice to me, or else I'll make *chutti* of you in my column."

Aasha Rani had stared, her eyes brimming with admiration. "Seven years? You enjoy your profession?" "*Theek hai, yaar.* It's OK; I get paid enough. I have my own place. I wear nice clothes; you like my outfit?"

Linda had lolled around some more and talked about herself. Not a question to Aasha Rani about her life. After half an hour, the studio hand had come back with a frantic message. Aasha Rani had pleaded with Linda not to leave. "I'll give the shot and come back. Don't go away—OK?" Linda had blown smoke in her direction and smooched the air. "Anything for you, light of my life."

Aasha Rani found Linda and her life fascinating. There was something about her that made her most attractive, even though she was not at all good-looking. Or even sexy. It was only her eyes, colored like molten caramel, that transformed her face. She wore her hair in a careless ponytail that tumbled down half a dozen times an hour. She wasn't a tall person, but the manner in which she carried herself, with her shoulders thrown back and her head in the air, and her jaunty stride as she walked into a room, commanded attention. Her figure was neat, but not special. She exuded vitality, a devil-may-care, throwaway confidence which she combined with an aggressive, overt sexuality that bordered on the defiant. In her own entirely unique way, Linda was striking. She reminded Aasha Rani of a tightly wound, swift-footed animal. A female fox or a she-wolf on the prowl.

Aasha Rani was flattered and privileged by Linda's interest in her. She genuinely believed she had finally found the friend she was looking for. A trendy, upmarket, Bombay friend. "I'm a survivor, *yaar,*" Linda loved to say. "In this *badmaash* city and this *badmaash* business, you have to be one. You are a real *bachchi*—a mama's girl. You should be on your own. Live life for yourself. Be like me—free!"

Amma had hated Linda on sight and had told Aasha Rani as much. "That girl is a bad influence on you. Don't mix with her.

Don't trust her. She will hurt you one day." Aasha Rani had brushed off the warnings. "*Amma,* you don't like my mixing with anybody. You don't want me to have friends of my own. I feel lonely, bored, I like Linda. She is nice to me. What has she done? She has not even written about me."

That was strictly true. Through all their meetings Linda hadn't ever taken notes or taped anything. In fact, she hadn't asked Aasha Rani a single question. And far from taking advantage of her, it was Linda who had given her presents. Nothing big—just sweet little things Aasha Rani felt very sentimental about, including a big handbag like her own. "You wait," *Amma* had said. "That girl is like a snake. One day she will strike, and only then will your eyes open."

"Let me do a cover story on you," Linda had finally said. It was two months since they had met, and Aasha Rani had been waiting for the suggestion. "I thought you were never going to ask." She'd laughed. By then they were meeting each other whenever they had the time, and jamming phone lines, talking for hours, when they didn't. Aasha Rani had even visited Linda's small flat where she lived with a cat called Roop Rani. Linda had shown her all the love letters she'd received over the years and had regaled her with amusing stories about all the randy heroes who'd made passes at her.

"Do you know," she'd say, her eyes dancing mischievously, "that big stud of yours—*garma-garam?* The first time I went to interview him, he asked me to sit down across a low coffee table. I was so nervous, being raw in the profession. He kept telling me to relax and all that. I didn't dare stare at him too much, so I began fiddling with the tape recorder. He kept looking at me with his bedroom eyes and then he said, 'Let's do the interview later, afterward.'

I still didn't understand what he meant. And then my eyes went down to the table. What do you think I saw? His fly was open, and there he was, raring to go! He'd placed his tool on the tabletop, and all the while I'd thought it was a cigar! I screamed with shock and jumped to my feet. He sprang up as well and lunged at me. I was hysterical. He put his arms on my shoulders and said, 'OK, OK, relax. I thought you wanted it; they all do!' That's when I discovered that he genuinely thought he was doing me a favor. He told me later how relieved he was when I said no. It seems the poor man had acquired such a reputation that women took morning flights from Delhi just to come and get fucked by him and went back on the evening flight. He asked me innocently, 'How can I disappoint them? I am a gentleman. It would hurt a woman's ego if I refused her. I could never do that.' We both laughed and got on with the interview. Now we are great friends."

It was through stories like these that Aasha Rani had gotten to know more and more about the industry. Linda had access to all the inside *khabar* (as she put it). Linda warned her about the wolves, informed her about potential rivals and told her which roles were worth angling for. Aasha Rani was thrilled that she had Linda in her life. It came to a point where she wouldn't make a move without her. "Should I sign this film? Should I attend that party? Should I go to the premiere? Should I ask for a better price? Should I wear a sari or a *salwar-kameez* for the *mahurat*? Should I, should I, should I . . . ?"

Linda indulged her. Now wasn't the time to exploit Aasha Rani. There were bigger and better stakes to play for. And she wasn't in any particular hurry.

* * *

THE NIGHT THEY REACHED Manali it was bitterly cold. The rest house had a log fire burning downstairs. After an early dinner she and Linda left the unit to their drinks and dirty jokes and set out for a walk. Once outside, Linda suddenly grabbed Aasha Rani, hugged her close and kissed her nose. "You are a real iceberg, *yaar*. All *thanda-thanda*. Look at your nose. Like an ice cube. *Chalo*, let's go in and have some brandy."

Aasha Rani hesitated. "I have an early morning call tomorrow—and what about Lucy, my hairdresser?" "Kick her out of the room, *yaar*. You are the only *bewakoof* heroine who sleeps with her hairdresser. I don't mean it literally. When do you have fun then? Don't tell me the hairdresser looks the other way when all the heroes come to your bed at night?"

Aasha Rani ignored the remark. She was feeling happy and relaxed without *Amma* around, and Akshay had, for a change, retreated to the dim recesses of her memory.

When they went upstairs to Aasha Rani's suite Lucy was already in bed wearing a frilly Dubai-bought nightie. "*Chal phoot*, get out of here," Linda said to her harshly, and pulled out a small bottle of brandy from her handbag. "Madam?" Lucy looked questioningly at Aasha Rani. "*Kya* madam-*vadam*. Just leave the room. We want to be alone." Lucy looked for a change of clothes. "Don't bother; take a pillow and go to the next room—there's a sofa there," Linda instructed her. Aasha Rani looked embarrassed but didn't interfere.

Once Lucy had left, Linda took off her leather jacket, pulled off her boots and threw herself on the bed. "Come here," she said to Aasha Rani. "Take a sip, come on, *yaar,* let's enjoy ourselves." She switched on some music and took a swig. Aasha Rani reached for the bottle and took one as well. "Good, nice feeling, no? I always remember my father when I drink brandy. He used to give it to me when I was sick. I used to die to get a cold so that I could drink brandy. Funny, certain childhood memories never fade. I remember his smell—Charminars, feni and some cheap scent. I used to love the combination—just as much as my mother detested it! They couldn't get along at all. My mother was *kaafi* sexy, *yaar*. Just like yours. I mean, I find *Amma* most attractive. But not as much as you." With that she pulled Aasha Rani down on the bed and kissed her on the lips.

It was a pleasant feeling, Aasha Rani thought. No rough bristles scraping her face, just smooth cheeks and soft lips over her own. A memory flashed in her head of the Thai masseuses. Linda's hands were in Aasha Rani's hair, expertly undoing the clasp that held it together at the nape. Her fingers began massaging Aasha Rani's neck as once again she bent over her to kiss her, saying, "Open your mouth; let me taste your tongue. I've been wanting to do this from the time I saw you nervously licking your lips the day we met. Your tongue looked so sexy and pink—relax, baby, relax. You will love it. Just leave it all to me. Trust me."

Her hands moved from Aasha Rani's neck to her breasts. She kept kissing her gently, probing her mouth with an eager tongue. Reaching under Aasha Rani's shirt she unhooked her bra. Aasha Rani tensed and tried to cover her breasts as they came free of their harness. "Don't stop me; it will be beautiful. Like nothing you have known before," Linda whispered. Her kissing was more passionate now, and her fingers rested on Aasha Rani's taut nipples. "Look, you want me. Your body can't lie." Her head moved down till her mouth found Aasha Rani's breasts.

There was no resistance left anymore. Aasha Rani's entire

body was floating—her mind was adrift. She let her arms drop to her sides as Linda's warm thigh wedged itself between hers and her hand moved between Aasha Rani's legs. "Close your eyes; let me do to you what no man could have done. Let me make you come like you've never come before. Stay loose, stay with me; you will forget men; you will forget everything you've known before. My hands, my mouth, my tongue, my thighs will set your body on fire. Enjoy it . . . enjoy it . . . oh . . . I've been dying for you all these months. And now you are mine at last."

Aasha Rani groaned with pleasure. Linda refused to stop. She'd become more aggressive now, and her hands pummeled Aasha Rani's body, exploring every inch of it. Unexpectedly she grabbed the bottle of brandy and poured some between Aasha Rani's open legs. "The only way to drink it," Linda said, and placed her mouth over the dampness, licking each drop as it trickled. The sensation was unbelievably arousing. Aasha Rani wanted to growl and scream with excitement, but she remembered Lucy lying next door, and suppressed the urge. "Come . . . come . . . come . . . not once but a hundred times!" Linda urged, her mouth still between Aasha Rani's legs. "But let me ride you first. Let me show you that I can take you like a man too." And she climbed roughly over Aasha Rani, whose head had fallen back, over the side of the bed.

"Do you like it this way?" Linda demanded gruffly, moving over her, rubbing herself against her, till both of them came together, shuddering and shaking, not wanting it to end. Aasha Rani collapsed with Linda over her. For a while they didn't say anything to each other. Then Linda began caressing Aasha Rani gently and kissing her fingertips. "*This* is love, understand? This is lovemaking, not what those bastards do to our bodies." Aasha

Rani was lulled to sleep by Linda's fingers stroking her. Yes, she thought, this is what it should be, tender, beautiful and erotic. In a way it could never be with a man.

Back in Bombay, as she lay in Linda's arms one evening, face divested of paint, her soft frizzy hair falling untortured and natural, her dusky skin aglow, Aasha Rani felt Linda's eyes boring into her face. "You're making me nervous, *yaar*." She giggled uncertainly. Linda continued to study her. "You know, without all that pancake on your face you're quite breathtaking," she said finally. "Kind of sensuous and ethnic—the type art-film wallahs would pawn their Golden Peacock awards for—I mean, has no one ever told you how gorgeous you look without that overbright, *ganwar*, Punjabi makeup?"

Akshay had. Often. But Aasha Rani said nothing. No memories of Akshay if she wanted to maintain her equilibrium. She watched as Linda suddenly rolled over the bed to reach for the phone.

"Who are you calling?"

"Guy called Suhas. One of those arty-intellectual types. He's making a movie. And I think it's time you landed yourself into parallel cinema. Who knows, you might even win an award or two."

They were shooting in Jaipur, and it was stiflingly hot on the sets of *Bechari Begum*. Aasha Rani was a little apprehensive about shooting her first art film. "Does one have to suffer to prove one's talent?" She giggled to the makeup man as he mopped her brow with an ice cube. "Remember, this is *serious* cinema you are doing now, not those rubbishy *masala* movies," he reminded her.

Aasha Rani was secretly thrilled when she had bagged the role of Emma in the *desi* version of *Madame Bovary*. *Amma* wrote a furious letter from Madras. "*Pagli!* Why did you sign without asking me? That crook is paying you next to nothing. You want to win some stupid award or what? *Arrey,* understand one thing, Baby: You are in the industry to make money, not win some two-bit award. Later in life when you become an old maid these awards won't be of any use. Not even the *raddiwalla* will pay you two *paise* for them. That is when you will remember your *amma*'s words. Now go and die in the studios. He will take every ounce out of you. Make you slog. You won't have dates for other producers."

Aasha Rani had told the Shethji the news. "Good for you," he'd said. "But watch out for that arty bastard, Suhas. All the industry girls jump into his Pathan suit for an intellectual fuck. They really believe it is different from the other ones." Aasha Rani had laughed. "Does he do it with his hooked nose . . . or does he have something inside the *salwar*?" "Wait till you find out for yourself," Shethji had retorted.

Now that the first few shooting schedules of *Bechari Begum* were over she was puzzled and a little disappointed by Suhas's lack of interest in her. He was a demon for work and drove his unit mercilessly, but toward her he maintained a cool professionalism that was beginning to drive her batty.

Suhas was attractive in a disheveled, unkempt sort of way. Tall and fashionably starved, with the mandatory stubble on his chin. Aasha Rani loved his hooded eyes and lazy charm. She also liked his hands, with their long, artistic fingers and generous square nails.

It was also a novel experience for someone from her background to be working with a team in which everyone seemed to know what *real* filmmaking was all about. She had a complete script in hand, and her dialogues for the next schedule were given to her well in advance. Suhas spent hours explaining the complexities of the role to her. He even presented her with a copy of *Madame Bovary*—noncommittally inscribed.

One evening the unit had gotten together to look at photograph stills. She was stunned by her appearance—without her usual batlike eyelashes, pancake and blush, without wigs and elaborate costumes she looked beautiful. Natural and altogether different. She squeezed Suhas's arm and whispered, "What have you done? Nobody will recognize me in your film." He whispered back, "That's the whole idea. I don't want people to recognize you. I want you to be reborn with this film." Aasha Rani was mesmerized by the lyrical appeal of Suhas's technique. The camera seemed almost fluid as it created visual poetry of the locales—and of her face.

Suhas had resisted the obvious by not exploiting her curves. He had shot her in tight, soft-focus close-ups, concentrating on her eyes and mouth. The effect was devastating. Aasha Rani was thrilled. The effort had been worth it.

Aasha Rani was made to eat with the rest of the unit—no special *khaana* for the star—and she went off to sleep in an ordinary room. No attempts were made to pamper her or treat her any differently from the others. Unaccustomed to what she'd thought was *ghatiya* treatment, Aasha Rani stormed into Suhas's room to demand an explanation. She found him relaxing on his bed in a *lungi,* listening to Vilayat Khan. A bottle of rum stood on the bedside table and a packet of Charms on the bed. He had funny-looking reading glasses on his nose and a heap of old, dusty books lying all over. Aasha Rani was wearing a black, flowing "after work" caftan, her hair streaming down her back.

"What is this nonsense, Suhasji!" she shouted. "I am a star. I can't eat with all these *kachra* people, all your *kachra* food. Please instruct the unit manager to provide me with separate meals. And I need a suite for myself, plus phone calls. What did that chap mean by telling me not to phone Bombay and Madras every day? My clothes, they have not been washed since we started shooting. I want fresh clothes tomorrow, and a thermos of Madras coffee on the set. My sister wants to join me here for a few days. And my journalist friend Linda—she will give you publicity. Please arrange for air tickets and their stay."

When she stopped for breath, Suhas put down his book and said, "Finished?" Then he spoke quietly: "If you are not satisfied with the arrangements, please feel free to walk out of the film right now. I'm not used to working with artistes who make demands and ask for preferential treatment. My unit works as a family. No discrimination. If it doesn't suit you, that's OK. I can look for another heroine. But if you are keen on proving your merit as an actress, then I suggest you concentrate on your role and forget all your old *nakhras*. They won't work with me. That's all I wish to say to you. Good night."

Naturally everybody got to hear of the tantrum the next day, since it was a small, twenty-room hotel with wooden flooring. But nobody said a word. Aasha Rani sulked for an hour and refused breakfast. But soon she was too hungry to concentrate on her lines. She asked her hairdresser to organize some coffee— and saw Suhas smile.

By the time the last scenes were being shot she had become used to all of them, though she still felt pretty much an outsider. They spoke a different language, they cracked jokes she didn't understand, they'd seen foreign films she'd never heard of, they'd read books she didn't know existed, they listened to music that was totally unfamiliar to her and they ate food which was inedible. They also smoked a lot of grass and bathed infrequently. Except for Suhas, who stuck to fresh *salwar-kurtas* with enormous pashmina shawls.

He was irresistible in a brooding, intellectual sort of way, conceded Aasha Rani, but he gave her a massive complex. Stripped of her "stardom," she felt stupid and ignorant in his presence. They had no common ground to speak of. What really puzzled her, though, was his choice of her as his heroine. Was he being polite just to get her to cooperate? Or was he interested in her? Why had he signed her in the first place when he could have stuck to his favorite harem—the gaudy *ghagra* girls in their ethnic sweeper-woman attire and masses of silver jewelry. The strictly no-makeup, dusky-is-devasting look.

He could have gotten Suhaila, his ex-wife, for the role. They'd recently had a "civilized divorce," which meant that they still slept together when the nights got lonesome. But someone from the unit said she couldn't have accepted it in the first place, as she was off to France to do a bit role in one of those "exotique" films on India.

Aasha Rani was fascinated by Suhaila and her relationship with Suhas. She'd visited the set on one occasion and sat around giggling with the unit, bumming cigarettes from the light boys and flirting lightly with the assistant director. She'd pretended she hadn't noticed Aasha Rani at all till someone had called out to her and asked her over. "Hello, Aasha Rani—or should I call you Aasha Rani*ji*?—Suhas has told me so much about you. I've seen the rushes, of course. You look fabulous." Usual noises over, she'd lit a joint, taken off her embroidered *jootis,* uncoiled her hair with a graceful flick of her head and had gone back to discussing Woody Allen with the men.

Suhaila dressed in one-of-a-kind handspuns, which looked most dramatic when combined with kilos and kilos of chunky, tribal jewelry. And she had her *bindis*—dots, dashes, paisleys and intricate designer combinations that never failed to evoke a minor discourse on critical art appreciation. Sometimes the black dots traveled from her forehead down to her chin or onto her cheekbones. Aasha Rani felt threatened by her. So she wrote a letter and bitched to Linda. "I bet Suhaila chews Suhas's balls off in bed. She has such spitfire eyes. And she is so full of herself." Linda wrote back at length: "I've interviewed her once. They were just married then and he was behaving like a lovelorn puppy. She was the one who kept talking about their plans and making fun of everybody else in the industry. 'What are they? Pimps and prostitutes. What do they know about filmmaking? They're only good at making money . . .' and all that pseudo crap. As if she could live without money. Two months later, I found out she was having a *maha* affair with a minister. Some crude fellow she'd known earlier. He was pretty powerful and totally crazy about her. He gave them their car, flat and all that. Also, he pushed Suhas's film into the festival when it had been rejected. He sent Suhaila to Paris, Nantes, Locarno and God knows where all, as an official delegate. She was a big hit abroad with all those weird *bindis-shindis*. People found her irresistible to look at—and not at all resisting when it came to getting into her bed! She was screwing around so much, they began calling her the great Indian thoroughfare! But she made a lot of contacts and signed on a couple of *chhota-mota* films."

* * *

A FEW DAYS LATER Aasha Rani overheard one of the unit hands telling the cameraman, "*Yaar,* Suhas *ka* birthday *hai.* We'll have to do something. *Daaru-sharu.* Some *dhamal-shamal* . . ."

Aasha Rani smiled to herself. Suhas deserved a very special present. Matters had improved between them. Now Suhas had taken to photographing her while the unit relaxed between takes. Naturally the pictures were offbeat and squalidly "realistic" ones: Aasha Rani sans makeup with her hair in curlers; Aasha Rani scowling at her image in a handheld mirror—even one of Aasha Rani picking her nose! The condescension remained, however: sly digs about her *anpadh* status; mean cracks about her synthetic attire; clever innuendo designed to confuse her—that sort of thing.

The hairdresser approached her for a donation, letting slip the fact that last time the heroine—Radhikaji—had stood the Scotch (*asli maal*) and had paid ten thousand bucks besides. Aasha Rani smiled magnanimously. "I'll pay for everything. It's a small token; I want Suhasji to know how much the film means to me."

Aasha Rani dressed very carefully for the occasion. No makeup. Just a smudge of *kaajal.* She chose a simple shot-silk Kanjeevaram and wore flowers in her hair. She toyed with the idea of an elaborate *bindi,* à la Suhaila, but decided against it.

Her sari blouse was decorously long with a narrowing vee neck that ended in a knot at her waist. No buttons. Just a tantalizing flash of cleavage when her *pallav* shifted from her shoulders. She finished with some strategic dabs of attar: behind her ears, on her throat, on her navel and between her thighs.

She arrived deliberately late and feigned a certain breathlessness. Suhas glanced up at her, trying hard to suppress his obvious interest. She smiled sweetly and did a coy *namaskaram.* "You look like a *devadasi* tonight," Suhas said. She smiled and beckoned to Lucy, who arrived on cue—carrying a silver *thali* set for an *aarti*. Aasha Rani lit the oil lamp and turned to Suhas. "This is a very significant day in your life," she said. "What *natak* is this?" he asked, darting sheepish glances at the staring unit. "This is my way of honoring you; this is how we do it in Madras," Aasha Rani said, moving the lamp-laden *thali* slowly around his startled face and chanting an invocation to Lord Ganesha. Finally, she lifted a *peda* from the silver *thali* and popped it into his (conveniently) open mouth. "May your life always be as sweet as this," she said, dimpling prettily as the unit clapped and said, "*Wah, wah.*" Then Aasha Rani smiled beatifically at everyone, spoke a few words to Lucy, wished Suhas well again and walked out. She went straight up to her room, undressed and climbed into bed.

It was almost an hour later that she heard a hesitant knock at the door. "Are you asleep?" Suhas asked drunkenly, a half bottle of rum gripped in his hand. "No, I've been waiting for you," she answered. Suhas let himself in and stood uncertainly by the door. "Come to me, come here; I have a present for you in my bed."

Suhas lurched unsteadily toward her as Aasha Rani flung the bedcovers off dramatically. "Surprise!" she said as she revealed her naked body. Suhas grabbed her. Extricating herself from Suhas's clumsy embrace, she said, "No, we'll do it my way today. I want you to remember this birthday of yours forever."

Aasha Rani steered Suhas to her bed and pushed him down firmly. Then she began to unbutton his *kurta*. One tug and the *lungi* was off. Suhas was small and limp. He tried to cover himself. She pushed his hands away. "Don't; let me excite you."

She took him into her mouth and bit him softly. "I need a drink," she heard him say. "Later," she promised. Experience told her that Suhas's seduction was going to pose problems. Expertly, she used her tongue, lips, fingers and teeth to arouse the man who lay passively beside her.

Aasha Rani plucked out a rose from the vase on the bedside table and ran it down the length of his body. He shut his eyes and moaned, "A drink, I need another drink."

"Let me fix you one," she said, filling her mouth with rum from Suhas's half-empty bottle and lying on top of him. "Open your mouth," she commanded, as she lowered her face over his. When her lips reached Suhas's mouth, she poured the rum straight into it. "Let's have the next one on the rocks," she suggested, placing an ice cube between her teeth. She passed it into his mouth the same way and then retrieved it. "Don't stop now," pleaded Suhas.

Aasha Rani reached down to feel him. He was still small. "No more drinks," she announced firmly. But Suhas's inability to perform made him crabby. "Do you try this trick with all your directors?" he demanded, peevishly indignant all of a sudden. "Only those whose birthdays are celebrated by the units." Aasha Rani smiled at him. "Bloody bitch!" he snarled. "Take your filthy fingers off me!" Aasha Rani sat back and surveyed him pityingly. "Poor Suhas! What a little boy you really are!" He leaped out of bed and frantically tied his *lungi*. "I'm not used to sleeping with cheap call girls like you," he spluttered. "Of course not," Aasha Rani said sweetly. "Even cheap call girls don't do it for free. Not even *do kodi* ones as cheap as your wife!"

She watched as he staggered out of her room, slamming the door behind him. And then she went to the bathroom to gargle. What a nasty aftertaste rum left.

* * *

AASHA RANI'S EARTHY "new look" publicity stills were plastered on the covers of not just the popular film magazines but also figured on the covers of the more "serious" newsmagazines that gave her gushing writeups to go with the sexy pictures. Reluctant snobbish critics switched from bitching about the "zero-talent sweetheart" to raving about her "amazing histrionic range." The awards followed soon after. "Bhavnagar Fan Club," "Bhubaneshwar Popular Film Awards Circle," besides dozens of Lions Club Achievement Awards sent through the mail or hand-delivered. The recognition that might have meant something to Aasha Rani still eluded her—she had yet to receive the National Award—but there was no doubt at all that she had cracked the commercial film jackpot. All this in less than seven years with not even twenty films in her bag.

Dressed in her favorite white outfit (an extravagant costume created by the industry's top designer), Aasha Rani stole the show at the *Bechari Begum* premiere. Perhaps it was all for Akshay's benefit. Even after the sordid way he had treated her, she still tried to phone him sometimes. But he refused all her calls. Linda advised her to lay off. "Keep some dignity, *yaar*. Don't go after him like a bitch in heat. There are other men, other cocks, if that's what you are looking for. I would have thought by now I'd converted you . . ."

She tried to explain that she sorely missed Akshay's company, the sound of his marvelously cultured voice, the music and books he sent her, even the makeup tips he offered. The success of *Bechari Begum*, and a little advice from Akshay which she had disdained earlier, had made her change the way she did her eyes these days. And she had stopped painting over her lip line. She switched from plastering her face with ghastly pink pancake in an effort to look "fair" and finally started using the bronze makeup that Akshay had picked up for her in New York two years ago ("All the black fashion models use it—try some. Great stuff"). It had made all the difference. Aasha Rani looked sophisticated now. Gone was the trampy, hungry, take-me-when-you-want-me come-hitherness. And it was all thanks to Akshay. Today their worlds were so different.

It was Akshay who had introduced her to *ghazals* and *shairis*. At first she couldn't understand a word. Hindi was tough enough. And now, Urdu! He'd corrected her when she went wrong with her English, or her accent slipped. Akshay had a certain superficial gloss which passed for class in the industry. He could pronounce words like "Bordeaux" and he'd heard of Frank Capra.

Aasha Rani had been an eager student. She had missed going to school, though *Amma* had tried, halfheartedly, to employ tutors for her. Aasha Rani was aware of her deficiencies. For instance, her diction, the tone of her conversational voice, was frightfully pleb. She knew she ought to modulate it and speak in the softly refined tones of society ladies she encountered at the health club. And it was Akshay who'd helped her to achieve this. Not by mocking her, but by helping her constantly, correcting her gently and encouraging her till she'd gotten it right. All these changes in her baby had upset *Amma*. "Who do you think you are? Sounding so silly. Speak up! Speak up! Why are you whispering? So many books, so much money. All those cassettes! Why do you want to listen to that music? Will it help your career? No! It is all that man's evil influence. First he ruined his wife's career and now he wants to ruin yours!"

Aasha Rani wondered whether Akshay would attend the premiere, and if he'd bring Malini with him. These days he'd become very conscious of his "family man" image. He even refrained from flirting with the extras on the sets. And his affairs on location were conducted discreetly. Often, Malini would accompany him on outstation jaunts. Once on location she'd see to it that they spent all their free time closeted in the suite watching videos. His recent interviews too were full of the joys of fatherhood. Aasha Rani tried to convince herself that the whole charade was for her benefit. That somewhere along the way, Malini had gotten him to swear off Aasha Rani.

But it would still be thrilling to see him at the show. And even more thrilling to have him see her. Did he keep track of her triumphs? Surely, he must have received reports about the incredible success of *Bechari Begum* and all the other hits? Did he know about her and Amar? Stupid question. The entire industry was aware of it. Would he turn his face away? Greet her as a stranger? Pretend he hadn't seen her at all? Aasha Rani wrote out a little love note anyway and tucked it into her bra—one of the early ones Akshay had gotten her. The kinky one without nipples. She felt sexy wearing it. Just thinking about the time he had put it on her made her nipples taut. Akshay still did that to her.

Aasha Rani coyly said her *namastejis* to everybody and quickly scanned the audience. No sign of Akshay. It was silly to expect him to be around. Unbidden, the image of Akshay as she had seen him last came to mind. He had looked so tired. Maybe he was unwell. She remembered reading somewhere that he was having problems with his health. She hadn't given much credence to the information at the time—given its improbable account of terminal cancer and imminent death—but now she wondered. He had looked thinner, less happy. A sudden inexplicable fear gripped her, and she forced herself to calm down. A police band was playing a restrained version of her LLKK song. She smiled and waved to them. Fat, overdressed Punjabi matrons with lipstick on their teeth came rushing toward her with autograph books. "Please write, 'For Bunty,' thanks, *yaar*," they said as she held her breath. She couldn't stand their "Punjabi smell," as *Amma* had dubbed it. A vile combination of onion-garlic on the breath, sweaty BO under the arms and gallons of stale perfume all over. Sickening.

Linda kept up a steady commentary. "I can see Supriya. She's looking ugh! Yellow *salwar-kameez*. And that chimpanzee Kiran with that *bhoot*! Look at Dara—no, don't look now. And Chunk the Hunk. He's with his mother. Also Anju and Anish. Quite cute. Tuck your paunch in—*saali,* are you pregnant or what? That lech is staring at you—Kanhaiyaji. Ignore him. Real *ghatiya* chap." But Aasha Rani's entire being was focused on just one person. And he wasn't there.

Luckily for Aasha Rani she met Abhijit Mehra that night. She'd never heard of him. Of his father, yes. Which Indian hadn't heard of Amrish Mehra? It was said he was as powerful as the prime minister, as ruthless as a hangman and as wealthy as the dictator of a banana republic. A.M., as he was known, was a legendary figure in business circles. An industrialist with a sprawl of businesses that spanned everything from heavy machinery to fine textiles. And Abhijit was his only child—heir to the A.M. millions. For Amrishbhai was a cold-blooded professional robot with just one known weakness—his son.

Abhijit had been raised to be a worthy scion of the Mehra empire. Amrishbhai had sent him off to Eton as a young boy, then on to Cambridge, where he read economics, and then to Harvard for the mandatory postgraduate degree in business management. Abhijit was an accomplished squash player, golfer and swimmer.

Plus, he had taken courses in classical ballroom dancing. He played polo whenever he could and windsurfed on weekends. He wasn't conventionally good-looking, but his sporty physique made up for that. He studiously cultivated a "macho" image—complete with two German attack dogs. His idea of a lark was to bring girlfriends home and impress them with his German. The only German he knew was the commands for his dogs. After seating the girl down in his superluxurious "pad" (as he called it), he'd order them to attack. When their bared fangs were barely a couple of centimeters from the terror-stricken girls' throats, he'd issue the countercommand and the canines would back off. Naturally his guests didn't try to test his German further, though some women found the "sport" wildly erotic. He used to boast that they tore off their clothes at this point and laid themselves down at his Gucci-shod feet.

He was stylish, all right, and physical. But a bit of a mutton-head despite the foreign degrees. Perhaps his father recognized his shortcomings. And that made him even more vigilant and protective.

Abhijit's mother, having put in her all and producing a son, had retired from the worldly life and pleasures. She spent all her time pilgrimaging to various shrines scattered around India. While in Bombay, Bakulben would retreat into the marble *mandir* in her duplex (yes, *her* duplex) and pray the hours away. She was rarely seen in public and nobody really missed her, least of all her husband. He traveled in a pack with the senior vice presidents of his companies. "We prosper together, work together, whore together and die together," he'd chant as he went through his daily body massage at his private health club. He inspired undying loyalty in his staff, who were willing to do anything for him—even commit murder.

The night Aasha Rani met Abhijit, he was the chief sponsor of the show. No, it was his father who had agreed to underwrite it. But Amrishbhai had had to rush off to Geneva on some urgent business. Abhijit was just standing in for him. Just as well, thought the sharks at the show. Amrishbhai was a prickly, egotistic bastard who invariably demanded his pound of flesh. It would have been difficult to refuse him if he, per chance, had fancied the star of the evening. There was no such possibility with Abhijit—who was younger and more sophisticated. But their calculations proved wrong.

Abhijit had taken one look at Aasha Rani and flipped. He'd summoned one of the organizers and told him he was interested in meeting her. And that had put everybody in a fix. What would the Shethji's reaction be? And Amrishbhai's? Or Aasha Rani's, for that matter? What if she snubbed the request and snubbed Abhijit?

It worked out differently, however. Aasha Rani very charmingly agreed to garland Abhijit on the stage at the end of the show. She noticed the outline of his body under the light Italian silk suit he was wearing. She took in his polka-dotted tie and the gel in his slicked-back hair. Like a gangster. An attractive gangster. She wondered what he'd be like in bed. Funny, she always wondered that about any man she saw. Any. He didn't have to be good-looking, and she didn't have to be attracted to him. He just had to be a man, that was all, and Aasha Rani's X-ray eyes would instantly undress him and get him into bed with her. What would he do to her? Or she to him?

With women, it worked differently. She stripped only those she was attracted to. And that didn't happen very often. Aasha Rani was far more discriminating with her own sex. But as she used to giggle with Linda, "It's so much more relaxed with women. Sex is fun when the person knows your body as well as she knows her own. Only a woman can really please another woman sexually. Only another woman knows where to touch, when to touch, how to touch . . ."

While garlanding Abhijit, she experienced a secret thrill as her fingers brushed past his ears. With her four-inch heels she was the same height, so their eyes were parallel, as were their lips. He bent his head to receive the garland and his mouth was near her breasts. She could feel his warm breath on her throat as he raised his neck, took his arms up to remove the prickly flowers and, in a smooth, spontaneous gesture, garlanded her back with the same. Nor did he stop there. He held her hands in his, leaned over and kissed her warmly on both cheeks to uproarious applause. Flustered, flattered and immensely thrilled, Aasha Rani stepped back and stared at him wide-eyed. He snapped his fingers in front of her face, winked and said, "It's OK. I'm for real. What are you doing later tonight?" "Not tonight," she whispered back. "Call me," Abhijit said, and passed a business card to her. "Meanwhile," he added before striding off the stage, "Love, Love, Kiss, Kiss. It's good for health!"

Abhijit Mehra 🙣

It was at a fancy jeweler's shop in Zaveri Bazaar that Aasha Rani ran into Abhijit again. She was busy trying on a pair of diamond *kadas* when someone placed a large hand over her slim wrist and said, "Tch! Tch! Poor woman. No bangles for the beautiful lady. So sad." She looked up sharply and saw Abhijit staring at her, laughter lighting up his eyes. "Very funny," she said, and laughed too. Outside the enormous glass windows she could see the narrow crowded street already full of fans who were being kept at bay by the burly *durban,* but (just about). She could hear the shouts of "Love, Love, Kiss, Kiss," followed by vulgar smooching sounds. She looked back at Abhijit, and he said, "Don't worry about them. I'll escort you out, and maybe you'd like to visit my home." She noticed a young girl with him. "My fiancée," he said. "Nikita. She's from London."

Aasha Rani looked at the fresh-faced teenager and said hello. She was lovely, with streaked hair and trendy clothes. "You should become a film star," Aasha Rani said to her. The girl stared coldly and in an accented voice replied, "No, thank you. I have better things to do." Abhijit tweaked her nose and admonished, "Naughty girl! Don't you know who you are speaking to? This is Aasha Rani, India's leading movie queen." The girl blushed deeply and apologized. "I am so terribly sorry. You must think me awfully rude. You see, I don't live here, and I haven't seen any Indian films. Forgive me for not recognizing you." "That's OK," Aasha Rani said. "But I still mean it. You should join the industry—you are a very pretty girl." Abhijit interjected, "Nikita happens to be a barrister. A *maha*-intellectual. Don't go by her looks. She is all brains as well." Nikita looked away modestly before asking, "What are all those people doing out there? God! There must be thousands of them." Abhijit smiled and said, "Oh, those? I've hired them for Aasha Rani's benefit. I thought she'd feel most insecure if she wasn't mobbed in Zaveri Bazaar." Aasha Rani gave him a friendly shove. He took her arm. "Shall we go?"

So they went off, the three of them, for a cup of coffee at Abhijit's favorite restaurant in Bombay—the Sea Lounge. They managed to get a table overlooking the Gateway of India. For a while nobody spoke. They watched the little boats of the Yacht Club bobbing up and down on the waves and the pigeons being fed by a group of Japanese tourists. The sky was aflame with the colors of the setting sun. The islands in the far distance looked lazy, and an impressive-looking oil rig suddenly floated into view. "It's so pretty out here," Nikita commented. Everybody was silent. "So how does it feel to be in a place like this where everybody pretends they don't know who you are?" Abhijit said finally. Aasha Rani looked around. It was true. Everyone else in the large restaurant was studiously looking away. The waiters, too, were behaving with the utmost discretion, neither hovering around too conspicuously nor neglecting their duties. "It's such a relief, actually," Aasha Rani said. "We film people can't go anywhere without being disturbed." "Doesn't that flatter you?" Nikita asked. "It did in the beginning but not anymore. Now it is a real *jhanjhat.*" "What is a '*jhanjhat*'?" Nikita asked. Both Aasha Rani and Abhijit laughed. "*Yeh to badi memsaab hai, yaar,*" he explained. Nikita flushed and protested, "Look, I understood what you just said. I know that much Hindi, you know. It's not a question of being a *memsaab.* I'm unfamiliar with local slang. I haven't ever lived in India, remember?" Aasha Rani smiled at her sweetly and said, "Just ignore the man. He's only teasing you. Now tell me, when is the wedding?"

Abhijit sat back and let Nikita gush. "Oh, we are planning it in December. It's a good time of the year, I'm told. Not quite this hot. God! I'm sweating all the time!" "Where is it going to be?" "The Turf Club, you must come." "I'll organize the fans and the police bandobast; don't worry. We must have a top star at the function; otherwise people will say we haven't really made it." Abhijit laughed. Then, turning to Nikita, he explained, "Film stars are considered status symbols in India." Nikita smiled at Aasha Rani. "In that case, you must come. And bring your favorite hero along." Abhijit winked and kicked her under the table.

When they came down to the foyer, Nikita excused herself and asked, "Where's the ladies'?" Abhijit escorted her to the door, then caught Aasha Rani by the sleeve and held her back. "I have to talk to you," he whispered. Aasha Rani stayed back and the two of them stood awkwardly in the narrow passage, while people pushed past them staring openmouthed at Aasha Rani.

"When can I see you?" Abhijit asked urgently. "You've been on my mind from the day we met at that ghastly show." Aasha Rani looked at him with surprise. "I thought you're getting married to that sweet, pretty child in December?" "That has nothing to do with my seeing you—it's an arranged affair. Our families have a business connection. I like her but I'm not in love with her." "You aren't in love with me either," Aasha Rani said. "Maybe I am. I don't know. All I know is that I've wanted you desperately from that day. I've even seen all your terrible films." "Thank you. I suppose I should be flattered that you took the trouble. But I'm really not interested. Besides, I'm very busy with my shooting." "We don't have time, Aasha Rani. She'll be out any moment. Say you'll see me. Let me come to you tonight. Say yes, wait for me, you won't regret it. I'll be there at ten thirty."

Nikita came out. She'd freshened her lipstick and had combed her long hair. "You look lovely," Abhijit said to her as he took her hand.

WHEN HE ARRIVED at Aasha Rani's house Abhijit was very agitated. "I need a drink," he said. "Go ahead; help yourself," she replied, pointing to the bar. "I'm so thirsty." Abhijit groaned, pouring himself a large Scotch as Aasha Rani watched. He looked so haunted, so troubled. "What's wrong?" she asked softly. "Everything!" he said, and collapsed into a deep chair. "I'm so fucked up. I hate my life, my job, my house, my father, Nikita. I hate everything—India, business, my dad, yes, him most of all. He'll go to any lengths to show me down. Today he yelled at me in front of his employees because we lost a two-crore contract. He blames me for everything. I hate him; God help me, I hate him . . ."

Aasha Rani went up to him and took off his jacket. Standing silently behind his chair she started massaging his neck. "Close your eyes . . . relax," she instructed. She unbuttoned his shirt, pulled off his tie and worked on his tense muscles. "Relax . . . relax . . . relax . . ." Gradually Abhijit began to unwind. He felt his tense musles slacken and his eyes began to droop. "That feels good. That feels *so-o-o* good," he said as her fingers moved deftly down his back and her thumb located the stiff spots on his spine. "Come and lie down here," she said, leading him by the arm. Once on the bed, she got to work seriously, sitting astride his bottom and working vigorously with her hands. Ten minutes later, Abhijit was fast asleep.

He woke up with a start at three a.m. and grabbed a sheet around his middle. He tried to reach for a light switch. Aasha Rani restrained him. "Ssssh, it's all right. You are with me, in my home." "Who are you?" he asked groggily. "And where the fuck am I?" She rolled over and brought her body nearer his. She placed his hands on her breasts and got him to cup them. "Guess . . ." she said.

Abhijit was wide-awake now. He laughed and pulled her to him, kissing her mouth tenderly. "Sorry, my queen," he said. "I had a nightmare. I get them every night. That's why I hate sleeping alone. Always have. Shall I tell you a little secret? This big, grown-up man in your bed is scared of the dark. Yes, he is. And he's also quite a crybaby. Don't laugh. If you shout at me or hurt my feelings, I will weep all over your lovely bed and ruin the sheets. Just be nice, OK?"

"How nice?" Aasha Rani asked, reaching down under the sheets and holding him. "This nice?" she teased, giving him a squeeze. "No, nicer . . ." He moaned as she slid down, her tongue leaving a wet streak along the length of his body.

For a while, Aasha Rani was sufficiently distracted by Abhijit's attentions. She thought of Akshay often but made no attempt to reach him. Often he would be shooting in the adjoining studio. She'd spot his van parked inside the gates and she'd tense with anticipation. Once they'd even crossed each other as she rushed from one set to the next, and she'd noticed how pale Akshay had looked.

Her attitude toward her work had changed. And she wondered whether it had anything to do with Akshay. She felt listless, distracted. Directors began to comment on her indifference. One of them suggested kindly that she should take a break. Go on vacation. Shop till she dropped in Singapore. But even that didn't turn her on. Who would she go with? What would she do? And just how much could she shop for? She'd lost interest in her cuddly toys too. She'd stare at her menagerie and cry for no reason.

THE NEWS OF ABHIJIT and Nikita's marriage was splashed on the front page of every daily. Every single paper and magazine carried photographs of the couple. Aasha Rani stared at Nikita's picture. She did look rather lovely. Abhijit looked handsome too—with an enormous *pheta* on his head and a smart ivory-colored *sherwani*. Amrishbhai had invited the entire city, but Aasha Rani had decided not to go—she was feeling too low and listless. Akshay was there; so were all the other girls, her rivals. She spotted Anushree in a photograph looking stunning in green. And Tanya, the latest temptress, who had created quite a sensation with her first film. She saw Amirchand's picture with the chief minister—looking every bit the mealymouthed politician in a *khadi churidar-kurta*. Little did the world know about his dirty secrets, Aasha Rani thought. Nitesh was there with his overdressed wife. And Ritaji, of course. Good God! What had she done with her hair? Malini's picture was with Suhaila—both of them trying to outethnic each other. Suhas, said the report, was away on location, shooting a film on the Bhils.

Aasha Rani had just about heard the names of the industrialist invitees. She certainly didn't recognize even one of them. That made her think of her *filmi duniya*. What an isolated, unreal world all of them lived in. A world built on illusions and Technicolor dreams. A world as phony as the films it churned out. She hardly knew a single person outside the film industry. Nor did she have the time to get to know the real world—whatever and wherever that was.

On the few occasions that she did meet non–movie people, she discovered she had nothing to say to them. They spoke a different language. Their interests were entirely alien. Their thinking was on a totally different plane. They were "normal."

There were times Aasha Rani wanted nothing more desperately than to be "normal," like she imagined those others to be. Studios, parties, photo sessions, dubbing—that was all. She felt self-conscious in the presence of non-*filmi* types and avoided contact with them because she didn't want to appear stupid; didn't want to be "found out." She knew she was unaware. But she also knew she was smart. Why should she allow these outsiders to judge her and call her stupid just because she was not interested in the same things? She could sometimes sense their hostility, their mockery. Especially at charity premieres for causes such as the Army Widows Welfare Fund. Women would come up to her on these occasions and make sly remarks like, "It must feel nice to make so much money for such little work. You girls are lucky, no responsibilities, no family, nothing. Just sing and dance and romance with the hero in Kashmir and get paid lakhs for it." "We are fortunate. God has given us so much," Aasha Rani would agree. And the women would zoom in for attack. "So much? *Arrey*—what about a family? What about a husband? Children? You may not miss these things now, but later, when your looks and popularity fade, then you'll think, 'My life is so empty and these women are so lucky.'"

They were right, Aasha Rani thought as she read Nikita's interview in a city glossy. "I'm the luckiest girl in the world," she was quoted as saying. Well, she'd certainly bagged a wonderful man. An unfaithful husband. But a terrific lover. Aasha Rani smiled at that. He'd promised to visit her right after his Hawaiian honeymoon.

ABHIJIT WASN'T THE SAME on his return. Or maybe it was her. She had no right to feel cheated. But somewhere along the line, she held his marriage against him. "My life is beginning to resemble the movies I act in," she told him. "You are like Devdas, and I, Chandramukhi." Abhijit didn't know what she was talking about. He hadn't heard of the classic. So she switched the VCR on for him, saying, "Watch! That is you and this is me." She disappeared to wash her hair and emerged half an hour later to find him crying. "Why are you torturing me like this?" Aasha Rani looked at him with surprise. "Me? Torturing you? I should be the one saying all this! You are a married man with a lovely young wife. And yet, you come to me. Why? For sex. Nothing else! What does that make me? Not even Chandramukhi—she was a courtesan. I'm just your celebrity fuck! I wouldn't turn you on as much had I been a nobody—just a sexy *Madraasi* girl with big tits. You aren't making love to me! You are screwing my image—my screen image. Get out of here, Abhijit. Go back to your wife and make a man of yourself! It's all over between us. I never want to see you again!"

Abhijit hadn't wanted to leave. "I've made a mistake," he whimpered. "I should never have married Nikita. I don't love her. She doesn't excite me. I needed booze, uppers, a sniff of coke on my honeymoon to make out with her. Each time I tried, I thought of you, Aasha Rani. Don't throw me out of your life like this! I need you." Aasha Rani looked at him pityingly. "Go home, Abhijit. I have my own life to lead . . ."

But did she really lead her own life? Aasha Rani wasn't sure. It seemed more and more like she was leading someone else's. As if the real her was trapped forever in the wrong movie, in the wrong role.

She was shooting with Tushar, a seasoned hero, who was still going strong after twenty-five years in the industry. It was an emotional scene. Aasha Rani was required to cry, but prettily, so as not to mess up her makeup. Tushar, playing a dacoit chief going in for his final encounter with the police (who'd surrounded the village), was holding her in his arms, saying, "Don't mourn after my death. Think of me as I was in life. And take care of my unborn child. He will be a son. I know that. Tell him about his father. Tell him about our love." That was Aasha Rani's cue to start crying, which she did, only she couldn't stop.

The director called out, "Cut," thrice. Finally Tushar led her gently away from the set. The director called for a cold drink, while the unit hands shrugged, switched off the lights, lit up cigarettes and waited.

Tushar sent everybody away and let Aasha Rani finish crying. "Don't worry," he said. "It happens to everybody at some point—this profession is such. Take your time. The unit can wait. You've been working too hard. Relax. Take a holiday."

Aasha Rani told him softly, "It isn't that. I don't work that hard anymore. I've stopped doing the third shift unless it's urgent. I don't work on Sundays. It's not the work. And it's not a holiday—I just had one in Madras. I don't know what it is. I feel depressed all the time. My heart is not in shooting. I come to the sets mechanically because I have given dates. Besides, if I wasn't shooting, what would I do? I have no friends. I suppose I'm just very lonely. I miss Madras."

Tushar held her hand tenderly. "I used to feel the same way years ago. I'd cry to go back to my village in Punjab. I missed the green fields, the food, my own people. But after five years, I got used to the industry. And to Bombay. This city is such—it isn't like any other city in India.

"People are caught up with their own lives. Nobody has time for you. You can die on the pavement and not a single person will stop to spit in your direction. All of us who come from other states feel shocked by this. Bombay is a cruel city. Only *matlab ki baat*. Do you think I have made friends here after twenty years? Do you think there's even one person I trust? No. I can never relax in Bombay. Never speak my heart to anyone. Nobody cares. They're only interested in what they can get out of you. The minute your use is over, you are over. So long as you are a success— at the top—people will flock around you. After that—*khalaas*.

"It is not a place for women. I know so many heroines who used to work with me ten years ago. Where are they today? No roles, no friends, no money. The lucky ones are those who escaped in time. Got married. Left this wretched industry and never looked back. That is what you should do. Find a good man, settle down. Have children, forget all this. How long will it last? Another two years? Three? And then where will you go? Make your money and quit in style. But one piece of advice I must give you—your time is right now. If you mess up your career at this point, you will be out. No hope after that. There are dozens of pretty girls waiting to take your place. Younger, better-looking, ambitious. If you start doing *nakhra* on the sets, keeping producers waiting, not showing up on time, forget it, you will be out. And if your films flop—again—out! Remember the industry rule—you are as good as your last film.

"Nobody cares if you've had ten silver jubilee films in the past. Nobody cares if producers have become millionaires because of your hits. The industry is also changing fast. It isn't what it was in my time. Video—that is our biggest enemy. You will see—there is a big crash coming. We will all have to lower our prices. Act in small-budget films. Compromise. Or we'll be driven out. Before that happens, you should finish your assignments and make another life.

"You are still young, beautiful, successful. Cash in on that now. Your market value is good. Any man will be proud to marry you. Two years from now, you will be sorry you didn't listen to a wise old actor's words. I tell you this because you are like a daughter. Do you know my son is older than you are? And see how ridiculous the whole thing is; I'm playing your lover in this film! That is how unreal, shallow and meaningless the industry is. *Chalo,* let's finish the scene. Everybody is waiting—the show must go on."

Aasha Rani 🙧

AASHA RANI DETESTED BOMBAY MONSOONS. IT WAS THE ONE time of the year that she seriously considered abandoning the city and fleeing to Madras. She hated waking up to a gray morning with the sound of rain pelting her windows. She hated the oppressive dampness. No building in Bombay, no matter how posh, was monsoon-proof. Moldy patches all over the house, the stench of carpets heavy with water. The walls wept, the windows leaked, and the rain seemed to seep into everything—including her mind.

The monsoons disoriented her completely. She couldn't judge from the light outside whether it was early afternoon or late evening. She disliked having the lights on at home all through the day. There was absolutely nothing romantic about the downpour outside, and no amount of listening to mood music removed the dark, gloomy clouds that hung over her. Most of all Aasha Rani loathed stepping out of her villa into the puddles outside.

The long drive to distant studios would get even longer as her van stalled every few meters. Traffic snarls were everywhere: raised voices and tempers, irate drivers honking in a vain effort to get everybody moving. As if the sound alone would blast the clogged drains and empty the roads of mounds of rotting garbage. Bombay stank during the rains. The three monsoon months seemed endless.

The producers took advantage of the weather to pin stars down to extended indoor shooting. The action had now shifted from suburban studios to suburban bungalows. Enterprising owners of these sprawling residences had discovered new avenues to raise money—film shootings. At over ten thousand rupees per day, they'd allow units into their homes to take the place over and shoot around the clock. Aasha Rani preferred these studios— at least there were decent loos to go to, unlike the smelly studio bathrooms, or worse, secluded spots behind rocks and trees during outdoor spells!

It was while her car was stuck at the Bandra intersection that she noticed Akshay's Mercedes right next to her. He was alone in the backseat reading *India Today*. She looked at him for nearly five minutes with longing and sadness. He wasn't keeping very well these days. It showed on his face. Why had he cut her out of his life so totally? Did his career matter all that much to him? Was it just Rita's and Malini's threats that did it? Or had he gotten tired of her? She had to know.

She lowered her window and tried to attract his attention. Her sleeve got drenched in seconds. Damn! Akshay's driver saw her before he did and turned around to inform him. Akshay looked up from the magazine and quickly looked away. Aasha Rani was crushed. Why? What had she done to him? It was so unfair!

Spontaneously, in the pouring rain, she opened the car door and jumped out. Before Akshay knew what was happening, she'd gotten in beside him. "You are dripping wet and ruining my car," he said coldly. "Akshay, please, not in front of—" And she indicated the driver. Her own was staring at the scene open-mouthed.

The lights had changed. Akshay's driver had to move, but he didn't have instructions. To the studios as usual, or . . . ? There was a deafening cacophony of car horns, and to add to the confusion, almost out of nowhere a crowd of half-naked urchins appeared and surrounded Akshay's car. "*Abbey* hero, Love, Love, Kiss, Kiss!" they hollered, thumping the windows and obstructing the windshield.

"You have no right to behave like this," Akshay said, his nostrils flaring with rage. Aasha Rani pleaded with him. "Please, all I want is one hour of your time. Don't turn me away. Don't create a scene, not here." Akshay glared at her. "I'm not the one creating the scene—you are. I'll ask my driver to pull up after the lights, and I'd be obliged if you got into your own car. There's nothing I have to say to you." Aasha Rani tried to hold his hand. The urchins screamed with delight and shouted, "*Chuma-Chuma.*" He pulled his hand away and said a sharp, "*Chalo,*" to the driver.

Aasha Rani knew she was running out of time. In desperation, she bent and touched his feet. "I beg of you, don't do this to me. You have humiliated me enough. All I want is an explanation. Tell me why you stopped seeing me, wanting me, and I'll never bother you again." Akshay looked into her eyes, and something about their expression made him change his mind. He told the driver to turn the car around and head for Holiday Inn.

It felt so good to be back in the familiar suite and the even more familiar bed. Aasha Rani clung to Akshay. She was dying to ask him why he had cut her out of his life. But she knew better. Their lovemaking was different too. No biting, clawing or frenzied passion. Akshay was gentle and unfrenzied. Aasha Rani didn't feel too much like a tigress herself. They hardly spoke. But both of them knew that the affair was on once more. That the self-imposed ban had been lifted.

The romance helped to see Aasha Rani through the monsoons. She canceled shootings and spent every moment she could get in the "secret suite" with Akshay. He didn't have too many films on hand. Aasha Rani noticed that he had dark circles under his eyes and that he didn't have the same energy, nor the zest for living that she had so envied. They spent time lying in each other's arms listening to music, eating, reading magazines. Once again gossip columns bristled with juicy tidbits about their affair, and Linda made it very clear that she disapproved. Aasha Rani didn't care. She was with him and that was all that mattered. They didn't talk about Rita or Malini either. It was no longer important.

BUT AASHA RANI'S PRODUCERS weren't all that sympathetic or understanding. She began receiving angry calls. One of them was from Gopal. He put it crudely: "*Dekho jaan-e-man,* we all know that your *chakkar* with Akshay has started again. *Chalo theek hai.* You are free to warm anybody's bed if you want to. But not on our time. We are the people who pay for your fun. Remember that. If you ditch us, you will be finished. Each time you don't turn up for shooting, we lose lakhs. You have already been knocked out of three big productions. Your reputation is mud. There are *hazaar* girls willing to take your place. Now listen to me: If you care about yourself and that *lafanga,* keep the dates you've given us. A lot of money is involved. If you don't, there are ways of dealing with you. Not even the Shethji will be able to help you then. All I have to do is to phone Amrishbhai and let him know about your *lafda* with his *pyaara beta. Phir to khatam.*"

Aasha Rani heard him out in stunned silence. It brought her to her senses, but not entirely. She knew Gopal and the others meant business. She'd overheard conversations at the studios also. But at that point nothing else mattered. It was Akshay she wanted. Just Akshay. All of him. All the time.

Fortunately for Aasha Rani, her next two films were hits. Nothing else counted in the industry. She knew that too. She took advantage of the situation to skip work even more. Her schedules became erratic. She was dubbed the most undependable star. She was warned that an industry boycott was being planned.

The showdown finally took place on Rajiv Behl's sets. Aasha Rani was playing a double role in his film, the usual one that revolved around twins separated at birth. She was expected to score a double victory with *Hum Dono, Alag.* But Aasha Rani's mind was not on the film at all. An elaborate mansion had been erected for the climax in which the rich twin comes face-to-face with the poor one. The shooting required complicated camera work. Everybody was tense, including the young producer-director whose maiden film it was.

The first time Aasha Rani failed to show up he was furious, but restrained himself when she arrived two days later. The second time he spoke to her firmly, but not sharply. The third time he threw a tantrum. Aasha Rani threw a countertantrum. The fourth time he asked her to get out. But Aasha Rani was too happy to care: "To hell with movies, *yaar.*" She laughed when Linda told her that film heroes were refusing to sign films if it meant acting opposite her. It was just the signal *Amma* needed to come back and take charge of her daughter's career and life once again.

Aasha Rani was rather glad to see *Amma* when she arrived unannounced from Madras. "Look at the house. A pigsty!" *Amma* growled as soon as she walked in. Aasha Rani hugged her and said, "I'm glad you are back. I need you." *Amma* ignored her and marched into the kitchen. "*Chhee!* It's a gutter," she declared. "And the new servants—loafers! Where did you get them all from—the slum colony next door?" "That's right," Aasha Rani admitted. "God knows you'll never be able to run your own house. You are disorganized, inefficient and sloppy. How did you manage for so long? What did you eat? There is nothing on the kitchen shelves. The fridge is empty. The whole place is stinking. Stale food everywhere. Rotting vegetables in baskets. Didn't you learn anything from me? And your career—what is all this nonsense I hear? You don't go for shooting? You keep producers waiting? Rajiv Behl has replaced you in his film. Is your secretary a *hijda*? What do you pay him a salary for? Is this the way to handle your affairs? What has happened to your money? Do you know? He must have swallowed it all up. And your taxes? Have you been paying up signing amounts? Who takes those, you or him? Irresponsible girl! Trying to show off with your own people. Fighting with your own *amma*. Not bothering to see *Appa* when he was sick. Wasting time with a fading actor. What can he do for you? Nothing!"

Aasha Rani heard her out and then said, "Now that you are here, everything will be all right. Tell me, how is *Appa*? I heard he was better. They brought him home, didn't they? And Sudha? How is she?" *Amma* looked at her. "Yes, *Appa* pulled out. It was a miracle. Nothing short of it. I know the reason—Shri Venkateshwara's blessings. I prayed night and day for his recovery. I made a vow to offer a *yagna*. It is a matter of faith, my girl. And yes, Sudha is very well. She is also receiving offers in Madras. But I don't know whether I want her to get into this dirty line. One child was enough. Sudha can be a dancer—a great dancer. She has gotten very good reviews. Or she can get married. I have protected that girl. She is pure. Any good Iyengar boy will be proud to marry her."

Aasha Rani listened to *Amma* without letting on how she felt. Well, at least *Amma* was being truthful. And she wished Sudha well. But didn't *Amma* stop to think for a moment how her words would hurt Aasha Rani? Didn't she feel a little ashamed admitting that she had ruined Aasha Rani's life? No. *Amma* probably had her explanations all worked out. In any case it was too late to mourn the past. Aasha Rani needed *Amma* to organize her future.

AMIRCHAND WASN'T HAPPY with the developments either. He sent for Aasha Rani after nearly three months. She knew what the meeting was for. Before he could say anything, she fell at his feet and said, "Forgive me. I have realized my mistake." Amirchand picked her up gently and put her on the settee. "Look here, I have been hearing stories, receiving complaints. All this is not good. You have to decide what you want to do with your life. Right now you are throwing it away. Your career is in a shambles. Producers, directors, financiers, even your heroes have come to me. I told them, *'Bhai*, she isn't my private property. Her life is her life. Why complain to me?' But they said, 'Shethji, only you will be able to help us. Only you can drill some sense into her head. We run at a loss if she cancels shooting. Today her films are still doing well. But we are gambling with our money on her future films. The public is fickle. Tomorrow there may be another craze, another heroine. We'll be stuck with unsalable films starring her which have gone overbudget because of her nonsense. *Usko* line *mein laga do.'* So tell me, what are you planning to do? Give me a straight answer. No *bakwas.*" Aasha Rani said, "OK, boss, no *bakwas.*" And she told him her plans. "Akshay and I have decided to get married."

The Shethji looked at her incredulously, his eyes popping out of their sockets. *"Tu bilkul pagal ho gayee hai kya?* Married? How? He is already married. That wife of his will never agree to a divorce. Even if she does, it will take years and years. You will be an old hag by then. You have lost your senses. Snap out of it! Concentrate on your career. Find the right man. If you can't, I will. This much I can do for you. But don't waste your time on that worthless fellow. He can't even keep you happy in bed. I hear he is very sick."

Aasha Rani fell back automatically into her old habit of pressing Amirchand's feet. "You don't understand, Shethji. I love this man. I really do. I want to marry him. Bear his child. We have found a way, but don't ask me what. I can't tell you. As soon as the ceremony is over, you'll be the first person I'll bring sweets for. But please do not try to stop me. This means everything to me, everything."

"All you women are just the same—bloody fools! How can you be any different from your mother? She ruined your life. Now, you'll ruin your child's. Don't you learn from mistakes? What did that father of yours do for any of you? He didn't even give you his name. What will Akshay do; will he recognize your bastard child? You are being cruel to an innocent life. To satisfy your selfish urges you will raise a baby whose father will disown it—mark my words. How will that child grow up and go to school? Have you thought of all these things?"

Aasha Rani started to cry. "Shethji, you know I have tried to get Akshay out of my life. I'd stopped seeing him in between. I went with other men, hoping I'd be able to get him out of my thoughts. But it didn't work. I'm willing to sacrifice everything. My career, my money, fame, *sub kuch*. All I want are your blessings. There is nobody else I can depend on in the world. Not even *Amma*. If she finds out my plans, she will kill me. She'll do anything to stop this marriage. Shethji, I beg of you, don't hate me for what I'm doing. And you can tell all my producers that I'll finish their assignments on time. Now that I know the course my life is going to take, I feel calmer. I feel secure. I won't ditch anybody. I'll turn up for shooting. But I'm not going to sign any more films either."

Without another word, she bent down to touch his feet, picked up her bag and ran out, tears streaming down her face.

THE NEWS THAT Aasha Rani was quitting films spread quickly. Linda was the first to phone. "Is it true?" she asked. "Yes," Aasha Rani said in an excited voice. "Why?" Linda demanded. "Are you asking as a friend or a journalist?" Aasha Rani asked. "Don't you know by now—there is no such thing as 'friendship' between journalists and film stars? A scoop is a scoop. It comes first—before anything else. Does that answer your question?" Impulsively Aasha Rani said, "Come and have lunch with me. We'll talk about it." Linda paused. "I'll be bringing a photographer along. Put on your makeup and wear something trendy." Aasha Rani groaned. "Listen, do you never stop working? I don't feel like applying makeup today. I want to relax, chat, gossip." "Forget it, in that case. I have loads of stuff to write. You know we are working on our annual issue right now. I'm not a lady of leisure like you. I work for a living. I can't waste time hogging *idlis* and listening to you mooning over that eunuch unless I can use your quotes!" Linda snapped. Aasha Rani was in much too good a mood to protest. "*Chalo theek hai,* see you in an hour."

Amma was suspicious. "Who was that on the phone?" she demanded. "Just Linda," Aasha Rani said nonchalantly. "Just Linda," *Amma* mimicked. "Huh! That girl is no good. I've told you before. She is not your well-wisher. She is a troublemaker. Why do you waste your time with her kind?" Aasha Rani smiled a mysterious smile and said nothing.

Amma had not been told about the marriage plans. She was furious when she heard Aasha Rani telling a producer over the phone that she was returning the signing amount of his forthcoming picture. "Have you gone mad? Why are you doing this?" she demanded. "I feel like taking some time off. I'm tired, *Amma;* I need a holiday," Aasha Rani replied airily. "What nonsense! At your age—tired? You look like a horse. There's nothing wrong with you. Now is the time to make money," *Amma* said scornfully.

"Money, money, money. That's all you think of. Well, I'm fed up with being your money machine. I've done enough for everybody—you, Sudha and the others—now I want to live for myself and enjoy life." *Amma* glared at her, eyes blazing. "Ungrateful wretch! I've sacrificed so much—my youth, my time, my energy. What for? So that I could make you a star. And this is how you treat your family? You want to throw everything away on some stupid whim, on some stupid man? Tell me, Baby, is that flop actor going to look after you in your old age? Is he going to look after your *amma* or your sister? We have to look after ourselves. Tomorrow, you won't have anybody willing to look at you. Today you are famous, successful. India is at your feet. But memory is very short. If you get out of films, other girls will get in, and the same fans who run after you today will be chasing them. That is the way the world is. Your arrogance won't work. Listen to your *amma*. Who else can tell you the truth? And don't open your heart to that evil girl. Never trust these journalists. They are snakes—vicious and poisonous. She will not think twice before biting you!"

"LET'S JUST DRIVE around the city or go to the zoo. Anywhere. We could take a launch from the Gateway of India and see the Elephanta Caves. I've been in Bombay for so many years, but I haven't seen anything. Just the inside of studios and five-star hotels. I want to wander around in the markets. Go shopping at Kala Niketan. Buy something at Chor Bazaar—have you been there? Akshay has told me so much about it. Let's have lunch at some sweet little Udipi place. Let me buy you a sari from Kala Niketan. Let's hunt for sandals at the Oberoi Shopping Arcade— let's do something different and exciting!" Aasha Rani said all in a rush to Linda as soon as she arrived.

Linda looked at her as if she were crazy. "Call that exciting? My dear woman, we do those things every day of our lives. Elephanta! Do you know it will take not less than five hours to go there and back? Even foreigners think twice before getting on the ferry. And have you thought of the crowds everywhere?"

"I won't wear makeup. Or I'll wear a *burqa*. I have one somewhere. I used to put it on in the early days when I went off to see my movies in theaters with the ordinary crowds. It used to be so much fun listening to their comments, seeing their reactions. Haven't done anything like that in years. *Chalo na.*"

OK," said Linda reluctantly. "But first, a deal. You give me an exclusive on why you are quitting and I'll come slumming with you."

"Deal," said Aasha Rani trustingly.

AKSHAY WASN'T CONVINCED about the marriage idea at all. "Ajay will kill me," he said to Aasha Rani. "Who is Ajay? Your keeper? Haven't you done enough for him? If you'd said Malini would get upset, I'd have understood. But right now, I don't want to think of anyone, not them, not *Amma,* not producers—no one. I want to concentrate on us. And our life!"

"Have you thought of the repercussions? There are laws in India—bigamy laws. We must consult some senior lawyers. But I can't talk to my man; he'll tell Malini and Ajay. He advises us on all matters. Handles the trust for the children," Akshay hedged, squirming in his seat. "I'll handle everything. I'll talk to someone. We will find a solution. You wait and see," Aasha Rani said.

She came back a couple of days later looking triumphant. "Akshay—I've got the answer! We can get married and it will be recognized by the whole world!" She waited to see his reaction. His eyes wore a guarded expression. "Well—aren't you going to ask me what I've discovered?" She laughed. "Tell me," he said. "Muslims," she announced. "We can both become Muslims! It's easy. First we get converted to the faith by a *Kazi,* change our names, and then perform the *nikah*—that's all it takes. That way, there doesn't have to be a divorce or anything! I'll be your legally wedded second wife. Muslims can have four, but you'd better stop with me."

"I knew you'd come up with that—it has been tried before, you know. We aren't the first film wallahs to think of it," Akshay said, not meeting her eyes. "Then," Aasha Rani reasoned, "so much the better if others have also done it. Nobody will raise eyebrows when they hear our news."

"You are so stubborn. And so stupid. Do you really think it's that simple? Or that it will be accepted by everyone without causing a sensation? Just forget it. Besides, I don't want to become a Muslim. I believe in my religion. I don't want to give up my faith. I was born a Hindu. I want to die a Hindu. I want to be cremated, not buried. I don't want to change my name to Aslam Khan or something. How could you think such an absurd plan would work?"

"I thought it could work because I wanted it to. But you, you couldn't care less! You've just taken me up again because your career is in the doldrums, and you're scared shitless of your wife. Damn you, damn you . . ." Aasha Rani collapsed on the sofa and sobbed uncontrollably.

WHEN *AMMA* FINALLY got the watchman to break open the door, she found Aasha Rani sprawled across the bed. *Amma* rushed to cover her bare legs first, knowing the watchman would be devouring the sight with hungry eyes. She took in the empty medicine bottle, the half-drunk glass of water. There was no time to waste. Who to call? The first name that came to her mind was Kishenbhai's.

He was there within half an hour. "This could become a police case," he said after checking Aasha Rani's pulse. "We've already wasted so much time—let's take her to that private nursing home close by. Do not inform anybody. This shouldn't get to the press. As it is, her career is shaky right now. Bad publicity will finish her off completely. Do you know some good doctor? Or shall I contact my family fellow? At least he won't talk outside. How many pills did she swallow? Why did you keep such things in the house?"

Amma wrung her hands. "*Baba,* how was I to know this foolish girl would do such a thing? I'd kept a few tablets for myself; I have trouble sleeping at night. *Hai Bhagwan!* Who would have imagined this foolish girl would do this? Shall we get an ambulance?"

Kishenbhai hastily said, "No, no. We'll take her in the van. Get the driver up. You and I will have to carry her. The best thing is to handle it all ourselves. The minute people get to know, Aasha Rani's career is over—take it from me."

"AASHA RANI'S SUICIDE ATTEMPT," screamed the headline in an evening paper. Linda's byline was prominently displayed. Not wanting to wait for a month before carrying the sensational news in her own magazine, Linda had sold the story to the paper on the condition that they front-paged the news and gave her a well-displayed byline. The short, snappy copy was full of statements that Aasha Rani had made to Linda strictly in confidence, feelings and ideas she'd let slip from time to time. She quoted Aasha

Rani on topics ranging from her disillusionment with the film industry to her decision to quit, to marry Akshay, and to have his baby. The last was the final blow.

Kishenbhai and *Amma* stared at the paper in disbelief. "Is this true?" Kishenbhai asked. *Amma* shook her head. "Aasha Rani has lost her mind. She has gone mad. No, I hope it is not true. She hasn't mentioned it to me at all. But these last few days she had become so secretive. She didn't tell me anything. I'm sure that she-devil Linda has made it all up to make her story sensational. Aasha Rani would not take such a step; I know my baby. That wretched woman. I'd warned Baby about her. Now her eyes will finally open. These journalists are all the same. I'll deal with her later—Linda *ki bachchi*. Poor, poor baby."

PART TWO

Aasha Rani ༄

AASHA RANI TOOK TWO DAYS TO COME OUT OF THE COMA. SHE was dopey and disoriented when she surfaced, but the moment the grogginess cleared she asked about Akshay: "Is he all right?"

Amma and Kishenbhai exchanged looks. It was then that Aasha Rani noticed Kishenbhai hovering in a corner. "What is he doing here? Who let him in?" Kishenbhai placed a restraining hand over hers and said, "Please don't exert yourself. Try to rest. Relax a little. It's all right. Everybody is all right." Aasha Rani tried to get up but couldn't. "Why am I in this horrible room? I want to go home! Take me home immediately. I'm not staying here!"

Amma put her arms around her. "You'll have to remain here for a few more days. I'll be here. If you like I'll ask Sudha to come from Madras. Don't worry about anything. Kishenbhai is here now."

"I hate him," Aasha Rani sobbed. "I hate him for getting me into the industry, for ruining my life. I will never forgive him, never. Now take me home. I want to go home!"

It was only a fortnight later that Aasha Rani was able to read Linda's scathing scoop. The phone at home had been ringing constantly with reporters hungry for the sordid details, but *Amma* fobbed off the journalists. Various publications had already written their versions of the suicide. She'd made it to the covers of all the leading film magazines and also rated a "newsmaker" item in a political weekly. Akshay's "role" in her suicide attempt had been unabashedly hyped, and there were quite a few boxed interviews with Malini, who had chosen to adopt the we-have-nothing-to-do-with-it line, making sure to speak in the plural—for herself and Akshay.

The stories veered from the plainly absurd to the truly vicious. Akshay and Aasha Rani had been dubbed a modern-day Salim and Anarkali *jodi*, and there were several snide digs about unrequited love.

The letters and flowers continued to pour in, including a bouquet and card from Linda. *Amma* looked at it and shuddered as if it held something contaminated and vile. Silently, she trashed the roses and tore up the card. "The cheek of the woman," Aasha Rani heard her say to Kishenbhai. "I'll deal with her. A defamation case will cost too much, and in the end our baby will suffer. But I'm going to talk to Amirchand. He'll set that *chudail* right."

In her statements to the press Malini had stressed the point that it was Aasha Rani who always threw herself at her husband, even after he had made it clear that he was not interested. Ajay too, had been quoted as saying, "My brother has so many women in love with him. Can he be held responsible if one of them tries to kill herself out of frustration?"

Only Akshay had refused all interviews. He'd become cold and unapproachable, withdrawing into an ominous silence. Aasha Rani was shattered by his indifference, by the way he neither confirmed nor denied any of the rumors. She was anguished by the fact that he had even refused to acknowledge their relationship. That he had not so much as mentioned her name. As if, for him, the suicide bid had indeed been successful, and she had ceased to exist. But Aasha

Rani still ached to see him. Still hungered for his touch. Still searched the bouquets and cards for his familiar scrawl. A word. A sign. She would ask *Amma* if there were any messages from him half a dozen times a day. *Amma* would pretend she hadn't heard and busy herself fluffing the pillows.

STRANGELY ENOUGH, Aasha Rani's suicide attempt gave a little boost to Akshay's career. As Kishenbhai explained it, "Aasha Rani has made him a hero once more. The very fact that she was willing to die for him makes him a big superstar in the public's eyes. They think there must be something to him if someone like Aasha Rani loves him—to this extent. *Chalo,* let him benefit. It must be his *naseeb.* We'll worry about our girl. She has to resume shooting within a month, or even her underproduction films will go."

Kishenbhai instructed *Amma* to make sure Aasha Rani got the right nourishment, enough fruit juice, curd and blanched nuts to get the color back in her face.

Aasha Rani, however, was not in a cooperative frame of mind. She was listless and unhappy, moping around the house, yearning for Akshay. She refused to look at new scripts or consider the offer she got for a prestigious TV serial. "It is work that will heal the scars," *Amma* said. "You must get back to the studios. That is the only way you'll forget. Who knows, if your stars are right, you may even meet the right man. Don't think I'm being selfish. I want you to get married. I want you to settle down. But before that, you have to organize your life. Don't wait for that bastard to change his mind. Men are all the same. He will never leave his wife. Now even his career is picking up, thanks to you. He doesn't need you anymore. The sooner you realize the uselessness of your obsession the better."

Aasha Rani knew *Amma* was right. But the memory of Akshay haunted her day and night. There was hardly a single waking moment when she didn't think of him and their time together. She broke down and told *Amma,* "It's no use. I cannot forget him. Don't abuse him in my presence. He is my *devta.* I worship him. If he is keeping to himself, he has his reasons. I respect his decision."

FOR HIS PART, Akshay left decision making to Ajay, and this time as well he respected his brother's advice. "Forget that woman," Ajay told Akshay. "She is no good for you: just a cheap gangster woman. I will get you better girls—younger, prettier. I'm not saying stay faithful to your wife. As India's biggest stud, it is your duty to have the world's most beautiful women. But leave that man-eater."

What Ajay and Malini could not counter was the mixture of guilt and loss that seemed to suck the life out of him. Akshay had started taking sitar lessons, and they were a convenient excuse to shut himself off in his room for hours on end. "*Riyaaz,*" he'd say, when Malini asked him what he'd been doing all alone. Moody, distracted and out of breath more often than not, Akshay had lost his looks, his personality. He was gaunt and hollow-eyed, a ruined, haunted man.

Rita came to see what the matter was. Her husband's money was tied up in a couple of Akshay productions. Malini let her in and tried to distract her with food. "Have another samosa. Some cold cofee?—It's the best in Bombay, *ji.*" Rita's mouth moved constantly as she popped one snack after the other, but her eyes were unblinkingly riveted to Akshay's door. Finally she said, "Let me get to the point, Maliniji. I've come about Akshayji. What is the matter with him? You know you can trust me. Nervous break-down or . . . ?"

Malini's laugh was strained. "Nothing of the sort. Akshay is just fine. He has been working too hard. But after a fortnight's rest, he'll be back in the studios feeling fresh." Rita helped herself to a *gulab jamun.* "You aren't hiding anything from me, are you? I've been hearing all sorts of stories."

"All rubbish, Ritaji," said Malini as she put another *gulab jamun* on Rita's plate. "Rumors, nothing else. People are all so jealous. Rival heroes are spreading all this nonsense. It's just not true. Ak-shay is a little fatigued; that is all. Did I show you my new Japanese pearls?"

But Rita was not to be diverted. "Does it have anything to do with Aasha Rani's *lafda?* I heard it was all because of Akshay."

"Nonsense! What has Akshay to do with that woman? We don't even utter her name in this house. It is all her fantasy. What can poor Akshay do? He has told her thousands of times, 'Stop dream-ing.' That too he stopped, thinking he might be encouraging her. She is a maniac. I think—we think—she needs psychiatric treat-ment. *Woh kuch paagal si hogayee hai,* she needs help. She has gone mad," Malini said more sharply than she had intended to.

"He had agreed to marry her, you know. Very reliable people have told me this," Rita said as she turned her attention to a plate of greasy cheese balls. Malini took her time pouring a cup of tea from the silver tea service and then spoke deliberately: "That woman will go to any extent to damage Akshay. And to ruin our family life. When she saw she was getting nowhere, she began spreading these absurd stories about their marriage. What marriage? Are we divorced yet? Akshay has never even uttered that dirty word in this house. Poor frustrated woman. I feel sorry for her. She lives in her own world. Marriage! Hah! As if my husband has gone completely mad."

Quite unexpectedly, Rita softened and took her hand. "Don't get excited, *yaar*. These things happen in a marriage. We've all been in the same boat sometime or another. No point in getting hysterical. We've had this chat before. But let me tell you something once again. If you want your husband back—I mean really back, not just physically around—then be good to him. Treat him with love. He needs it. He seems a lonely, lost man.

"*Dekho yaar,* you can say it's none of my business. And you can try to bullshit me. But what would be the point of that? I'm your friend—I'm the entire industry's friend. I want all of us to do well, live well, be happy. Apart from the business angle, where I admit I have a *matlab,* I'm concerned about both of you as an older *didi* who has seen life.

"These men, our *filmi* men, are very insecure, no matter how successful they are. In fact, the more they succeed, the worse they feel. Take my husband. Each hit makes him more miserable. Immediately, his mind goes to the next one—'Will I make money on that or will I lose everything?' It's the same with your husband. 'Will my next film flop. Or be a hit?' 'Will producers still flock to my door?' 'Will my fans desert me?' This is the time a man needs an understanding woman.

"Our problem is that we have become greedy. Very greedy. And we expect some great things out of marriage. Look at me. Over twenty years with this fellow, and yet I expect him to remember my birthday, our anniversary. Get presents. Have a party. Stupid. I tell myself, 'Don't be silly, *yaar.*' Men forget such things after the first two or three years. We want romance like we see in the films. We want our husbands to sit at our feet while we sing songs and feed them grapes. We want them to be our slaves and listen to our every word. And what do we tell them? 'The maidservant didn't turn up today.' Or 'Darling, the jeweler has to be paid.' We think of fantasies. We demand communication, attention, pampering. *Arrey baba,* forget it. We should be happy if they don't beat us, burn us, torture us, insult us, discard us. That is all."

By the time she finished, Rita had Malini's attention completely. The older woman affectionately put an arm around Malini and said to her, "Let's go and meet Akshay. He might be feeling lonely."

UNDER *AMMA*'S SUPERVISION, Aasha Rani's health was picking up. But she seemed totally switched off and uncommunicative. "*Amma,* take me to Madras," she kept pleading. "I want to go to Tirupathi. I want to beg of God for the one thing I was willing to give up my life for. You shouldn't have saved me, *Amma.* You should have let me die."

Amma wasn't unduly worried. She told Kishenbhai confidently, "She's feeling weak; that's all. How can I take her away now? As it is her producers are shouting. Aasha Rani has some responsibility toward them."

Kishenbhai tried hard to get *Amma* to change her mind. "Madras will do her good. She will get home-cooked meals. She will be among her own people. Let her take a break. Also, she'll be away from all this nonsense—Akshay, Abhijit." But *Amma* wouldn't hear of it. Within ten days she'd pushed Aasha Rani back into the studios. "Work, my dear, work. Best cure for everything."

Aasha Rani dreaded waking up each morning and setting off on the unending drive through crowded roads and narrow streets.

Off to brave the hot lights and cold expressions of people who didn't understand her. The only stretch she enjoyed was the area around the small Mahim bay, where the road turned off for the airport. She remembered how fascinated she was when she had come to Bombay with that fishing village there and the sight of the billowing sails at sunset. How happy the fisherfolk looked, and how industrious. They seemed unconcerned about the world beyond their boats. Just a few meters away was the city's main thoroughfare, choked with cars at any time of the day or night. If they heard the constant honking of trucks, taxis and cars as they waited impatiently at the intersection for the lights to change, they didn't show it. Total absorption was written on their faces. The women dried shellfish straight on the hot tar of the main road, with naked babies playing nonchalantly as enormous goods carriers whizzed within centimeters of them. Did these women ever worry about their future? Aasha Rani often wondered, especially when she saw them huddled inside their grounded *dhows* during the rains.

Once, on an impulse, she decided to stop off at the Mahim Church. She had a Goan maid at that point, who, on the day of her interview for the job, had just made one thing clear: "Madam, I need two hours off every Wednesday evening." Aasha Rani had asked why. "Novena," she'd stated simply. "Novena?" Aasha Rani had wanted to know. "Madam, you don't know 'Novena'? We go to the Virgin Mary at the Mahim Church and ask for something. She sees us only on Wednesdays. We make a vow and we then give her a present once she gives us what we've asked for—after twenty-one Wednesdays. Madam, all sorts of people come there, not only Catholics. The Mother is very kind. She gives to everybody." Aasha Rani was taken with her maid's obvious sincerity and faith and arranged to visit the church the next Wednesday. When she'd entered the shrine she'd been overwhelmed and felt curiously humbled by the number of people thronging the place. People carrying plastic limbs, wax infants, toy houses, candles, garlands. She had gotten swept along inside the vast interior and had gasped when she'd looked up at the main altar. It was so beautiful and yet so unfussy. And the crowds were organized and disciplined, each person absorbed in his or her faith. Each one fervently wishing, hoping, praying, that the sad-eyed Virgin would answer their heart's desire. It had reminded her of Tirupathi. Or rather, the accounts of Tirupathi that *Amma* had given her. That evening she'd asked for nothing. Just done a simple *namaskar* and driven home.

But today she was there to beg for her life, for Akshay. To her dismay she thought she saw an unsympathetic frown creasing the Mother's forehead.

ABHIJIT HAD RUSHED to Aasha Rani's home on hearing the news about the suicide, but the chowkidar had refused to let him in. Ever since, he'd been sending flowers and notes every day. *Amma* was going by Kishenbhai's advice: "Abhijit is still a child. His father is a *dada*. He'll destroy us if he finds out about all this nonsense. I've heard Amrishbhai's *bahu* is expecting her first child. Don't let that young goat come here!"

He finally caught up with Aasha Rani at the Film City studios— where she was playing Sita to Tushar's Ram. At the sight of Abhijit standing there twirling his car keys her eyes lit up momentarily. She'd been so desperately lonely now that even Linda had bowed out of her life. Linda, her one big contact in Bombay, with Bombay, was gone. And her one link with the film industry—Akshay—and her one incentive to remain there—Akshay—were gone too.

Abhijit looked pretty good, she thought quickly. Marriage obviously suited him. He walked up to her and said warmly, "So good to see you. You look well. Like a million dollars, actually. I tried to see you several times while you were . . . well, you know, when you weren't too good. But . . ." "Marriage suits you," Aasha Rani said brightly, trying to change the subject. "Not marriage," he corrected her, "Switzerland. I've been away for a couple of months. Just got back. Couldn't wait to see you. Are you free, I mean, once you are through with all this? Sita, huh? Not bad. You'll have all of India prostrating itself at your feet after this movie. A real goddess!"

"It's no longer the same story. We've made Sita into a modern woman with lib ideas. But anyway, I'm enjoying the role." Aasha Rani laughed. "Trial by fire too?" he asked. "Not yet. Maybe we'll think of some new version. OK, let's meet after this shift."

Abhijit looked delighted. "I can't believe I'm hearing right," he said. "I was sure you'd ask me to get out. I won't tell you how much I bribed your *gurkha* to allow me onto the set. Top security work here! Maybe he thought I was a spy from a rival producer's camp. So, do you want me to wait or shall I come by later? By the way, are there any nosy reporters around? I'm terrified of them. Don't want the old man to know. He thinks I'm off inspecting a factory he is planning to take over. Had to get rid of the driver too. Bloody fellow is a real *jasoos*. The old boy has hired him just to spy on me and my activities. Or maybe he's on Nikita's payroll. Who knows. Fucking pain in the ass!"

Aasha Rani smiled indulgently. "See you in a couple of hours. Why don't you drive around? It's pretty pleasant here, especially now, after the rains. Everything's so green and lovely."

"No, thanks. I think I'll wait for you at the Leela Kempinski.

I like the Waterfall Café there. Tell you what; I'll check into a suite and you join me there. How does that sound?" Aasha Rani hesitated. "*Amma* is with me these days. She'll send a police party out if I'm not home. She's more than a bodyguard. Baba—your driver is nothing compared to *Amma*."

"You work on her. And I'll work on us! See you soon; you look beautiful. And sexy. I can't wait to tear your clothes off."

Abhijit took Aasha Rani's mind off Akshay. He insisted on her having a drink with him when she got to his suite. "Let's celebrate," he said, popping a champagne cork. Aasha Rani resisted, but ultimately gave in when she saw how important the occasion was to him. She hated the stuff. It wasn't the first time she'd tasted it, but each time she'd sipped a glass, her reaction had been the same: "Why do people drink such *khatta* stuff?" Champagne made her gassy and giddy. Abhijit told her, "You film wallahs don't know how to drink it. It's not *tharra* that you just knock back. It's delicate and refined. Champagne is more than just a drink; it is a state of mind. I will teach you to appreciate it, love it. Champagne is a celebration. There are champagnes and champagnes. Let me begin with lesson number one. For instance—this glass. It's all wrong. Champagne has to be drunk from a fluted glass so that the bubbles stay in. Look at this bottle and the way it's being chilled. All wrong. The vintage is wrong too. But never mind. We'll get to all that later. Those are finer points. All you have to know is that with champagne, you are never alone—there are all those millions of bubbles. Now, be a good girl and take a ladylike sip without tilting the glass too much. Move the champagne around in your mouth with your tongue, look, like this. And take a bite of what I'm giving you. Have you tasted caviar before? Never? Good God! What kind of a *jungli* woman are you? No, these are not papaya seeds. I'll teach you to like caviar too. Don't ask me what that is. If I tell you, you'll probably throw up, waste my champagne and ruin the carpet.

"There's a big, big world out there that you know absolutely nothing about. And I'm dying to share it with you! Come away with me. Someplace where nobody knows us. No pesky press, no besotted fans, no daddy's moles, where I can fill a tub with champagne and bathe you in it. Where we can wake up in the morning together and gargle with it. Where I can shampoo your hair with bubbly. Let's see—where? Not London—too many Indians, plus all of Nikita's clan. Not New York—too full of nosy *desis*. Not Paris—I don't speak enough French. Where? I know! In fact, even the old man won't suspect a thing—New Zealand—that's where! Let's go to Auckland. It's full of sheep—that's all. It's unlikely any of them will have seen your films—you can say 'baa' to them if they have. Plus, we have a vague project my old man has been presented with. I'll have to find out more, something to do with state-of-the-art sheep rearing and sheep farming. I'll tell him I'd like to check it out. He'll believe me. As for your *amma*—you handle her."

AASHA RANI HADN'T THE FAINTEST IDEA where on earth New Zealand was. On their next evening together Abhijit gave her a world atlas and told her to locate it on the map. It was the first time that she had seriously studied a map. It embarrassed her to discover she didn't even know where, broadly, to jab her finger. She knew Indian cricketers went there to play matches. And the only reason she knew that was because she had once had a brief thing with a fast bowler.

She remembered the time she'd hooked off for a one-day match to Dubai with Ramesh, her gallant sportsman. It hadn't lasted for very long. A few months at most. But the two of them had blazed headlines internationally, especially when she'd shown up for the match in a miniskirt ("un-Islamic and improper," the local press had hissed). And what had made it a truly memorable relationship was the fact that Ramesh was the best lover Aasha Rani had ever had.

It was rumored he took special shots to keep going for as long as three hours, but that, Aasha Rani had soon discovered, was just a team joke. Aasha Rani found him a very attentive and sensitive partner. The best she'd had. He took his time arousing her gently, and what was more, talked tenderly to her. Such a change from the crude, grunting intercourse she'd become accustomed to.

Ramesh really did it in style: He usually started with a bubble bath, during which he had soaped her all over, taking time to massage the back of her neck, her toes, calves, and the insides of her knees. He was also the only lover to shampoo *and* condition her hair expertly. She remembered one particularly exquisite night. The mood was right and so was the music. There was champagne by the side of the sunken tub and delicate canapés to munch. He dried her off with a huge, fluffy towel, rubbing her down firmly, cleaning behind her ears, patting between her legs, and finally chivalrously draped a bathrobe around her and took her to bed.

There, too, his manners had been impeccable. Unbelting her robe, he had powdered her like a baby and watched as she luxuriated in his ministrations. He had dabbed Guerlain on her pulse spots and waited for the fragrance to envelop her whole body.

"Want to try something different?" he had asked. Aasha Rani giggled, game for anything. He had gone to the cupboard and brought out three or four silk scarves. "Take your pick," he'd said. "What will you do with these?" she'd asked. "Ssh . . . You'll find out. Just don't hold back; that's all." With that he had swung her arms over her head and bound them loosely to the bedpost. Aasha Rani had started giggling some more. "Why are you tying me up?" "It's more fun this way . . . believe me. You'll love it," he'd answered, and bent down to tie her ankles. "Do you like doing it with your eyes open or closed?" he had asked, kissing her softly all over. "Let's try both options," she'd said, surrendering totally.

The next thing she knew, he'd bound her eyes with a scarf and whispered, "Relax; let me show you something new, something exciting. It won't hurt; trust me." And he had started stroking her slowly with two other scarves twisted together to form a rope. At first, the feel of silk against her naked skin had felt strange, but soon a different consciousness had taken over.

Helped by the blindfold Aasha Rani had lost herself in a new, forbidden world. Ramesh had crooned erotic words of love and desire as the stroking became steadier and stronger. Her skin had started to tingle deliciously. She could feel Ramesh as his body moved skillfully over hers, and his hands continued to lash her with silk. It was a pain so exquisite, Aasha Rani had moaned with pleasure. Ramesh had stopped abruptly. She could hear him panting. She heard herself say, "More, don't stop."

She was pulled out of her reverie by Abhijit taking hold of her hand and jabbing her forefinger down on New Zealand. Her finger traced the outline of the country. What tiny islands, she thought. What do they do there? Madras seemed vast, and India a giant in comparison. "It's so tiny. We could swallow it up in one gulp, like an *idli,*" she said to Abhijit.

AMRISHBHAI GOT TO HEAR of his son's escape only after Abhijit and Aasha Rani were safely airborne. Malini told him. Not directly, of course. But through a common source. "Your son's life is going to be ruined," Kapal Singh told Amrishbhai at the latter's gigantic office in a South Bombay high-rise. "He is having an affair with that cheap actress, that harlot Aasha Rani. She has already ruined other men and other marriages. Now, she has got her eyes on your son. You have to intervene and stop this ridiculous *maamla* at once. If *bhabhiji* finds out—that too, in the condition she's in."

Amrishbhai was enraged by the news. He had become extremely fond of his young *bahu* and had left instructions that in her delicate condition, her every wish was to be catered to. "An heir is to be born in our family," he'd said proudly at a board meeting at which Abhijit had been present. When his father made the announcement Abhijit had modestly looked down into his lap and accepted the congratulations. He was glad for Nikita, but the news of the baby hadn't made much of a difference to him. In a way he'd felt relieved. "Thank God, *yaar.* Now at least she'll stay out of my hair. It will give her something to do," he had informed his squash buddy.

After his visitor left, Amrishbhai sat for a long while in his office. Now everything fell into place: his son's absences from his house in the evenings when he should have been with his wife; Nikita's reliance on him when she should have been looking to her husband for support; his son's casual acceptance of the fact that he would soon be a father. Amrishbhai's brows creased with fury. How could his son do this to his wife? Betray her, in her condition, with that slut who'd sleep with anyone provided the money was right? He needed to come up with a plan if he was to save the family honor, prevent the scandal from blossoming. But most of all, he knew it was only he who could save his young, defenseless daughter-in-law. He instructed his secretary not to put through any calls. Strictly no interruptions or visitors. It took Amrishbhai three hours to arrive at a decision. Close to midnight he phoned his travel agent. Personally. The man jumped when he heard Amrishbhai's voice. "Get me on the next flight to New Zealand—any route, any airline, any class. It's an emergency."

Amrishbhai was already waiting at Auckland airport when Abhijit and Aasha Rani landed there, after a shop-till-you-drop stopover in Singapore. Abhijit was the first to spot his father standing in the lounge. "Oh my God!" he said, clutching Aasha Rani's arm. "He's here!" "Who?" she asked carelessly. "My father! It's him. Bloody shit! How did he find out? Oh hell—I hope nothing has happened to Nikita or the baby. Why the fuck would he be here otherwise?" If Abhijit had had his way, he would have bolted from the scene. But that was impossible. Aasha Rani was nervous too, but didn't want to show it. She tried clinging to Abhijit's arm, but he shrugged off her hand and snarled, "Are you crazy? Take your hands off me. He's looking." Numbly he collected their luggage and walked slowly out to meet his father.

Amrishbhai ignored Aasha Rani altogether. But he greeted Abhijit affectionately. "Don't worry—nobody is dead. Come on; let's go. Where are you booked?" Abhijit looked helplessly at Aasha Rani and stuttered, "Look, Dad, I can explain . . ." Funnily enough Aasha Rani was enjoying Abhijit's discomfiture. She felt removed from the whole scene as the tough old man put an arm around his son, who, she noted, almost dropped at the touch, and walked him away like a small boy.

Six hours later Abhijit walked into their suite. "It's all over, darling," he said in a small, broken voice. "There's nothing to explain or say. Dad has said it all. I'm exhausted. Please don't ask questions. I'm checking out. Dad wants you to stay here as long as you want. He's left instructions that all your bills be settled. He has also left you money for shopping and traveling. There'll be more when you get back to Bombay. His guys will be in touch with you. I don't have to tell you that this is good-bye."

Aasha Rani looked at him wordlessly. She felt intensely sorry for the pathetic, scared man standing in front of her. She would have stayed out of Abhijit's life for free, but since a gift package was being thrust at her she'd be a fool to turn her back on it. Coolly, she held out her hand. "All the luck in the world," she said, "and thank your father for his generous offer. Tell him I accept."

A man she met in the hotel coffee shop suggested Wellington, and she thought, Why not? "What will I do there?" she asked him. "Well, you could take long walks, look at the sprawling farms, drink milk, eat cheese and count sheep. What else do kiwis do?"

Aasha Rani spent ten days in Wellington. Ten whole days to herself. She hadn't ever been alone before. Entirely alone—like she now found herself. In the beginning it felt strange. She thought everybody was staring at her. They were, of course, but that was because of the clothes she wore. She decided to blow some of Amrishbhai's money getting herself a new wardrobe. She chucked all her *salwar-kameezes,* saris and *dhoti* pants and went shopping for sleek, well-tailored shirts, skirts and dresses. She decided to change her hair and rework her makeup while she was at it.

The salon in the hotel may not have been the best in Wellington, but the young girl there was friendly and helpful. She picked up Aasha Rani's long tresses and sighed. "Split and abused. You need conditioning, love. And a new look. Leave it to me." Snip, snip, snip; the scissors ran through her hair in seconds. Aasha Rani stared at the strands lying on the floor and felt like crying.

"It took me ten years to get it this length," she complained. "My producers will kill me. What about continuity, oh God! My hairdresser will die when she sees me." "You're talking like a blooming movie star." The young girl laughed. And that was when it occurred to Aasha Rani that she was truly a nonentity in this country. The young girl's lighthearted remark had driven home the point.

Nobody knew her here. And nobody cared who she was. It was a realization that exhilarated her. She could pass for anyone! She squeezed the hairdresser's hand gleefully. "It's great. I love it." "Ooh, watch it, love—I could have nicked you there." "Go ahead, streak it, frost it, bleach it, do what you want; I'm going to have fun." Aasha Rani's eyes were shining with mischief.

"Your boyfriend won't recognize you," said the hairdresser worriedly. "That's the whole idea," Aasha Rani said. And laughed.

Jamie (Jay) Phillips

She met Jamie (Jay) Phillips on her sixth day in Wellington. It was a Friday night and the local disco was crowded. Aasha Rani sat at a corner table with some newly acquired friends from the hotel. The deejay was in cracking form mixing music, playing old favorites with the latest chartbusters, urging people onto the kerchief-sized floor.

Aasha Rani was enjoying herself, laughing with abandon and guzzling beer. She was smoking a cigar, more as an accessory to her hot pink sequined dress than anything else. For the past hour or so she'd noticed a tall, slim man observing her, but she didn't pay him much attention; she was used to being stared at. People came up to her and asked all sorts of questions. With her new hair and crazy clothes she resembled Tina Turner gone wrong. Then, during a temporary lull in the music, the stranger walked up to her. "Listen, this may sound completely crazy and over the top," he said, "but aren't you Aasha Rani, the movie star from India?"

The half-puffed Davidoff fell out of her fingers. "How do you know?" she asked incredulously. "Allow me to buy you another cigar, and I'll tell you," he said in an accent that was hard to place.

She allowed herself to be led away from her group and they settled down at a tiny glass table. There he introduced himself and confessed that he was an unabashed Hindi film buff, in fact, had been one for a few years. She still didn't get it. Where on earth did he get to see Hindi films? How did he understand them?

"Oh, it's a long story," he answered, "but I don't want to shout myself hoarse narrating it to you in here. Let's go someplace else, shall we?" Aasha Rani went back to her friends and winked. "I have met a fan—here, of all places!" They didn't really get the joke but they laughed anyway and waved her off.

At a little garden restaurant Jay told her his story. He had an old Indian connection in his grandfather, an army general, who'd spent four long years in Imphal commanding troops during the war. He'd brought the family back to India regularly after that. The India link didn't end there. When Jay was at university in England he'd met and had a brief affair with an Air India stewardess. They'd stayed in touch—more out of a warm friendship and kinship than anything else. When she got posted to London, he'd moved in with her and had been introduced to the gaudy world of Hindi films. Samira was hooked on them. Her reading was restricted to junky fan magazines, and her idea of a great evening at home was to root herself in front of a VCR and watch her favorite film artists dance, sing and ham in the hottest new potboiler. During their off-and-on association, Jay, too, had gotten the habit. He amazed Aasha Rani with his knowledge of films and film stars, quoting dialogues and recalling lyrics. She laughed and laughed when he mimicked her and did a takeoff on Akshay. "Married the guy, didn't you?"

Aasha Rani shook her head sadly. "He backed out." "Still single?" he casually asked. "Unfortunately." "In that case, lady . . ." Jay announced with a flourish, "would you do me the honor of marrying me? I am yours; single, AIDS-free and considerably well-off. I've been a little in love with you for years, and this seems like a dream come true. Would you make me very happy and be my wife?"

Aasha Rani was taken aback. For a country whose main claim to fame seemed to be its sheep, people did seem to work fast. "This is all a bit too unexpected," she said.

"How long are you staying?" Jay asked.

"Two-three days more," she replied.

"Well, how about letting me know by four in the evening Thursday?"

"Deal," she said.

JAY PROVED TO BE AN ARDENT, passionate and imaginative husband. Aasha Rani felt relaxed and secure enough with him to teach him one or two tricks of her own. He was game for anything, dubbing her kinks "oriental love games."

"What kind of a girlfriend was she—that Samira of yours? She taught you nothing at all," Aasha Rani would tease. Jay laughed her remarks off as he concentrated on pleasing her. Once Aasha Rani told him, only half joking, "Actually, if you must know, I prefer girls. They are so sensitive and soft. This, only another woman can know—how to turn a woman on. Can't you find me a sexy girlfriend here?" Jay thought for a minute before answering, "Well, I don't know about a female sex companion for you. But you could try sheep—or dogs or something. Considering how lusty and insatiable you are, you'd probably enjoy the experience." Aasha Rani pretended to consider it before sniffing. "No, not for me. Too smelly." "Don't knock it till you've tried it," Jay said, tweaking her nose playfully.

Five months into the marriage, Aasha Rani discovered she was pregnant. Jay whooped with delight when she broke the news. He picked her up and twirled her around deliriously. "Wonderful, wonderful, wonderful! Where do you want to have the baby? What shall we do? What names have you thought of? Do you want me to phone and tell your mother? Do you want to call her over? Shall we go to India?"

Aasha Rani waited for him to quiet down. "I'm a strong girl. My mother had no problems with her pregnancies and deliveries. I don't think I will either. No, I don't want to go back to India. In fact, I never want to return. We'll have the baby here. It's going to be a girl. I know it. We'll call her Sasha. I like the name; it's so cuddly and sweet—like she will be."

Jay wasn't too happy about Aasha Rani's decision to have the baby on the farm. "Let me at least call my mother or one of my sisters across," he suggested. "No way!" Aasha Rani put her foot down. "That will make me tense and uncomfortable. Didn't you see how they behaved at the wedding? They find me weird— I know it. They think I'm some sort of savage you picked up. A colored, who doesn't eat with a knife and fork. Who speaks English with a funny accent. Who wears strange clothes. And an actress! *Baap re baap*—the worst possible woman. They don't like me at all. They haven't accepted me—but I suppose I can't really blame them. If they came here, I would have to look after them and be hospitable—or at least pretend to. No. I'd rather go through this alone. We have each other; that's enough. There must be hundreds of couples in your country just like us, with no family members around. We'll manage. And for God's sake, don't let *Amma* know. She hasn't forgiven me and never will. Just see— not one letter, card or telegram from her—nothing. I've written so many times. You've written—we've sent photographs; we've tried everything. She does not want to have any contact with me. I know that. So let her be. I don't care either. All my life she has exploited me. I've known only harshness and punishment from her. Nothing else. Today, she has no further need for me. Why should she bother whether I'm alive or dead? Please, Jay, let me do this my way, please."

Jay gave in, as he did to most of Aasha Rani's whims. Each passing day of her pregnancy was making her bloom and look even more beautiful. He couldn't get over the fact that she was soon going to be a mother. He clicked hundreds of photographs as she waddled along the garden, or puttered about the house, taking one heavy step at a time. He filmed her on video and assiduously kept a progress chart of each month—detailing all the changes in her swelling body.

The first time the baby kicked, Jay's heart nearly stopped. "Jesus! Holy shit! What is the little princess up to?" he asked with his hand placed gingerly over Aasha Rani's belly. "You are a good man, Jay. I want to make you a good wife. And I promise you, I'll be a good mother to Sasha," Aasha Rani said, smiling and kissing him gently.

SASHA WAS BORN on a beautiful spring morning with Jay holding Aasha Rani's hand. "She is like a lovely little primrose," Jay said tenderly, stroking Aasha Rani's hair. "Just like you, darling," he continued. "You were wonderful through it all. I'm so proud of you. I wish my parents—and yours—had been here."

Aasha Rani was far too exhausted to respond. She gazed at the little perfection lying snugly across her breasts and kissed her daughter's screwed-up face. "I'm tired," she said to Jay. "I need some sleep." Jay sat next to her bed right through the day, occasionally cradling the baby and crooning long-forgotten lullabies to her. He watched his sleeping wife and marveled at their being there together, married and now parents. It was destined, he told himself. How else would anybody explain their having met the way they did? Maybe he had been a Hindu in his last life. He felt a desperate urge to go back to India with his small family.

The next day he suggested it to Aasha Rani. Her face clouded over and she snapped, "Nothing doing, no way. I never want to go back. And please don't give *Amma* the news. I want to protect Sasha from her. I want to bring her up with all the love in the world. I never want her to meet her grandmother. Never!"

Jay was surprised by the vehemence in Aasha Rani's voice. He kept quiet, putting her outburst down to post-baby blues. But her attitude remained unchanged even after she'd settled in with the baby. Nothing mattered more to her than her little girl. She told Jay, "It would have been so different back in India. Sasha would have been handed over to a succession of *ayahs*. I would hardly have seen her. *Amma* would have pushed me back into the studios to do any role that was going. I'd have ended up playing mother roles to forty-year-old hunks before I touched thirty. And then I'd have graduated to being grandmother to the very same hunks. No, thank you. I'm better off here. I feel happy, relaxed and . . ."

"Bored," Jay completed the sentence for her. She smiled at him. "Yes, a little, sometimes, but that can't be helped."

"Do you miss your old life? Your old friends? Akshay?" Jay asked gently. Aasha Rani thought for a while before answering. "Yes and no. I didn't really have friends. I had one, but she turned out to be worse than an enemy. The others? Let me see——I think of Amar sometimes. I knew he was using me but he was sweet. I think of Ramesh—that was one of the few no-strings-attached relationships I've had. Perfect while it lasted. Abhijit, I just feel sorry for him; that's all. I wish him well. And Nikita too. I suppose we were using each other too—he for his reasons and I for mine. The old letch, the Shethji. I think of him often. He didn't harm me. I think he was quite fond of me, really. And Akshay— yes, I do think of him. And miss him. I've never understood my obsession for that man. Or the hold he had on me. Maybe it was his image that swept me off my feet initially. I was so completely overawed, so overwhelmed that somebody like him—a top hero—would notice someone like me. Even after his films started flopping and mine were hits, I couldn't get over him. He was so cultured and civilized compared to the others. He recited poetry. He read books. He ate exotic food. He dressed well. I felt like a villager in his presence. It's not even as if he was a great lover or anything. But there was—there is—something between us. Why should I lie to you? I often wonder what he's doing, where he is, how his films are faring. His health had started failing him—poor man. He needed an understanding, warm woman by his side. Instead, he had that bitch who was so harsh to him. I hate her. I'll hate her till I die. I learned so much from Akshay. I wonder if he knows how grateful I feel. You don't mind my talking about him, do you?"

Jay had been listening to her monologue quietly. He shook his head. "Go on. You'll feel better." But Aasha Rani changed her mind. It was as if she'd had enough of the past.

"I'm sorry. Let's talk about you. Actually, even after all these months, I still don't know too much. You never speak of your earlier loves, besides the air hostess. What about white girls? You must have had several local girlfriends?" Jay shook his head. "I was shuttling back and forth far too much to fall seriously in love with anyone. Besides, this may sound strange to you—it does to most Asians—we white men are not exactly sex maniacs. And all white girls aren't nymphos. Why do we have such awful reputations? This used to happen to me in India, in Bangkok, Hong Kong, even China. Women would be wary of me, and all of them would assume I was looking for quick sex. I have my preferences. I have my moods. I'm not into sex for the sake of sex. As for love—it doesn't happen to me that easily. But I knew the moment I saw you in that tacky disco that you were the one. I wanted you—not just in a superficial, physical sense, but I wanted to make you my wife. I wanted to spend the rest of my life with you. Does that sound corny? And I was so confident it would work. It has, hasn't it? We have pulled it off, haven't we?"

Aasha Rani's eyes were full of tears. "Don't cry," Jay said. "You make a wonderful wife and mother. I must be blessed. My only regret is that our families don't know how happy we are. I'm sure my father would be filled with joy to see our Sasha. Perhaps someday they'll come to terms with our decisions."

Aasha Rani had a hard look in her eyes. "I don't really care. This is my life—our life—and for the first time I'm living the way I want to. I certainly don't miss *Amma*. As for Sudha, by now *Amma* must have pushed her into enough producers' beds to get her a few roles. That's all over now. It's behind me. My life belongs to Sasha; she will have the best of everything. I'll see to that."

SASHA AT FOUR was an unusually pretty child. This didn't surprise Aasha Rani, who'd point out to Jay that nearly all children born of mixed parentage turned out to be exceptionally good-looking. But her little girl was something else. She'd inherited Jay's gray-green eyes, Aasha Rani's features, and their joint coloring. Her skin glowed like milky cocoa; her hair was like burnished copper.

Sasha was precocious for her age, but that was because she didn't have companions to play with. Her "friends" were farm animals, and her favorite a pony called Trixie. On weekends Jay and Aasha Rani made it a point to take her for outings, but these occasions weren't enough to satisfy her lively and curious mind.

Aasha Rani had put on some weight. Not too much. But she was no longer lithe and firm, and her breasts hadn't shed the extra fat even a year after she'd stopped nursing Sasha. Jay brought home the latest workout tapes and urged Aasha Rani to take up a sport—go riding or swimming. But she was reluctant to move out, preferring to spend the day playing with Sasha and watching TV soaps. It seemed unnatural to Jay that she was so indifferent to the life she'd left behind. She refused to watch Hindi films, read Indian magazines or even dress and eat Indian. She was practically unrecognizable with her bleached, permed hair, nondescript clothes and uncertain accent. Jay would try to joke her out of her lethargy by saying, "Come on, girl, I didn't marry a chichi farmhand. My bride was an exotic, oriental beauty. An absolute knockout. How about wearing a sari for me tonight? Who knows, I might get turned on enough to produce a brother for Sasha." Aasha Rani would pretend she hadn't heard and turn on the TV.

She found Jay's preoccupation with India—and his idealistic image of it—hard to swallow. It was obvious that he hadn't been there for a long time. The crowds had multiplied; the pollution was even more rampant. And the Bombay film world—one brush with that and he'd never talk about India again!

Jay bided his time. One day when Aasha Rani was in a particularly good mood he broached the topic of India again: "Feel like a trip to India? Or London? Or both?" Initially she said nothing and carried on putting the final touches to the salad she had fixed for lunch. He didn't push the issue and started playing with Sasha. After five minutes, Aasha Rani spoke, almost to herself: "We'll be in time for Holi if we leave next month. Sasha would love that. I used to enjoy Holi as a child."

Jay was delighted. He went and kissed her, saying, "That's my girl. I'll talk to my travel agent. But tell me—London or Bombay?"

Aasha Rani put some mayonnaise on his nose and said, "Let's do it in stages. First stop London, then Bombay and then perhaps Madras!"

LONDON, AFTER A BREAK of nearly five years, made Aasha Rani nervous. She remembered her last visit there and shuddered involuntarily. She'd come with an entertainment troupe to raise money for some cause or another. The organizers had promised them a good time, shopping money and a token payment. This was a standard summer ritual in the industry. A way for stars to cadge free holidays abroad from devoted NRI sponsors, who made up their costs five times over with the ticket money and local advertising. For their part the stars didn't mind spending two evenings monkeying around onstage, singing songs, dancing, repeating hit "dialogues" and posing with delirious fans. Often it was Indian grocery store owners from Southall who enthusiastically arranged these programs. The formula was the same year after year—one playback singer, one top hero, one up-and-coming heroine, a couple of cabaret dancers, a mimic and a few sidekicks. The top-bracket stars got to stay in suites at fancy five-star hotels and went home with VCRs. The smaller fry had to make do with makeup kits and St. Michael's T-shirts. Fancy heroines took chaperones along at the organizers' expense and ran up enormous bills phoning boyfriends left behind. But nobody cribbed. Everything was "covered."

Aasha Rani had been the up-and-coming supernova on the scene with three major hits running simultaneously. *Amma* had insisted on tagging along, but so had Linda. This had led to some confusion, since *Amma* had demanded a suite, leaving Aasha Rani no choice but to share Linda's poky little room where there wasn't even place enough for her vanity case. But the overall experience had been thrilling—with hysterical fans mobbing her wherever she went. She'd been interviewed on Channel 4, wined and dined by a notorious NRI, made it to a profile in the *Observer* and generally felt like the screen queen she then was. Swarms of young, lusty men had gazed at her with something like reverence as she'd performed her superhit dance number from *Chaalu Cheez,* swaying her hips and stomping her feet to the strains of *"Mujhey kehtey hai chaalu . . ."* The crowds at Wembley had gone wild and had demanded an encore. Aasha Rani, flushed and excited by all the adulation, had flung her *dupatta* into the audience, driving them to further frenzy. Her trip had been a major feather in the organizers' cap, and they'd booked her for the following year as well.

Aasha Rani had enjoyed London on that visit. She had liked being recognized by shop assistants at Harrods and being asked for autographs at Selfridges. But most of all, she had enjoyed walking through Hyde Park, feeding the ducks and pigeons by the lake. Aasha Rani had not minded the attention local Indian businessmen showered on her. She always had a chauffeured Rolls-Royce at her service and was received like royalty in their opulent homes, where other prominent London-based Indians clamored to pose for photographs with her. And the lavish gifts she'd received! They'd arrive at her hotel by the carload—chocolates, flowers, champagne, baskets of goodies from Fortnums, expensive lingerie from Victoria's Secret, Fendi furs, CD players, video cameras, innumerable French chiffons and perfume by the gallon. The presents she most looked forward to, however, were the soft toys. It was well-known, thanks to all the film magazines, that Aasha Rani had a special weakness for them. Besotted admirers arrived with pandas, cats, koala bears, elephants and teddies. Her passage through customs on landing in Bombay had been colorful in more ways than one.

WHEN JAY AND FAMILY landed in London, Sasha was exhausted and cranky. Aasha Rani wasn't feeling much better. It was left to Jay to go through all the motions before depositing them at the St. James Court hotel near Buckingham Palace. The choice of the hotel had been Jay's. "You'll feel more comfortable with the baby and all that. It's run by the Taj people." Aasha Rani was a little skeptical but went along.

Living in "propah" British-run hotels in London had not been one of her best experiences—especially when she'd taken *Amma* with her. All that fuss made by housekeeping over something small like asking for a mug in the bathroom. *Amma* didn't like taking showers and she hated bathing in a tub. Plus, *Amma* with her fussy vegetarian hang-ups drove room service wild with her questions and demands. She suspected everything, from the cheese sandwiches to the mushroom soup, and embarrassed everyone by sniffing all the food on the buffet table.

But Aasha Rani had overlooked one major disadvantage of checking into St. James Court. Within minutes the news was out that she was staying there. Barely half an hour after they had set their bags down, flowers and fruit arrived from the general manager, welcoming them to London.

Aasha Rani was flattered and apprehensive. She'd been so insulated from this sort of attention in New Zealand. Her days as a movie star had been converted into memories. Memories that she didn't really care to rake up too often. She had no idea what sort of an impact her abrupt exit had made on audiences back home, or whether she'd been missed at all. She wasn't even aware whether her marriage had made headlines or if people knew about Sasha. She had cut herself off so successfully that it came as a slight shock when the staff at the hotel recognized her. Jay laughed. "Did you really think you'd be forgotten in such a hurry? You—the 'Sweetheart of Millions'?"

"Oh come off it," she said, brushing him off. "It has been nearly five years since I last made a film. At the pace the industry was moving when I quit, at least ten 'sweethearts' must have surfaced by now. Besides, audiences are so fickle, so cruel. Once you're out, you're out; that's it."

Jay shook his head. "Certainly doesn't seem so. Look at how rapidly news of your arrival spread. You can bet the press will zero in on you. So get some rest, put on your best face and I'll get you some new clothes. The show is on, darling, and you are the star!"

Aasha Rani signed her first autograph in years, the next morning, while they were breakfasting downstairs. The young woman who came up to ask for it was from Bombay. "I couldn't believe my eyes," she gushed. "I wasn't sure it was you, so I checked with the manager. Gosh! You look so different! I saw your last film five times and cried so much when we learned you'd left India."

Jay smiled sympathetically and asked her to sit down. "Coffee?" he asked, while Aasha Rani glared at him. "Is this your daughter? My, she's *cho chweet*. Like a real *gudiya*. Will she join films like you?" "Never," Aasha Rani snapped. "Why not?" the woman insisted. "She's so pretty. She will also become famous like you and her aunty."

So, *Amma* had made a star out of Sudha after all. "How is my sister doing? Do you see her films?" Aasha Rani couldn't resist asking. The woman was thrilled to be answering the questions. "Oh my, Sudha Rani is just too good, *yaar*. I love her dancing. *Kya* disco *karti hai*—don't mind, but she beats you hollow, *yaar*. Her latest film was *Disco Baby*, and I liked it so much I bought the original tape for my library. She and Amar are fabulous, *yaar*. He's also great!"

Jay was watching Aasha Rani's face for reactions. The fan kept up her chatter: "You must come to India, *yaar*. Your fans are really missing you. The mags keep writing stories. All rubbish, *yaar*. You know how these gossips are. One mag—I think it was *Showbiz*—said you were dead. Then that Linda, big bitch, *yaar*, she said you'd gone mad and were in a mental asylum. Someone else said you'd committed suicide. All *bakwas, yaar*. I told my friends, 'Never. Aasha Rani must be alive somewhere.' I thought you'd had an accident. Don't mind, but the gossip was really too much. I'd also read that someone had thrown acid on your face—you know that businessman—the papers said he'd caught you with his son and threatened to kill you! Anyway, poor fellow, his *bahu* lost her first baby. We all said, 'Good! God is punishing him.' Then we read you had had plastic surgery to change your face, and you had also changed your name. Such crap, *yaar.* Don't mind.

"One mag said their reporter had met you while you were passing through Bombay and you'd shown him your new face through the burqa by lifting up the flap. He said you looked like Dracula *ki ma.* All scarred. That same fellow said you'd gone crazy and you kept imagining that the businessman was going to kill you for destroying his son's family. There were rumors he'd paid international *goondas* lakhs of rupees to murder you. *Chalo,* I'm so glad all this was rubbish. Now that I've seen you, spoken to you, I'll phone and tell my sister in Bombay. You don't mind if I bring my relatives here tomorrow for autographs and photographs, do you? My nephew used to be your big fan. We called him a *chamcha* because he kept all your photographs and he'd also met you at Wembley. He'll be so thrilled, *yaar.* He'll come running. *Achcha,* so, see you."

Jay put his hand on Aasha Rani's. "It's OK, darling. It was bound to happen sooner or later," he said. "You couldn't have stayed cooped up and hidden away all your life. These are your people. They love you. They want you. How can you turn your back on them? Cheer up! Let's go shopping."

She was besieged again while they were buying toys for Sasha at Hamlyn. They ran headlong into a group of Indians, who screeched, "*Arrey, yeh dekho kaun hai*—Aasha Rani!" and lunged toward her. They were aggressive and rude as they jostled Jay and Sasha to get closer to her. "We thought you were dead," they said cheerfully, while Aasha Rani smiled wanly and signed slips of paper hastily pulled out of handbags.

Later, while they were looking for wooden blocks at Mothercare, Aasha Rani thought she spotted someone familiar. She turned to have another look, to make sure. It was her, all right.

Malini looked a little different but not much. Clad in an ill-fitting fur coat, her hair in a neat nape bun, her expression as unpleasant and severe as always. What was she doing in London? And was Akshay with her? Aasha Rani ducked into the toys section. She didn't want to be seen.

Malini was with another Indian woman, someone younger and obviously pregnant. A local sponsor's wife, Aasha Rani guessed. One of those pretty Punjabi girls who'd always lived in London and dreamed of India. She was sure Malini hadn't noticed her. She caught Jay's arm, grabbed Sasha and hissed, "Let's get out of here." But the young woman saw them just as they were exiting. "Aasha Rani!" she squealed, clutching Malini's hand. "Hey! Aasha Rani. We know it's you!" Aasha Rani pretended she hadn't heard and rushed out of the store and onto Oxford Street.

She was breathing heavily when they emerged outside, and Sasha was most puzzled. "What's the matter with Mommy?" she asked Jay worriedly. Jay comforted the child and put his arm around Aasha Rani. She pleaded, "Let's get out of here. I'm suffocating. Please, let's not go to India. Oh God! Why did we come here?"

When they went back to the hotel, there were two messages for them. One was from the local TV channel, the other from Akshay. "Call him," Jay urged. "Go on, ring him up." "No. I don't want to see him ever again." But the phone rang within minutes of their getting into the room. And it was Akshay.

"Here, take it," Jay said, handing the receiver to her. "It's all right. He can't hurt you. Not after all these years. Tell him you are happy. Tell him I'm with you."

Aasha Rani's hands were shaking as she picked up the receiver. She could barely say hello. Her voice sounded strange and unnatural. His too. She sensed something was wrong the moment he uttered her name. And she panicked.

"Akshay! What's wrong?" she demanded. There was a pause. A long one. "I'm dying," he said to her slowly. "Don't! Don't say that," she said, her voice almost a sob. "It's true," Akshay answered calmly. "I'm surprised it has taken this long; that's all. Perhaps God willed it this way. Perhaps we were destined to meet for one final time. Will you come and see me? Bring your husband and daughter. Malini told me she saw all of you today. I couldn't believe it. Now I know, it's a miracle. All these years, I've been living for this moment. All through my bad days, one thought kept me going. I knew I had to see you. I couldn't leave this world without saying good-bye."

Aasha Rani's composure threatened to desert her completely. "Tell me you are lying. It's another one of your tricks. I don't believe what you are saying. If you are seriously ill, what was Malini doing shopping on Oxford Street?" Akshay explained patiently, "Aasha Rani, we live here now. After my last hospitalization, when the doctors in Bombay gave up on me, we decided to move to London. We have to shuttle between Geneva, Paris and here for my treatment. It is easier to maintain a base in Knightsbridge—which is where I am. The young girl you saw is Ajay's daughter-in-law. That's right! His son got married last year. Malini had taken her to buy some baby things. Our children are at school here too. But all this can wait. When will you come?" Aasha Rani looked at Jay and repeated the question si-lently. He nodded and mouthed, *Tomorrow.*

When Aasha Rani replaced the receiver, she was cold and numb. Jay left her alone and kept Sasha out of her way. He knew Aasha Rani needed time. He needed it too.

"Dying?" Aasha Rani finally asked Jay. "What could he be dy-ing from? I don't believe it. I just don't. He was sick when I left India but not that sick. Or at least, I didn't know about it." "Sounds like cancer," Jay said slowly. "Perhaps it was in its early stages then." "Cancer?" Aasha Rani all but screamed. "How can Akshay get cancer? He was so fit, so healthy."

Aasha Rani sat still for a long time. It hadn't sunk in. She didn't want it to. Cancer doesn't hit people you know, she thought. It doesn't kill your loved ones. It happens to others. You read about it in the papers. Someone tells you about a relative who is dying of it. And that's all. This was absurd! Jay was wrong. And Akshay was playing his usual tricks. He just wanted to see her; that was all. Maybe he wished to apologize. All things considered, he had behaved very rudely toward her. Unnecessarily so. That was it. Akshay wanted to say he was sorry. It had taken him five years to realize his mistake.

She repeated her theory to Jay. He kept quiet for a while and then said, "No, Aasha Rani. I don't think so. Akshay wouldn't jest about something like this. You'd better go and find out to-morrow." "Come with me," Aasha Rani pleaded. "I can't handle this on my own." "You're a big girl now. Of course you can han-dle it. Meanwhile I'll take Sasha to see the queen."

* * *

AASHA RANI THOUGHT she was seeing a ghost. Akshay was virtually unrecognizable. Painfully thin and dark. Much darker than she remembered him. His voice had changed too. He spoke in a rasping croak. Aasha Rani rushed to sit by his bed. He didn't have the energy to lift himself up. Malini stayed for a while and then left them alone. "You didn't bring her," Akshay whispered. "Who?" Aasha Rani asked. "Your daughter. I heard you had a daughter, a beautiful daughter. I wanted to see her."

Aasha Rani felt the tears stream down her face. "Sasha, her name is Sasha."

"Nice name," he said. "And your husband. I wanted to meet him too." "Jay. I mean Jamie, that's his name." "Yes, I'm happy for you. I really am. You look well. Different from what I remember you. What has happened to your hair? Cut it? And your clothes. I suppose you had to change, married to a *phirangi* and all that. How does it feel? Do you like living abroad? Tell me everything. I want to know all about your new life. Where you live. How you live. What you do. *Chalo,* start *karo.*"

Aasha Rani spent the next two hours talking to him softly. Telling him about New Zealand and their sheep farm. He dozed off from time to time, but waved his hand weakly to say, "Go on," when she stopped. It seemed to comfort him to hear her voice. She wanted to stroke his hair—the little that was left of it. And she wanted to bend over and kiss him. But more than anything else, she wanted, once again, to hear Amjad Ali play in the background as she sipped his wine and took a drag or two of his cigarette, staining the tip with her lipstick, wetting the filter and hearing him say irritatedly, "How many times have I told you not to touch my fags?"

But the man lying helplessly in front of her was already far away. She wasn't sure if he was even listening to her words. After a while he slipped into deep sleep. She bent low over Akshay and kissed his forehead and then his lips.

He didn't stir.

Sudha Rani

"*LOOK, SASHA, LOOK!* THAT'S YOUR AUNT—MY LITTLE SISTER—Sudha! God! She's splashed everywhere! And that's Amar—old *chikna* face. They seem to be monopolizing every hoarding in Bombay," said Aasha Rani excitedly as they drove down to the Sea Rock Sheraton.

So *Amma* had pulled it off. Sudha—or Sudha Rani, as the hoardings screamed—had made it! Sudha Rani—what a name. Must have been Kishenbhai's idea, she thought to herself, vastly amused.

Aasha Rani felt herself relax as the familiar sights of Bombay slipped by. She hadn't been looking forward to this and had begun feeling apprehensive right at Heathrow.

But the moment she stepped out of Santa Cruz airport she had felt the tension draining away. Aasha Rani's homecoming had coincided with Holi, and that had added to her delight. But Jay lost all his enthusiasm for India the moment they stepped out of the plane and somebody threw *gulal* on him. Sasha, too, fell back in fright.

"Bloody buggers. I hate the bloody stuff. I remember it from my early trips to India. Grandfather used to enjoy himself and join the natives. But my parents and I—not us. We hated getting all that muck on ourselves. Tell these rogues to get lost before I sock one of them," he had snarled as a group of revelers had come toward him with fistfuls of colored powder.

"It's nothing," Aasha Rani had assured both of them. "It won't hurt. We can wash it off when we get to the hotel." But Sasha had hid behind her father and covered her face, while Jay had tried in vain to shoo them off. "It's Holi," Aasha Rani had kept repeating. "This is all a part of the celebrations. These people don't mean any harm. They are only trying to get you to join in. Go on, be a sport; all they want to do is put a dot of red on your forehead. They'll go away after that."

Jay had reluctantly bent down and waited for one of the men to put a *tikka* between his brows. "Barbarians," he had muttered under his breath. "Drunk buggers! What is this crazy festival about, anyway? I remember seeing your bloody films with you cavorting around in filthy clothes and lots of filthy color on your face."

Aasha Rani had laughed at his discomfort. "Don't ask me complicated questions. Read your guidebook. We are in India now. We are home. Holi is our spring festival. You'll see all the fishing boats when we pass my favorite village. They'll have bright new flags over their masts. From today the seas will be safe for sailing till the horrible monsoon."

Jay had been even more hassled when it came to getting a cab. "Where are all the taxis?" he had asked sharply.

"They're probably celebrating Holi. Most cars stay off the streets today. Sometimes the crowds can get a little aggressive," Aasha Rani had tried to explain. "Well, thanks a lot. I suppose we couldn't have picked another day." Jay had been barely able to disguise his irritation. "I used to love Holi," Aasha Rani had told him. "The industry always celebrated it in a big way. In fact, the biggest all-day party used to be at Akshay's bungalow. The entire industry would come there and fool around. Akshay would fill his swimming pool with colored water, and everybody would be thrown into it on arrival. Have you ever drunk *bhang*? I tell you, it gives a bigger kick than tequila. You should try it. People drink *bhang* on holiday. It's some kind of a milk-based drink with lots of pistachios and nuts made into a paste and dissolved in it."

"Since when have people started getting drunk on milk and nuts?" Jay had asked petulantly.

"Oops, did I forget to mention the ground marijuana leaves and the copper coin? It's the coin that gives the kick," Aasha Rani had said, trying to amuse him. "Sounds exciting," Jay had said, sounding most unconvinced. "It is fun when you are with the right people. I used to look forward to Holi parties. In fact, on the night before Holi I always made it a point to go to the fishing village in Bandra and join the people there as they danced around a huge bonfire. Their food was delicious. I'll take you there sometime." "Thanks, but I think I'll pass."

They had finally found a cab, and as they had neared Bandra the hoardings with Sudha gracing them had started sprouting. The sight set off a train of memories, and Aasha Rani attempted to revive her sullen audience with stories of the days when she was the star attraction at filmland Holi celebrations.

"In our time, promising newcomers were also invited, along with the top heroes and heroines. It was a good occasion for them to meet everybody in an informal atmosphere. Big producers kept a lookout for fresh talent. There was so much music and dancing, it was always easy to spot someone who had the makings of a future star," Aasha Rani explained excitedly. "Can you imagine all of us, drenched to the skin, wearing clinging white clothes—at least, they used to be white to start with—and then dancing the bhangra and discoing on the lawns with all those important people ogling us? *Amma* used to come with me and force me to go on dancing alone, even after the others had stopped. All the magazines used to carry my solo pictures because I was the best!" "I bet you were," Jay said, and gazed out of the window onto the highway. "God! It's getting worse by the year, isn't it?" he said. "Look at all those squatters. Look at those slums! Filthy! Was it always this bad?" "To my eyes it looks just the same. Maybe we get used to the crowds and the dirt. I don't really mind. Look how happy the people seem. Look at all those kids throwing color and enjoying themselves," Aasha Rani said as she looked out.

"Yes, they're having so much fun, they're likely to get run over by all the trucks speeding by," Jay said darkly.

"Oh, go on. These children grow up on the streets. They know how to take care of themselves."

But even Aasha Rani had to admit that Bombay looked shabbier and dirtier. Even while the aircraft had been poised over the runway, awaiting permission to land, Aasha Rani had stared aghast at the proliferation of shantytowns all along the edge of the airport boundary walls. She'd noticed the satellite townships of Bombay with thousands of ugly housing complexes arranged mechanically in cramped squares, the buildings with peeling distemper and rusting water tanks on the roofs. Such a depressing sight, especially the mountains of uncleared, rotting garbage dotting the suburban thoroughfares, dense hutment colonies along open drains and—the most amazing sight of all—hundreds of TV antennae like metallic skeletons atop one-room tenements fabricated out of gunnysacks, corrugated sheets, plywood and assorted rags. Bombay was squalor at its most advanced.

"Mommy, why are all the children naked? Don't they have clothes? Why are they so dark and thin?" Sasha asked her. "Well, darling, that's because they are poor." "What's 'poor,' Mommy?" And Aasha Rani had realized for the first time that her daughter was a foreigner to India. And she had no one to blame but herself. It was she who had insulated her and protected her. Not wanted her to know about her mother's country. Or her mother's past. Jay exchanged glances with his wife and said, "You answer that. You tell her what's 'poor.'"

WHEN THEY REACHED their hotel Aasha Rani wasn't sure she should phone *Amma*. Ever since London, she had heard stray rumors of how *Amma* had vilified her after she'd fled Bombay. Perhaps it would be best not to reestablish contact. It was Jay who was insistent. "It's been so many years. Come on, she's your mother, after all. And it's important for Sasha to get to know her grandma and other relatives. We can't go on cutting her out of our lives like this. Besides, I thought the whole idea of coming here was for you to reestablish contact with your family."

Aasha Rani, as it turned out, didn't have to make the first move. Kishenbhai phoned her "on *Amma*'s behalf." Aasha Rani was faintly irritated by that. "Why couldn't she call herself?" she asked. "*Jaaney do.* We are all happy that you are here. We read it in the evening papers." "What papers?" Aasha Rani demanded. "I didn't talk to anybody. Nobody knew I was coming here." "Maybe. But some reporter saw you at the airport. He was there

to photograph a minister who was also returning from London—
same flight—and a few members of the cricket team after their
England series. He recognized you and phoned the papers. Also,
your London trip was reported here. You must've met Indians
there; see, the public doesn't forget that fast. Your fans still want
you back. I get calls, many calls . . . if you are interested."

"Don't be silly. When I quit films, I quit permanently," Aasha
Rani said, dismissing the idea of joining films again. "But tell
me—how's *Amma*? And Sudha? And everybody else?"

"Great lady, memsahibji, why don't you come and find out for
yourself?" Kishenbhai said. "*Amma* will prepare hot-hot *uttapams*
and *kaapi* for all of you. Then I'll give you the news—everything.
Bachchi kaisi hai?" "*Achchi hai,*" Aasha Rani said. "How did you
know about Sasha?" "*Arrey,* don't worry. We get to know everything sitting here. We have our spies."

Aasha Rani smiled to herself. Some things never change, she
thought. Indian inquisitiveness is like Indian slums. Nothing is
private. Nobody has a right to secrets, especially in a family. It
was such a contrast from the world of white men. It was only
when she got back to India that it struck her how much of an alien
she was in New Zealand. She had tried to adapt, adjust and accept. And she thought she had succeeded. Now, back in familiar
territory, she realized just how far her self-delusion had gone.
No. She didn't belong there. This was home. And home was Holi
and Diwali and fisherfolks with gaily painted boats beckoning her
to join them as they lurched drunkenly around a gigantic bonfire—
lit in the same manner, year after year, over several centuries, to
commemorate the destruction of the demoness Holika. Aasha
Rani couldn't wait to meet her people. To catch up with all
the news.

The news of Aasha Rani's marriage had sent shock waves through Bombay. *Amma* had been the worst affected. "How dare she?" *Amma* had asked Kishenbhai, her voice choked with rage. "That girl has let us all down. What am I to say to her producers? What about all the pending contracts? Who will dub for her? Finish the incomplete films? Wretch! I always knew that she would ruin me one day. Ruin all the plans I've been making for her all these years. First, she disappears with someone else's husband. Then she marries a strange man. A white man. What about his character? Who is he? *Chhee, chhee*—must be eating beef. Now she'll never be able to enter our home, our temple. She is defiled. I refuse to call her my daughter. She has betrayed my faith in her. If anybody from the press phones, put them on to me. I'll be happy to give interviews and tell everybody what sort of a daughter I gave birth to—a witch, a demon woman. Seven generations of sin have led to this fate. I ask God, what have I done in my past lives to deserve such a daughter? I cannot show my face in Madras. What shall I tell *Appa*? Viji has disgraced us all. I should have known from the beginning." Kishenbhai had tried to console her by saying, "At least she must be happy." "Happy?" *Amma* had snorted. "That girl will *never* be happy. My curse is upon her."

The phone had rung then. Linda. All honeyed charm and glib persuasion as she'd urged *Amma* to grant *Showbiz* an exclusive. Not that *Amma* had required any urging. She had had her quotes all worked out.

The next week had been full of *Amma*-isms. Hoardings all over the city had blazed headlines such as, "My Daughter Is a Whore," "Aasha Rani Betrayed Me." "Mother Disowns Aasha Rani," "Sweetheart of Millions Turns Vamp." Spewing anger and bitterness *Amma* had lashed out at her daughter, providing intimate details of her life and cataloging all her affairs. *Amma* had begun to revel in the spotlight. It had given her quite a thrill to feel wanted. She had experienced a hitherto unknown sense of power each time she picked up the phone to grant appointments to scoop-hungry journalists. She'd even had a photo session with one of the regular film photographers so that she'd have a set of pictures ready when the reporters arrived.

The first thing *Amma* had done after she realized that there was nothing she could do about Aasha Rani's marriage was to place a call to the Shethji. "You must have heard the news about my foolish daughter's sudden marriage, yes, yes, to some foreigner in some country I don't know. God has really let me down. I worry about her future. I don't know where she is, how she is, but I have also to worry about my other child. Yes, Shethji, I have one more. What is a helpless woman like me to do all alone? Aasha Rani has conveniently run away from her responsibilities. But I can't do that. That is why I'm phoning you, Shethji. No, not to ask for favors; I only want to present my younger daughter to you. I'd be honored if you made a little time to see her. Yes, I know you are busy with the elections, but try to squeeze us in, *bahut meharbani,* Shethji. Sudha is young, and innocent—you will not be disappointed. Aasha Rani, in any case, is dead to us. I have to take care of Sudha's future now. You are very kind, Shethji. God will shower his blessings on you. It's not for nothing that all of Bombay says Sheth Amirchand is the only man who cares for his people. I now put the younger one into your hands as well, since I know that you alone will take good care of her."

Sudha had been sent to the Shethji's house with Kishenbhai. But she was spared the torture Aasha Rani had been subjected to.

The Shethji had summoned both of them into his room. He had taken a good, hard look at Sudha. Then he asked her to wait outside while he spoke privately to Kishenbhai. "I like the girl," he had told him. "In fact, she's better-looking than her sister. Fairer also. Figure is good, everything is good. But *kuch jamta nahi hai*—there's something missing. Aasha Rani had sex appeal. A man had only to take one look at her and he'd feel aroused—like an animal. I know men who couldn't wait to tear off her clothes. She had such a powerful effect on them. This girl is OK. *Chaalu cheez*. But I don't want her. Maybe I'm getting old. Prostrate problem *bhi hai*. And all this elections *ka jhamela*. You know how it is. But that girl Aasha Rani, I liked her. She was clever. She understood men. She knew how to please them. *Khair,* I will help this one—what is the girl's name? Sudha? I'll help her, only because I liked her sister. Their mother is a shameless woman. An unfeeling bitch. She has ruined her innocent children. But I'll let God take care of her in His own way. You stay in touch and tell me what I can do for this *ladki*. Party-*sharty* to be arranged? Any other *tamasha*? I can call her for our functions. We can always do with pretty girls. What else? I'll introduce her to my producer friends. After that, it's her destiny. Tell her mother not to bother me. But if you hear from Aasha Rani and if she requires any help, I'm always there. *Achcha,* business over. This girl has my blessings. You can drop my name to introduce her around; Sheth Amirchand still counts in the right circles, *theek hai*?" Kishenbhai had touched his feet before leaving. He knew Sudha was made. And he had been glad she hadn't had to go through what her sister had. Very glad.

Kishenbhai was getting on himself. He'd given up his old dreams of becoming a full-fledged producer after a couple of disastrous efforts in which he had lost just about all he had. Now he was only a small-time distributor. Occasionally he took on individual star aspirants. But the days of running around and putting deals together were over for him. Funnily, he didn't miss them one bit. It had seemed inevitable for Sudha to move into the roles vacated by Aasha Rani. That was what *Amma* had wanted, so that was the way it had worked out.

Kishenbhai had smoothly moved in to perform the job he had already handled for Aasha Rani. "I made her a star then," he told *Amma*, "and I'll make Sudha one now—a bigger star than her sister. That is my challenge. And my goal." Sudha had initially been nervous about stepping into her *akka*'s shoes. "Will people accept me?" she had tearfully asked *Amma* as she faced her first camera in Bombay. *Amma* had shut her up quickly, "Don't ever say that, understand? People accept anything. You have to prove yourself worthy; that's all. Do you think audiences are loyal? Do you think they really miss their favorites once they're out? No. Ask me. Audiences are fickle. They have short memories. They don't care who is on the screen as long as they are entertained. Now, you must always remember that. Forget about *akka*. She is dead to us. Forget what she did on the screen. You are a better dancer, a better actress. You have a better figure, and you are fairer. What was *akka*? Just a dark lump! It is we—Kishenbhai and I—who made her into what she was. Plus, that girl was lazy and indifferent—obsessed with that womanizer. You are not like that. You have everything in your favor—age, looks, talent. Make the most of them. Don't throw your career away like your stupid sister did. She could have made so much money. Achieved so much fame. But what did she do? Spent all her time on useless men. And now? She has gone and married some white farmer! Can you imagine the life she must be leading? He must be making her work night and day. Clean bathrooms, cook, polish the windows, sweep, scrub, do dishes. I tell you, that man must have been looking for an *ayah*, not a wife. And that foolish girl went and got caught in his trap. But you—you listen to your *Amma*. Stay away from men. I will be with you all the time. Speak to nobody. Trust no one. Whatever you want will be given to you by me and me alone. Kishenbhai will handle your other work. He will deal with your producers. But I don't want you to speak directly to him either. You keep your mouth shut and do your work. That is all. We will make you the biggest heroine in the film industry. Just you wait and see."

AMMA's WELCOME TO AASHA RANI was guarded but not hostile. She greeted her daughter and son-in-law with a traditional *aarti* to welcome them home. Aasha Rani stared at her mother's face over the dancing flames of the oil lamps in the silver *thali* and wondered if this was the same woman who had been so vicious toward her. With an enormous effort she shrugged off the past and smiled at her mother. What a sad life she led, really. Still suspicious, still cautious, still worried that someone—even her own child—would get the better of her. Aasha Rani wanted to hug her mother, fall into her arms, hold her close and say, "It's all right. Whatever happened, it's over now. All is in the past. Let's forget everything. Let's just enjoy each other's happiness." But she didn't dare.

It was ages since there had been any physical closeness between the two of them. But watching her mother's frown of concentration as she meticulously performed all the little rituals of welcome, she felt protective toward her. And forgiving. *Amma* looked old and tired. There were lines around her eyes and mouth. Her breasts sagged inside the ill-fitting sari blouse. And *Amma,* ever frugal, was obviously still washing all her Kanjeevarams at home, Aasha Rani guessed. Aasha Rani sighed. Even after all these years of living luxuriously *Amma* still saved on laundry bills!

There was the usual fuss over the child. Sasha was smothered by half a dozen people—all at once. She was completely bewildered by the strangeness of the experience. The language was new, and so were all the persons hugging and kissing her. She began to cry. "Mommy, I want my mommy." That led to a new rush of ladies dying to comfort her. They marveled at her accent, touched her hair with disbelief and kept repeating, "Just like a dolly! So fair and with golden hair!" Aasha Rani hastily looked at Jay, checking to see whether he was embarrassed. But he seemed unperturbed. He was watching the proceedings in amused silence, waiting for the fuss to subside. *Amma* told her son-in-law, "We have kept her room exactly the way it was. The same. No change. Pink. Everything pink. We knew she'd come back, and then she'd get upset if anything was different." "I hate pink! Always have," Aasha Rani had protested mildly. But Jay caught Sasha's hand and said, "Let's go and see Mommy's old room. She has lots of toys in it." After he'd left, *Amma* fixed Aasha Rani with a look that dared her to lie. "Is he a good man?" Aasha Rani looked back at her steadily and said, "Yes, *Amma.* Jay is wonderful. You can say he saved my life. I don't know what would have happened to me if I hadn't met him. I didn't want to come back to India. And I couldn't have stayed there." *Amma* nodded and then said: "Your *Appa* is old now. Very old. He knows you are in India. It will make him happy to see you and his grandchild." Aasha Rani said nothing. *Amma* waited for her to say something. "Well?" she finally demanded. "I'll think about it," Aasha Rani said, "but first, tell me about Sudha. Her pictures, her price—what are they paying top heroines nowadays? Five lakhs?" *Amma* laughed. "Baby, days are different now. Sudha gets double that—about ten lakhs." Aasha Rani gasped. "Ten? My God! How many films were released this year?" *Amma* said smugly, "So far only five—two hits. Four more in the next few months. Big release at Diwali opposite Amar."

"Why didn't you move out of this place if she's earning so much? Or does she hoard all her money? Are you still looking after her earnings?"

Amma hesitated before answering. "Well, actually Sudha's affairs are handled professionally by a banker friend of hers. He tells her where and when to invest. They have what is called a portfolio. I don't interfere. Stocks, shares, property, Sudha takes care of it herself, along with her secretary and Amar." Aasha Rani thought for a while. "What about you? How do you manage?" "Well, we had some of your money, you know, when you left, the collection continued to come in. And now Sudha gives us a fixed allowance. She is very generous. We have more than enough to live on. Sudha doesn't stay here; she has bought a grand bungalow at Vile Parle. She is with Amar there. God knows what is going on. No marriage plans, nothing. They simply stay together. Shamelessly. But what can *Amma* say? I don't utter a word. That girl was always so jealous. You know, Baby, she hates you."

Kishenbhai joined them. He sat slouched in a chair. "Why did you cut your hair?" he asked Aasha Rani. "Now you look like a pucca *phirangi*."

The servant brought in the coffee and snacks. Aasha Rani

noticed the frayed napkins, the plastic trays and the unbreakable cups and saucers. Kishenbhai caught her observing the air of general seediness about the place, and when *Amma* had left the room to check on Jay and Sasha, he said quietly: "Aasha Rani, things are not what they used to be when you were here. *Amma* has been having a lot of problems. Your sister is not like you. She's different. Selfish. Very selfish. And hard on *Amma*. They fight all the time. Over money, over everything. Even if *Amma* wants a new sari, she has to ask Sudha's permission. That hopeless fellow she's involved with . . . I don't have to tell you about Amar; you know what he's like—a bastard number one. Now he has become a big star. His head is also big. Too big. They think nobody can beat them. They think nobody knows about their plan! There is no love between them. It is all a pretense. Every day she needs a new man. And Amar goes to common prostitutes. He says he doesn't like film girls. But they stay together to show the world they are a team. He is a smart, shrewd businessman. Nothing is kept in India. Everything abroad. *Havala* transactions. *Saala,* he's so smart, he can't be caught; all *benaami* business. His investments are solid. *Ekdum* solid. He doesn't have to bother about films. But films are a *nasha,* a madness. You can never get out. Unless audiences throw you out. Unless you are rejected by them." Kishenbhai paused for breath and looked at Aasha Rani. "Tell me, Aasha Rani—what are your plans? *Chalo,* now you have a husband, a nice daughter. What do you want to do? You are still young, and don't mind my saying—sexy. Producers were asking me . . . I said, 'Baba, let her first come to India; then we shall see.' You have a good chance if you want to come back. Your fan mail still comes. People have not forgotten you.

"Sudha gets asked questions about you. And *Amma*. If you get the right role in the right film, you should do it. *Chalo,* you'll have to lose some weight first. But that is not the problem. We could get Saroj, your old dance director—your dancing must have become a little *dheela,* you know; don't get me wrong. But we can organize all that. The most important thing is—do you want to come back? And your *miya?* What is his opinion? Will he mind? You'll have to think. Don't answer me now. But remember, even your fans can't wait forever. You'll be too old later if you change your mind. And look at the competition. Young girls not much older than your child—not even menstruating! And they're playing heroines opposite heroes old enough to be their grandfathers! Two films, four films and they're out. There are two hundred others waiting to take their place. But you were different. You had a following. You were a national craze. You really were the 'Sweetheart of Millions.' People still sing your songs. They go crazy when they're shown on TV. For you it will be easy. Niteshji was wondering . . ."

But Aasha Rani was far away. She'd heard every word—but only just. She was thinking of her last days in Bombay. Of Abhijit and Akshay and the state she'd been in. Of *Amma's* harsh words, and Amirchand's unexpected support. It seemed so unreal, so far away. And here was this man, this fixer (he wore funny dark glasses these days, and his hands had a tremor) tempting her to jump right back into the well from which she had barely escaped. "No," she said abruptly. "No. I'm not interested. I'm very happy where I am; I like my life there. I want to be just a wife and mother. I want to bring up my daughter well and look after my husband. That's all. There's no question of a comeback!"

Jay walked in just then. He'd heard the last few words, "Comeback?" he said quizzically. "What's all this about a comeback?

Aasha Rani, are you thinking of going back into films?" Aasha Rani rushed toward him and put her hands around his waist. "No way, darling. I just told Kishenbhai that." Jay looked at her indulgently. "She's tired today," he said to Kishenbhai. "It's been too much for her, all the excitement of getting home, meeting everybody, seeing her family. She needs time to rest and time to think. Maybe we'll go off to Goa for the weekend. The change will do her good. And I could do with some sun."

AASHA RANI WELCOMED Jay's idea. Bombay after five years of being away had overwhelmed her. Particularly the insistent suggestions from Kishenbhai that she should consider a comeback. "I am tempted. I'd be lying if I said I wasn't flattered by the attention," Aasha Rani had confessed to Jay as their plane wobbled along to Dabolim Airport. "It makes me feel wanted. Is there something wrong with that?" "Of course not, baby," Jay had reassured her, saying, "I'd have been surprised if you hadn't been affected by all this. That wouldn't have been normal. You are only human, Aasha Rani. You have experienced the sort of adulation and success that very few human beings experience. I'm amazed you haven't missed it in all these years that you've been away. Unless you have and you haven't told me."

Aasha Rani gazed out at the stunningly beautiful coastline below her. She pointed out the palm trees and sandy beaches of Goa to Sasha, whose nose was pressed to the window. She tried not to think of Bombay and what Kishenbhai had told her. She didn't want to confront the dilemma. She didn't want to make any decisions. "I was very happy in New Zealand," she finally said.

Jay smiled. "Was? You spoke in the past tense without realizing it." Aasha Rani hastily corrected herself: "Oh! I didn't mean it that way. I was just saying——" Jay interrupted her. "It's all right, my darling. I knew when I married you that New Zealand was only going to be a stopover. A restful phase. You needed it. You'd earned it. Like Goa right now. Only difference being Goa is five days and New Zealand was five years. A matter of perspective. That's all." "How can you say that?" Aasha Rani asked Jay, genuinely puzzled. "I haven't made up my mind about the comeback. I haven't even thought about it clearly as yet. All I said was that I felt flattered people still want to see me on the screen."

The plane had begun its descent. They could clearly see the whitewashed churches standing out like chalky dollhouses amid the lush paddy fields. "Oh look!" Aasha Rani said. "How beautiful it is. I had almost forgotten what a lovely place it was. *Baby Doll* was filmed here. Not all of it, but quite a bit." "I know," Jay said. "Shall I sing that famous song where you were dressed like a Goan fishergirl and were trying to seduce that stud; I forget his name—Umesh?" Aasha Rani giggled. "You've seen that silly film, then?" "I've seen all your films, darling." Jay laughed. "Some of them five times over."

Sasha was very excited. "Look, Mommy, look at the sea! Just like in Sydney." The stewardess came up to tell them to fasten their seat belts. Suddenly, she noticed Aasha Rani. "Oh, I'm so sorry. I didn't know you were on this flight. What a surprise! I'd read you were back, of course, and also that you'd signed up for a few films." Aasha Rani was astonished. "Where did you read that rubbish?" she asked irritatedly. "Oh, it was in a trade paper. One of those, I forget."

Aasha Rani caught hold of Jay's hand. "That bastard! Must be Kishenbhai—nobody else knows about our conversation. He couldn't even wait to check with me before rushing into print. I'll kill him. How dare he! Let's book a call as soon as we get to the hotel."

Jay said quietly, "Calm down. Look at it this way; he has made the decision for you. Now there is no going back."

Aasha Rani looked steadily at him. "Is that really what you want for me?"

"I think it's what you want for yourself," Jay said quietly, "only you are afraid to face it. And face me."

By the time they got back to Bombay, it had been decided—Aasha Rani was back. Back to the world she had thought she could escape. And Jay was the one who pushed her into it. As *Amma* pointed out, "Baby, you are a lucky woman. No Indian husband would allow his wife to act after marriage. Look at *Appa*. Look at Akshay. I can point out so many other examples. Our men are hypocrites. They want to go out and have all the fun while their wives stay at home. Jay is an understanding husband. He doesn't need your money. He doesn't need your fame. But he knows you. He knows what you want. And he wants you to have it. Jewel. He is a jewel. *Navratna*. I hope you realize that." Aasha Rani nodded, smiling to herself at *Amma*'s abrupt revision of her opinion of Jay. *Amma* carried on. "But what about your marriage? Your daughter? Have you thought about it? How will it work if you are here and he is there? Think a hundred times. Your *amma* has changed. I have realized my mistakes. Now I'm no longer thinking of your career; I'm only thinking of you and your happiness. You know what this industry is like. It is vulgar, cheap, cruel—not meant for decent people. And certainly not meant for married women!

"For heroes it is different. They can be married five times over and it makes no difference. But for you, you have responsibilities now. Your own daughter. How will you deal with all the filthy men? The drunks? The distributors? I know what you have gone through. I know what I myself put you through. I'm ashamed of all that now. It's too late. Sudha opened my eyes.

"Look at your sister—she is hardhearted and vicious. She has turned on her own *amma,* not realizing that whatever I did, I did for her. She wanted to be a big star. She wanted to beat you. That was her ambition from the very beginning. That is what she told me when she came to Bombay. '*Amma,* make me a top heroine. I want to be bigger than *akka.* I want to be the best. I want people to forget her. I am better than her—I can prove it.' Yes, that's what she said to me. I'll never forget it. And she didn't want to stop at anything!

"*Hai Bhagwan!* Such ambition. Such cunning. She would have sold her *Amma* if she had to. That girl has no feelings, nothing. She is only after money. I wonder who she's taken after. Money, sex and fame. *Bas.* She gives not a penny to me. I have to beg her. Beg her for even a blouse piece. 'Be thankful,' she says, 'that I've given you a house to live in.' It's your house, Aasha Rani, not hers. But she still says that. She doesn't care for anyone. She has no love in her heart. God will punish her one day. I'm not cursing her; I'm her *amma,* after all. She may have forgotten that, but for me she will always be my child.

"But you—you are different. You have a soft heart. You are kind and good to people who have done so much for you. I know you will not throw out your *amma.* You will look after her in her old age. Where can I go now? How will I live? Lord Venkatesh knows the hardships I've suffered to bring you children up. Am I not entitled to some rest now?

"I'm tired. My joints pain me. The doctor says I'm suffering from hypertension. I've got diabetes. God knows how many more days I have on this earth. But I'm not complaining. I want to live in peace."

Aasha Rani heard her out in complete silence. She didn't want to tell *Amma* what she really felt. The woman was broken in body and spirit. Aasha Rani was willing to overlook her sly, self-seeking speech. We all have to look out for ourselves in the end, she thought tiredly. Each person finds his or her own way to survive. Poor *Amma*—her only hope is me. And as for me, I'll find out soon enough.

Later in the day, *Amma* came to Aasha Rani's bedroom carrying a cup of coffee. "Baby, I was thinking, we should hold a big party to announce your comeback. Give interviews. But only to top magazines. That way your price will also go up. Producers will give you more *bhav*."

Aasha Rani sleepily shooed her off, saying, "Later, *Amma*, later, I've still to make up my mind."

Ten minutes after that conversation the phone rang and Aasha Rani picked up the extension. With a slight shock she recognized Linda's voice. "Well? What did she say? When can I come?" Linda was asking in her usual aggressive fashion. "Ssh! I don't know; she didn't say anything. Later," *Amma* whispered, "I'll talk to you later. She might wake up and hear us." Linda snapped, "I can't wait forever. We have our deadlines. The great *maharani* wants to play hard-to-get, does she? Tell her from me, it won't work. She is the one who needs all the publicity she can get at this point. Remind her it's we who will be doing her a favor by featuring her. And not the other way around. By the way, does she know I'm the editor now? Anyway, you know the deal—we get the exclusive. If I see any other writeup, it's off." *Amma* assured her she'd talk Aasha Rani into it and hastily rang off.

Aasha Rani emerged from her room and found *Amma* talking to Kishenbhai in the living room. "So, nothing really changes, huh?" she said. "I heard you talking to that bitch. *Amma,* how could you? I don't care if I don't ever sign another film, but I'm not going begging to that woman. She can go to hell with her magazine! I don't need her. This time, if I come back, I will do things my way. Kishenbhai, I'll let you know my decision in a couple of days. Meanwhile, please do not make any moves on my behalf. Is that clear?" *Amma* and Kishenbhai stared dumbly at her. Aasha Rani rang the bell and ordered fresh coffee.

JAY WAS BEGINNING to get restless. And bored. Now that he was actually in the thick of Hindi cinema he had lost his fascination for it. He tried watching the latest releases on video, but they bored him. "When are we going to Madras?" he asked Aasha Rani, adding, "And then after that we, I mean I, shall have to think about getting back."

Aasha Rani didn't say anything. She spoke to Sasha. "Darling, do you want to go and meet your grandfather in Madras?" Sasha looked at her with those beautiful gray-green eyes. "I didn't know I had a grandpa in Madras." Aasha Rani patted her head and replied, "Well, now you know. He's my father and he's very sweet. You'll like him." "Your father?" the child asked. "You didn't tell me you had a father. What does he look like? What is his name?"

"I call him *Appa*. He is very old now and sick." Sasha thought for a while and then asked, "Is he going to die, Mommy?" Aasha Rani hugged her and replied, "I hope not, darling."

They took the first available flight to Madras. Jay was excited about going there, since it was a city he hadn't been to before.

And he was curious about *Appa*. Aasha Rani had told him enough about her father to arouse his interest. But she'd left the details sketchy. He hadn't pushed either, thinking it was a touchy, unpleasant aspect of her life that she didn't particularly want to be reminded of.

"Nervous?" he asked her after their plane had landed at Meenambakkam Airport. "No," she replied. "Just hot and sweaty." Jay laughed. "You're sounding just like a kiwi on her virgin trip to the Orient. You were born here, remember?" "Yes, of course I remember," she said a trifle testily, "but I was never comfortable with the heat, always hated it, still do. Some people never get used to sweating; I'm one of them." And with that she started speaking in rapid-fire Tamil to the porters surging around them as they emerged into the hot Madras air.

"Mommy, what are you saying?" Sasha kept asking her. Getting no reply, she turned to her father and said, "Mommy's acting so strange. I can't understand her language. What's the matter with her?" Jay kissed Sasha and replied, "Nothing, your mommy is just happy to be going home; that's all."

ON THE LONG FLIGHT TO MADRAS, Aasha Rani's thoughts had been full of Sudha. She had been flipping through Linda's magazine and had found unflattering pictures of herself prominently splashed in their much-read gossip column. "Have You Heard the Latest Scandal?" Oh God! Aasha Rani had felt terrible reading all the muck and seeing her photographs so spitefully distorted. There was a long interview with Sudha that Linda had written. It was a vicious, malignant piece in which Sudha had said something like: "*Bechari akka.* I can understand how she must be feeling. Now I am the star and she is a nobody. Poor thing—how did she imagine that she could get heroine roles at her age? Someone has misguided her. She should be happy living a retired life, now that she's married and a mother. Why not give others a chance? She has had hers. OK, so she made so many mistakes and got involved with the wrong men. But she should have realized what she was doing. Akshayji, after all, was a married man. She should not have tried to ruin his marriage. And also Abhijit's. Now all those curses are on her head. In her place I would be very scared. It is better to remain unmarried and untouched than to get into *lafdas* with men who belong to other women. I have also learned from my older sister's mistakes. I will never get involved with a married man. And I will take my time before I decide to settle down, not marry the first stranger—that, too, a foreigner who just comes along! Don't ask me any more about all that. After all, he is my brother-in-law. At least, that is what *akka* says I must call him. Who knows whether they are really married or not? Nobody from our family was there. I haven't been to Australia or Timbuktu or wherever they live to find out. I've heard his family does not accept her. But that may be a rumor. What I am saying is that I believe in our customs and conventions. I'm an old-fashioned girl. For me, the *saat pheras* are sacred. Let my *akka* live her life as she wants, but my values are different. I shouldn't be saying this, but I find her relationship with her so-called husband also very *ajeeb.* Maybe I'm conventional, but I was surprised when that foreigner came to my house uninvited and kept calling me out— alone! I refused flat, saying, 'What will *akka* feel?' *Chhee, chhee, chhee,* in our country *devars* don't behave like this! I was so shocked!

These foreigners think all women are like their women—cheap and without morals. I put him in his place. Anyway, it is her life and I can't interfere; I pray that she is happy, now she can't hope to come back also, you know the audiences will never accept her. As it is, last time she ditched all her producers and fans and disappeared without any warning. That is not a professional way to behave. Thank God I was there; otherwise who knows what might have happened? So many lakhs, even crores were depending on her name. She just ditched everybody and went away. Fortunately, directors had confidence in me, and all the films were hits. Now, poor lady, not even mother roles will come to her. Who knows, she might ditch again, even if it's a small role; producers can't reshoot all the scenes. What about continuity and all that? *Bechara* financiers also. They came to me asking me to guarantee that *akka* won't let them down. I said, '*Baba,* how can I promise anything on her behalf?' After all, she's an elder sister. Much, much older than I am. In fact, I could be like her own daughter. That is the sort of respect I have for my *akka*. I can't tell her, 'Don't do this, don't do that.' Now the rest is up to God. I don't know whether she still believes in Him, but in our family, we are all very religious and go to Tirupathi every year."

AFTER SHE HAD FINISHED reading the piece Aasha Rani wondered what had turned Sudha against her. Why was she so hostile, so bitter? What had Aasha Rani done to her, after all? Were the rumors really true that *Amma* had poisoned her mind against Aasha Rani? Why would *Amma* do that? Weren't they both her children? Or was *Amma* really such an unfeeling, ruthless woman?

Was she *that* greedy that she would use one daughter against the other just for money? What a horrible thought. And was it only because of the way *Appa* behaved with her that *Amma* had turned into such a monster? Whichever way one looked at it, there was always a man in the picture. A man using, abusing and finally discarding a woman.

Appa ❧

AMMA HAD INFORMED *APPA* ABOUT AASHA RANI'S VISIT. HE
was confined to a wheelchair now, with nurses attending him night
and day, and his mind had been affected by the multiple strokes
he'd suffered. But *Amma* had also told Aasha Rani that he had his
lucid periods. Aasha Rani was both apprehensive and scared about
the meeting. She had almost forgotten what her father looked like.
The man she remembered was the stranger in family albums. A
robust, virile person dressed in a starched white *mundu* with an
angavastram over his shoulders. But she also remembered the play-
ful father of her childhood, who was away more than at home. Who
always showered the children with extravagant presents on Diwali
and teased their mother to distraction.

JAY'S FIRST REACTION to her home city was revealing. "It's
much cleaner than Bombay. But the people are shorter and
darker." But by the time they had gotten to the center of town,
Jay was clutching his head. "This is insane. What's going on? Is
there a carnival somewhere? Or a religious gathering, a conven-
tion of some kind?" Cyclists, buses, cars and pedestrians were all
over the place. "Mommy, look at all the bright colors!" Sasha said

excitedly. "And those pretty skirts. Mommy, get me one like that."

Aasha Rani found the crowds choking the streets of the bustling Mylapore area pretty hard to take herself. But she enjoyed the sight of the women heading for the temple, carrying brass *thalis* full of pale orange flowers and pretty white jasmine. Jay was fascinated by the white caste marks worn by the men and their *mundus*. "How comfortable they look in their sarongs," he commented, prompting Aasha Rani to correct him: "Those are not sarongs. This is our traditional dress. It's very practical, you know. When it rains, they just hitch the *mundus* up to their knees and carry on. You'll see; *Appa* wears one too." Sasha giggled. "They look so funny, Mommy, all these men dressed in long skirts." Aasha Rani didn't bother to explain anything to the child. As her meeting with her father drew nearer, her head seemed ready to explode from the tension.

She dressed carefully at the hotel. *Amma* had picked out one of her old saris from her trunk and given it to her—a bright yellow one with a vermilion border. "*Appa* likes these colors," she told her. "Now, don't go without a *pottu,* bangles and a *thali.* You are a married woman and must look like one. *Appa* will feel disappointed. And here, take this; he'd given it to me long ago, just after you were born. Wear it. Let's hope he can recognize it." And *Amma* had put a heavy gold necklace around Aasha Rani's neck. "You left all your jewelry behind when you left India," she'd said. "I tried my best to look after all your things. But after Sudha came . . ." And she'd let the sentence trail. "How much of my stuff did she steal?" Aasha Rani had demanded angrily. "I have a right to know—I worked very hard for it. Tell me, *Amma,* what did she take?" *Amma* had looked embarrassed. "Well, it wasn't all her doing. After all, when she came to Bombay, she had nothing. We had to show the producers that she was also a big star. All her money from Tamil films had been spent on other things. Poor girl. She needed a few nice pieces of jewelry for parties and all that, so I gave her yours. How was I to know she wouldn't return them? It was supposed to be a loan!"

Aasha Rani had seethed with anger. "That girl. I'll deal with her when I come back. She's a thief. She has cheated her own sister! Does she really think she'll get away with it?" And with that she'd slammed the door in *Amma*'s face.

THE DRIVE TO *Appa*'s home seemed interminably long. Aasha Rani kept fidgeting with her sari and hair. She'd strung flowers into her improvised plait and had tried to pin down the perm. She looked absurd and knew it. A few people at the hotel had recognized her and made some tentative inquiries. She was in no mood to indulge them. "No, you've got the wrong person," she'd snapped angrily, leaving Sasha looking most bewildered.

Jay was busy staring at the enormous cutouts of film stars and politicians lining the roads. "These are incredible! I've never seen anything like this in my life! Look at that one, and that! Monstrous! I wish I'd brought my video camera. People back home are never going to believe this. And these temples—just look at the way they've been painted. It's pop art, you know, unconscious pop art."

But Aasha Rani was far too preoccupied to respond.

Sasha couldn't get over the cows strolling casually down the streets or settled comfortably bang in the middle of busy traffic intersections. "Look at the moo-moos, Mommy!" she kept repeating. "Why aren't they inside a ranch?" Aasha Rani told her, "There are no ranches in India." "Who do the moo-moos belong to?" Sasha persisted. "To everybody," Aasha Rani answered shortly. "Who feeds them?" "Everybody does." "Where do they get the grass from?" Sasha wanted to know. But Aasha Rani's patience had snapped. "Stop asking stupid questions." Jay placed a restraining hand on her lap and said, "Take it easy, darling. She's only a child. She's naturally curious." "You answer her in that case," Aasha Rani snarled. "I'm sick and tired of replying to her endless questions."

They drove past the famous Marina Beach, and Sasha commented on the color of the sea. "It's different," she cried. "So pretty. And the beach is so crowded! But why is everybody wearing clothes? Oh look—they're going into the water with everything on; they'll catch a cold!"

Jay looked out, amused. It was a pretty funny sight. Entire families, covered from head to toe, were wading into the sea, holding rubber *chappals* aloft. "Don't they have swimsuits?" Sasha went on. "Nobody in India, in Madras, wears swimsuits," Aasha Rani informed her. "Yes, they do," Sasha said. "I saw them in our hotel pool. I saw bikinis and other swimming things." "Oh, but those were foreigners," Aasha Rani said. Sasha looked very puzzled. "No, they weren't. They were like us. *Those* are foreigners," she said, pointing outside. Aasha Rani hugged her daughter. What a clever child, she thought, but what a lot I have to teach her. But could Sasha really be blamed for her remark? Who was she? An Indian? A New Zealander? Mixed breed? Someone without a real identity? It was time Sasha learned about her Indian roots. Her mother's country, her mother's religion, her mother's language and, most important, her mother's people—starting with her grandfather.

Aasha Rani was shocked to see *Appa*. He was virtually a vegetable, not the tall, proud man she had fixed in her mind. She wished *Amma* had prepared her for this. Told her a little more about the state *Appa* had been reduced to. And the house he now occupied! A broken-down hovel with poor ventilation and no lighting. It was more like a makeshift shed with an outhouse where the lavatories were. The woman taking care of him was an illiterate—some destitute from the nearby slum colony. She looked like she probably had lice in her hair, and her clothes stank of urine. She stood there sullenly scratching her scalp and disinterestedly fanning the flies off *Appa*'s face. Where were the nurses? The medical help he was supposed to be getting? Aasha Rani went up to him and called out, "*Appa?*" He heard her voice, all right, since he moved his head in the direction of the sound. But she wasn't sure he recognized it, or her. She put her hand gingerly on his shoulder and repeated, "*Appa.*" An ill-kempt parrot in a wire cage hanging from the rafters squawked once, as if in reply.

Appa was completely motionless and silent. The servant girl stood aside, bewildered by the scene. "Didn't *Amma* tell you I was coming?" Aasha Rani cried. "*Appa*, look at me—listen to me. It's me—Viji—your daughter. *Appa*—talk to me!" For five minutes or so, she just sat there at his feet, gazing at him helplessly. "*Appa*— say something, please. Look, I've brought your granddaughter, and your son-in-law—my husband. *Appa,* look at them." Nothing. Jay came to stand beside her. "It's OK, darling," he said. "I'm sure he can hear you; I'm sure he knows you are with him. Maybe the whole thing has been too much for him. Let's leave him alone for a while—let him absorb the shock." But Aasha Rani refused to budge. "I can't believe this is *Appa*. What has happened to him? He used to be so tall and handsome. You've seen his old photographs. Now he looks like a ghost, a shadow. Why didn't *Amma* stay here to look after him? And where did all the money go? I used to send *Amma* quite a bit for his care—who took it?"

Sasha had disappeared somewhere. Aasha Rani looked around for her. "Where's Sasha?" she asked, alarmed. Jay strode off to look for her. Just then, without warning, she heard *Appa's* voice—"Is that really you, Viji?" he asked. She thought she was hallucinating. The voice was not as feeble as she'd thought it might be. It was her *appa's* voice, all right. Firm and strong. She grabbed his hands and cried, "*Appa!* You recognized me! You know I'm here with you . . . yes, *Appa*, it's me, Viji." *Appa's* eyes came to rest on her. "*Amma* told me you were coming," he said. Aasha Rani hugged his knee. "*Appa*—what is this? Where are you living? And why are you living like this? I will not allow you to stay here for one more minute. Who put you in this hell? Why isn't anyone looking after you?"

Appa was silent. She looked up at his face and there were tears streaming down his cheeks. "I'm so happy," he said, "so happy. Now I can die in peace." Aasha Rani cradled his head in her arms, repeating, "I'm here now, *Appa*. I'll take care of you. Don't worry about anything. Now you are with me. I'll make all the arrangements." Jay came back with a disheveled Sasha and stood motionless, watching the scene. "Grandpa's talking, Grandpa's talking," Sasha screamed, jumping up and down. The parrot began squawking. The servant woman slipped silently away.

AASHA RANI DECIDED to remove *Appa* to her own house in Madras. But when she got to the place to make the necessary arrangements for the ailing old man, she discovered it was locked up and in a shambles. The old caretaker who lived in the garage was lying drunk on a *charpoy,* with his harassed-looking wife fanning him. Aasha Rani was stunned to see how dilapidated the place looked, with weeds growing all over the garden and bird droppings covering the windows. "What is this?" she demanded furiously. The old man, Krishna, was too far gone in a drunken stupor to reply. He looked up at the visitors from the *charpoy* and said: "Who are you? What do you want? Go away. Nobody lives here. They've all gone. Gone to Bombay." His wife, Laxmi, recognized Aasha Rani and stiffened. Then she ran into the garage and looked for the keys in an empty oil tin, rushing to open the door. She let them in, apologizing constantly and begging forgiveness. "*Amma* has stopped sending money," she said hesitantly. "What could Krishna and I do? We barely survive somehow. I do housework in the area—he just drinks away whatever I earn. We are starving. The children are hungry all the time. One of them is dead. Two are scrounging around on the streets, begging, picking up leftover food from dustbins." Aasha Rani asked her to calm down and tell her exactly what had happened. "About a year ago the money suddenly stopped coming. We wrote letters. Many letters. But no reply. Krishna wrote to Sudha *akka* also. But no reply. Then he borrowed money and took a train to Bombay. He met *Amma. Amma* said, 'What to do? I also don't have money.' She sent Krishna to Sudha *akka*'s house. But she refused to meet him. He went back twice, thrice. He spoke to her as she was leaving the gate for shooting. She said, 'That is not my house. This is my house. You get the money from Viji. Or *Amma.*' We did not know what to do, where to go. *Amma* said, 'Manage somehow.' Krishna came back. He told me, 'At least we have a place to stay. I will become a watchman. You find work washing clothes and utensils. We will pull along and wait for Viji *akka* to return.' For some time, I tried to keep the house clean. I used to open it every week. We also looked after the garden after the *mali* left. But then my health failed, the child died and Krishna started drinking."

Aasha Rani heard her out. There was work to be done. Lots of it. "We are going to stay here for some time," she announced.

TWO MONTHS LATER, Aasha Rani received an unexpected call from Rita. "Hello, *ji*, I'm in Madras," she said cheerily. "We have come for a *mahurat*. I was wondering, Aasha Rani, if you could come as the chief guest and sound the clapper? It will be a good way to relaunch yourself. Bring your husband—Jay, isn't it? You'll get a lot of publicity. You know the entire unit is here from Bombay, so many of your old friends. Also, the press wallahs—you'll recognize some of them. Your favorite publicist and photographer are here too. We heard you were staying in Madras to look after your father, so sweet. Very good, very good. *Amma* told us where we could contact you. How is your little baby? What do you think, *ji*? It's a very prestigious film . . . multistarrer . . ." She trailed off vaguely.

Aasha Rani was alerted at once. "Is my sister Sudha in it?" she asked. Rita coughed nervously. "*Hahn, hahnji* she's there. But there are three other heroines also. You know, new girls. My husband has always given a chance to newcomers. And there are new boys. *Bahut badhiya* production *hai*. Something to be proud of, Aashaji." Aasha Rani asked, "Who's the hero opposite Sudha?" Rita hesitated before replying, "*Bas,* the same one—you know him, of course—Amar. They are the hit pair now, you know. My husband thought, Why not make another big film with them? These days top stars come and go. Five films and finish. Public bore *ho jati hai.* Too many problems in the industry now. *Ammaji* must have told you—Video-*shideo, pata nahi* all these problems with piracy. My husband has a court case—*arrey* Supreme Court *tak gaye hain.* Still. Financing also has changed. *Baba,* this television nuisance is too much. Nobody wants to go to see films in theaters. Prices are going to crash soon. Everybody is saying the industry will collapse next year. *Khallas.* Distributors are reducing rates per territory. *Chalo,* why should I bore you with all these things? You must be knowing already. Your father, poor fellow. Look what happened to him. I tell you, the film business is very dangerous. One day you are a king; next day you're a beggar. See your poor father. Just a few years ago he was a *badshah* in Madras. And now. At least you are there for him. That is good. *Ammaji* was saying you might be interested in coming back. *Sach hai?* I can talk to my husband. But first, do this much for me—say yes to the *mahurat* shot. Publicity guaranteed. First time you two sisters will be seen together; think of that. *Arrey* film magazines will go crazy. Cover page *ho jayega!*" Aasha Rani couldn't begin to imagine the sheer gall of the woman. Surely she must know the depth of the enmity between Sudha and herself. And to think she would go slinking over to the *mahurat* to be eclipsed by her vicious little sister. Why, she had resolutely refused to visit Sudha in Bombay, even though *Amma* had suggested it. The silly bitch must be stark, staring mad to think she'd do it. And then it struck home with an almost physical force. But, of course, the best revenge would be to go and show she was completely unfazed by that little vixen.

"Fine. I'll be there. Give me the details and send the car to pick me up," Aasha Rani said into the phone.

Rita seemed slightly taken aback that Aasha Rani had agreed to the request, but she recovered swiftly and gave her the details of the function that would take place the next day.

The moment she put the phone down, nervousness took over. What had she put her foot into? What had Rita talked her into? How was she going to deal with Sudha? And Amar? But, most important—what was she going to wear? She hadn't had the time to shop for anything. Her old saris looked faded and shabby. Her perm was well past its prime, and hung limply. Even her otherwise glowing skin looked drained of color and patchy in places. She decided to concentrate on herself for a change. Only, she didn't know quite where to begin.

The sari part was easy enough. There was just one shop everybody went to—Nalli's. The blouse would take some fixing, but Laxmi offered to copy one of her old ones for her. "*Akka,* I had started stitching for the neighbors when nobody was in Madras. All I need is a sewing machine." As for her face, Aasha Rani decided to leave it to the experts. Without a second thought she called up the beauty parlor at the Taj Coromandel and fixed an appointment.

When Aasha Rani was finished dressing on the day of the *mahurat* she looked stunning and knew it. She'd picked a simple white-and-gold Mysore georgette for the occasion. Her hair was styled in a sophisticated French braid. The beautician had applied her makeup with care: just enough to get her sallow skin to look brighter. Surveying herself in the full-length mirror, she was pleased. Laxmi looked at her admiringly and told her she resembled an *apsara.* Aasha Rani preened in front of *Appa* and Jay. Both of them approved of her appearance, and Jay even whistled. Aasha Rani bent over *Appa*'s head and kissed him. "Wish me luck," she said. "I'm nervous." His eyes said it all.

* * *

THE STUDIO CAR DROVE UP at the dot of eleven. She noted with some amusement that it was a local Ambassador minus air-conditioning. The imported Toyotas were only for the real stars, she explained sarcastically to Jay. She decided to get one up on them by deliberately staging a late arrival. She'd show them. Stupid fools, indulging in their cheap power games! A star's worth was gauged by the number of hours he or she could keep a unit waiting. Well, now they could wait for her. After all, these were the little tricks she'd learned from them. Around noon, she drank a glass of water, took a final look at herself and stepped into the waiting car with Jay. The driver stared at her in the mirror. "Weren't you also a star?" he asked in Tamil. She smiled sweetly at him and replied, "I still am." He laughed uneasily, and she imagined him thinking, "Not another one of those crazies."

He screeched to a halt at the studio gate for the usual bumbling identification ritual. He turned to her and said, "Name, please," in broken English. She rolled her window down and said, "Viji Iyengar." The security guard looked at her curiously and waved the car on. She was surprised at herself. Why hadn't she just said Aasha Rani? This was the first time in her professional life that she had actually used her father's name. Still wondering about that, she got out of the car.

Rita came waddling up swathed in sea green sequined chiffon, her eyes quickly sizing up Jay. She still had the sprayed helmet of hair, only now the color was different. It was nearly blond! She patted it self-consciously into place and, before even saying a perfunctory "Hello, *ji*" to Jay, asked, "Like it?" Aasha Rani smiled. "Very much." Rita burst into relieved peals of laughter. "My, my, Aasha Rani. *Kamaal hai.* You talk just like a *memsaab* these days. *Bas,* Mr. Jay, what have you done to her? In five years you have changed her completely, huh? Accent-shaccent. Forgotten all of us? Forgotten you are Indian?" Aasha Rani refused to react and waited for Rita to calm down. "*Wah!* Look at you," Rita continued. "Still sexy. Very good. One child, no? Daughter? Good. Girls are nice. They care for you. Not like sons. Naughty fellows. *Badmash hotey hain.* Everybody is waiting for you, madam. You haven't forgotten your star *nakhras,* no? One hour late! *Arrey,* things have changed now. Nobody waits for anybody. There are no superstars anymore. Nothing. *Sab log* same to same. You come on time, do your work and go. No *nakhra.* No *khit-pit.* You don't like to work like that—OK, hundred other boys and girls are ready. *Chalo*—let's meet everybody. You must be dying to see your sister. She's too good, *yaar.* Everybody's favorite."

Aasha Rani stepped into a blaze of flashbulbs. Once inside the studio it was as if she'd never been away. It all came back: the peculiar smell of burning wires, the haze of the strong lights, the precarious scaffolding on which the light boys scampered around nimbly, the sweat and the stench of urine, the dirty floors, the enormous pedestal fans whirring noisily, and above all, the impersonal eyes staring, staring, staring. People crowding around, dying to touch you, get near you, smell you. Stale perfume on the women, extrastrong aftershave on the men, wobbly sets with pink nylon lace curtains, tackily dressed extras in mustard satin and black net slinking into the background, living for that split second the camera swept over them, and there, away from everything, the stars with their hangers-on. Someone to light a cigarette, someone to fetch a cold drink, someone to produce a chair to sit on, someone to fan the flies off. Aasha Rani sighed nostalgically. She missed it all. She took a deep breath and looked around for Sudha.

Her eyes were still searching when she felt a tap on her

shoulder. "*Akka,*" a voice said into her ear. Aasha Rani whirled around. There she was—Sudha Rani herself. There was just one word to describe her. Gorgeous! Aasha Rani gazed at her kid sister and tried to see her through the eyes of a stranger. My God! She looked fantastic! And every inch a star. A superstar. How she had changed—not her looks as much as her expression. The haughty way she carried herself. She stood tall and proud, with a slight sneer on her lips, her eyes half-closed. Despite everything between them Aasha Rani hugged her warmly. Spontaneously. She was still her little sister, after all. For Aasha Rani was embracing the pigtailed girl who used to hold the edge of her *pavadai* and trail her everywhere, who used her old lipsticks and climbed into her discarded costumes. A girl who skipped endlessly in the courtyard singing some silly song. A girl who ate twenty *idlis* at one go and bashed up most of the neighborhood boys. Also, a girl who cried easily and was scared of the dark. A girl who came to her in a terrified state at her first menstruation, convinced she was going to bleed to death. How could Aasha Rani ever forget that little child? Sudha returned her hug cautiously so as not to smudge her makeup or muss her hair. She was dressed in a shocking pink outfit. Her head was a mass of golden curls. Her makeup was pink and gold. She looked devastatingly sexy. And Aasha Rani told her so.

Sudha pouted engagingly. "So, *akka,* you aren't angry with me—are you?" Aasha Rani smiled and shook her head. "You look stunning. Absolutely beautiful. I wish *Appa* could see you now. How proud he'd be!" Sudha's expression changed immediately. "Don't talk to me about that man. Or *Amma*. I hate them both." Aasha Rani didn't have the time to react because they were both suddenly besieged by photographers clamoring for "together" pictures. "This is a big reunion, *ji*." Rita cackled. "Let's celebrate with *pedas*." The *pedas,* when they arrived, looked as if a million flies had already sampled them. "Have, have," Rita said, thrusting the box in Aasha Rani's hands. "Take, take," she urged Sudha. "Why doesn't Aasha Rani feed Sudha?" one of the photographers suggested. "Good idea," Rita said, and Aasha Rani obediently picked up a *peda* as Sudha opened her mouth just wide enough to keep her lipstick from cracking. Once again the photographers went wild.

Aasha Rani spotted Amar. He was dressed like Indiana Jones. She saw him clapping enthusiastically. He caught her watching him and raised his cap. He hadn't changed all that much, Aasha Rani thought. He'd put on some weight, but it suited him. His face looked broader too.

Sudha saw her staring. "Looks handsome, no?" she asked. Aasha Rani nodded. "Too much booze." Sudha giggled. "Look at his stomach—full of beer. This morning also I said to him, 'Darling, don't drink just now. We have to go for the *mahurat*. And *akka* is going to be there. What will she think?' He is very naughty. He said, '*Theek hai,* I won't kiss your sister. That way she won't know what I've drunk.' See—he's staying far away from you. He's scared."

Aasha Rani smiled. Sudha had managed to cleverly insinuate all that she had wanted to. Little sister had grown up. The industry had done a good job on her. She had become like one of them—scheming, devious and manipulative. Although she wasn't prepared to forgive her, Aasha Rani didn't quite blame her either. For in the film industry you were either a star—or nothing. And everywhere people waited like vultures for just one flop, one false move, and *khatam*—they'd pounce on you viciously and rip off your flesh before you even got a chance to struggle back to your feet. It was a cruel world. And Sudha had learned how to survive in it. Even thrive in it. Aasha Rani could gauge that just from the way the others reacted to her. The way Rita's husband danced to her tune. Even the way she handled the press—with charming insolence. Sudha was playing queen. And playing it convincingly. She was probably the smartest person in that room. And she knew it. Aasha Rani got the impression that Sudha wanted her to know it as well.

Aasha Rani gazed admiringly at her sister. She was surprised at her own reaction. There was no anger of the sort she had imagined she would feel when she came face-to-face with her sister. Bitterness, yes. Envy, perhaps. But no jealousy or fury. Sudha was tossing off quotable quotes for the benefit of the copy-hungry reporters:

"I am where I am because I deserve to be here"; "Rivals? What rivals? My only competition is me"; "Heroes need me more than I need them"; "Strip? What for? The whole country goes crazy when I show just my ankle"; "Marriage? I don't need it. The poor man would die of an inferiority complex"; "Politics and me don't go together. You see my one-point program ends with me." Aasha Rani watched her with a smile on her lips and acknowledged to herself that Sudha, her little sister, had left her far behind.

"I WANT TO GO HOME," Sasha said, bursting into tears. "I want Trixie; I want to go back to the ranch. Mommy, please let's go home." Aasha Rani tried to shush Sasha but couldn't manage. She'd had a stomach upset—probably the water—and had been cranky ever since. *Appa* was parked in the living room, staring impassively around him. He didn't say a word. Jay took Aasha Rani aside. "It's unrealistic to expect a little girl to understand what's going on here," he said firmly. "Sasha has suddenly been exposed to a world she never knew existed. She is troubled by all the changes. You can't think she'd be able to live here. I mean, I know it's your old home—but just look at it! It's a dump! It will take weeks to set it right. What if Sasha falls sick? What if I do? Or you? We don't know any doctors. We don't know anybody. And now you've taken on the responsibility of looking after your sick father. How do you propose to do that? We need to discuss things. I realize this is a very emotional moment for you. But think in rational, practical terms. Do you intend to stay here indefinitely? What about our home? What about Bombay? I can't hang on much longer—I told you that. Wait, before you say anything, I have a plan. I think it would be best if I took Sasha back with me till you are in a position to make up your mind. You have a great deal of sorting out to do.

"I wish I could have stayed and helped you. But I have to go home. We were supposed to be on a short vacation. But things have turned out differently. I don't blame you. How could you have foreseen these developments? But I love you, my darling, and I want you to be happy. I know you'll be miserable if I drag you back at this stage. I know how much it has cost you to come back to India and confront the life you'd left behind—ran away from. I won't force you to choose. You need time—and you've got it. I will be there for you whenever you need me, and for whatever purpose. You can count on me. You know that. But Sasha must go back with me. She needs a proper education, a proper home. Don't worry about her. I can take care of her. She's a big girl now. Plus, I can always get a responsible nanny."

Aasha Rani had heard him out attentively. She now chose her words with care. "Jay, you have been wonderful all these years. In a way, you saved my life. God knows what might have happened to me if I hadn't met you in that disco. I was sick of living. Sick of deception. So many people had betrayed me so many times. And I too had lost my head, become a loose woman. You never questioned me about my past. You didn't question me about the other men, other affairs. You helped me to put my life back together again. You showed me that another, better life was possible for a woman like me. In India, no man—that is, no decent man—would have married me, given me his name, looked after me the way you have done. If I had found a husband, it would have been some scoundrel after my money, or marrying me for fame. Most probably I would have ended up like *Amma*. Maybe Amirchand would have kept me. Or another Abhijit would have come my way. With you, God gave me the chance to forget my old self, my old sins, my old friends, everything. How can I ever repay you for all that?"

"Oh, come on, you make me sound like one of those early missionaries out to convert the tribals and show them the light. Rubbish, girl! I didn't marry you to 'save' you. I did it for myself. I find you impossibly sexy, and yes, exotic. I was sick of bland white girls from proper English schools, speaking with proper English accents. I liked you the way you were, with your funny Indian English and singsong accent. That's what attracted me in the first place. I miss that old you—do you know that? I miss your saris and all those fussy clothes. And all the little rituals and *pujas* you used to perform in the beginning. Now you have started looking and behaving like one of us, quite forgetting that if I'd wanted that, I would have married the neighboring rancher's boring daughter. Silly girl! I love you very, very much. And I still find you indecently sexy!

"We had to come to India, and we had to find out. You were hiding in New Zealand. Now your exile is over. You are no longer afraid of yourself. This is where you belong. And your father needs you desperately. Do you think I can't see that? It would kill you if I forced you back. It would also finish off our marriage. This way, we still stand a good chance. If we both want it, we can make it work. You stay here till you've worked out what you want to do with your life on a long-term basis. If you want to take another crack at your acting career—go ahead. I believe a person should not live with regrets. A frustrated person is an unhappy person. If you don't grab your chance now, it will be too late. I want my old lady to be a contented girl. I want to be able to sit on the swing out in the garden when we are both ninety and say, 'That's my girl. I'm proud of you.' I want our grandchildren to see pictures of you in your prime—glittering, gorgeous, successful, with the world at your feet. So chin up, cheer up and let's feed the old boy something before he collapses on us."

IT WAS HARD on Aasha Rani after Jay and Sasha left. She felt desperately lonely and ready to quit. There was so much to be done. Of course, money, lots of it, solved problems that much faster. And Jay had transferred a generous amount into her account. She had also gotten in touch with her old accountant and gotten a garbled statement on her own affairs out of him. *Amma* called and solicitously offered to come to Madras. Aasha Rani calculated that she would only add to the costs and be of little or no help. She didn't need a liability around, not with the absolute mess she found herself in the middle of. Her first priority was to get a competent nursing staff for *Appa*. That was simple enough. And then on to setting the bungalow right and weaning Krishna off his drinking habit.

The *mali* was lured back with a hike in his salary. Soon, the garden was cleared of all the undergrowth and began to look tended. The house required massive restructuring, and Aasha Rani called in a firm of contractors, who said they would take care of everything: waterproofing, plumbing, electricity, etc. "Everything must be completed before the monsoons," she said firmly. "OK, *Amma*," they chorused, none too convincingly. Aasha Rani suppressed a small smile. When had she made the transition from *akka* to *amma*? She looked at herself in the mirror. Was she matronly already? Oh hell, she hadn't had time to fix her hair, the perm had grown out, and she felt like a golliwog. She also needed to get back into shape; she knew the tiny tire around her middle was no hallucination. This won't do, she told herself sternly, and planned a rigorous aerobics program for herself.

Within a fortnight she had the kitchen running efficiently, though she made a conscious effort to steer clear of Laxmi's crisp *dosas* and fluffy *idlis*. She warned her, "No *rasam-sambar-bhaat* in this house. I don't want to balloon out like a cow; you understand? Even *Appa* needs a different diet, not all this. I will see to his meals." She stuck to buttermilk, fruits and cereal—occasionally treating herself and *Appa* to ice cream. *Amma*'s calls came frequently and always with the same refrain: Sudha said this, Sudha did that. Finally Aasha Rani told her to stop running up phone bills. "I will deal with Sudha when I get to Bombay—whenever that is. But please don't waste my time and money talking about her."

One day, after she had finished her usual frugal lunch, eating alone in the dining room, the nurse came up to her and spoke under her breath. "He seems a little agitated today. I don't know what the matter is. I think he wants to talk to you." "Of course," Aasha Rani said. She went with Stella, the nurse, to *Appa*'s bedroom and then told the girl to leave them alone. "Ring the bell when you need me," the nurse said, and left.

Appa was definitely not himself. His eyes looked too animated. Shining and alert. This was the first time in so many years that she'd seen him this way. Certainly the first time since she got back. He beckoned her to come closer. Aasha Rani picked up a low stool and sat by his feet. He kept looking at her as if he wanted to say something, but couldn't. Aasha Rani stroked his hands that lay passively in his lap and encouraged him to speak. "What is it, *Appa*? Tell me. Take your time. I'm here to listen to you." Finally, after what seemed like an eternity, *Appa*'s voice emerged in rasping whisper: "Come near me," he said to his daughter. "There are things I have to tell you. Things I should have told you years ago. When I thought I was dying—you remember that illness a few years ago—that's when I wanted to see you, touch you, tell you how sorry I was for whatever had happened. I had done all of you great harm. Behaved unforgivably. Cruelly.

"Your *amma*'s life—I destroyed it. I know that. But I was too busy being a great man to care. Too busy running my studio, showing everybody how powerful I was. Nothing, nobody mattered to me. Nobody. Not my children, my wife, my mistresses. I thought nothing or nobody could touch me. That the gods would protect me from all harm. Why? Because I saw myself as a religious man. I went to Tirupathi—shaved off my hair. I went to Sabarimala and did penance. Observed all the rules. I even went to Gangotri. I was sure all these pilgrimages, the donations to temples, charity to the needy, hospitals, all my 'good deeds,' would ultimately save me. They didn't. Do you know what I asked the mighty gods to do for me in return? To save my skin. To make me still richer. Still more powerful. Still more successful. I prayed for myself and myself alone. I tried to do business with God— can you imagine that? I tried to bargain with him. I'd tell him, 'Look, I'm giving so much to make a new gold *mookoot* for you. Isn't that nice of me? Now, what will you give me for that? I promise you more money, a *yagna* also, if my next film is a hit. And if my studio prospers, I will open a dispensary for slum dwellers in your name. I will get an ambulance for the poor. I will provide free education. Anything. But you keep to your side of our partnership.' I believed God was on my side. That I could never fail, never. I thought I could buy anybody, anytime. That it was only a matter of settling the right price. But I was wrong. Do you know when I realized that? After the fire. You don't know anything about that, do you?

"We were shooting a mythological film in the studios. Even for that scene I was cashing in on God. It was a film about Anusaya— the wronged woman. The opening shot showed Lord Venkatesh- wara's image with me performing a massive *puja*. A beautiful *bhajan* played in the background. I thought God would be pleased. The film was dedicated to him. I'd announced I would give part of the profits to improve the courtyard of the nearby temple and to put in a pump for the well there. I'd even agreed to repaint the whole thing. I told God, 'See, I'm doing such a lot for you. Every- body will remember me for that.' Anyway, for one of the scenes we had to build new sets with a small hut in a forest. The villagers were supposed to gather around a fire. We had composed a special song and dance for that. The girls danced with sparklers and fire torches. One of those foolish girls dropped a sparkler on her flowing skirt. Made of nylon. She lit up like a torch and was gone in seconds. Her body fell on a heap of straw and that caught fire. In no time, the flames were everywhere . . . shooting right up to the sky. It was all over within ten minutes. Burned. Completely burned. Nothing left. Eight people died. The studio was finished. Forever.

"I had borrowed heavily for this film—the previous two had lost money. I was sure of this one's success. I'd told all the creditors I'd pay them back with heavy interest, no problem. I still had people's faith. But what happened? I should have burned with the others and died. I would have been spared this. But God wanted to teach me a lesson. He wanted to reduce me to this helpless state. He wanted to see me bankrupt. Who could have imagined God would be so vengeful? That was the end for me. I lost everything. Every penny I'd made.

"The creditors came swooping to my doors like vultures. They didn't care about my problem. All they wanted was their money. Money—hah! I'd worshipped it till that day. My dream died, Aasha Rani—it went up in flames.

"But after seeing you again my hopes have been reborn. I can tell myself, all is not lost yet. You have a daughter. A clever daughter. She will do it. She will revive your banner. She will reopen the studio. She will once again restore that lost glory of your name.

"Please, Aasha Rani, you can do it. And you must. Do it for a father who is dying. Who is broken. Who is a very unhappy man. I had lost the will to live or even to speak. But now, with you by my side, I feel strong. I feel young again—in my mind, at least. In my lifetime, what remains of it now, I want to see the studio prosper once again. Become the pride of the industry." It was the longest speech the old man had made since she had come to Madras, and clearly it had exhausted him. But the glow in his eyes remained as he gazed upon his daughter. She rang the bell for the nurse.

Jojo ❧

TWO AND A HALF MONTHS AFTER SHE HAD LEFT BOMBAY AASHA Rani returned. But she was not alone, for she had decided *Appa* would return with her. *Amma* was accepting of her daughter's decision, especially as Aasha Rani sensed that her mother had plans that could succeed only with her older daughter's cooperation. She hadn't long to wait, for the day after her arrival in Bombay, Kishenbhai showed up with an offer. "There's this new producer," he began. "You don't know his name. But good. Two hits. He is interested in casting you for his latest film. Solid story. Heroine-backed role. Shall we see him?" "Why not? Let's find out what kind of a market I have." Aasha Rani was casual.

The producer came over that evening. She was pleasantly surprised. He was so entirely different from the sort of producers she was familiar with. This man was young, good-looking, smart and well dressed. He could have been a movie star himself. He spoke with a trace of an American accent, and had come armed with a complete script. His attitude was casual but businesslike. He even looked like he'd been to college!

As it turned out, Jojo (short for Jitendra) Mehta had just returned from the University of California after studying filmmaking and philosophy. He was full of bright ideas and jargon. The script he'd brought with him was his own effort ("I'd taken a few courses in screenplay writing while I was at it") and from what Aasha Rani gathered he'd gotten an interesting project together. It was a thriller, a slick, offbeat murder story. Perhaps he'd plagiarized it. But the adapted version was pretty good. Aasha Rani was puzzled by just one thing—she didn't know where she fit into the script. There were three female roles—a mother-in-law, her daughter-in-law and the murdered "other woman." After reading the synopsis she asked Jojo where she was supposed to come in. "Oh, you play the mother-in-law," Jojo said smoothly.

"Mother-in-law?" Aasha Rani exploded. "That's absurd. I'm not old enough to play anybody's mother-in-law! Do you know that till I signed my last film I was only doing college girl roles? Not even married women—and here you are asking me to play a bloody mother-in-law! There must be some mistake. Do you know how old I am? I'm not yet thirty!" Jojo put up his hands. "Relax, lady. I didn't mean to offend you. It's a meaty role. I thought you could do justice to it. That's all. No hassles, OK?" Aasha Rani was still fuming. Gesticulating to Kishenbhai, she took him aside. "What is the meaning of this?" she demanded. "This man is insulting me. You must have known about the role. Why didn't you tell me before bringing him here and wasting everybody's time?"

"Aasha Rani, things have changed in the industry," Kishenbhai said quietly. "In just five years? That's all it has been—five lousy years! Has there been a revolution or something?"

"I'm sorry, Aasha Rani. But the public is demanding younger and younger heroines. You've seen the posters and magazines. What is the age of hit heroines? Fifteen! You can't compete with them. In a year or so even Sudha will have to switch to character roles. The demand is like that. I thought it was an interesting proposal. Jojo is a respected filmmaker. He's very professional. Pays on time. His films are technically top class. People think it's an honor if he asks them to work in his films. It's OK. I'll understand if you aren't interested. I'll tell him." Aasha Rani stopped Kishenbhai. "Wait, let me think it over—I'll tell him myself." She walked up to Jojo and turned on the charm. "Well, Jojo, I've been thinking. It's not a bad project. In fact, it's pretty good. Mother-in-law? Why not? I've known some sexy mothers-in-law. Besides, it's up to me and you to interpret the role, isn't it? I can still look glamorous. You could put in a song. We could do a few sexy close-ups. Not bad. Let me read the script tonight and get back to you tomorrow. How about that?" Jojo held out his hand. "Done." At the door he turned around. "By the way, I think you are gorgeous. They were right about you, all those swooning, drooling idiots; you are the best. No one to touch you. No one."

"Thanks," Aasha Rani purred, and blew him a kiss.

Aasha Rani went to *Appa*'s room and found him dozing off. "*Appa?*" she said softly. Groggily he opened his eyes. He seemed disoriented. "I heard the conversation outside," he said. "Which conversation?" Aasha Rani asked. "The one with that producer. Don't do it. Don't take the film. It will be a mistake." Aasha Rani was stunned. She couldn't believe that *Appa* was capable of not just overhearing but understanding a conversation being conducted in the next room. "Why not?" she asked *Appa*, more out of curiosity than any need for advice. "I told you—it's a mistake. You'll hurt your image. Your career. After that if you ever want to return as a heroine, it will be impossible. Nobody will take you; audiences won't accept you. Don't listen to these fellows. They are new to the game. New to the industry. They come here with their American ideas and try all their stunts. People get impressed. By fluke one or two films become hits. That's all. After that they disappear and nobody hears from them again. Why do you need this film? Not for money? If it is your ego, then wait for the right film. A big film. Where you are the central character. Audiences should be dazzled by you. They should feel excited. People should queue up at the theaters to see your film. It should be Aasha Rani's film. No one else's."

Aasha Rani looked fondly at her father. She was touched by his concern. And to discover that he was all there. "*Appa,* I am not going to jump into anything in a hurry," she assured him, "but I am bored. Films are all I know. What else can I do at this stage? I'm not educated. I'm not a clever businesswoman. How many choices do I have? Soon Sasha will grow up and go away. After five years, I still feel an outsider in New Zealand. Jay's family does not accept me. There's nothing I can do there. Jay needs me, he loves me, but he's a fairly independent person. He can also manage very well without me. Sometimes I feel lonely and restless. I miss the hectic life I had before. I miss the attention, the lights, the people, everything. I just want to try a film or two to see whether I enjoy the experience and whether audiences still want me. Look at other actresses who are my age, who started out with me. Where are they today? I'm still getting offers.

"Producers are not fools; they aren't doing me a favor. I'll take my time, but if I don't grab this opportunity, I'll always regret it. So many old actresses commit suicide, get depressed, start drinking. I don't want to end up like that." *Appa's* eyes rested on her with gentle understanding. When he spoke again he'd changed tack. "That girl, Sudha, even though she is my own flesh and blood, I'm afraid of her. Don't trust your sister. She's dangerous. Stay away from her," he said.

Even though *Amma* had accepted *Appa*'s arrival, it was clear, as the days went by, that she was not overjoyed at having *Appa* around. At first Aasha Rani thought that she didn't want to be saddled with a sick and broken man. An unnecessary impediment. But there was more to it than that. *Amma* had begun moping around the house. She was listless and easily distracted. Aasha Rani found it strange that she no longer barged in to make her decisions for her, when she discussed work with Kishenbhai and Jojo. Perhaps age was finally catching up with her, though she couldn't have been more than fifty. Mostly, Aasha Rani thought, having to stay under the same roof with *Appa* made her nervous. She had never forgiven her "husband," nor forgotten that he was the father of her children.

"Why don't you go to Madras? Krishna and Laxmi never work properly unless they have someone overseeing their work," Aasha Rani said. *Amma* hesitated. Aasha Rani could see she wanted to go. "I'll look after *Appa,*" Aasha Rani promised.

SUDHA CALLED AND ASKED her over. Aasha Rani tried making excuses, but they sounded lame even to herself. Sudha wouldn't take no for an answer. She called again and again till Aasha Rani gave in, reasoning that she'd dealt with tougher adversaries in the past. She was aware that among the many reasons she was putting off going to Sudha's house was an immediate problem: She wanted to avoid meeting Amar. She still experienced a tiny twitch of irritation when she thought of him and their short-lived affair. Of course, she'd gotten involved with him only to show Akshay she could get a new lover—a much younger one. Amar, too, had used her as his springboard to stardom. And she hadn't held it against him ("I've used Amar, too," she'd said to Linda—strictly off-the-record, but it had promptly jumped into print). Still, the thought of meeting him now, in the company of her younger sister, made her uncomfortable. In the end, she decided to overcome her feelings and accept the invitation. Besides, there were a lot of things she needed to sort out with Sudha. Several scores to be settled. Aasha Rani reminded herself to keep *Appa*'s warning in mind and not let Sudha get the better of her. No matter what. When Sudha phoned that evening she agreed to have tea with her the following day.

Aasha Rani reached Sudha's bungalow and took in the landscaped lawns, the artificial pond with the rockery and waterfall, the smartly dressed *durwan* at the gate, and the rest of the liveried staff. Sudha, she had to admit, had class.

Hearing the car roll up the driveway, Sudha rushed out to greet Aasha Rani. "I'm so happy to see you, *akka*," she said warmly. Aasha Rani hugged her back, and they went into the house. An involuntary gasp escaped Aasha Rani as she surveyed the luxurious home of her little sister. "All this. And so quickly?" she heard herself say. Sudha smiled. "I worked hard for it, *akka*," she said, and took Aasha Rani by the hand. "Let me show you around."

The conducted tour revealed things about her sister Aasha Rani would never have suspected. Sudha's home was grand—but not vulgarly so. Aasha Rani gazed openmouthed at the muted splendor around her. "Did you buy all these things yourself?" Aasha Rani asked. "No," Sudha answered easily, "I wouldn't lie to you. We got hold of a Delhi designer—he was involved with the Festivals of India in Paris and New York. Ranjit Jain. He's terrific. Very talented. Actually, Akshay Arora was the first to discover him. After he got his house done all the heroes and their wives wanted him." "How did you get him to agree?" Aasha Rani asked.

"Simple." Sudha smiled. "First, I slept with him; then I asked him to do my house, but Ranjit wanted Amar more than he wanted me. Don't look so shocked, *akka*. Anyway, I told Amar, 'If you want the best-looking bungalow in the industry, do it.' It's hardly as if it was the first time for Amar. Everyone knows about his weakness for the fishermen of Marvé and the fairer *chhokra* boys on the sets. Amar has also had a long affair with Hanif—you remember that villain? So, to cut a long story short, Amar agreed, quite willingly, and we got Ranjit at a discount," Sudha reminisced as she traced her fingers over an antique silver *jhoola* with Pathani pillow covers.

All of a sudden Aasha Rani was knocked over by a huge dog. She screamed with fright. Sudha said, "Down, Jackson, down." As she fondled the Great Dane's enormous head, she explained, "We need him for security. Too many fans, some of them quite crazy. They climb over the walls. Once I found a lunatic in my bedroom in the middle of the night. He said he'd come from Jalandhar only to get my autograph! I was so scared, I couldn't even scream."

As casually as she could, Aasha Rani asked, "Oh, really? So where was Amar?" "Amar was on outdoor location that night."

"And today?"

"Oh, today he's in town but not here. I sort of thought, you know, I didn't want to . . ."

"Want to what? Embarrass me?"

"*Akka,* please, let's not fight. You know how much it means to me to have you here. I want us to be friends."

"Friends? How can we be friends? When you say all those hateful things—and sound off to Linda in print?" Aasha Rani shot back angrily, quite forgetting her resolve to remain unruffled.

"You have stolen my money. Stolen my films. Stolen my lover. Been unkind to our parents. Lied, cheated and deceived everyone to get where you are today. And you want to be friends!"

"*Akka*, calm down. That magazine article—Linda just has something against you. Why are you losing your temper and blaming me, me alone? You don't know what *Amma* did to you. The sort of things she told me about you. The lies she made me tell just to get your roles. I was young. And innocent. Do you think it was I who schemed against you? Am I capable of it? It was *Amma* who threw Amar at me. She practically locked us up in a room together, like that song from *Bobby*. What could I do? He was the first man I got to know in Bombay. And, let me be frank, I did feel attracted to him. I thought, 'If *akka* found Amar so great, then he must really be something.' *Amma* sent me to the Shethji also. But he wasn't interested. You want to know something else? When *Amma* saw Jay, she phoned me the same night and said, 'He's very good-looking. Why don't you make friends with him? Call him to your house.' Actually, she forced me to phone him once or twice when you were out. Didn't he tell you? Ask him if you don't believe me. And your husband. I don't know whether I should tell you. I mean, he didn't exactly snub me or anything at the *mahurat* in Madras. I chatted him up. He sounded quite interested. Though he kept saying, 'Your sister will kill me if she finds out.' He even suggested that he route his flight back to New Zealand through Bombay. But fortunately Amar was at home on the dates that he suggested so I had to put him off. Amar can be jealous. *Bas*, that was the end. So, don't worry, nothing happened. You wanted to hear the truth; now you've heard it. *Chalo*, let's have tea. I've made your favorite *medhu vadas*."

Aasha Rani was shaking. She didn't know whether it was

shock, rage, frustration or disbelief. It wasn't possible, she told herself. Nothing else mattered. Not all the other betrayals. But Jay! Could Sudha be telling the truth? How could he have done this to her? And if he'd really done all that right under her nose, what must he be doing back home? Alone? She couldn't think straight. There was just no one she wanted to talk to. Especially not Sudha. She went through the evening numbly, making small talk, discussing Sudha's films. She wasn't an actress for nothing. But inwardly, she couldn't wait to get home and put a call through to Jay to find out the truth. Was it Sudha or was it *Amma*? Or was it both of them? Who was lying to her? And why?

THE PHONE CIRCUITS were down all evening and till late into the night. Aasha Rani couldn't sleep. Sudha's words had burned a hole through her heart. There was no one she could turn to. Aasha Rani realized how friendless and alone she really was. She stared out at the dark sea and she saw the distant lights of Marvé twinkling through the smog. She longed to hold Sasha. If only the bloody operator would get through. She started pacing around her house searching for something, anything, that would calm her nerves. Her eyes fell on the crystal decanter Akshay had once given her. It was beautiful, especially when the lights caused sparks to fly from it. Why not? she thought, and helped herself to a drink. It tasted foul. How old was the whiskey lying in it? Not even Scotch, something sour-tasting and awful. She nearly gagged. Akshay preferred single malts. Jay stuck to beer. Amar drank anything, even horse piss. Maybe the servants had finished the Scotch and refilled the decanter with hooch from the nearby "Aunty." And the sudden memory of Aunty made her laugh.

She remembered going to Aunty's illicit hooch corner with Akshay late one night and asking for a drink. Aunty had nearly had a heart attack seeing the two stars outside her humble bar. She'd hastily produced two chipped glasses and her best "*narangi*"—a potent drink made from fermented fruit skins, picked by garbage collectors and sold to distillers like Aunty. Akshay and Aasha Rani had gotten roaring drunk that night and had set off in search of *boti kababs* and *kalejis* at the small road-side grill outside the enormous Mahim Mosque. There was a fair on, and the small road alongside was packed with open-air food stalls selling everything from fried sweetbreads to entire charcoal-grilled goats. They'd gorged themselves, finishing off their meal with *malpooas* straight out of the large frying pans. "I want to be able to get into my costume tomorrow," Aasha Rani had giggled. Akshay had pinched her tummy and said, "Forget it. Let's both bunk and go to Lonavala."

How she missed Akshay. And the evenings they'd shared. She took another swig and switched on some music. Ghulam Ali. They used to listen to his *ghazals,* lying contentedly in each other's arms after making feverish love. Abruptly she stopped the music—and stopped herself from dissolving into tears.

This was hopeless. There was no point in waiting for the phone to ring. She didn't even feel like cross-examining Jay. In the state she was in, she knew she would handle it all wrong. Spit out words she'd regret later. Accuse him instead of asking him. No. That call could wait. On the spur of the moment, she picked up the business card near the telephone and called Jojo.

* * *

JOJO ARRIVED HALF AN HOUR later. Raring to go. "Do you want to waste time performing a mating dance or shall I start reading you bedtime stories straightaway?" he asked cockily. "Straightaway," she said, pointing to her room.

He was out of his T-shirt before she had shut the door. Brisk and businesslike. Worthy of any American professional. He climbed out of his jeans and folded them neatly. Once he had stripped and settled comfortably in bed, he looked around. "Yech!" he said. "What a ghastly room. And that pink! No wonder you can't sleep!" Aasha Rani had stripped down to her panties. "With me here so close to you all you see is the color of the room. What's the matter? Fag or something?" Jojo grabbed her hand and placed it on his erect penis. "Is that fag enough for you?"

There were no preliminaries, no sweet love words, no teasing, nothing. It was over in minutes, practically before it had even begun. Aasha Rani was very disappointed. "Is that all?" She pouted. Jojo lit a cigarette and said nonchalantly, "For starters."

"How long before the main course?" she asked. "Don't be greedy. Work up an appetite first," Jojo replied, and went back to his cigarette. "Anything decent in this pink house to quench a thirsty man? Perrier, Pernod, Chablis?" he wanted to know. Aasha Rani said coquettishly, "A pink gin goes best with the atmosphere, actually."

Aasha Rani tried to talk Jojo into changing her role as they lay in bed. "Why don't I play the other woman?" she suggested brightly. "Why don't you adapt the script a little so that she's not a teenager. I don't mind doing a negative role provided it's young." Jojo patted her bottom and said, "Don't try your little tricks with me, sweetheart. I'm not in the market for the world's oldest con. It's that role or nothing. If you want to withdraw your sexual favors in that context, you can do so right now. No hassles. But save your little number for someone else." Aasha Rani admired his cool, emotionless pragmatism. "You win," she said. "Where's the dotted line for me to sign on?"

THE MOVIE WAS A MISTAKE. The press was horribly unkind to her after the announcement appeared. Journalists dug out old photographs and jeered at her decision. "It's not fair," Aasha Rani fumed to Kishenbhai. "Why are they being so cruel? It's not as if I'm fifty. Look at that other female—the divorcée with the two kids—she's playing heroine roles and nobody is objecting. Why can't I?"

"This is the fate reserved for those at the top. You were a craze, not just an ordinary heroine. And then at the height of your fame, you ditched everybody and went away. Your fans felt let down. You can't do that with audiences," Kishenbhai said, trying to console her. "Journalists also felt *maha* let down. They are angry. They want to teach you a lesson. You should ignore all of them and do your role well.

"People can be fickle. Today they hate you. Tomorrow they'll love you. The industry works on this rule. That's why they call it a gambler's profession. Who knows, if your first comeback role clicks, you'll get another, better role. It all depends on the people—only they accept and only they reject.

"Gopal had come today—that bloody son of a bitch. He was making inquiries. Cheap inquiries. Saying, 'Aasha Rani must have come down to earth now. I hope she has swallowed her pride.' He was meaning something dirty, some *faltu* thing, you know what I mean. As if you are so hard up that you've become a call girl. I told him to go to hell. But he is in a powerful position. He has a standing in the industry today. Not like the old days. He may contact you directly and invite you to private parties to entertain clients and all that. But be careful. He mixes with dangerous people these days. All *goondas*. Amrishbhai is also in touch with him. You know about Abhijit, I suppose."

"No, I don't know anything about him. I lost touch completely. How is he?" Aasha Rani asked.

"Not good. He has turned out to be a wastrel. Amrishbhai did everything, tried everything. But the boy is now beyond help. Drugs, women, *sub kuch*. Gopal and his *goondas* have been hired to amuse and protect him. Keep him out of bigger trouble. They control his life totally. Supply him the girls and the drugs."

"What about his wife?" Aasha Rani asked. "She nearly lost her life during the delivery. Stillborn. Amrishbhai was with her throughout. Best doctors, best treatment. They gave up hope . . . But she pulled through somehow. Now she has another son, Aniket—Amrishbhai dotes on him. Since his father is canceled out, Aniket will inherit everything. Trust-*vust* all in his name." "That's interesting. Maybe I should try to meet Abhijit," Aasha Rani said almost to herself. Kishenbhai looked alarmed. "Do you want to die? Amrishbhai will murder you. Don't go near his son. He blames you for everything. His daughter-in-law's health included. Poor girl, she found out both of you had gone together. That night itself she started bleeding. And you know, she wasn't even in Bombay at that time. They brought her to the Breach Candy Hospital by a special helicopter. They thought she'd go that night itself. *Bahut* panic *ho gayaa*. She pulled through somehow, but the doctors told her they couldn't save the child. Now she spends all her time at Amrishbhai's office. He has made her the executive director of his other company—the one that manufactures textile machinery. Workers like her. She does a lot for them. So that is their life."

"But where does Abhijit stay?" Aasha Rani asked curiously. "He has been given a separate wing. Full bandobast, security and all that. Four, five times they've sent him abroad to cure him of his drug habit. For a few months he is all right. Then back again he falls into the pit. That is life."

THE CALL TO JAY came through three days later, by which time she'd slept with Jojo thrice, excluding two midday quickies. When she heard Jay's anxious voice at the other end, her anger dissipated. In any case, after Jojo, she had mentally tuned herself into believing that they were now "equal" somehow. When he finally heard her voice he shouted, "Sasha and I both love you and miss you madly. But don't worry. You just go ahead and do what you have to. How are *Appa* and *Amma*?

That was just the chance she was waiting for. "Aren't you going to ask me how Sudha is? After all, she's also family." There was an infinitesimal pause before he said, "Sure, so how is your sister?" Aasha Rani tried to restrain her words but they tripped out involuntarily. "I thought you might know."

"How might I know? Or are you trying to tell me something?" Jay said.

"I think you need to explain a few things to me first, Jay, darling." Aasha Rani was sarcastic. "Or am I going to be the last to know?"

"Know *what?*" Jay hollered.

"Look, darling, let's not play games. I want to hear it from you, and I want a straight answer. Is it true that you had an affair with my sister?"

"Are you completely crazy?" Jay all but exploded. "Me and Sudha? What's the matter with you? Have you been drinking or something? Whatever gave you such a mad idea?"

"She told me," Aasha Rani said, beginning to crumble, "that you and she had arranged to meet in Bombay while I was in Madras, and that Amar's presence spoiled it all."

"The bitch is lying! Sudha is lying. I don't know why she is doing this; perhaps she wants to hurt you. But you mustn't believe her. Do you have such little faith in me? Do you really think I'm such a lowdown heel that I would cheat on you with your own sister? Come off it, darling—it's you. There's nobody else. You must believe me. Don't let Sudha ruin your peace of mind. Ignore her. And if you like, I can join you next month. Sasha would like that very much," Jay said sincerely.

"Where is she? Is she asleep? I want to speak to her," Aasha Rani said, beginning to cry.

"Mommy, I need you. Come back. I don't like my nanny. She isn't like you. I don't like her cooking. I don't like anything!"

Aasha Rani's heart went out to her little girl. "Oh, my baby, I'm so sorry; we'll be together soon, but if you don't like your nanny why don't you ask Daddy to change her? I'm sure he could find another one." Sasha cried, "No, he can't. He won't. He likes the nanny. He told me so. They are together all the time and I'm alone. Mommy, please come . . ." The sentence remained unfinished as Jay suddenly came back on the line.

"Poor Sasha. She's really upset. You know your calls always

do that to her. She starts imagining things, making up stories. She's doing fine. Don't believe a word of what she just said. Her grades in school have gone up. And she's looking better than ever. I'll send you some pictures. Don't worry your head over us. You need to concentrate on your life right now. Tell me, have you signed that new film? The one you told me about last week?"

"Yes, I have. I signed it last week," Aasha Rani said slowly.

Aasha Rani was perturbed by Sasha's childish candor. Her daughter was a smart kid. Perhaps she was much too young to catch the real implications of what was happening between her daddy and the nanny. But soon, she'd cotton on. Aasha Rani wanted to protect her from that. She had no peace of mind these days. Jojo was a bedmate of sorts, but she didn't really like him. He treated sex like a casual sport. His bed manners were awful. And he did nothing for her ego as a woman. He made it clear he was there to use her as and when he felt like it. "Everything on my terms, baby," he said, making her feel like a hard-up, frustrated discard. The shooting hadn't started. She had all the time in the world. And *Appa* had once again withdrawn into his secret, silent world.

THE STREETS OF BANDRA were unusually crowded. Oh yes, she remembered, it was that time of the year—the Mount Mary Fair must be on. She checked with one of her Goan servants and he confirmed it. On an impulse she decided to brave the crowds and go. It was going to be a long, hot, arduous walk up a steep hill, jostling thousands of devotees on their way up to the magnificent church for a split-second glimpse of the Madonna. Like the

Mahim Novena, this annual event too attracted people from all faiths. The Mother was supposed to be extraordinarily generous in granting boons to true believers. Aasha Rani didn't really know what she wanted from Mother Mary—besides peace of mind.

What would she offer her in return? The others lit candles, took flowers and the usual wax images. It didn't matter. Aasha Rani wanted to forget herself, even if only temporarily. She wanted to smell the flowers, get scalded by the molten wax, and feel the thrust of sweaty bodies pressed against her own as the mass moved up, carried along by its own momentum, with stick-wielding *havaldars* to nudge the slower ones along.

She dressed in casual pants with a tucked-in shirt and put on a pair of sunglasses. She was just about to step out of the house when the phone rang. She sensed somehow that it was bad news. Who was it? Jay? Sasha? She heaved a sigh of relief when she heard the voice. It was neither. The caller, who refused to identify himself, spoke urgently: "Akshay is critical. He needs your prayers. He has been asking for you. Pray for him." Click. Whoever it was disconnected.

Aasha Rani felt her heart thudding against her rib cage. Oh God! So, this was it! She'd postponed thinking about Akshay ever since she had left London. She hadn't wanted to imagine what he was going through. She refused to acknowledge that he was never going to be well again. And now this call. It was uncanny. She shivered under her shirt and felt the hairs on her arm standing on end. If the caller had phoned even half a minute later, he would've missed her. Without waiting another minute, Aasha Rani rushed out of her house, knowing what she'd be asking the Mother for.

* * *

BANDRA HAD CHANGED so much in the time that she'd been away that she could no longer find her way around its tiny, labyrinthine lanes. She veered the car desperately in and out of unfamiliar bylanes as the news of Akshay began to sink in. Every familiar corner had been converted into either a clothing store or a restaurant. As if the locals lived only to shop and hog. Perhaps they did.

The car crawled along on its way to the Mother. The tiny fishing community had managed to hang on to its property, resisting all the attempts of real estate sharks to gobble it up as they'd gobbled up the rest of Bandra. Very few of the original little bungalows now remained. Aasha Rani remembered telling Akshay that they should buy one of those charming cottages with rosebushes in the front garden and a vegetable patch in the back, as their secret hideout. Akshay had laughed and said, "Consider it bought. You can have it as your next birthday present." Now, "Mon Repos" the tiled bungalow they'd jokingly picked out, had been replaced by an ugly high-rise. She was hypnotized by the clothes hanging from every possible display point, including the trees outside. At night, before all the neon was switched off, the garments waving and flapping in the sea breeze from hangers strung up on low branches looked like skeletons performing the dance of death. Or like shadows in a discotheque—depending on your mood.

Today, she could barely concentrate on the trendy boutiques with names like Anjusan, Bada Saab, Rich Bitch and First Lady. Beauty parlors, cake shops, croissant counters, video libraries, high-rise luxury apartments called San Remo, Hawaii, Sea Gull, Sea Wind and other equally evocative names. She looked toward Sea Rock hotel—where the action had shifted recently. Gone were the glory days of the old Juhu places. Nobody went to Sun 'n' Sand anymore except the loyalists. Sea Rock got all the big parties and all the big names. Srilalitha, the new star from the South, who was giving Sudha some hot competition, lived there permanently. So did Krishnakanth, the South's answer to Akshay. The rocky beach with the necking couples was still there, and Aasha Rani felt her heart lift as she saw stray couples necking between the crannies.

Once near the church she inched along in her car, with devout pedestrians banging on the rear windscreen. Although she knew what she was going to ask the Virgin for that evening, she knew her wish wouldn't be granted. It was too late.

Later she learned that Akshay had died at around the same time (she liked to believe it was the precise moment) that she stood in front of the main altar, praying fervently for his life.

AKSHAY'S DEATH WAS given the usual treatment. Fulsome front-page obits in the dailies, a sixty-second mention on Doordarshan's news bulletin with an additional sixty seconds devoted to industry reactions. Colleagues mouthed platitudes, costars cried prettily into their *pallavs*. The standard condolence messages from the chief minister ("Akshay Arora's death is a great loss to the film industry"). A message from the PM ("In this hour of grief we send our heartfelt sympathies to Mrs. Malini Arora, his grieving widow, and the other members of his family").

Watching Akshay's funeral proceedings on the TV set in her bedroom, Aasha Rani smiled bitterly. Nobody ever thinks of condoling the other woman. Nobody sympathizes with her. Not even in death.

She had known Akshay as nobody else had. And she had loved

him more than anyone else ever did. But today not a single person phoned to ask her how she had taken the sad news. She remained in Akshay's death what she had been in his life—a woman without status. A shadowy nobody. How silly she was being, she thought to herself. Why should anyone call on her? And then she began to laugh.

What was she grieving about? Someone should tell Yama, the God of Death, that he should have spared her the heartache, this overwhelming sense of loss. After all, what was Akshay to her? For in the eyes of the world, if he wasn't her husband he was nothing. Their closeness, their sense of belonging to each other, their unique chemistry, was of no interest to anybody. That part of her that reacted to Akshay was a part of her that only he culled out. That it had died with him concerned nobody. Because it was a facet of her that nobody even knew existed.

IT WAS ABOUT A FORTNIGHT after Akshay's death that the doorbell rang in the early hours of the morning, about three a.m. Aasha Rani didn't hear it for a long time. Finally, the insistent pounding on her pink door woke her up. It was *Appa*'s night nurse. She looked terror-stricken. "Madam, some men are outside. I didn't want to open the door but, but . . ." Before she could finish her sentence, three burly men pushed past her, demanding, "*Kahan hai woh kutta?*" She grabbed a bedsheet to cover herself and said, "*Kaunsa kutta? Idhar koi nahi hai.*"

The men walked in and started searching the room, looking under the bed, opening her cupboard, looking into the bathroom. One of the men ordered the others to check the entire house. Aasha Rani was paralyzed with fear. But she knew she had to do something. As surreptitiously as she could, she tried to open her side drawer, where her revolver was hidden. The man watching her lunged. She saw the glistening blade of his knife just in time and ducked. It gashed her arm, but not deeply. He caught her by the hair and dragged her off the bed. The other two had joined him by then, alerted by the scuffle. The man holding her said: "Jojo Saab's wife sends her *salaams* with this message: Stay miles away from Jojo—or the next time I'll spread open your legs and slash your vagina." Then he reached into the pocket of his denim jacket and produced a small bottle. "Acid," he told her, "*thobdé ke liye.*"

Just then *Appa* appeared at her door in his wheelchair. Aasha Rani screamed, "*Appa,* what are you doing here? Go back into your room." The men jostled the wheelchair roughly and jeered, "*Saala buddha*—do you want to watch while we rip your daughter to pieces? She is a *chudail,* a *bhootni,* after other people's husbands! Already killed one man and widowed our *bhabiji!* Now she wants to murder another victim!

"Don't be foolish enough to go to the police," they told the terrified man. "If you try any tricks, we'll get your daughter. We'll find out where she is and we'll find her even if we have to go to the ends of the earth. Neelum *memsaab* is a millionairess. Money is no problem." Then, very dramatically, the leader pulled out some papers from inside his jacket and showed them to Aasha Rani. "Your contract, *khatam,*" he said, as he flicked a lighter and, lighting it, tossed it at her. Aasha Rani jumped back and the flaming papers fell on her synthetic carpet, which burst into flame. The nurse had fled. *Amma* was in Madras, and the servant's room was much too far. There was no one to stop the ruffians who sauntered out casually.

It was only after they had left that Aasha Rani got her wits about her and rushed *Appa* out in his wheelchair. "Fire!" she screamed. "Please, someone, help!"

The two of them ran out on the deserted street. Aasha Rani felt numb with shock. *Appa*—oh my God! Would he be able to stand the shock? He looked terrified and bewildered. He was staring at her, his eyes wide with fear. God, a car, yes. That was what they needed immediately. Just then she heard the wail of police sirens. She didn't want to be there to explain anything, to fill out forms, to answer a million humiliating questions. She grabbed *Appa*'s wheelchair and pushed it faster and faster into the night.

When she was too tired to take another step she parked the wheelchair by the curb and, sitting on the pavement, put her face into her hands and wept uncontrollably. *Appa*'s fingers were in her tangled hair. "Don't cry, Viji," he whispered. "We'll find a way; have faith. Have faith in God." Aasha Rani turned to look at him. "God! What has he done for me, huh? Or you? Or *Amma*? Or any of us? We are finished, *Appa*; there is a curse on our family. Finished!" They were still sitting on the same pavement, with dawn breaking gently over a sleeping Bombay, when a car rolled up. It was full of teenage Bandra boys returning from a late-night party. They were pleasantly high. One of them stared at Aasha Rani and gulped. "Jesus! This looks like Aasha Rani." The others gazed at her drunkenly. "Can't be," one of them muttered. "Let's go before the cops arrive." They were about to drive off when Aasha Rani stopped them. "Please get us to Sea Rock," she pleaded. "It's just there—see? Two minutes away." Reluctantly they folded *Appa*'s wheelchair and squeezed them both inside the already packed car.

* * *

AASHA RANI CHECKED in with *Appa* and phoned Kishenbhai. She didn't feel like talking to Sudha or explaining anything to anyone. There were practical problems to be tackled first. She didn't even know where the property papers were or whether the house had insurance coverage. As it turned out, Kishenbhai didn't have a clue either. He told her vaguely that since Amirchand had been involved in the transaction, the papers were likely to be with him. When she phoned the Shethji, he didn't come on the line, but asked one of his goons to tell her to come over. Immediately.

This was their first meeting after five years. The first thing Aasha Rani noticed was how rapidly he had aged. He seemed bent and weak, as if he had shrunk physically. He thumped his chest and croaked, "Asthma. It's killing me." She touched his feet respectfully, as she had always done. "Problem *kya hai?*" he asked. She told him.

The Shethji shook his head. "You will never learn. Always getting into *lafdas* with the wrong men. First Amar, or was it Akshay? *Phir woh* Amrishbhai *ka bachcha*. I thought after your marriage you'd settle down. Get some sense. What are you doing with your life? I'm old now. Even my *goondas* have aged. The underworld is no longer what it used to be. There is no honor left. The old code is gone. All the rules are broken. Nobody cares anymore. Nobody even knows who is in charge. In the past, we had five main gangs and all the *dhanda* was divided fairly between them. Now, it's a free-for-all. New gangs come in, kill the old ones and take over the business. Politicians have lost their power. We need the *goondas* more than they need us. Do you understand? We can't fight elections without them. They are the ones who tell us what to do. Anyway, my advice to you is, get out. Go back to your husband and child. There is nothing for you here. Your *zamana* is over.

Nobody will give you roles. The market has changed. People want young *chidiyas,* not married women with children. If you ask me, you wait till your daughter is slightly older. Wait ten years and then make her a star. A *shandar* star."

Aasha Rani heard him out. His words were brutal. But accurate. She decided then and there that she would first fly to Madras and deposit *Appa* in *Amma*'s care. Then she would plan her trip home.

When Aasha Rani reached Madras, there was more bad news. *Amma* was not just depressed. She required medical attention. Aasha Rani felt exceedingly low. The doctors insisted *Amma* had had a nervous breakdown and needed hospitalization. "Forget it," said Aasha Rani. "My money's running out. Plus, I won't be able to shuttle between the two—a wheelchair patient at home and a hysterical woman in hospital." Laxmi was the only person who behaved in a supportive, helpful fashion, assuring Aasha Rani that she'd manage the house on her own, leaving her free to handle outside affairs. Finally, she phoned the Shethji and asked him to arrange for her Bombay house to be rented or sold. She told him she needed the money; the Shethji told her not to be hasty and that he would advance her however much money she needed. She should give the matter of selling her house some thought, and if she finally decided to do so he would help her. She was touched by and grateful for his magnanimity.

Sudha astonished everybody by not even bothering to phone. It was as if her family did not exist at all. Aasha Rani was far too preoccupied to bother about her, but she was bitter. Sudha had achieved her goals and didn't need her family any longer.

She wished Jay were around. If not Jay, then any other man. She loathed acknowledging her dependence on men, but at times like this they had their uses. She wasn't even sure she really wanted to go back to Jay. To Sasha, yes. But Jay? Had she ever loved him? Jay had been an out for her, an escape route. Perhaps he'd known that all along too. Perhaps she had been an out for him as well.

Aasha Rani had had ample time to think about and analyze her marriage. She was honest enough to admit that the years she had shared with Jay had been far better than any she might have shared with a film man. Or an Indian man, for that matter. Film men were the world's worst husbands. But their wives dared not squeak. How often had she ended up listening to sob stories of sadism, mental cruelty, physical battering and plain humiliation? She remembered a small-time actor's wife telling her, "*Bas* all these macho men are the same. One hit and they think they are supermen. My husband was a decent fellow till that film of his clicked. After that you should have seen the airs he put on, the *bhav* he *lagaoed*. One day he came home after shooting and I teasingly asked him, 'So how many heroines did you screw today?' Without a second's pause he struck me across the face and yelled, 'Bloody bitch! How dare you talk to me like that? Do you know who I am? The industry is at my feet. I have a fan club in Aurangabad. And you, what are you? Nothing. Keep your mouth shut in the future, understand? Or pack your bags and get out.' He said that with such hatred, I couldn't believe it. I was so stunned, I kept quiet. Then I said, 'Am I a maidservant in this house that you can dismiss me at will?' He looked at me and spat, '*Naukrani nahi to aur kya hai tu?*' My two young children heard all this and they started screaming with fright. 'Am I not the mother of your children?' I asked him. 'From this day that is all you are in this house. A glorified *ayah*. And remember, this is my house. I pay all the bills with my hard-earned money. If the arrangements don't suit you—get out. Look for someone else to shelter you.' Fortunately, I had my parents. And they didn't turn me out of their home. I went there with my children the same night. He didn't bother to find out where we'd gone or how we would survive. I've taken up a job in a boutique and manage somehow. He has become a drunk with not a single film in hand. Serves the bastard right."

Aasha Rani's fate wouldn't have been all that different. First she would have had to give up her career "for the sake of the marriage." And then, the hero in her life would have rapidly changed into a villain. She'd seen enough of that. Men heady with power and success, treating their wives like dispensable commodities. Why did these men ever marry? she wondered. Why did Akshay? "For status, prestige and acceptability," Kishenbhai had once told her. "A successful man in any field needs a grand home. A wife to look after it. Two good-looking children—a boy and a girl—and all the other domestic trappings."

The bigger the hero, the more miserable his wife, mused Aasha Rani. In fact, she hardly ever saw him. Some visited their husbands on weekends, on outdoor locations. But it inhibited the heroine and made the hero tense. So the wives were pulled out of obscurity only on "important" functions such as premieres, festivals and other VIP affairs which called for social conformity. Then she was expected to reflect her husband's position in the industry and behave in accordance with his status—small, tight smiles for lesser beings, floor-sweeping *namaskars* for the biggies, blank looks for the small fry.

Aasha Rani shuddered at the memories of all the stages, recalling in particular her experiences when she was a nobody, not even a glorified extra in the industry. How different the very same people had been when she became a star. Fawning and fussing all over her. Including those slimy photographers. Two-*paisa* chaps who didn't bother to look in her direction when she'd hang around the studios. Suddenly they were there with flashbulbs popping, pleading, "Aasha Raniji, *bas iss taraf.* Thank you, *ji.*"

It was Akshay who had taught her to tackle them all. "Fix the bastards who treated you badly," he had said. "Teach them a lesson they'll never forget." He'd been through it all himself. And Akshay was one person who rarely forgot. Or forgave. What would her life have been like if she'd married him? At one point that thought used to obsess her. She'd made such a fool of herself. Journalists had noticed and commented on her *mangalsutra, sindhoor* and bangles. Akshay had admonished her, embarrassed by all the show: Are you crazy? Why are you doing all this? For heaven's sake, stop it. What is all this rubbish? You want people to jump to the wrong conclusion or what?" Aasha Rani had smiled a secret smile and answered mysteriously, irritatingly, "Have I told anyone that you gave these to me? Think of me as a madwoman. If someone asks, I say I bought the *mangalsutra* for myself, and I wear *sindhoor* in my hair because I want to start a new fashion. Why should it embarrass you?"

"Do what you want then. Suit yourself. If Malini asks me anything, I'll deny even knowing you. Or I'll tell her you have gone mad. Crazy. See a psychiatrist in any case—you need help," Akshay had snapped. Now, looking back on that phase, she realized how impulsive and immature she'd been. How foolish and naive. Even her "second marriage" plan. Sure, other women in the industry had done it. Successfully, too, people said. But to the world they remained single women and unmarried mothers leading bleak lives without legal sanction. And what did the farce add up to publicly? Did their men acknowledge them? No. What about the children of these unusual arrangements? They were all still too young. They'd know how it felt to be illegitimate later. As she had.

Sometimes she felt like asking *Appa* why he'd treated her mother that way. Once she'd tried. *Appa* had shaken his head sadly and replied, "Men are cruel. Very cruel. There is no justice in this world. And no equality between men and women. Don't believe that a marriage alters that balance. Sometimes it only makes it worse. Power lies with the purse—remember that. Whoever controls that controls the relationship. When you review your own marriage, you will realize the truth of what I'm saying. The only difference is that some men can control their true feelings of superiority. These men are called 'cultured.' Other men display them openly. They make their wives feel under constant obligation. That is the best way to keep them suppressed. Your husband falls in the first category. But wait, maybe a day will come when you will have more money. And then you will see him change. Take my advice; start something to call your own. Do not remain dependent on him indefinitely. It's been all right so far. Now your child is older. You have more time. You are intelligent. And still young. Come back to live in your own country amidst your own people. Come back to Madras. Revive the studio. You will make a success of it. I'm sure."

Aasha Rani had hung on to those words. Maybe *Appa* was right. But she lacked the will to push herself into anything. She was afraid of failure and rejection. Jay had taken care of everything for five years, and she'd enjoyed that. It was true that she had no idea about the state of their domestic finances. Jay hadn't been forthcoming about such things. "Why do you want to bother your pretty little head with all that? Leave it to me. You just relax, enjoy yourself, make me a good wife, be a good mother. That's what being a woman is all about," he had said.

Aasha Rani had been grateful for that. It had felt like an unheard-of luxury to have someone take charge and take over so completely. She was so tired of running at that point.

But today was different. She lacked confidence. And it was true she was exhausted by all the problems that seemed to have converged on her, but, strangely, she'd never felt better. Perhaps the Jojo thing was what had jolted her out of the rut. Made her come to terms with life as it was. No illusions. No pretense. Her career as a movie star was unambiguously over. That much she accepted. She was even prepared to confront the fact that her marriage was over. At least, the old familiar marriage. If Jay and she were to go on, it would be on a fresh footing. With renegotiated terms. Maybe he'd want to opt out of the new deal. Maybe she would. But at least a few things were clearer. She had to come back to India. And more specifically, to Madras. She belonged there. Not Bombay. And certainly not Wellington. Madras. Madras with its unbearable summer heat, the crowds and chaos. Suddenly Aasha Rani knew she would want to hear temple bells for the rest of her life. Temple bells, fragrant jasmine, *upma* in the afternoon and crisp *dosas* at dawn. She wasn't running anymore. But first, there was unfinished business to attend to.

Reluctantly, she booked her flight back to New Zealand. Then she called Kishenbhai and asked him to keep an eye on her house while she was away. On an impulse, she bought a silk *pavadai* for

Sasha and some cheap trinkets to go with it. Aasha Rani imagined her daughter in the traditional long skirt little girls all over South India wore with such grace. Sasha would look charming in one. She bought her silver anklets, hair ornaments, bangles, necklaces, sandalwood soaps and a tiny elephant with holes in its back to hold joss sticks. Would Jay find all this strange? Why should he? He was no stranger to India. He claimed he loved it. Wasn't that why he'd married her in the first place?

Gopalakrishnan

AASHA RANI HATED FLYING ALONE. AND THIS TIME SHE WAS even more resentful than usual. Her homecoming was making her jittery. And she was feeling wretched about what she'd left behind. The stewardess came up solicitously once or twice to offer her the usual pampering first-class passengers took so much for granted. "Champagne? Orange juice? Caviar? Extra pillow? Blanket?" Aasha Rani waved her off wearily. Her mind was on Sasha, the little girl she no longer seemed to know. Just then Aasha Rani heard a voice at her elbow. It was the stewardess again, carrying a glass of chilled wine. "I'm sorry to disturb you, madam, but the gentleman in row four asked me to send you this glass of wine with his compliments." Aasha Rani turned around to look.

Oh God! Aasha Rani groaned. Not another letch who has recognized me and wants company on the flight. She smiled politely at the stewardess and declined the drink. "No, thank you, I don't drink. And I *am* awfully tired." The stewardess shrugged and took the glass back. The big, burly man—a swarthy, bearded Indian—looked disappointed. But undeterred. He unbuckled his seat belt and ambled over with a big friendly grin on his face, his hands raised in mock defense. "Look," he said in Tamil, "before you say anything or ask me to get out . . . I'm an old friend of your father's. Gopalakrishnan. No, that's not correct. Not a friend. I used to work for him as a production assistant. I left him just before the tragedy, the accident, his stroke. I decided to go west and start my own production company to make documentaries and other programs for cable TV. I also have a side business in garments. I live in New Jersey with my family. My wife is American. She helps me. We have two young children. I'm on my way to Papua New Guinea. New markets, you know. We people can't stay in one place. I'm on the move all the time. And you?" Aasha Rani wasn't at all sure she wanted to get into an extended discussion with this stranger. She didn't even believe his old yarn about knowing *Appa* and all that. She figured he was a rich, lonely businessman on a lonely trip to some foreign land. Seeing her, he'd decided to invent a small story just to break the ice and get talking. There were a lot of hopeful men out there, as she'd discovered a long while ago. Men who chatted up strange women on the off chance that they could jump into bed later. If not, it was still time better spent than reading *Fortune* and drinking martinis, with calf muscle cramps and swelling feet.

Aasha Rani wiggled her toes encased in the airline tube socks. At least this man spoke Tamil. Of course, there was no rule that a friend of one's father was necessarily a gentleman with paternal inclinations. On the contrary, she'd experienced distinctly nonpaternal vibes from *Appa*'s friends ever since she could remember. In those days child abuse was not an issue. In India it still wasn't. Aasha Rani looked again at the stranger and noticed his strong white teeth. He reminded her of *Appa*'s old friends and colleagues. Somewhat like the man who had taken her to the circus when she was no more than seven years old.

She remembered queuing up outside the enormous tent with

this man holding her hand. Soon her hand had been slyly slipped into his *mundu*. And his hand had been replaced by what felt like a firm, hard stick. Aasha Rani had wanted to scream. But she was terrified. She knew instinctively that there was something wrong with the way this "uncle" was behaving. But what could she do? She was much too terrified to let go in case he hit her. So she had hung on for what seemed like an eternity. Finally, he had turned limp and she had felt her small hand go damp with something sticky and smelly. He had nonchalantly wiped her fingers on his *mundu* and started to chat about the performing elephants and tigers. She had felt sick. Physically sick. Finally, she'd turned to him and said, "*Anna,* I want to go home. I don't want to see the circus. I'm not feeling well." He'd picked her up and asked solicitously, "Not well? What's wrong?" "Nothing," she'd answered, scared. "My stomach is paining." She thought he'd looked very relieved as he'd said, "All right. In that case, let us go home."

And now here was this man with his American wife left behind in New Jersey asking her if he could sit in the empty seat beside her. Actually, it was unimportant whether or not he was married. Whether he had a Wendy or a Lindy waiting for him in Upper Montclair with blueberry muffins and Yankee coffee. This was now, and she decided that maybe it wouldn't be a bad idea to have him keep her company. Get her mind off her problem.

The stranger did most of the talking, asking her about her life, even though it was obvious he knew quite a lot about it already. The stewardess came back to check whether they needed anything. Gopalakrishnan asked for champagne. There were just four other people in their section. "Cheers," he said, holding his glass aloft, "to our reunion." She found that funny and said so: "Why reunion? We haven't met before." "OK, cheers to our union then." Gopalakrishnan laughed as they clinked glasses.

By her third glass, Aasha Rani was feeling distinctly woozy. As a rule, she rarely accepted a drink on flights, since she knew how dehydrated it made her feel. But tonight was different. She needed something to lift her spirits. To help her forget Bombay. And the fact that Akshay was dead.

She didn't know what she was going back to. But it felt safe up here. She wanted to remain like this—forever in limbo—soaring high with an attractive, caring man who flashed his white teeth and tucked a blanket around her knees. "Just relax," he kept saying. "Here, give me your feet; I give an excellent toe massage." Obediently she removed the armrest between them and, sliding sideways, swung her legs over. He placed an air pillow under her head. "Close your eyes. Don't be tense." He spoke slowly, hypnotically. "Leave yourself in my hands. I have trained with Chinese experts. I know all the pressure spots, especially in a woman's beautiful body. My wife often tells me that if our business fails, I could always set up a relaxation center and give erotic massages to lonely dowagers."

Aasha Rani wasn't even listening. She had succumbed totally to the tips of his magic fingers. He pressed the balls of her feet, caressing the arches with his strong thumbs. Soon his hands went higher. Up, past the the ankles and on toward her calves. Oh, that felt wonderful. She felt herself relax. Her shot nerves were tranquilized, her aching muscles lulled. His fingers had magical powers. Gently, surely, expertly he rubbed her legs till they felt like jelly, all tingly and soft. Now he was working on her lower thighs. She felt herself drifting off while, below her waist, something incredible was happening. He stayed at that spot for so long that finally she grabbed his hands and placed them between her legs and over her belly. "Do it," she moaned. "I can't bear to wait."

"No," he said firmly. "There is more. You aren't ready yet."

"Not ready?" she asked in genuine surprise. "Look at this," she said, and parted her legs. She took his hand and inserted it into herself.

"Not yet," he repeated obstinately, and licked the hand that had entered her so easily. He continued massaging her thighs and belly while she arched her back and demanded his hand once more.

Aasha Rani had never experienced such hunger, such intensity. She wanted this man. Passionately. She hated the thought that she'd have to restrain herself and not scratch, scream and thrash around with him inside her. "Finish me off quickly," she pleaded, "or I'll die." "No, you won't," he said, and his head disappeared under the blanket. Now she could feel his hot tongue on her—probing, searching, stabbing and withdrawing just as she was ready to come.

"Pass me my glass," he ordered. He took a sip of champagne and then plunged his cold tongue into her. "Do you like that? Does it burn?" he asked.

"I prefer your taste. I like your hot breath, the feel of your beard; don't stop now!" she cried.

"Go to the loo and wait for me there," he ordered.

"I can't. My legs will collapse," Aasha Rani groaned.

"No, they won't. It will be worth it."

She tottered to her feet and just about made it. A minute later he had joined her.

"Sit there," he said, and plonked her near the washbasin. "Now open your legs wide." She obeyed, and with one swift, smooth move he was inside her, thrusting expertly. "Hold my neck. And I'll hang on to your bottom," he said, and slid his hands under her, almost lifting her up and carrying her in his arms like one would a child. "Now, let yourself go. I'll rock you back and forth and you contract in time with me." They began a swinging motion that was so perfectly coordinated, Aasha Rani felt they'd done away with gravity. They seemed to be afloat in space, flying weightlessly. Both of them came together, with such force that the tiny toilet shuddered noisily with the impact.

"First time?" Gopalakrishnan asked her with a wicked smile. "No, second," she lied, then corrected herself. "There are two firsts, actually. One, at thirty thousand feet and two, a Tamilian."

"Let's celebrate then." He laughed. "No," said Aasha Rani more soberly. "Let's not. Let's just forget it ever happened." "Why?" he asked, pushing back a strand of hair from her damp brow.

"Because, oh, I don't know, what's the point? Life is complicated enough anyway, and I know I'll never see you again. Perhaps that's how it was meant to be." "I'm not so sure," Gopalakrishnan said tenderly, and released her.

THE HOMECOMING WAS MORE PLEASANT than Aasha Rani had expected. Jay and Sasha both looked delighted to see her. As she hugged and kissed them, Gopalakrishnan stopped his baggage trolley next to Aasha Rani and handed her his business card, saying, "Just in case you ever need to consult a Chinese expert again." She glared at him and slipped the card into her handbag. "Who is the stud?" Jay asked.

Aasha Rani feigned puzzlement. "Stud? Oh, that was a friend of my father's."

Jay looked disbelievingly at the broad back clad in a natty business suit. "That man—*Appa*'s friend?"

"Yes," said Aasha Rani sweetly, "and an ex-employee."

"What was he teaching the old man—Chinese?"

"In a sense," Aasha Rani replied. "He specializes in certain healing techniques he picked up from a Chinese master."

"I'll be damned," said Jay, shaking his head.

Sasha had been staring at her mother. "Mommy, you look different."

"Why? What's so different about me?" Aasha Rani laughed.

"I don't know . . . no, yes, I know, you look Indian," Sasha said.

Aasha Rani stared at her in surprise. "Well, darling, that's what I am."

"No, you are not. At least, I didn't think you were till Alice told me. And Granny too. So then, what am I?"

Aasha Rani looked at Jay. "Ask your father."

"He told me to ask you," Sasha insisted.

"Well, darling, let me see, your dad is from New Zealand and your mommy from India. I guess that makes you half-and-half."

Sasha suddenly stomped her foot and cried, "I don't want to be a bloody Indian. I don't want to be a blackie."

Aasha Rani was too shocked to respond. She hugged her close and whispered into her hair, "It's OK, darling, it's all right. You can be anything or anyone you want to be."

Sasha was sobbing. "Alice told me you'd say I was Indian. She told me. Well, I hate being Indian. I don't like Indians. I don't like India. And I never want to go back."

Aasha Rani continued to hold her while Jay tried to change the subject, saying, "Come on, big girl. Aren't you going to show Mommy all the flowers we have gotten for her? And the 'welcome home' cake in the oven? All the horses are waiting. And the dogs. We're going to have a big barbecue party tonight, aren't we, doll?"

But Sasha wouldn't stop crying. "I don't want a party. I don't want anything. I hate my mommy. I hate her clothes and her tummy showing and and everything."

"I suppose it really is my fault. I should have told her from the start. I should have behaved like an Indian. Been myself. Now she is feeling let down," Aasha Rani said worriedly to Jay when they reached home. "She thinks I lied to her all along. And in a sense, that's true. I *did* lie to her. God! I'm feeling so guilty and awful. What am I going to do?"

"Well," said Jay patiently, "to begin with, you are going to take a long, hot shower with me. And dress up for the party. I've invited a few of our neighbors, Mum and Dad, Alice—Sasha's nanny—that couple we'd met a few times in the Italian restaurant. Remember them?"

Aasha Rani was exhausted. And ready to cry. "Jay, darling, couldn't this have waited? I mean, it was a long flight and I am feeling pooped. A party? Tonight? Since when have you started hobnobbing with the neighbors?"

"Oh, we've been to a couple of dances, you know, and Halloween parties, costume things. I thought it was important for Sasha not to be lonely. She needs friends. We are isolated enough out here as it is."

"That's true. It was sweet of you to arrange all that for her. By the way, who is the 'we'?" Aasha Rani asked. "Sasha and her nanny, Alice?"

Jay tried to kiss her. "Don't be silly, darling. How could I handle the child all on my own? Besides, Sasha insisted on her coming along."

"Handle Sasha on your own? You've done it before. And she was much younger then. What is there to 'handle' now? She doesn't wear nappies; she's perfectly potty trained."

"It's not that. I think she needed a mother figure," Jay explained.

"Sure," said Aasha Rani. "And you, I suppose, needed a wife figure. Or am I being bitchy?"

"No, you're not. You are just being jealous. I can understand. But wait till you meet her nanny. She's such a sweet girl. She's the one who got all the flowers and arranged to bake the cake, getting Sasha to help her with everything. Even the barbecue was her idea. I thought that was really great, especially since Mum and Dad agreed to come. And Sasha's aunts, cousins. Family, after all, is family."

Aasha Rani was too tired to get into an argument. She nodded. "You are right. I'm being ridiculous! Poor Sasha, and poor you. Managing all by yourselves while Mommy was away."

Jay kissed her on the forehead and said cheerily, "That's my girl. Come on; take off your clothes. I'm dying to get you naked and look for all those moles."

Sasha didn't want Aasha Rani to wear a sari for the party. "It looks awful, Mommy," she kept saying. Aasha Rani decided to please her and wore jeans instead. Jay looked happy about the decision as well. "A sari, well, it's a bit too exotic for the locals, you know, all the tum-tum showing. And your sexy belly button! It's such an informal crowd. Let's keep the sari for our special evening. You haven't forgotten the wedding anniversary, have you?"

Aasha Rani hadn't forgotten. But she found no reason to be enthusiastic about it either.

Alice, the nanny, showed up at six in the evening, all fresh and sweet in a summer dress. She was wholesome-looking—like newly baked bread. Clean, well scrubbed, with flushed cheeks and eyes the color of bluebells. Sasha clung to her skirt excitedly. "Where were you today? Why didn't you come in the morning? I didn't eat breakfast when I didn't see you," she chirped.

Jay looked embarrassed and left the room to do some last-minute shopping for the party. Aasha Rani looked the young girl coolly in the eye. "You were sleeping with my husband, weren't you?" she asked. "Don't worry. I'm not going to ask him. And I'm not going to hit you or anything. But I want you out of this house and out of our lives this minute. I'll mail you your wages. But get out now!"

Sasha began weeping, even though it was obvious she didn't get the true import of the conversation. But the hostility in Aasha Rani's voice had been apparent, and the fact that she'd asked Alice to leave. She was enraged and shaking with hostility. "Mommy, you can't do that. You can't ask Nanny to go. I'll tell Daddy. I'll tell Grandma. I'll tell everybody. If you don't like her, you go. Go back to India. Go and wear saris there and act in all those silly films. I don't want you. I don't need you. I only want my nanny. I want to cuddle with her in the night and go to Daddy's room in the morning to wake her up. I hate you, I hate you, I hate you."

Aasha Rani tried to hold Sasha's hand. But she pulled herself away violently. "Don't touch me. I'm not your daughter. I don't want to be your daughter." Aasha Rani knew it was no use trying to reach out to her. Sasha needed time. Lots of time. Aasha Rani only hoped that she'd get it from her.

When Jay got back an hour later, he was shocked to find Sasha sulking in her room. Aasha Rani was sitting calmly tinkering with the piano in the living room. "What happened?" he demanded. "Where's Alice?" "I sacked her," Aasha Rani said, still playing the piano.

Jay strode over and grabbed her arm. "What? What do you mean, you sacked her? Who are you to do that? What about Sasha?"

"You mean, what about *you*? Sasha will be fine eventually. She's a little upset now, which is understandable. But you? How will you manage?"

Jay sank into a deep armchair and said calmly, "Look, darling, we need to talk. Tonight is the wrong night. Still . . . I won't bother to deny that she and I were having an affair—well, it's a little more than that. I won't even try to pass it off as a fling, a passing fancy. I love the girl. She loves me. And she loves Sasha. Things just worked out that way. I hadn't planned it. I love you too, but differently. We've grown apart. We've been drifting off for quite a while now. I guess it was Sasha who was the common factor. Now that she's older and has a mind of her own, we should allow her to choose the sort of life she wants for herself.

"Baby, I know you. I get the feeling you want to go back to India. More specifically, to Madras. Your exile is over. You don't need to hide thousands of miles away any longer. You are ready to face India and your people. Perhaps on your own terms this time. It's going to be difficult. More for you than for me. I'll be there no matter what. I will provide all that is required to re-settle you, get you back onto the fast track. But it's over between us as husband and wife. I think you are realistic enough to ac-knowledge that much. Let's not make it any harder on ourselves than is necessary. We've both been bruised—in different ways and by different people. I'm ready to start all over again. I know you can do it too."

Aasha Rani stared at the framed photograph of herself on the piano. She wanted to smash it. Wreck everything. Set the house on fire. Destroy Jay. Kill the nanny. And finally maybe take her own life. But there was Sasha. Poor, innocent Sasha. Trapped in this messy web of adult lies and deceit. No. There was no real choice. Aasha Rani had to accept what Jay was telling her. But first, there was the barbecue to enjoy. And Jay's family and friends. Aasha Rani would dazzle and disarm them all tonight. She would show them she was not just a "bloody native," some tribal woman from the back of the beyond.

Aasha Rani went back to her room and chose a flashy sari—the sparkling pink one with sequins all over—and wondered whether the blouse would fit her fuller figure. She tried it on. A bit tight over the bust, but wearable. She applied her makeup carefully, making sure to match the *bindi* with the tiny turquoise motifs embroidered on her sari. She did her eyes differently—lining them with *kaajal,* accenting them in a way that was a far cry from the way the haughty models in those Revlon/Dior ads did. But there was something missing. Jewelry? She didn't have much here. Flowers? Oh yes. She plucked a large rose from a vase and tucked it in her hair.

Jay looked up when Aasha Rani walked down the stairs. It was early evening, and the light was beginning to fade. "My God, darling, you look dazzling!" he said, drawing in his breath. She looked at him evenly and said a soft thank-you. They both knew that what she really meant was farewell.

Sasha came running up but stopped short at the sight of Aasha

Rani. "Mommy!" she protested. "I told you not to wear that. I told you, I told you, I told you," she wailed. Aasha Rani tried to calm her. She didn't want to get provoked or provoke the little girl further. "Darling, I changed my mind . . . Besides, I couldn't get into my old jeans; I've put on too much weight," she said, trying to placate her distraught daughter. Sasha flounced off and began fussing with the plates.

The guests began to trickle in. She recognized a few of them from her outings into town. They were polite but distant with her, though they were boisterous and friendly with Sasha and Jay. Aasha Rani watched her parents-in-law enter the living room briskly, accompanied by Jay's unmarried sister. She noticed the shadow that crossed their faces and the way their expressions changed when they saw her. Jay's mother smiled tightly and said, "Good to see you, Aasha Rani. Sasha sure missed you a whole lot." It didn't skip Aasha Rani's notice that she hadn't included her son. At least she was being honest. The father stood back and surveyed her. "Well, well, well, my dear. Aren't we looking grand. Just like an Indian movie star, ha ha ha," he guffawed. Aasha Rani joined in his laughter and took his hand. "Let's fix you a drink," she said.

Years of golf and riding had ensured Jay's father a slim physique. He was an extremely fit sixty, whose vivid tan was in sharp contrast to his skeletal wife's ghostly pallor.

Jay was being charming to everybody and was getting the barbecue going. Aasha Rani helped herself to another glass of Chardonnay. "Nice wine, huh?" she heard someone at her elbow say. It was her father-in-law. Jay turned up the music. It was an Australian rock band singing a cover of "Love to Love You, Baby." Complete with the moans and groans.

Jay's father wiggled his bottom and shook his leg. "Dance?" he asked. "Later, perhaps," she said. He took her by the arm and led her to the edge of the patio. "You're a very beautiful woman," he whispered into her ear appreciatively. Aasha Rani looked him in the eyes. "Thank you. That's the first nice thing I've heard since my arrival here."

They sat down and watched as more people strolled in and exchanged raucous greetings. Some of them had begun gyrating on the floor. She felt her father-in-law's hot breath on her neck. "You're a sexy woman," he said, his eyes gleaming. Reaching across the small folding table, he placed his hand over hers. "Jay is a lucky guy. We always thought he was a sissy, shy with the ladies, if you know what I mean. And look at you! I mean, I'm sure you need a really hot-blooded man in your bed." His hand over hers tightened its grip as he squeezed it suggestively. She felt his knees rub against hers—the rough texture of his jeans cutting through the flimsy layers of her sari. He was staring at her partially exposed cleavage, and she watched as his thick tongue darted out and ran over his lips. Contemptuously Aasha Rani thought of the fashionable bag of bones her father-in-law went to bed with every night. Of Jay's flat-chested sister. And her own spineless husband who was doing the Birdy dance on the small wooden floor with Sasha.

She felt her father-in-law's free hand feeling her thigh under the table. The trees began to whirl around her. She saw undisguised desire in his eyes as he leaned toward her. "What's the matter, dear? Feeling giddy?"

She nodded her head. "It's the wine, oh God, the bloody wine. It's everybody and everything. I hate it; I hate you." Aasha Rani tried to get to her feet, but she lost her balance and spilled the contents of her glass on Jay's father. Aasha Rani began to giggle. "There, that should cool you off, you horny son of a bitch." And she chucked what remained in her glass right onto his bulging crotch.

AASHA RANI HAD ALWAYS RESISTED wearing ethnic ensembles abroad. She just found it so much simpler to merge with the masses than to be ogled like some leftover exhibit from the Festival of India. Not that adopting a Westernized appearance had helped. It had just confused her little daughter. Maybe someday Sasha would forgive her—maybe even understand and accept her, as she had *Amma* and *Appa*.

She was waiting in the departure lounge with Jay and Sasha. Sasha was holding on to Jay's hand and was watching her mother adjust the pleats of her brilliant blue-green Kanjeevaram sari. The flight to London was announced, and the passengers got ready for the security check. Aasha Rani went up to Sasha and hugged her tight. Her baby. How she would miss her. Sasha quietly handed her a folded, grubby piece of paper—and was gone. It was as she was walking to the plane that she unfolded the paper. On it was a clumsily drawn picture of a lady with a huge *bindi,* in a sari. Under it Sasha had printed, "My Mommy," in shaky letters.

Shonali ≈

AASHA RANI STARED OUT OF THE WINDOW AS HER CAB ROLLED
through the still-deserted streets of London in the early hours
of the morning. London had been a decision that she hadn't fully
thought through. All she had known at the time was that after
her showdown with Jay, she couldn't bear going back to Madras
with the problems of *Amma* and *Appa* and an empty house in Bombay. She'd felt defeated and utterly alone, and all she'd wanted to
do was run and hide. London was as good a place as any. And then
Jay had come up with an unexpectedly generous offer. He had a
tiny flat in London, and she was welcome to stay there for as long
as she wanted. Plus he offered her an allowance. Unmindful of the
damage to her ego, she'd not taken time to grab the lifeline he offered. Now that she was here she would have to make some hard
decisions. The first was an obvious one: If she was planning to stay
here for a while, she would have to find a job that would not only
supplement Jay's allowance but also keep her occupied. Perhaps a
crash course in hairdressing or one in makeup and grooming. The
world was full of opportunities and possibilities. The trick was to
grab them at the right time.

As it turned out, Aasha Rani didn't have to slog or scrounge at
all. Within the first month in London, on a gray, drippy day, as

she drifted from one Harrods makeup counter to the next, trying on the latest in lipsticks and eyeshadows, a stunningly attractive Indian woman—very chic and very well dressed—walked up to her. "You're Aasha Rani, aren't you?" she asked. "I would have recognized that incredible face anywhere."

Aasha Rani took in the sleek, smiling, superbly groomed creature standing in front of her and smiled uncertainly. The woman held out her hand. "Hi! I'm Shonali Leclerc; I'm from India too. Originally. Now I live and work in London, Paris, New York—you know."

Aasha Rani didn't quite know how to react to this stunning stranger. Her outfit was so elegant and yet so trampy. She could have been a countess or a hooker. Cream-colored crepe de chine with ropes and ropes of faux pearls. The jewelry was somewhat exaggerated, but the overall effect breathtaking. Aasha Rani noticed her silk stockings and the tiny feet fitting neatly into beige shoes with four-inch heels. The bag looked expensive, as did the professionally done coiffeur. Shonali was as dusky as Aasha Rani, but her makeup was done to a high gloss, giving her a sheen that blended with her clothes. She was exotic but not obviously so. Her figure was ripe and full, with the smallest waist Aasha Rani had ever seen. The polished buckle of her belt drew attention to its perfect proportion and emphasized the shapely hips that flared under it. She moved gracefully, like a Thai dancer, and smiled with her eyes.

Aasha Rani just kept staring stupidly. Finally she heard herself say, "Oh, I see. So nice meeting you."

"Are you alone? Busy?"

"Not really," Aasha Rani said.

"Shall we have tea somewhere?" Shonali asked.

She wished she'd bothered a little with her own appearance that morning. She was looking like an absolute hag, she knew. She'd woken up feeling depressed. Her face was puffy, thanks to the pills she'd popped, and the day was drippy and miserable. She didn't know what she wanted to do with herself that day. Not that the morning was any different from the ones that had preceded it. Over two weeks in London and still looking for the key to the future. She'd applied to a few salons. All the courses cost a packet. But money was not really the problem. She just couldn't seem to shake off her apathy. She'd even toyed with the idea of phoning Malini. Now, with Akshay out of the way, perhaps she'd be less hostile. She'd heard Malini had tentatively resumed her career and was giving small concerts in London. She was also going back to recording some of her old hits. Apparently she'd pulled out of the tragedy quite unscarred. Not that that surprised Aasha Rani, who'd always found Malini cold and unfeeling.

Aasha Rani had dialed her number a couple of times and then rung off. And now, here she was with a gorgeous stranger having tea at Churchill's just off Oxford Street. Shonali waved to a couple of Arabs who came over and said a few soft words in Arabic. Shonali introduced Aasha Rani to them. Later she casually told her that they were her "clients."

Aasha Rani took some time to pluck up the nerve to ask her newly acquired friend what exactly it was that she did. Shonali lit a cigarette with a fancy gold lighter before she replied. "I run a PR agency. A worldwide affair. We represent a lot of VIPs, you know—socialites, princesses, sheikhs, movie stars, showbiz personalities, television tycoons, that kind of thing. It's very exciting. In fact, the moment I saw you, I said to myself, 'Wouldn't it be spiffy if I could get her in?' That is, if you are at all interested in looking around for something different to do? Why don't you give it a bash? I could introduce you around, no strings attached. And then you decide if it's for you. I know just about everybody there is to know in London—journalists, editors, politicians, royalty. We party together all the time. The job involves a lot of traveling, and frankly, darling, I'm exhausted. Too, too, but too tired. I'd love to pass on some of my special assignments to someone like you. I mean, look at you—you are like an orchid. Exotic, passionate, sensuous. You'd be sensational! I'm already jealous. I can see all my admirers deserting me once they see you. Plus, you have a name! You were a siren, a screen queen. You are famous. And young. And sexy. I mean, how lucky can a woman get? I take it you are here alone. You look alone."

Aasha Rani nodded.

"Splendid! It's settled then," Shonali said, and put a gloved hand over Aasha Rani's bare and cold one. She brought out an expensively embossed business card and a tiny notebook encased in gold. "Tell me, darling, where can I reach you? When can you and I get together, you know, to firm things up?"

Aasha Rani was too nonplussed by the speed at which Shonali was going to say a thing. "But I don't know if I can do it. I don't really have any experience. What exactly does the job involve?"

"Details. Details. Don't be a bloody bore, darling. Those can always be worked out later. Just say yes and let's meet for a drink at the club tonight. I'll introduce you to a couple of my good friends. We can make a party of it. What fun. Come on, smile; let's see those gorgeous teeth of yours. Remember, in the PR business there is no room for women whose mouths droop at the corners! Why don't I drop you off so you can get some beauty sleep before putting on your glad rags for tonight? Hey, listen, we are here to have a good time. Trust me. I have great instincts. You and I are going to get along just fine. I feel it in my bones. We were destined to meet. And, by the way, wear a sari tonight. You look awful in those pants. Where on earth did you pick them up, anyway? A jumble sale?"

Aasha Rani didn't quite know what to make of the encounter. The whole thing had happened far too rapidly. There was nobody she knew in London with whom she could've exchanged notes. Who was Shonali? And what exactly was her game? Aasha Rani was intrigued and attracted. She decided to meet her that night— and find out.

Aasha Rani wore a peacock blue sari with a backless *choli*. The blue did great things for her, especially when it was teamed with the right accessories and a golden *bindi*. She stuck on lots of gold jewelry and decided to wear golden stilettos. Surveying herself in the mirror, she was more than pleased. She looked like her old self—sultry, sexy and desirable. Very much the "Sweetheart of Millions."

Shonali gasped when she came around to collect her, "Ravishing! You horrible woman. How dare you do this to me? I look like a blooming maid in comparison! Or was that the whole idea?"

Aasha Rani smiled a mysterious smile. "Maybe," she said.

Shonali, too, was dressed to kill—or perhaps slaughter—in a black miniskirt topped by a sequined jacket. Her hair was slicked back into a tiny swirl secured with a black velvet bow. Aasha Rani looked admiringly at her long legs encased in sheer black silk stockings. The shoes and bag were fuchsia pink to match her lipstick.

"So, where are we going?" Aasha Rani asked her as they walked down to the car. "You'll soon find out, darling, that with me there's never a dull moment. By the way, the man in the Bentley is Lord Ashley. He's sweet, just a touch kinky, like most Englishmen, but great fun. We're seeing a couple of his friends for drinks and then on to the theater, with a late supper. And after that, well, who knows."

The man in the car was buried in the leather upholstery but perked up at the sight of the two women. He was around fiftyish and very distinguished-looking, Aasha Rani noticed. His voice was slightly high-pitched and his hands like velvet—with long, mani-cured nails. The rings on his slim fingers glinted in the dark. Sho-nali introduced Aasha Rani as a "tribal princess from one of the remote villages of India." Before Aasha Rani could react to that, Shonali nudged her and whispered, *"Chhup raho."* On the way to the party, she made up an incredible story about her which sounded more improbable than all the films Aasha Rani had ever acted in.

"What if someone finds out you're fibbing?" she asked Shonali casually in Hindi.

"Don't worry, darling, we'll think of something as we go along. We can say your father remarried a wicked woman after your mother died giving birth to you at age fifteen. And that your father and your witchlike stepmother threw you out of the house, since you weren't the son they wanted. You were forced to come to Bombay, where an eagle-eyed talent scout spotted you, and that's how you became a famous movie star. We can also add that your horrible stepmother died an unnatural death—ritualistic murder or something—and that her only son killed himself by ODing on coke while studying in Paris. That left just you. And now you are the rightful claimant to the throne and an heiress in your own right."

"Then what would I be doing hanging around in London?"

"Oh, India bores you. You like action; you do the scene—the Riviera and all that. And you have your tribesmen to look after your affairs back home. Your kingdom will pass on to your son, when he's born. The Brits love these *Far Pavilions* type of stories. They fall for yarns about the Raj, lap them up; we could sell your story for thousands of pounds. Maybe get a television series out of it. Now, it's up to you; just play the part. And don't talk too much. Men don't like women who yak-yak. Listen a lot. Look interested and keep telling even the toads how handsome and wonderful they are. The worse they look, the more they'll want to believe your lies. Flattery, darling, is the key. It gets you anywhere and everywhere. Watch me in action tonight and you'll learn fast enough." Lord Ashley appeared to have gone to sleep. Shonali pressed Aasha Rani's hand, then his lordship's, and began flirting with him in English.

For the rest of the evening Aasha Rani observed Shonali closely. She was quite something. Her modus operandi could teach a few of the film women a trick or two. Aasha Rani deliberately played herself down. She didn't want to reveal to Shonali that she too had a few tricks up her sleeve.

The people they met that night couldn't keep their eyes off Aasha Rani. Shonali took her aside and whispered, "Darling, you're a hit. A smashing hit. I can see it, sense it. Everybody wants to know more about you. I've changed the story here and there, but basically it remains the same. If someone asks you which royal state you belong to, think of some tongue twister that they'll never be able to catch or pronounce. That way you'll be safe. There are quite a few 'highnesses' floating around London society, and they seem to know just about every royal family in India.

We don't want you caught out. I mean, we are dealing with real snobs here; the last thing we want is a fraud on our hands. And tonight you go home like a good girl—alone in a cab. Refuse all offers to bed you. Tell them you don't go for that sort of thing. That will arouse their interest still more. I'll call you tomorrow. We can plan things."

SOON AASHA RANI FELL headlong into an endless whirl of parties, country weekends and small jaunts across the Channel. This was the high life in London (or the low), and Shonali, without doubt, was the reigning empress on the social circuit. Aasha Rani was more impressed than she cared to admit. Shonali had sass, style, spunk and sex appeal. Plus, she was intelligent. With her coaching Aasha Rani learned rapidly and well. Her accent changed along with her thinking. This was certainly better than slaving at some seedy hairdresser's.

If Aasha Rani found the Brits more than a little strange, it seemed inconsequential when weighed against the compensations. Within six months she'd moved out of Jay's apartment and into her own smart Knightsbridge flat. Shonali lived in a sprawling apartment in Carlos Place, where, she insisted, all the *real* action was. Aasha Rani partied there often and longed to acquire something similar for herself. Her daily routine revolved around shopping and beauty care by day and wild parties by night. She reveled in the attention she received as someone mysterious, unusual and immensely sexy. She'd even received a couple of mentions in trendy magazines which referred to her as the latest "heat and lust" import from India. Shonali was very proud of her discovery and enjoyed flashing Aasha Rani around, describing her as "the Jewel in the Crown" princess who'd abandoned a hundred richly caparisoned elephants back home to enjoy the good life in England. "It's so boring, darling," Shonali usually added. "I mean, there's just so much one can do with elephants!" This got the usual laughs, and the people turned to Aasha Rani with additional interest in their eyes.

Shonali preferred to handle all the "transactions," saying, "Leave it all to me, darling. I have the setup for it. You know, secretaries, tax men and things. You concentrate on being beautiful. I'll make sure you get rich in the meanwhile."

Aasha Rani didn't object to the arrangement. Besides, she trusted Shonali. These days Shonali let her go solo on dates, saying, "I have a couple of things that need looking at. Why don't you carry on, have a good time, tell me all about it tomorrow. Don't leave a single dirty detail out . . ." Sometimes Aasha Rani felt guilty about the people she'd abandoned, to all intents and purposes—*Amma, Appa,* Sasha—but she would quickly remind herself that the only way she could help them was by helping herself. Also, as the months went by she had less and less time to herself as the engagements piled up.

Shonali was a remorseless critic and guide as Aasha Rani plunged into her new life.

"Darling, you are wasting your time. You *must* educate yourself. Keep up with the news. Read the papers. Catch up on books, current affairs. Improve yourself. These people we meet are very sophisticated. They want good company, intelligent conversation, humor, amusing little stories. After all, we aren't in the Lady Di league as yet, and even *her* admirers complain how dumb she is after a point. If you want to keep your new friends, you'll have to stop seeing all this junk."

Sometimes Aasha Rani resented Shonali's pep talks. But she dared not rebel. It was true that the men they met were not all that easy to please. There were evenings Aasha Rani felt hopelessly inadequate. Particularly when the topic turned to politics. Shonali seemed clued-in and more than merely well-up. She often threw in a nugget or two of information that was considered classified. Aasha Rani noticed how shrewdly she timed her little bombs. And the way she assessed the impact. Once Aasha Rani even asked her about it. Shonali replied casually, "Oh, I have friends in high places, you know, editors and people. And that minister you've met a few times at my place? A real sweetie, but gay as a coot. I listen to every word. Sometimes these men let on more than they should. Especially after a couple of cognacs. After they leave, I jot down some of the information—you never know when it might be of use. But I am the soul of discretion, darling; I keep my lips sealed. It's strictly 'no names.' Even my diary doesn't have any. But I've got my secret codes. I can decipher it all. One day my jottings are going to fetch me a fortune—just you watch!"

Aasha Rani didn't want to know more. She respected Shonali's privacy and expected her to respect hers. She knew Shonali kept secrets well, since she'd never caught her compromising anybody. Men relaxed in Shonali's company. She had a knack for making them talk and reveal more than was good for them. And she did it all without coming on too strong, without being aggressive. She encouraged Aasha Rani to imitate her, saying, "You disarm people far better than I can. These men who seek out our company are powerful, rich and influential. They control the world. They find us relaxing, charming and desirable. We are doing them a favor—they spend their days under stress and tension.

Their lives are complicated, their wives are bitches, their children hate them and their English girlfriends use them. We are safe. We give them what they want. That's why we are successful. Do you think others don't try? They'd love to be in our position. People come to me offering vast sums for information. They want me to tap all my conversations, record everything. I refuse to do it. Who needs complications? The reason I'm telling you all this is simple. Why don't you get into the act? You'll soon be on your own. Frankly, darling, you don't need me anymore. You have your besotted admirers—hordes of them. I only made the introductions. You could capitalize on the idea if you want to. I have friends who can wire your place up. It's easy. Nothing to it. You're good at making men talk. Use your talent. There's a lot of big money involved. You know how these Arabs are with cash. They're willing to pay the earth. Do it for a year, and then, when you've made your pile, you can opt out. Retire to the country. There are some wonderful seventeenth-century estates going. I could put in a word. Or you could go back to India and start something there.

"For me the situation is slightly more difficult, darling. I live here. I don't have any other place to go. I hate the United States. I detest the French; by the way, always remember to carry a disposable razor in your handbag when you are out with a Frenchie. They all love to sixty-nine. It's almost obligatory. And it isn't much fun if you have a mouthful of hair! In any case, I hope you do use hair conditioner down there with every shampoo. An absolute must, darling. Men prefer it nice and silky . . . so, as I was saying, all my friends are here. We could work out something; think about it."

Aasha Rani did. But she was scared. She didn't want to mess

with shady characters on her own, especially after her encounter with the *goondas* dispatched by Jojo's wife. They all seemed so far away. But the image of the *goondas* still kept recurring in her dreams. Till now, she'd managed to keep the more suspect "clients" in London at bay, and she wanted to keep it that way.

Shonali never discussed their "profession" explicitly. They had a tacit understanding about that. Not even oblique references were allowed. Their nights out were called "entertaining." Shonali would call and say, "I'm entertaining tonight. Feel like a foursome?" Aasha Rani too kept up the charade. Not even to herself did she acknowledge that she was nothing more than a high-priced whore. London was full of them. Aristocratic call girls who settled in kind if not in cash, though most preferred the liquidity provided by the latter. There was no shame in it, Aasha Rani reasoned. No *real* shame. She was providing a service; that was all. Occasionally she even enjoyed herself. Besides, it was difficult to sniff at the perks of the job. She'd managed to stash quite a chunk away. Plus, she'd gratefully accepted jewelry from some of the men. Jewelry she never intended to wear but had gotten evaluated nevertheless.

Over the days Shonali kept at her with the suggestion that she go solo. And with the real big fish—the shadier the better, for that was where she said the real money lay. Gradually she wore Aasha Rani's resistance down. And, in a way, the idea excited her the same way her first few years with the Shethji used to turn her on. But now she was alone—without a godfather, without a protector, without a cover. No. She felt far too exposed and vulnerable. She told herself she was not smart enough for these sorts of high stakes. She also felt Shonali was keeping things from her. For instance, their "chance" meeting at Harrods seemed suspicious in retrospect. Had someone set it up? But who knew about Aasha Rani's whereabouts? And how would she ever know if that was how it really happened?

She decided to ask Shonali directly. She knew her well enough by now. If Shonali tried to feed her a line, she'd know that too. All she needed was the right opportunity. Aasha Rani didn't have to wait long. And what was even better, she didn't have to ask. The answer was provided automatically the minute Aasha Rani's eyes fell on Gopalakrishnan.

GOPALAKRISHNAN WAS TALKING to a group of English bankers in a quiet corner of Shonali's living room on one of their party evenings. She saw his profile, lit up by the glow of burning logs in the fireplace, the minute she entered Shonali's apartment. Initially, she got a start. What was he doing here? Then the whole thing fell into place. Of course. It was he who'd orchestrated the whole thing. Aasha Rani walked up purposefully and tapped him lightly on the shoulder. "Remember me?" she asked huskily. He raised his glass and smiled broadly. "How could I ever forget? It was the best glass of champagne I've ever had." The bankers looked at Aasha Rani and then back at him. He introduced her easily as "a friend of our hostess, Shonali."

Excusing himself as fast as he could, he took her away from the group, saying, "How wonderful to see you again like this. You look even better than I remember you. Irresistible too." Aasha Rani looked steadily at him. "It was you, wasn't it? You were the one who got Shonali to track me down? Bump into me 'accidentally' at Harrods? Go on, admit it."

Gopalakrishnan chucked her under the chin and said in Tamil,

"If you already know so much, why waste time on another inter-rogation?"

"How did you know I'd be in London? And did you have people following me all the time?"

"Shonali is a very enterprising woman. She doesn't require my help. But yes, in your case, it's true. I was the one who alerted her. I thought you needed a break. I knew you were going through a bad patch. I made discreet inquiries through my associates in Wellington. They kept tabs on you. I was told you were headed for London. We had some more people involved from that point on. The rest was easy. Shonali is an old friend."

Aasha Rani was stunned by the information. She wanted to know more. But Gopalakrishnan was in no mood to talk. In any case, he was hardly left alone that evening. There were all sorts of people going for his attention, some of whom Aasha Rani hadn't met at Shonali's earlier parties. She asked her about a couple of guests. Shonali replied vaguely. "Darling, who knows, diplomats, I think."

Gopalakrishnan seemed to know everybody. From time to time he'd disappear into the study with someone or another.

Shonali kept the party going. She'd invited a couple of Danish girls who were top models in London that season, and there was a Moroccan princess, an arty film actress from Argentina along with her stable of polo players, a TV anchorwoman from New York and all her other regular party girls.

Despite the constant stream of acquaintances whom she kept running into, a single thought dominated Aasha Rani's mind: Go-palakrishnan. Who was he? What did he do? It bothered her that she couldn't figure him out. Or the other Indian who'd come along with Gopalakrishnan. The stranger stood in a dark corner throughout the evening, with a sullen face that had a pair of very watchful eyes shining out of it. He didn't drink, smoke or talk. Everybody, including Shonali, left him alone.

When Gopalakrishnan came back into the room, Aasha Rani asked him the stranger's identity. "That man? He's my body-guard," Gopalakrishnan answered shortly. Before Aasha Rani could ask any more questions, Gopalakrishnan disappeared with a new group into the study. Aasha Rani decided to leave. She was confused, upset and tired.

THE NEXT MORNING, there was a knock at Aasha Rani's door. Sleepily she went to see who it was. Generally the milk was left outside and nobody ever disturbed her till well past eleven, which was when she woke up. Cautiously, she opened the heavy door, making sure the safety chain was in place. She found Gopalakrish-nan outside, a broad smile on his face. "*Vanakam!*" he greeted her heartily.

"What on earth are you doing here?" she asked groggily.

"Won't you let me and my friend in?" he said.

"Which friend?"

"You met him last night. It's Bhaskaran." Bhaskaran was the mysterious sullen stranger she'd noticed at the party. She let them both in and noticed that he looked less menacing by day.

Aasha Rani clutched her velour dressing gown around herself and went unsteadily into the kitchen to make some tea for all of them. They followed her there, and all of a sudden Gopalakrish-nan pulled out a gun.

"Relax, I'm not shooting you. This is just to let you know that Bhaskaran will be spending the night here with you. You don't have to fuck him—but you do have to keep your mouth shut. He'll be here about a week. Thanks so much. I knew you wouldn't say no." Gopalakrishnan smiled as Aasha Rani sank down wordlessly on the kitchen stool.

"There are people after me—my enemies. I have to go back to India, but Bhaskaran cannot leave England. Not right now. I need fresh papers for him. All that is going to take time. I have to organize funds as well."

"I don't know what all this is about. Who are you, and who is this man? Why have you come here?"

"Don't let that worry your pretty little head. All I can tell you is that it would be extremely unwise to squeal to the police. My men are posted everywhere; they're all armed. And they are all dangerous! By the way, we're keeping an eye on your daughter. Beautiful child. It would be a pity if anything happened to her."

"Does Shonali know about this?" Aasha Rani asked quietly.

"Let's just say she knows as much as is good for her. She has very good contacts. She knows influential people in the British intelligence and some international arms dealers. Two of our consignments for the IRA have been intercepted. We know who is betraying us. Bhaskaran is here to track that person down and eliminate him. But I have to go back. Nobody will dream of looking for Bhaskaran here."

"Had you singled me out as a potential victim when you took that flight with me from Bombay?" Aasha Rani asked flatly.

Gopalakrishnan pulled her to himself roughly and looked into her eyes. "I noticed you on board. I knew who you were. And I liked what I saw. When I gave you my card, I was teasing you. But in my line of business you never know when someone can come in useful."

Bhaskaran still hadn't opened his mouth. His gaze was steady and alert.

Gopalakrishnan moved to the curtained window of her apartment and parted the fabric just a chink. He looked back at Bhaskaran. "All clear. Safe," he said. "Safe for whom? What if someone finds out this man's whereabouts? I don't want my apartment bombed or trashed or anything," Aasha Rani screamed hysterically.

Gopalakrishnan came up close and said, "Honey, be thankful you're alive. Oh, by the way, no men friends over for slumber parties, please. How many of the people you see regularly know your address?"

"About half a dozen—those who drop me back after a party. Generally, I drive myself, or a chauffeur drops me."

"That's good. How busy is your schedule next week?"

"Let me look at my diary—the appointment book, I mean."

As she went toward the telephone table where she had her appointment book, Gopalakrishnan spoke urgently to Bhaskaran in Tamil. Aasha Rani strained to listen, but he spoke in such a low voice that she couldn't catch a word. She came back and informed the men that she was booked through the week except for two days—Tuesday and Friday.

"Excellent!" Gopalakrishnan said. "Now listen carefully. No extra milk in the house. Nothing different about your routine. Keep the answering machine on all the time—even when you are at home. Bhaskaran hasn't brought clothes with him so that there should be no washing to dry that isn't yours. You will not get any food into the house that is in any way different from what you normally eat. Your curtains will be adjusted in the regular way. You will naturally not open the door to anybody you don't know.

Bhaskaran will remain in the guest room throughout. He is a trained guerrilla fighter, so he doesn't require food or drink for hours. When he does, he shall knock or tap softly on his door and you will give him what he asks for. In case you are leaving the house, tap on his door and he will know you are gone. Tap once again on your return. You neither have to see him nor talk to him. Leave the food and water on the table outside his door. He requires it only once a day. On the right day, he will let himself out of this house and slip away. You won't see him again. Or me. But then, if you open your mouth, you'll be too dead to see anyone." With that, Gopalakrishnan abruptly left the house.

AASHA RANI WAS LEFT ALONE with a complete stranger. A silent one who watched her every move and caught even the extra breath that escaped her when Gopalakrishnan shut the door behind him.

Bhaskaran's catlike movements and incredible agility fascinated Aasha Rani. She tried to dig out some clues about Gopalakrishnan's past, but he told her abruptly, in Tamil, that he wasn't in her house as a social guest and would prefer it if she left him alone and followed Gopalakrishnan's instructions about food and water. Rebuffed, Aasha Rani went off to her room to worry and go over the dramatic happenings of the morning. It was useless trying to fit the pieces of the puzzle together. She guessed that Gopalakrishnan was an arms dealer of some sort who supplied weapons to anybody who wanted them: terrorists, banana republic dictators and all sorts of subversive forces. All she had to do to get him behind bars was to make an anonymous call to the police. But the thought of what might happen to Sasha held her back. Goddamn the man. She had never had any scruples about sex. But this was an exception. The idea of having made love to a man who murdered for a living repulsed her.

Aasha Rani's phone generally started buzzing by late afternoon. Today she had the answering machine on. Shonali had gotten her to redo her message at least fifty times till she'd gotten it just right. Now her voice came across sexily, confident, teasing and with the right accent.

Aasha Rani was getting edgy and restless. What a fine mess she had gotten herself into. Maybe she should cook herself a meal. She had never been a great one for cooking. Jay used to tease her about that, when she fixed all of them her "one-dish dinners," as she called the main meal of the day. Poor Sasha, she'd gotten used to munching nuts, raw carrots and cookies throughout the day.

But now she needed to divert her mind from the stranger who lurked in her house. Aasha Rani decided to run down to the nearest supermarket and pick up bottles of mango pickles, high-fat yogurt, basmati rice and mixed curry powder. She tapped lightly on his door before leaving.

She was surprised when she stepped out and discovered it was one of those unusual London days, all blue and bright and shiny. It reminded her of Fisherman's Cove and Goa. She breathed the air in deeply, stared at the clear sky and wondered how to tackle the danger that seemed to loom all around her. As she walked along, she caught sight of herself in a storefront. God! What a mess her hair looked! And her face—like she hadn't slept a wink. Maybe a shampoo and blow-dry would relax her. She was in no particular hurry to get home to her surly guest, so she thought she'd spend time in the salon. She had all the time in the world today. The party at night was one of those spiffy galas where Princess Anne was to be chief guest. Tonight she was going to share a table with Shonali and her parliamentarians. If Shonali's high-powered friends ever found out who was sharing her flat these days, she would be out of Britain in a shot.

WHEN HER CAB DREW UP in front of her apartment, she glanced up at the windows as she generally did, more out of habit than anything else. That's funny, she thought. The curtains were open. She'd made sure to draw them before going out. She ran up the stairs swiftly and inserted the key into the lock.

She was stunned to see the state of her flat. It was trashed—completely devastated and torn apart. In the center of the living room, impeccably dressed, sat Shonali. Aasha Rani looked at the pool of blood on the floor. "Bhaskaran's dead," Shonali said finally. "And you had better get out of here fast. Here's your plane ticket—the flight leaves in two hours. Don't stop and start trying to pack. You know, darling, you're lucky to be alive."

Aasha Rani didn't quite know what to say. She silently surveyed the destruction about her and realized for the first time that she could have been killed. The tall, handsome stranger she'd innocently befriended on the flight to New Zealand had meant business. Shonali came up to her and embraced her. "I'm sorry it had to end this way—I rather liked you. But you're in deep shit and had better start running." "But . . . but . . . what happened? Gopalakrishnan . . ." she managed to stammer out before Shonali motioned her to be quiet.

"No names," she said grimly. "No names, no memories, nothing. You don't know what happened, you never saw anything, you've never lived in this place. Be thankful I have friends all over the place. So far as the world outside is concerned nothing has happened. And I've managed to fix it so you won't be followed or harassed. Make no mistake, I'm doing this as much for myself as for you, as there's no profit in rocking the boat too much. But you have to get out. Now. Come on; I have a car waiting. Get your passport."

It was only after Aasha Rani found herself on the British Airways flight that she got the chance to review the rushed events that had, once again, overtaken her life. Strangely enough she didn't regret leaving London. Or the fact that she'd left behind a vault full of furs and boxes of jewelry. Though she wondered why the powers-that-be had helped her get away instead of whisking her off to some torture cell somewhere or bludgeoning her to death. There were so many unanswered questions in Aasha Rani's head, and Shonali's mysterious explanation had served only to confuse her further. Now, as she sat sedately sipping a glass of port after a typically uninspiring "oriental dinner," she wondered about Gopalakrishnan and Bhaskaran. About the man with the sexy teeth who had made an ordinary, boring, tedious, airline flight so memorably exciting for her. Him, a wanted man, a killer?

Aasha Rani shut her eyes. Her thoughts drifted to Sasha. The threat to her life had really thrown Aasha Rani. She shivered as she recalled Gopalakrishnan's warning. Sasha. How she missed her little daughter.

She arrived to an empty house in Bombay. A servant, obviously new, opened the door and stammered nervously at the sight of Aasha Rani—he didn't recognize her, but kept repeating, "Go away, go away. Nobody home. Everybody is in Madras. *Appa* serious. *Amma* not well." Aasha Rani sighed. She didn't care to stay in that huge, empty house alone. She was exhausted. Jet lag was the least of her discomforts. She nodded to the servant, went back to the taxi and told the driver to take her to the Sea Rock.

In the morning, after a lousy cup of ready-made tea (she'd rather begun enjoying weak English tea), she phoned Kishenbhai. He reacted as if she had arisen from the dead. His voice was high-pitched and hysterical. "Good you have come. This is destiny. *Appa* is very serious. Sudha is in trouble. *Amma*'s condition is worse. Too many problems. Your husband phoning. Daughter phoning. Saying, 'Mama, *Mama*.' We don't know anything, where you are—nothing. Good you are here. Now everything will be *theek-thak*." Aasha Rani urged him to calm down and come over to the hotel. She booked calls to Madras and Wellington.

Waiting for the telephone to ring, Aasha Rani realized with a sense of finality that she was back. The telephone seemed to represent everything she felt about India, about Bombay, about Madras, and home. It sat there so smug and impassive. There was nothing she could do to make it ring. It controlled her. Was it being perverse and obstinate or just plain inefficient? The phone made her irritable, frustrated her, drove her into a rage. She had tried slamming down the receiver, banging the instrument violently, even chucking it angrily across the room. She had ignored it, turned her back on it and pretended it didn't exist. Eventually, she slumped down beside it and wailed.

The perfect way to handle it, she'd learned through trial and error, was to be humble, patient and grateful, if it condescended to ring. The only way to cope was to accept the phone, no-ring, engaged tone, plain-dead and all.

But today, the phone proved it could perform miracles if it chose to. She got Jay's call through within the hour.

Jay sounded anxious. "We received a couple of strange calls asking about your whereabouts. Sasha was worried. She has been crying constantly. No, I couldn't say who they were from. The voice was muffled, and the accent was strange. The sort of accent we heard in Madras. The man wouldn't say anything, but his tone was menacing and he suggested that your life was in danger. He also threatened us—Sasha in particular. Are you all right? What on earth have you been up to?"

Aasha Rani assured him she was safe and that the whole thing had been a misunderstanding.

"It isn't drug-related, I hope," Jay said sharply.

"Come on. I have never done drugs. You know that."

"It's just that we'd heard stories about your lifestyle in London," Jay explained. "I knew I hadn't forked out that kind of money. Naturally, I was puzzled. There were reports of you having been seen cruising around in Bentleys and Jaguars; that's all. Anyway, the important thing is that you are safe and well and back at home."

Aasha Rani asked him how he was. "Things are working out splendidly. Sasha misses you, of course. She's looking more and more like you, as a matter of fact. Everybody says so. She misses you, darling—it's true. Here, speak to her." And he handed the phone to Sasha.

For a second or so there was no sound. Aasha Rani repeated, "Hello, my kitten, hello, love, hello, my darling baby," over and over again. She knew Sasha could hear her, that she was listening. Finally, Sasha responded in a tiny voice, "Mommy, Mommy, I want you. I need you."

Aasha Rani crooned back, "I want you too. I love you, my darling. We'll be together soon. I promise you that."

Sasha ❧

"*SUDHA IS RESPONSIBLE* FOR EVERYTHING. SHE'S THE REASON everything is in such a mess," blurted out Kishenbhai the moment he walked in. Aasha Rani made him sit down, gave him a glass of water and told him to calm himself before telling her the story. When it was finished, she marveled at the astonishing sequence of events that had taken place during her seven and a half months in London. And to think, she had been blissfully ignorant of it all!

It had all started with Sudha borrowing money heavily for a film that she wanted to launch for herself and Amar. Instead of going through the usual producers like Gopal to raise the capital, she'd decided to approach the reigning underworld don, who was just waiting to grab control of film financing in any case. Sudha had guaranteed him a hefty percentage of the profits. The film had gone haywire on its production costs and overshot the original budget four times over. She'd gone out and borrowed some more cash after mortgaging everything she owned. The film was finally released five months behind schedule. Fortunately for her, it had turned out to be a hit. A megahit.

Her problems would have been over with the box office receipts, but Sudha had foolishly decided to fudge receipts and manipulate accounts. She was insane to do so and everybody, including Kishenbhai and *Amma,* had advised her against it. But Sudha was too giddy with success to listen. Even Amar had been overruled. Sudha, in her greed, had refused to yield.

"It's all my money. The film is mine, the idea is mine, the story is mine. I have acted in it, the credit goes to me; why should I part with more? I took the risk. I gambled. Now I'll decide what to do with the money I've earned," she had said emphatically.

It wasn't long before the word was out. She had ignored the phone calls, even one from the Shethji warning her about the potential danger of the game she was playing. The underworld don had phoned personally to tell her to come clean with the accounts, or else. "I make more in two hours than the amount you are risking your life for. Think carefully—is it worth all this?" he had said to Sudha. Sudha had lied through her teeth, saying she'd played it straight. The don had rung off after delivering a final threat: "We'll find out whose *hisaab-kitaab* is right." Soon after, things started going horribly wrong.

Sudha's van had been speeding along the eastern highway when she'd found the road blocked. She'd thought there was an accident and told her driver to honk. He'd realized before she had that it wasn't an accident. He'd tried to swerve the vehicle to the other side of the road, spin it around and get away. But before he could, the two front tires of the van were blown out and it had skidded and overturned.

Sudha had scrambled out frantically and started running, shouting for help. She could see the squatters' colonies along the edge of the road, and a taxi stand just twenty meters away. The highway wasn't deserted. The usual midmorning traffic of goods-laden trucks, interstate cars, company buses, auto rickshaws and pedestrians flowed past as they did every day. At least five hundred onlookers had watched as two armed men chased after her, firing shots in the air. Nobody had bothered about the driver, who had been trapped under the van. Sudha had stumbled as her sari kept getting caught under her feet. Then she fell as the heel of her sandal snapped.

The men had ambled up. One of them slowly pulled out a hip flask from his back pocket and poured it over her. Whiskey. Then, lighting a match, he had tossed it casually on her and sauntered off. The other man had waited to make sure her clothes were on fire before he too laughed and moved off in the direction of the waiting Maruti. Sudha's heart-wrenching screams for help had been heard by dozens of people: shopkeepers along the highway, the slum dwellers from the swampy, marshy colonies on the other side, and motorists driving by, carefully diverting their vehicles to avoid the burning bundle in the middle of the road. It was only after the Maruti disappeared from view that a few people had ventured to come to Sudha's rescue and to see what had become of her driver.

Sudha had been admitted to the nearest hospital with sixty percent burns. A shopkeeper who had a tiny cold-drinks stall along the highway was the only one who had displayed great presence of mind by pulling the tarpaulin off his shop and swathing her in it. Meanwhile, somebody had phoned for an ambulance. A passing police control van spotted the crowd and drove up to find out what was going on. At the sight of the police, the crowds melted away. Nobody was willing to give a statement. Nobody wanted to get involved. Sudha had been identified easily enough because of her van. Along that highway everybody knew precisely which car belonged to which star. It was a familiar sight for them, particularly the urchins, who harassed the stars daily when their cars stopped at the traffic lights. Sudha's driver was dead. She herself was in no condition to tell the police what had happened. And, as was standard in Bombay, there were no witnesses.

The police tried to bully the shopkeeper who'd saved her life to describe the sequence of events. But he begged and pleaded with them to spare his life, saying, "If they find out who told you—I'm finished. I'm dead. I have a family—small children. Have mercy. I didn't see anything. I don't know anything." It was impossible. Nobody would even divulge the number of the car in which the killers had gotten away. The police tried to induce some of the children who'd been present to give them more details. They were sure the kids would be able to recall the plate number of the Maruti. One child started repeating it, but was immediately silenced by an older brother, who slapped his wrist and dragged him away. There were no leads.

Amar had lapsed into deep shock after the incident. It wasn't clear, though, whether this was on account of what had happened to Sudha or the thought that he would have to face a police interrogation. The police had a tough time getting him to speak. Finally, the doctors advised sedation, and he was admitted to a clinic near his house. It was feared that somebody might try to get him as well, and so his room was guarded by armed policemen.

AMMA HAD INITIALLY ARRIVED to stay in the hospital with Sudha, but her frail physical health meant that she was more hindrance than help. *Amma* was told to return to Madras. Finally, it was Kishenbhai who had done all the running around as Sudha hovered between life and death for over a fortnight. Her fans maintained a day-and-night vigil outside the hospital. Bottles and bottles of blood were willingly donated by total strangers. News about her attempted murder made it to Doordarshan. Progress reports were issued daily. The film industry rallied around too, which surprised everybody. Daily statements were issued by costars, producers, directors and others, voicing their concern and support. But the message was clear: Sudha was out of the film industry—forever.

Sudha had sustained severe burns all over, including her face. She was to have plastic surgery after the skin grafts. When she was declared out of danger *Amma* had taken her to Madras for further treatment.

AFTER KISHENBHAI LEFT, Aasha Rani sat numbly for a long time. The news had devastated her. Sudha's incredible ambitiousness had toppled the family. Kishenbhai was right. Almost everybody in the film industry would see it that way. But could they really place all the blame on poor Sudha? Hadn't they all a share in it? *Amma, Appa,* Kishenbhai . . . and she herself?

She tried to calm down, but she could feel only despair. Nothing could get worse than this. And all this while a single thought kept surfacing: It was up to her to resurrect the family. She couldn't do it, she thought despairingly; she didn't have the strength, the resources, the courage. But what could she do? She couldn't go back to London, to the mercy of the men (the High and Flighty, as Shonali called them) she had entertained. She couldn't revive her marriage. What then? Perhaps she could go to Australia. There were so many people like her there: displaced, moneyed, lonesome. She'd be one more immigrant. That was all. An oddball, yes. But she was doomed to be that anyway. Perhaps she'd be an even bigger one here in Bombay.

New York? Never. It reminded her too much of Akshay and his plans of running away from the Bombay film industry. Making it big in America together as hotshot producers of those dreadful ethnic programs. Fleetingly she thought of Akshay. Remembering the time he had come to her, escorting two brats with streaked hair, streaked jeans, streaked American T-shirts and, possibly, streaked minds. She'd complained about it to him later and had told him that he sucked up to the *goras*. "OK, in that case, why don't you and I make films for them? Good films. Classical dance, music, temples, monuments. Let us show them our country as it is!"

"As it is?" She'd laughed again. "Are you joking? We'd have to show all the rubbish in that case. We can send them our art films—why should we bother to shoot anything? Let them see the filth, poverty, disease, corruption."

Akshay had looked away at the sea and said dreamily, "That is the trouble with you. No romance. No idealism. You see only ugly things, remember ugly things. India is also beautiful. We can make it beautiful, you and I."

From her hotel room she could see the same sea that had captivated Akshay so many years ago. As always, the rocky coast was full of young couples, some hiding under sun umbrellas, and others seeking what little privacy they could by hiding behind the woman's sari *pallav*. Foolish people, Aasha Rani thought. It couldn't be too much fun making love here—not with tiny crabs scuttling out of the crevices and biting unwary toes. And the urchins! Merciless.

Yet Aasha Rani envied them. She had all the privacy in the world, a luxurious, air-conditioned bedroom, music at the touch of a button, fluffy pillows, but not a person in the world to turn to. Slowly the scene in front of her eyes blurred as her mind occupied itself once more with the problems that threatened to engulf her. In the late afternoon she made her decision. She wouldn't run again.

At the Indian Airlines office, the queues were never-ending. Indifferent clerks sat around chatting and paid not the slightest attention to passengers thumping the counters. "Computers are down," they announced indifferently before disappearing somewhere. Nobody was sure when the flights were due or likely to take off—if at all. An A-320 had come back after a tire burst; another had reported a bird hit. It was hot beyond belief. The air-conditioning had malfunctioned. Aasha Rani nearly suffocated on the combined stench of stale cigarettes lying uncleared for days in ash bins, sweat evaporating from polyester shirts, sticky betel leaf spittle, and the damp odor of carpets continually soaked by leaking machines. God, it was all so depressing. How was she to cope with what awaited her in Madras?

Things were even worse than she had imagined when she got home. For one thing *Appa*'s health had deteriorated badly. When she saw him lying very still in bed, his eyes hooded and his breathing irregular and heavy, she knew he wouldn't last much longer. The realization was almost too hard to take. He hadn't been much of a father, but in the last couple of years she had begun to accept him. Even understand him a little. The anger, the sense of betrayal—had vanished. Not just toward him, but *Amma* too. It was just that her parents didn't know better. They'd tried in their own foolish way to bring up the children as doughty street fighters, something they themselves must have been in their early years. But with Sasha in her life, Aasha Rani knew that parenting wasn't only about survival lessons. It was also about something called love. Maybe in their twisted way, they too had loved their children, but there was no memory of it in Aasha Rani's mind. The bitterness had gone, however, and was replaced with something that was nearly affection. And *Amma?* The feisty old battle-ax was reduced to a bag of bones. A depressive with fading memory and humiliating incontinence. Two wounded veterans waiting to die.

Appa, however, still had a few tricks up his sleeve. Sensing someone standing beside his bed, he slowly opened his eyes. Seeing Aasha Rani he grew excited and agitated. He managed to convey to her that there was something he wanted her to read. He told her where she would find it.

Locked away in a tiny tin box full of peculiar odds and ends, she found a sheaf of papers. The handwriting wasn't *Appa*'s—he'd obviously dictated it to someone. Aasha Rani read through it slowly in *Appa*'s presence. Then she read it once again. *Appa* was watching her face throughout, his eyes shutting, in spite of himself, from time to time. It was a letter—a farewell letter. In it *Appa* had begged her forgiveness and tried to explain some of the circumstances in his life that had led to ugly decisions. Decisions that had hurt her and her mother and the others. Aasha Rani had tears in her eyes as she read her father's words. She wanted to comfort him, hold him in her arms and say it was all right. And that, in any case, it was much too late. She didn't expect him to make amends. Not at this stage. She had made her peace with him.

It was the last paragraph that stunned her. *Appa* outlined his master plan in it. The studio was hers. It had been hers all along. Only the solicitors knew it. Not even the creditors. When he closed it down, the title stayed with him. He was bankrupt, the studio was boarded up, all the movable assets sold—but the name and the premises—they were both Aasha Rani's. He had refused to sell both. Oh yes, there had been offers. Many offers. From the other owners of studios in Madras—the Big Eight, as they were called. The goodwill was there. The banner still carried weight. People continued to see his old films when they were reissued. He held all the copyrights. There were people in the industry who were willing to back the name—the name that had given so many superhits—the name that now belonged to Aasha Rani.

There was one condition. She was not to sell the property. It was built on land that would fetch a phenomenal price—but he hadn't kept the studio all these years for her to sell the ground it stood on! Oh no! He could have done that a long time ago. When he desperately needed money to pay off his debts. When he was forced to sell his house and move into a shabby little shack. When he didn't have the money to foot his hospital bills. But he held on. And waited for the right time.

Aasha Rani had to promise him that she would resurrect the family banner and reopen the studio. The film industry was thriving. There were more films being made than ever before. The market was buoyant. And he was confident she could do it. She would immortalize their family and make a permanent contribution to cinema. That was his legacy to her. The only legacy he had left to give.

Aasha Rani didn't know what to say or what to think. How

could *Appa* do this to her? It just wasn't fair. How on earth could he think she'd want to get involved in this racket just to keep his banner flying? What did she care? Her own experience with the film industry had been foul. It was riddled with unscrupulous people: sharks, thieves, blackmailers and double-crossers. She didn't want *Appa*'s studio and all the groveling that went with it. She didn't even want to be associated with an industry which had given her nothing but pain, hurt and anguish. Didn't *Appa* realize what he was putting her through? But looking at the old man lying there, pinning her with his rheumy eyes, she knew she had to put on a brave front, if only to ensure he could die in peace. "This is fantastic, *Appa*," she said softly to him. The old man nodded and shut his eyes, contentment on his face.

Alone in her room, the doubts returned to plague her.

If only there were someone sensible she could have discussed them with! Someone she trusted. Whose judgement she valued. Jay? What would Jay know about running studios in India? Besides, she doubted very much that he cared one way or the other. Not in the way husbands were supposed to care. How *were* husbands supposed to care? Aasha Rani wondered. She thought she knew. Though it was something she was unlikely to experience. It was also something that had passed *Amma* by. Yet, ironically, nearly every film she'd acted in extolled the husband-wife relationship and spoke of the perfect understanding that two committed people shared within this sacred relationship. Baloney—as her Brit friends might have said.

She hadn't seen a single happy marriage. Not one. You either used or got used. You dominated or got run over. It was that simple. *Amma* talked of her own parents and their wonderful love. But Aasha Rani had never known her grandparents. At times, she'd observed "ordinary" people going about their mundane lives. They seemed satisfied enough. Perhaps it was the environment in the film industry that bred a certain madness. Nobody, not a single person, was "normal" or even reasonably at peace. She used to wonder about that sometimes. There were other jobs in the world which were equally stress-ridden, equally demanding, but those people weren't crazy. Film people were. Everybody said so. The trouble was, film people met only other film people. And they really believed that it was everybody on the outside who was crazy. How often she'd heard them say that everyone who couldn't get into the film industry was jealous and criticized them because they were jealous. Everybody in the great out-there wanted to join the movies. Become film stars. Those who made it were somehow privileged. And those who didn't were forever condemned. All criticism was inverted envy. *Bas.*

At one time in her life, she'd been a party to the delusion too. She wasn't sure when she'd jumped out of the cuckoo house and discovered exactly how lopsided her views were. How far removed from reality. She'd felt sorry when that had happened. She had wanted to run out and hug all the old fantasies, the old defenses, to herself. She wanted to hear the words, the great upper film people constantly repeated to each other: "You are great, *yaar.* Too good! You are the best. No one to touch you." She used to think so too. The best. Too good. Yes—that was her. Aasha Rani—Sweetheart of Millions.

She remembered meeting an old actress once. The woman had frightened her with her hollow, empty eyes and bitter words. She'd been number one in her time. Stunningly beautiful and a good singer too. Now on the wrong side of fifty, she was still single ("a bachelor girl," as she preferred to describe her status), still looking for a dashing middle-aged Prince Charming. She used to come for the odd film function, escorted by an octogenarian mother who would survey the room with her cataract-ridden eyes ("Everybody is after my girl; I have to be careful," she'd say). And while Savita (who was actually a Muslim with an assumed Hindu name, as were many other stars of her generation who thought they wouldn't be accepted if they were called Iqbal or Shaheen) continued to mourn the only heartbreak in her life, her contemporaries mocked her, called her a hag, a *buddhi*. Maybe she would have been better off with her first love, a Hindu hero with whom she'd started her career in the industry's biggest Technicolor production of that time. But her mother had objected violently. Two years later he had married another heroine, leaving Savita to wallow in regret and longing forever.

How grotesque she had looked. Still playing the eternal coquette. Her makeup was antiquated, her hairstyle the same as during her first hit. Loaded with jewelry and clad in frenetically overdone saris, she had looked like a faded and faintly batty bride whose groom had stood her up at the altar. Thank God, Aasha Rani thought to herself. She'd spared herself that, at least. She had married. Her womb had been filled. She had a daughter. She had escaped.

THE NIGHT AASHA RANI MADE UP HER MIND to see Sudha, it rained in Madras. She woke up to the sound of thunder outside. She'd been dreaming she was dancing on an enormous stage. She was alone—no musicians, no audience. In her half-awake state she thought the gods were providing the percussion. It was a *mridangam* from heaven that broke her trance, and she found herself wide-eyed, alert. The thunder was followed by lightning. How beautiful it must be on the beach, she thought. She breathed in deeply. Her nostrils filled with the fragrance of damp earth and she was back in her childhood, huddling close to *Amma*, giggling with Sudha, conspiring how best to sneak out and get drenched. Unseasonal rain. What was it? A squall somewhere else? A depression in the Bay of Bengal? Predictably, the weathermen had not mentioned rain.

She got out of bed. Laxmi was up as well. It must have been four or five in the morning. The sky was beginning to lighten. It turned out to be a spectacular storm. While Laxmi hurried to get her a cup of coffee, Aasha Rani sat by the window and watched. The jasmine bush right outside had been laden with flowers the night before. Now the delicate white blossoms lay on the wet earth like tiny stars fallen from the sky. Lightning streaked across the sky. Funny. She used to be scared of lightning in the past. Really, really scared. This was the first time she was looking at it. And it was beautiful.

The storm must have lasted about forty-five minutes. When she looked up at the sky, dawn was breaking gently. A pretty dawn, all pink and flustered. Like the bride she would have wanted to be. The rain clouds had moved on. The sky was silent. The cosmic dance was over. God had put his *tablas* away and gone to his green room to rest.

Aasha Rani went to the telephone. There was so much she had to do. She had to speak to Sasha. Perhaps she'd be able to get through quickly today. She had to see *Appa*. Talk to the solicitors. But more than anything else, she had to see Sudha. Touch her, talk to her, hold her, forgive her. And, for the first time in the last couple of days, she could see a glimpse of how the future might work.

* * *

THE MOMENT SUDHA SAW Aasha Rani standing next to her bed, she held up her scarred hands to shield her face. "*Akka*—no! Don't," she said brokenly. "Please . . . please, go away. I don't want you to see me like this. I want to die. I don't want anyone to see me. There is nothing left to live for. Please, *akka*, I beg of you. Whatever it is that you've come here for—I don't even want to know. God has punished me. It is nothing else but that. I deserve it. I have been evil. I have sinned. Heaven knows what made me do it. I have done you so much harm. You don't have to forgive me. Just let me die. I'm reduced to this; I frighten myself when I look into a mirror. Why did I not die then? That would have been better. I would have been released from this. Take everything I have. It is rightfully yours; I grabbed it from you. There is nothing I want. Take the bungalow, take Amar, my jewelry, whatever there is. But please, do me a favor. Get me some pills to end this agony. Please, *akka*. These people here bring me one sleeping pill for the night. I had a plan. I pretended I was swallowing them but was actually hoarding them away. I wanted enough. At least forty or fifty. But they found them under the bed last week. Tell them, *akka*, tell them not to keep me alive like this. Nobody expected me to pull through. God knows why I did. And now they want to send me abroad—Switzerland, they say. For further grafting. What's the use? Will I ever look the same again? No. Please, I have had enough. No more pain. Infection, septic wounds, pneumonia—there is no strength left in my body. After they graft every piece into place—what will happen? Will someone give me a role? Will any man marry me? Will anyone even want to look at me? Have I no right over my own body, my own life? *Akka*, what am I to do?"

There were no tears left either. Sudha was dry-eyed through it all.

Aasha Rani moved closer and put her arms tenderly around her sister. "I'll tell you what to do. But first you have to promise me one thing—that you will stay with me. I will look after you, and you're going to help me. The two of us together will reopen *Appa*'s studio—our studio. We will make films, good films, and we will survive. Not just survive, but prosper. We will make our banner the greatest banner the south has known. We will modernize the studio. Get all the latest equipment. Hire the best people. You will come with me to Singapore, Hong Kong, Tokyo to buy whatever is needed. Ours will be the most up-to-date, high-tech studio in India. You have excellent business sense. I will need that. I will concentrate on the technical side, handle production details. *Appa* will be proud of his daughters. *Amma* too. Look at me, Sudha. This is our chance, yours and mine, to start new lives, begin again. We are going to do it. Do you hear me? We are going to succeed and never look back. As for my daughter, Sasha, I have plans for her too, but those will have to wait. Are you ready, Sudha? Sudha, are you with me? You're going to make it. Make it just fine. There is nothing good plastic surgeons can't do today. And I'll be with you, for however long it takes and wherever in the world it is that we have to go. Show your face to me, Sudha, my dear little Sudha. Let me look at you."

Sudha refused to move her hands away. Aasha Rani bent over her sister and carefully pried away her stiff fingers. Then, very, very gently, she leaned in and kissed Sudha all over her face.

* * *

APPA WAS OVERJOYED when she told him her plan. He couldn't really express himself clearly, but Aasha Rani could understand his delight from the feeble pressure of his hands as they pressed hers, and from the tears that were steadily flowing down his leathery cheeks. "Everything is going to be perfect, *Appa,*" she kept repeating. "It rained last night. Good omen. Did you know it had rained?" He nodded slowly. "And, *Appa,*" Aasha Rani continued, "We will all go to Tirupathi soon. Very soon. As quickly as the doctors allow Sudha and *Amma* to be moved. And as fast as Sasha can get here. I'm going to call her now and tell her to come over. I know she'll like that. I just know it. Then, with Venkateshwara's blessings, we will all start again. You will see your banner flying high once more and feel proud. Very proud. Our name will rule the industry and the studio will regain its glory. I promise you that . . . You will see that I shall do it and prove it to you."

IN BED THAT NIGHT, in the twilight state between waking and dreaming, Aasha Rani thought of Sasha. It was Sasha who needed her the most, she told herself. Sasha. Her beautiful daughter with her tawny skin and those special eyes that had the sun and the sea dissolved in them. Eyes that danced and dimmed like a thousand constellations. Sasha with her innocence and guilelessness. Sasha would come and live with her. Together they would conquer the world. Together, her little daughter and she would carve themselves a niche. With no one telling them how to live life. No heartbreaks, no disappointments, no compromises. And as her beautiful daughter rose up in her mind she knew it was all going to be easy. Sasha would live life on her own terms. And she would bring her up as *Amma* never had. Aasha Rani suddenly imagined her daughter's fresh, innocent face gracing movie hoardings and gossip magazines. Sasha had the makings of a star. An unforgettable star. The Golden Girl of the silver screen! Oh yes, Sasha would be tomorrow's Lover Girl!

It was Diwali tomorrow. The festival of lights. She would need to tell Laxmi to prepare the *diyas*.

Bollywood Nights

Shobhaa Dé

A CONVERSATION WITH SHOBHAA DÉ

Q. What made you write Bollywood Nights?

A. I was the founder/editor of India's first fanzine called *Stardust*. From that privileged position, I got a ringside view of Bollywood. *Stardust* remains the market leader till today, combining as it does a lot of spicy masala (showbiz gossip), with bold exposés and candid interviews with the top stars. Bollywood is a pretty fascinating place and our stars are amazingly colorful. More than ten years of monitoring their lives via *Stardust* editorship provided all the material I needed for the novel. I wanted to tell the real story of Bollywood, warts and all.

Q. How important is it for a writer to know the subject? How well do you know Bollywood?

A. A good story can only be told well from a position of strength. A writer must know his/her turf intimately. The author's "voice" has to be real . . . credible. I knew Bollywood better than most, having seen it from the inside out. I understood the grime behind the glamour. The tears behind the plastic smiles. Maybe I've seen Bollywood for what it really is, stripped of its gaudy facade. It was a story worth telling and sharing.

Q. How different is Hollywood from Bollywood?

A. There are the obvious parallels—both are populated by larger-than-life characters, egotistical monsters and adorable rascals. Both deal with fragile egos and monumental insecurities. Both entertain millions of fans worldwide. Other than that, Bollywood has its very own identity—it is a very special place and functions by its own crazy codes and rules. Like Hollywood, the star system and the savage pecking order, determine everything.

Q. Why do you think Bollywood is gaining in popularity across the world?

A. Bollywood is one of the fastest-growing brands out of India. It has achieved global recognition during the past five years. Film buffs seem to enjoy its unique formula of song-and-dance romances, interspersed with melodrama. It is an attractive fantasy that doubles up as escapism of the most entertaining kind.

Q. You are credited with having invented "Hinglish," which combines English with local colloquialisms. How and when did that happen?

A. It happened quite naturally when I was editing *Stardust*. I decided to incorporate "street speak" into one of its most popular columns ("Neeta's Natter"). The language was spicy, racy and colloquial . . . so catchy, in fact, that today it has gone mainstream. Readers of *Bollywood Nights* will find the novel peppered with Hinglish words and phrases. . . . That's the real flavor of Bollywood.

Q. Why do your books shock India so much?

A. The books broke a lot of rules. . . . They were not conventional by any standards. The language was raw, and the content provocative—a surefire formula for generating controversy.

Q. *Are your characters in* Bollywood Nights *based on real-life movie stars?*

A. Yes and no. Some of them are definitely inspired by real-life movie stars. That is inevitable. Avid followers of fanzines might be able to track the similarities. But the story itself is entirely original and does not reproduce the life of any one movie star.

Q. *What do you want the book to convey about Bollywood to the rest of the world?*

A. I want the book to arouse curiosity and provide a window into a very intriguing world peopled by some incredible characters. Bollywood is unique. This is its real story.

Q. *So does the casting couch really exist in Bollywood?*

A. You'll get the answer in the book!!!